Master of the Opera

Also by Jeffe Kennedy

The Twelve Kingdoms:
The Mark of the Tala

The Twelve Kingdoms:
The Tears of the Rose

The Twelve Kingdoms:
The Talon of the Hawk

Published by Kensington Publishing Corp.

MASTER OF THE OPERA

jeffe kennedy

LYRICAL PRESS
Kensington Publishing Corp.
www.kensingtonbooks.com

LYRICAL PRESS BOOKS are published by

Kensington Publishing Corp.
119 West 40th Street
New York, NY 10018

All Kensington titles, imprints, and distributed lines are available at special quantity discounts for bulk purchases for sales promotion, premiums, fund-raising, and educational or institutional use.

Special book excerpts or customized printings can also be created to fit specific needs. For details, write or phone the office of the Kensington Special Sales Manager: Kensington Publishing Corp., 119 West 40th Street, New York, NY 10018. Attn. Special Sales Department. Phone: 1-800-221-2647.

LYRICAL PRESS and the Lyrical Press logo are trademarks of Kensington Publishing Corp.

ISBN-13: 978-1-61650-948-4
ISBN-10: 1-61650-948-1

First paperback edition: August 2015

10 9 8 7 6 5 4 3 2 1

Printed in the United States of America

Passionate Overture

1

Anything could happen. Anything.

The sky soared impossibly blue, studded with cotton clouds worthy of a Georgia O'Keeffe painting. Driving with the convertible's top down, Christy soaked up the Southwestern sunshine as she planned to do with absolutely everything.

The wind blew her hair, the short ends whipping around her face, stinging her skin with the perfect thrill of being alive and the mistress of her own destiny. *No more classes, no more books*, she thought to herself with a grin. No more East Coast gloom and city pressure. Free to be her own person, she zoomed down the highway and into her brand-new life.

The Santa Fe Opera House came into view, the elegant, arching lines of it an extension of the red rock cliff it perched on. Like a raptor of copper and steel, it gazed over the vast basin, a temple to pure sound, a place for the worship of ancestral theater.

Following the signs, she found the backstage area and parked. Grabbing purse, cell phone, and tablet, she swung her legs out of the car. They looked damn decent, thanks to the time she'd put in at the gym. The new stiletto heels she'd squandered some of her graduation money on helped enormously. She strode toward the building and around to the back apron, ready for her first day on the job.

The vaulting ceilings of the open-air theater, designed to look like swathes of fabric but made of steel, cast a deep shadow that made her shiver from the abrupt chill. Pushing her sunglasses onto her head, which also served to hold back her wind-ruffled hair, she opened the back door and peered into the gloom of below stage.

No one seemed to be about, though the door had been unlocked. Her heels clicked on the poured concrete floor, echoing in the perfect acoustics of even this dark working space. Here and there, shrouded stage pieces loomed with dusty magnificence. Where a cover had been shrugged off, a shoulder of gold filigree gleamed. In the deeper shadows, a mirrored sapphire elephant raised its trunk, forever frozen.

"Can I help you?"

Choking back a startled shriek, she whirled on the man who seemed to have crept up behind her. She threw an accusing look at his soft sneaker treads and he gave her a rueful smile.

"Sorry about that. Charles Donovan—Charlie—general manager of the opera. And you're Christine Davis?"

"Everyone calls me Christy." She shook the hand he offered. "Sorry—I wasn't sure which way to go to find your office."

"Some days even I don't know." He flashed her a comfortable grin and tucked his thumbs in the loops of his faded Levi's. "For all that this theater isn't as old as the European opera houses, somehow it ended up with labyrinths below stage. This way."

She followed as he wound back in the other direction. "At least there aren't catacombs or ancient sewers to get lost in."

He chuckled, arriving at the door to a tiny office, bright with fluorescent light, and gestured her inside. "No. But to hear the New Agers talk, there's plenty of Native American burial sites, hidden tunnels, subterranean dwellings, and so forth."

"Here?"

Charlie shrugged and wedged himself behind the tiny metal desk, piled high with paperwork. Sticky notes covered every surface, including the glowing screen of an apparently ancient laptop perched precariously on one corner.

"You'll find there's every kind here, Ms. Davis. Hang around long enough and you'll find someone who believes in it. Sacred spirals, peyote, reincarnation. You name it. And then there's the talent."

"Theater people tend to be superstitious, my dad always says. The smart manager learns to work with that."

"You have no idea. Ah well, we're here to keep 'em happy, if only for the season."

"Mr. Donovan, I—" She'd rehearsed this speech and it came out in a rush. "I want you to know that I'm here to work hard. My dad might have arranged for me to take this apprenticeship at the last minute, but that was just the right opportunity. I want this and I'll do what it takes."

"Don't worry about that. Apprentices are slave labor. You'll put in your sweat and blood." He extracted a file folder with surprising efficiency from one teetering pile. "You already have the show schedule. Here's a preliminary list of prop and set items for each opera. And . . ." Charlie spun his chair around to the sagging industrial bookcase behind him and yanked out an enormous three-ring binder, dropping it on the desk in front of her with a bang and a poof of dust, ". . . our inventory."

She stared at the binder in dismay. "On paper?"

Charlie grinned and poked a finger at the laptop, which was making an ominous grinding noise. "I've been meaning to get to it. And Tara—well, she was only a few days into it before . . ." He trailed off, scratching his scalp. "Most of the staff starts arriving next week—you ought to have a chunk of it done by then. I have Tara's notes. They might help."

With a sigh, Christy propped the tome on her lap and flipped through the yellowing pages. "The letters and numbers indicate location?"

"Yeah, in theory. That's where you come in. The L number is the level. The other codes indicate the exact storage room. Here, let me grab you a map." Charlie spun back around to frown at the shelves.

"Am I interrupting?"

"Roman!" Christy grinned at her old friend. "I was wondering when I'd get to see you."

Handsome as ever, Roman leaned in the doorway. He looked to be doing well, from the expensive cut of his chestnut brown hair to the sleek shoes peeking out from under his impeccably tailored suit. He returned Christy's smile with familiar charm. "I had to stop by, see my sweet girl. But I see that I'm interrupting."

"Not at all, Mr. Sanclaro!" Charlie popped up from his chair, dusting his hands off on his jeans and leaning over to offer one in welcome. "You know you and your family can stop in anytime. How's your father?"

"Busy as ever," Roman replied easily, then turned to Christy. "How about a hug—or are you too grown up for that now?"

"Don't be silly." She returned the light embrace, accepting his polite kiss on her cheek—something her ten-year-old self would have sighed over and embroidered into fantasies for weeks. "It's so good to see you again."

"I knew the Davises and Sanclaros have long jointly owned the property," Charlie commented, "but I didn't realize the families are close."

Roman rolled his brown eyes. "When Christy and I were growing up, our fathers used to joke about our betrothal—that it would at last resolve the logistics of the Davises owning the actual opera house and mineral rights, while the Sanclaros own all the surrounding property."

"It wasn't funny," Christy put in. That was putting it mildly. Any time Domingo Sanclaro and his son visited them in New York City, she'd been torn between a frenzy of anticipation at seeing her lifelong crush and dread at the older men's teasing. They were two of a kind, Carlton Davis and the elder Sanclaro, living for the business deal. It never occurred to them that needling an adolescent girl who imagined herself in love with the dashing college boy family friend was so cruel. Roman had always been so patient, however, treating her like a little sister. His sweet girl.

With a rush of warmth, Christy realized she had a hand on Roman's arm. She let go and grabbed ahold of the unnaturally blue plastic binder.

"Have you seen much of Santa Fe yet?"

"No—I've barely just arrived. I'm surprised you even knew I was here."

He winked. "Your dad told my dad—I'm to look after you."

"I'm not twelve anymore," she replied with a bit of irritation. Which immediately melted when Roman's grin shaded to sexy and he swept her with an appraising look.

"No. You've definitely grown up. Let me at least take you to dinner tonight. We have more five-star restaurants per capita than any other city in the U.S, you know."

"I didn't know." Roman Sanclaro was flirting with her. Her adolescent self would never forgive her if she didn't go. "Yes—I'd love to."

"Excellent. At least we can appease the fathers. Shall I pick you up around eight, then?"

"Perfect. I'm at the El Rey on Cerillos until I find a place."

Roman raised an eyebrow at Charlie. "Nothing but the best for our new staff?"

Charlie shook his head. "Not much of a budget for apprentices."

"Surely your dad can spring for better than that place? I'm surprised he'd let you stay there."

She maintained the easy smile on her face. She'd kept the car because that was practical, but the rest she was determined to do on her own. *Daddy's girl.* One only needed to hear that so many times in a lifetime. "It's nice. Clean. I like it. Eight o'clock, then?"

"I'm looking forward to it. And I'll get out of the way now." But he hesitated.

"Did you need something else, Mr. Sanclaro?" Charlie had his thumbs tucked in his belt loops, all courtesy for the son of the opera's patron.

Roman glanced at her. Back at Charlie. "My father is wondering if there is further word about . . . our little problem?"

"No. The police have no leads. Tara's family is pushing to have the lower levels searched again, but Detective Sanchez thinks she took off. Official stance is no evidence of foul play, there's nothing more they can do."

Roman cleared his throat and Charlie raised his eyebrows. "I'm sure Ms. Davis is perfectly well aware of what became of her predecessor."

"I don't want you to worry." Roman turned to her, his brown eyes warm. "All the fuss will die down. Tara was a bit flighty. Probably thought she fell in love and took off for Acapulco, eh, Charlie?"

Charlie nodded in slow agreement, a line between his bushy gray brows. He seemed about to say something but stopped himself. It hadn't occurred to Christy to be concerned. Her father had made it sound as if Tara, the previous apprentice, had simply run off, much as Roman described.

"Is there reason to be concerned?"

"Would Carlton Davis send his daughter here if there was?"

Roman waved his hands as if encompassing the greater world, then sobered, giving her a very serious look. "Besides, I'll protect you. From the theater ghost."

Christy laughed and Charlie shook his head. Every theater had some kind of ghost or legend. It was as necessary as lighting and curtains.

"They say," Roman's voice dropped an octave and he flicked his eyes dramatically at the floor, "that he lurks below, scarred, deformed even. At night, after the audiences have left and the stage crew is cleaning, they can hear him sobbing, calling out the name of his love, who had drowned in the underground lake. "*Christine*," he keened the name. "*Christeeen.*"

The hair stood up on the back of her neck, a shiver passing over her.

"Was that her name?" she whispered.

Roman grinned at her. "Gotcha."

"Oh!" Christy clutched the notebook to her chest, hating that she'd been so gullible. She tried to smile.

"New girl initiation—don't be mad."

"I'm not," she assured him. Silly. He'd always been able to sucker her into his jokes. Apparently she hadn't grown up *that* much.

"I'll see you tonight." With a jaunty wink and a wave, Roman left. "Sorry about that." She turned to Charlie, hoping she hadn't seemed unprofessional. "I really had no idea he'd stop by."

He shrugged. "We're pretty low key around here. And I'm not going to argue about anything that keeps the Sanclaros happy."

Christy took the map and the inventory book and gave herself the tour. Right after Roman left, the phone had rung and Charlie had rolled his eyes, shrugged his helplessness, and waved her on her way. Her dad always said managing a theater was 95 percent soothing ruffled feathers and it seemed that was what Charlie did.

The enormous freight elevator looked like standard institutional issue. She stabbed at the cracked down arrow and waited. The gears cranked more ominously than Charlie's laptop, accompanied by the screech of a tormented belt. When the doors shuddered open—the floor of the elevator a good hand's length above the one she stood on—revealing the garage-like interior, which smelled as if feral cats had pissed inside, she decided to save using it for transporting heavy stuff. And only when there would be a *lot* of people around to hear her if she got trapped in it.

Instead, she found the central spiral staircase and descended into the dimly lit lower levels, deciding to start at the bottom and work her way back up. The hollow clanking of her heels echoed through the silent rooms. In another week the space would teem with people and noise. Bursting with energy and excitement.

She couldn't wait.

Until then, silence and peace reigned, which was why she took advantage of the time. Tomorrow she'd be back in jeans and tennies—and geez, maybe a sweater—ready to dig into the deep and dusty layers. Today was for orienting, despite the ultimately unnecessary interview outfit, which now felt way too skimpy in the chilly bowels of the opera house.

She flicked on another set of lights, the fluorescents taking a moment to catch, then flickering on with an insectile buzz. Beyond it, she caught another sound, a whisper of movement. A draft of colder air brushed past her, making the small hairs on her arms stand up and her scalp prickle.

Mice or rats, most likely. Or pack rats, in this area. The woman who ran the hotel had warned her about the pack rats.

Still, for a moment, she thought she'd heard music.

An echo, perhaps. The expectation of the space, the perfect acoustics. She fancied that the building absorbed all the music and played it back to itself when everyone was gone, the timbers saturated with it.

Soon, real music would crash through—out of tune, cadence, and context. The same phrases repeated in cacophonous opposition to someone else's practice run. Chaos and tumult.

There it was again. A whisper of song. A honeyed tenor.

Curious, compelled, she followed it down the corridor, passing the various storage rooms, holding their eclectic treasures in darkness. The hallway ended abruptly in a dead end, a good thirty feet past the last lightbulb. Christy consulted her map in the dim light. If this was the right level, the hall should keep going to another set of storage rooms.

It didn't.

She retraced her steps, frowning at the map, then at the end of the hall again. The featureless wall hadn't changed. Had the door been covered over or sealed? She set the map and inventory note-book down and walked back to the end of the hall, ran her hands over it. Not drywall, but solid plaster, cool and damp to the touch. If it had been closed off, it didn't seem to be recent.

Her fingertips caught on a small flaw in the smooth surface and she bent to see it better in the shadowy green light. A circle cut into the plaster, with what appeared to be a set of links dangling from it, like a collar and chain. It was crossed by a whip, the braided design painstakingly worked in.

She gasped, then swallowed it, glad no one had heard her.

She glanced around, uncannily convinced that someone watched, listened. Unable to help herself, she traced the emblem with her nail, wondering what it meant and why it was here.

And why something about it thrilled her, sent her blood perco-lating with intrigue and a desire to know more. Along with a strange familiarity.

A breath of cold air swept across the back of her neck again, and she stood abruptly, spinning on her heels and putting her back to the wall.

Nothing.

No one was there.

And yet . . . that tenor voice, golden and sweet, sang somewhere far in the distance, too distant for her to make out the melody, but the notes strummed across her stimulated nerves, soothing and arousing. She wanted to find it, to hear it better.

The song ended in a soft laugh. And then a whisper.

Christine.

2

She showered before her date—for the second time that day. By the time she got back to her little room, she'd felt covered in grime and the crawling sensation of cobwebs on her flesh. Turning the water on as hot as she could stand it, she reveled in the burn, heating her skin, loosening her muscles, and driving away that odd uneasiness.

Though she'd wanted to ask Charlie about that sealed-over door, he'd been on the phone—still or again—when she finally found her way back to his office. Now, with a bit of distance from the place, she thought maybe she wouldn't bring it up. Nothing was listed as stored on that level. Maybe the rock walls had become unstable or something.

No sense letting Charlie know they'd spooked her. Imagining the theater ghost, crying *Christine*.

The hotel shower gel smelled of pine needles, a surprisingly sensual fragrance, like the depths of the forest, where no light filtered through. She rubbed it into her skin, enjoying a long-held fantasy about how it might be to have the devastatingly handsome Roman Sanclaro finally kiss her.

She updated it in her mind. He'd grown up, become more fully a man now, with his MBA and a more worldly air. He was the type to ask first, with that ironic smile to show his nod toward the gentlemanly thing. His full lips would be warm, maybe with a hint of after-dinner brandy on his breath. It would be everything she'd dreamed about, way back when.

The image of the carved whip and collar floated through her mind, dark and taunting. It worried her that she seemed fixated on it. Not a good sign. But all of this was new to her. Feeling a little emotional and uncertain was natural. What mattered was how she handled it. With rationality, not obsession.

She pushed the image away, locking it in with the other bad thoughts she no longer allowed herself to have. Those days were past. She could be normal and happy. "I control the environment of my mind," she said out loud, repeating what the counselors had helped her affirm.

With a last rinse, she made herself turn off the gloriously hot water and step out of the shower. Toweling off briskly, she rubbed in the lotion that matched the body wash but didn't linger over it. On the counter, her little diamond watch—another graduation present from her dad—showed she didn't have much time left. Fortunately her pixie bob would dry fast, with a little gel and some tousling. Her father hadn't been thrilled about the change, but she loved the spunkiness of it.

He did *not* know about her tattoo. Never would, if she could help it.

She went for the standard little black dress. That should be sophisticated enough for wherever Roman took her. The short skirt and her splurge stilettos made her tanned legs look long. Adding a pair of dangly earrings—silver spirals with a pinpoint of turquoise that she'd gotten for a steal at the Indian Market—she spiked up her hair a little more, then did her eyes up all smoky.

Perfect.

"Look out, Roman Sanclaro!" she told her reflection. The new, grown-up her was saucy like that.

Unfortunately, the new her didn't have a matching coat—and she was pretty sure her usual bubble coat made her look twelve. Not what she was going for. Oh, well, hotel to car to restaurant, right? She could pull that off.

Roman pulled up in front of the lobby at exactly eight o'clock. Before she got to the passenger door, he'd come around the car and opened it for her with a reproving smile. "Allow me."

She slid into the low-slung sports car—quite a trick in the short skirt not to flash the guy standing *right there*. Pulling on her seat belt while he walked back around the car, she took in the glowing lights of the dash. The gentlemanly thing seemed nice enough, but it was weird to sit and wait like this. For lack of anything better to do, she folded her hands in her lap.

"You look gorgeous." Roman flashed her a grin as he settled into his seat. He trailed a light finger down her bare arm. "But we're at pretty high altitude—spring comes late here. Won't you be cold?"

She wouldn't have been, if he hadn't made her wait while he opened the door. "Not unless you're making me eat outside. And thank you. You look spiffy yourself."

He did look good, in his sleek gray suit jacket and matching shirt, open at the neck. They zoomed down Cerillos toward the Plaza, then around and up Canyon Road. There Roman was forced to slow, weaving his way past the narrow, crooked turns and laughing tourists enjoying the darkening spring evening, despite the snow-chilled air sliding down from the snowy slopes above.

At a one-story white building, sandwiched amid the galleries, he handed the valet a folded bill and escorted her with a guiding hand on her lower back.

"Geronimo is one of my favorites," he murmured in her ear. "I thought it would be suitable for your introduction to Santa Fe dining."

Roman didn't have to say a word to the hostess—they were seated immediately in a cozy candlelit booth, nestled between curved, low white walls. A waiter showed Roman a bottle and uncorked it at his nod of approval, pouring for her first. When he left, Roman raised his glass in a toast.

"To the most beautiful girl in the room."

She clinked her glass against his, hoping she hadn't blushed. The wine tasted surprisingly good.

"It's good. I don't usually drink red."

He sat back and slung an arm along the top of the curved seat, his tailored shirt tightening against his pecs. "It's one of their best— I knew you'd appreciate it."

The waiter returned, setting down a plate of hors d'oeuvres.

"And you already ordered."

"I hope you don't mind." He gestured at the plate with his wineglass. "I called ahead, to make sure they'd have all my favorite things. So tonight would be a special treat for you."

Even in her sweetest fantasies, she hadn't imagined this kind of thoughtful attention from him. Though that stuff on the crackers looked suspiciously like raw meat. Her father didn't hold with food he couldn't identify the ingredients of from five feet away.

"Steak tartare." He snagged one and popped it in his mouth, eyes closing in pleasure as he chewed. She took one and put it on her little plate, resisting the urge to poke it with her finger, hearing her father's voice in her head.

"It won't bite you." He watched her, a laugh sparking in his brown eyes. "Just try a taste."

That's why she was doing all this, right? The new, adventurous, anything-is-possible Christy. She took a bite.

It *was* raw meat. But, as with the wine, the flavor spread in her mouth, rich and full, tingling her senses. She smiled at him. "Delicious."

"Me? Or the steak tartare?" he teased her.

"Both."

He picked up her hand and kissed her fingers, a warm and sensuous press of his lips. "I was hoping you'd think so. I've always wanted a chance for us to get to know one another, outside the family stuff. Remember when I took you to your senior prom?"

Remember? She would never forget. Her boyfriend had dumped her a week before and she'd felt the ground shifting beneath her, the shimmering sense of that old instability, like the slow loss of blood into hot bathwater. Unable to deal, she'd declared she wouldn't go, despite her father's blandishments. In a fit of anger, she threw the dress she'd bought onto the fire, to end the arguments once and for all.

And then Roman had taken the train down from Harvard that afternoon, bringing her a sequined dress that one of his girls told him was all the rage. Like a prince in a fairy tale, he'd rescued her.

"It was the best night of my life." Christy swallowed some wine to clear the tightness in her throat. "I'll never forget it. Though it must have been awful for you—having to hang out at a high-school prom with a teenage girl."

"Not at all." He stroked her hand thoughtfully. "You were so adorable. Besides, every girl should go to her prom."

"How did my dad bribe you?"

Roman's eyes flashed with a bit of surprise, then he shook his head ruefully. "It wasn't really a bribe, but I was fighting with my dad then and he'd cut me off. The spending money came in handy.

Don't be mad." He widened his brown eyes into a sad puppy look, then smiled when she laughed.

"I knew something like that had happened. I didn't mind. I just felt kind of bad that you got stuck with me all the time, like a bratty little sister."

"I'm not being bribed now," he murmured. "And you are all gorgeous girl."

His polished charisma filled the small restaurant like a rich cologne. A woman at a nearby table even snapped their picture surreptitiously with her phone, clearly thinking they might be celebrities.

The rest of the evening followed suit. Roman offered her plate after plate of exquisite food, as pleased with her responses as if he'd made everything himself, flirting shamelessly. The waiter seemed half in love with him, bringing out extra tidbits and blushing at Roman's extravagant praise.

Christy dreamily watched the lights roll by as Roman drove them through the streets that wound through the adobe houses. She was a little drunk on wine, sated with excellent food, and warm from her dream date's attentions. Roman suggested after-dinner drinks at a great little bar he knew, but Christy begged off, thinking of an early morning and that massive inventory.

The carved image of the whip and collar returned, along with that haunting tenor. Was it the theater ghost?

Stop thinking about it.

Roman pulled into the hotel drive just then and she was suddenly sorry she'd declined drinks. Now she'd be alone with her thoughts. She nearly said she'd changed her mind.

"Thanks," she said instead. "I had a really good time."

He undid his seat belt and opened his door. She did as well, and he pointed at her. "Wait." He smiled. "I'll get your door."

It still seemed silly, but she waited. He lifted her up out of the low seat and ran warm hands down her arms—and silly became romantic.

"I'd like to see you again."

"Okay," she agreed easily. Hopefully not too eagerly. Innocent twelve-year-old Christy was jumping up and down for joy.

His eyes glinted warmly at her under the hotel awning lights, his full lips curving with pleasure.

"And I'd like to kiss you."

"Okay." She breathed out the word, unable to think of something more articulate.

The kiss was even better than she'd fantasized, a brush of his lips that deepened, hot and sensual. He put his hands around her waist, pulling her close, while she slid her hands up behind his neck, toying with the shorter curls there, just as she'd always wanted to do.

"Mmm." He pulled back. "The sweetest thing I've tasted all night."

She giggled. So not sophisticated, but she felt too giddy to care.

"I'll call you." He opened the lobby door and watched her go inside. "Good night, sweet girl."

In the morning she arrived at the opera house ready to tackle the inventory in truth. The bright, sunshiny day helped. Plus a steady replay of Roman's kiss. She might even have sung along with "Call Me Maybe" on the car radio on the way in.

What other people didn't know wouldn't get her laughed at.

"Good morning, Charlie!" she sang out, imagining herself as one of the Angels. She could totally be the Lucy Liu character, in a non-Asian way and with lighter hair.

Charlie took in her worn jeans, sweatshirt, and cross-trainers, nodding in approval. He pointed at her iPad. "What's that for?"

"It's a newfangled computer thingy. I'm going to create what us kids call a database."

He glared at her, chewing on his lip to hide a smile. "Cute. You're sure frisky this morning."

"Just happy to be starting my new job."

"Uh-huh. What if I don't want the inventory in a database?"

"Don't say that! It'll be so much better." She laid her tablet on the desk and tapped it meaningfully. "It'll be *searchable*."

"Searchable, huh?"

"Yesss." She drew out the word, nodding along and giving him a manic smile.

He laughed. "Ah, the vigor of youth. Well, I won't hold it against you if you give up halfway through."

"I'm converting this inventory to electronic if it kills me."

A shadow darkened Charlie's face and the room chilled. *Christine.*

Did she hear that—or imagine it?

"Did you—"

Charlie cut her off. "Don't worry. I'm sensitive, what with Tara's people so convinced something happened to her. Just look after yourself. Her office is still sealed by the police, but I found you something else that'll work. Not fancy, but . . ."

"I don't need fancy."

Charlie huffed a laugh. "Good thing."

He had a point. The office turned out to be hardly worthy of the name. It was more of a closet—or a vestibule between other rooms—barely big enough for a student-sized desk, and three of the "walls" were closed doors. One opened onto the long, curving main corridor, all the way around the bend from Charlie's. "Shouting distance," he'd called it, but an uneasy feeling in her stomach doubted he'd hear her, even if she did shout.

One of the other two doors led into a studio with floor-to-ceiling mirrors along one wall and a ballet bar inset. The last opened into a minuscule closet, barely big enough to wedge her body into. But it did give her a place to hang up her coat. Plus, a couple of battered posters from previous seasons stood rolled up in the corner. She stole a few thumbtacks from the empty bulletin board down the way and hung the posters on the bare walls—one on the door to the studio—to liven up the place.

Then she could delay no longer. She tucked a pen behind her ear, grabbed her tablet and the Big Notebook of Doom, and headed down the stairs.

She started out on the second-lowest level. Not that she was avoiding the lowest one, creepy though it might be. No, she told herself, there simply wasn't any point in going down there again since that corridor had been walled off. Surely the inventory items listed for that level would be in other rooms and no one had updated the massive list.

This, she smiled to herself, was why they needed a database.

She unhooked the massive ring of keys Charlie had given her from her belt loop and sorted through it, looking for the correct room number. The lock in the institutional-style door didn't want to turn but finally gave way to total gloom and a muscular, musty smell reminiscent of the elevator. Feeling around for the switch, she wished she'd thought to bring a flashlight with her. *Please don't let a spider bite me.* God or a scorpion. Did they have those here?

The overhead light came on with a snick and a whirr, as in the old gym in her high school. The one that hadn't been rehabbed. Sure enough, it was one of those gray metal kind, with a frame to protect the bulb. Odd that such old lights would be on a motion sensor, but she hadn't found the switch.

Feeble light chased away most of the shadows, showing a room packed with boxes upon boxes—some cardboard, some wood—and none labeled. With a sigh, she thumbed on the iPad and started a list of things she needed: flashlight, fat Sharpie markers, gloves.

She started with the box nearest the door, sitting on the floor to sort through the contents. Mostly folded cotton kimonos in this one. Or the under kimono, rather. Whatever those were called. Flipping to the correct level and room in the Big Notebook of Doom, she scanned the list for something like that.

This was going to take forever. Maybe this was what had scared Tara away.

She hoped that Tara had indeed run off to Acapulco with her boyfriend. Maybe she'd taken one look at the BNoD and run as fast as she could. If Roman Sanclaro invited *her* on a sexy little beach vacay, she might be entirely tempted.

Tempted, but she wouldn't do it. After the season is over, she'd tell him. They could go in the winter, when the opera house had closed up.

Half daydreaming about the fantasy beach trip—how good would Roman look in swim trunks?—and concentrating on checking things off her list and entering them into the tablet, she lost track of time.

Humming along with the music, she became aware of the crick in her neck. Then her head snapped up and she winced as her muscles caught. Music? No, there wasn't . . . Yes. There. That golden tenor wafted down the hallway through the open door, now clearly audible, then gone again. She knew the tune but couldn't place it. Something sweet and sad, a song of longing. Of love lost and never forgotten.

Mesmerized by it, she followed the sound into the dim hall. The bare bulbs opened small gaps of light down the hallway for a few doorways, then gave up against the darkness beyond. Her sneakers making soft whispers against the grit on the cement floor, she chased the tantalizing wisps of song, pulled into the deeper shadows.

Just when they had faded beyond hearing, the golden notes surged again, teasing, beckoning, offering . . . something. Like the singer, she longed for what she'd never had, yearned for it with a deep, sexual need, feeling as if she'd lost something precious, never quite grasped, always barely beyond her reach and now—gone forever.

She had to place her hand against the near wall to guide herself in the deep gloom, feeling her way across the floor. Intent on the music, senses roused in response, she barely felt the chill concrete, nearly desperate to find the source. *Wanting*, a bone-deep need, surged through her, overcoming everything else.

Christine.

Her breath shuddered out, wanting to call back to him.

Christine.

"Who's there?" Her voice bounced back, unbearably loud and jangling after straining to hear each whispered note.

"Christy?"

She whirled around, heart clenching, to crash straight into Charlie. A little shriek escaped her.

"What the hell are you doing here in the dark?" His industrial-strength flashlight pointed down toward the floor, light bouncing back up to illuminate his genial cowboy face so that he looked more like a kind of evil gnome. "Who are you talking to?"

"Ah—" Her voice came out on a squeak and she had to swallow it down. What *had* she been doing? "I, um, thought I heard music."

Charlie looked past her, as if he could see something in the impenetrable black. "Echoes of the techs, probably, from upstairs. The acoustics in this place are funny that way. I came to see if you wanted to break for lunch."

"Yes!" The prospect of getting out into the sunshine dispelled the sticky web of neediness that still stirred uneasily inside her.

"C'mon, then. I have a hankering for green chile." Charlie turned decisively back to the weak lighting down the hall, a pale gleam at the end of the tunnel. "And next time bring one of the flashlights. It's not safe."

"I thought you said Tara ran off—that she couldn't have . . ." *don't say died* ". . . disappeared down here."

Charlie grunted but didn't reply.

3

They rode in Charlie's rattling pickup down the road to Tesuque. Under the overpass, the Native American symbols in colorful shapes danced on the walls.

"What do they all mean—do you know?"

"Some of 'em. Some are so old even the tribes don't know."

"How can that be?"

"Well, nobody around here is original to the place, if you go back far enough. Santa Fe might be one of the oldest cities in the U.S.—just had our four-hundred-year celebration—but that's when the Spanish arrived. The tribes that were here at the time—the Nambe, the Tesuque, the Pueblo, among others—they moved into the abandoned dwellings left by even more ancient Indians."

"Like the Anasazi at Mesa Verde."

Charlie chuckled. "Yeah, same people, but you're not supposed to use that name anymore because it means something along the lines of 'ancient enemy,' and modern folks figure that's not really fair. Go visit Bandelier and read up on it."

"I thought we're not supposed to say 'Indian,' either."

"True, true." Charlie pulled into a dirt parking lot alongside the road, in front of a ramshackle building with a wooden porch. "But the Indians all say it, unless they're being formal, so I slip into it over time."

The small dining room looked like the inside of a log cabin cook shack, which it probably started out as. By the register, a long hall took a crooked turn to become a sort of grocery store/gift shop. People were crowded in around linoleum-topped tables, a mix of locals and tourists armed with maps and brochures.

Charlie nodded at them. "People come over here to see the ironworks and the sculpture garden. Worth a wander through, if you haven't yet."

The menu was as simple as the setting. No steak tartare here. Christy ended up ordering a burger with guacamole and green chile strips, which Charlie assured her would warm her right up. Those lower levels could be cold this time of year.

"Not a five-star place, but the food is good and you can't beat the prices."

"Mr. Sanclaro took me to Geronimo last night," she told him, deciding to answer the question he wasn't asking.

"Nice."

"It was."

They lapsed into silence. She suspected he was torn between treating her as any apprentice and standing in for her father.

"We're old friends—as you know—but if it gets to be more, um, I mean, if it's not kosher for me to see a patron, you know, romantically . . ." To her horror, she found herself blushing, remembering that very yummy kiss. In front of her new boss.

"No, no. It's not that." Charlie drank from his mug of coffee and wrinkled up one side of his mouth, chewing on the words. "I feel I should warn you. Which is all kinds of inappropriate and you have the family connection and all. But if you were my daughter, I'd want to tell you that fellow is—well, he has a bit of reputation around here. He sniffs around all the pretty young apprentices, and the actresses, too. He gets around."

Okay, that was a fair warning. "I'll be very careful not to let him break my heart." She tried to sound solemn, but Charlie shook his head with a wan smile.

"All right. Make fun of an old man."

"You're not old."

"Old enough to know some things."

"Do you believe in the theater ghost?" The question sprang out before she realized she was thinking it.

Charlie sat back in his chair and scratched an ear. "Depends," he finally said.

Not the answer she'd expected. "Really? On what?"

"Well . . ." He gazed at the ceiling, shifting to the side when the people clearing the table next to them brushed past. "See, I believe there's more to this world than meets the eye. Like the opera house—there's all these levels below levels and hidden crannies. You don't live in a place like this without knowing that the intangibles make it special. You know the artists all moved here because of the light?"

"Like Georgia O'Keeffe?"

"Yeah, she was one of the first, but they all followed because they agreed. There's something special about the sky and the light."

"Okay."

"But how can that be?" He nodded thanks to the harried woman who refilled his coffee. "I mean—same sun, same atmosphere, same planet. How can the light be any different here than, say, in Denver? Or Reno—any of those places with the same altitude?"

"I don't know."

"Exactly!" Charlie thumped down his mug. "Because there isn't any reason, but it's still true. We see it. We feel the difference in our bones. Same as the new Indians who moved in and took up the sacred symbols of the ancient Indians before them. Something in us recognizes magic when we encounter it. Whether we believe in it consciously or not. It affects us and the choices we make." That same expression of worry crossed his face, as it had when he spoke of Tara.

The waitress dropped off their food with a cheerful exhortation to enjoy it. Finding a way to open her mouth wide enough to bite into the thick burger, dripping with green chile stew, gave her some time to think. Charlie seemed to forget his somber thoughts and happily plowed into a smothered burrito.

"So, you're saying the theater ghost exists whether we believe in him or not?" She wiped her mouth on a paper napkin.

"I'm saying there are more things in heaven and earth than are dreamt of in your philosophy."

"Horatio," she inserted automatically, and Charlie tossed off a two-fingered half salute. "And I don't think I have a philosophy."

"Well, you're young yet. It takes experience and paying attention to build a good philosophy."

"What's yours?"

"Just told you, didn't I?"

"I think I heard him—the ghost. Singing. That's what I was doing."

"Ah."

She waited, only halfway through her burger and already stuffed. But he didn't say anything else. Didn't call her crazy.

"That's it?"

"Well, I already told you to be careful. And to take a flashlight. What else can I say?" Charlie no longer seemed his cheerful self but defensive. Resigned? Maybe afraid.

"Did Tara hear the ghost?"

"Now why would you ask that?" Charlie snapped up the check in uncharacteristic irritation. "If you're done, let's go. My treat."

While he waited in line to pay at the register, Christy browsed the shelves of the market. The place was kind of like those out-of-the-way convenience stores, with odd assortments of necessities, comfort foods, and items you couldn't imagine anyone needing—like tapioca pudding mix.

A ceramic bowl held polished stones that fit in the palm of her hand, inscribed with different animal symbols. She recognized one from the bridge—a humpbacked bear—carved into a shining black rock. Charlie waited impatiently by the door while she paid her five dollars and change for it.

"You shouldn't buy that Indian crap," he huffed.

It lay in her palm, surprisingly warm. "Why not? Maybe it's good luck."

"Maybe it's a rip-off, too. Not all of 'em feel friendly to white folks either. Could be they wrapped some bad juju in there, to make you a little miserable."

"Which is it, Charlie?" She laughed, hoisting herself into the truck, glad not to be in yesterday's narrow skirt. "Bad luck or worthless?"

"Don't get smart with me."

"I think it's lucky. It feels lucky," she decided.

Charlie pointed the truck up the river road and the early afternoon sun streamed in on the cracked dashboard, illuminating the dusty old blue so it glowed. The budding limbs of the trees stood out against a sky of the same creamy color. It all looked other-worldly, beautiful and full of sensual promise.

"You might find—" Charlie cleared his throat, staring stead-fastly at the narrow road. "If you think you hear the ghost, go the other way."

"You *do* believe in him." She pounced on his words.

"Didn't say that, did I?"

Oh, but he had. That much was very clear. "Do you think—is it possible he hurt Tara, after all?" The stone burned hot in her palm, a tiny sun of its own.

Charlie glanced at her before turning up the winding drive, past the gated communities of the wealthy, that led to the opera house. "There's no reason to think Tara did anything but run off. It didn't surprise me because she was the type to be easily spooked."

He pulled into the backstage lot and cut the engine. Reaching over, he tapped the back of her hand, and she opened it, showing him the polished stone. "Are you easily spooked?"

The carving of the bear seemed subtly different. Had one paw been curled up, as if about to take a step, before? And its head was turned in semiprofile, looking up at her. A wash of hot-cold ran over her scalp and her skin prickled with golden sparks, that feeling of being crazy, of blood draining away.

"C'mon. That inventory beckons, kiddo."

She had to scramble to catch up with him. "Thanks for lunch!" she called to his back.

He turned, holding the door open. "Remember what I told you. And take a damn flashlight."

4

Nothing unusual happened that afternoon. If Christy put on a playlist of dance tunes to drown out any potential otherworldly melodies, who would blame her? No cell or wireless signal down here, but she had her iTunes library to pull from.

Maybe she turned up the volume louder than usual. Not like she'd be bothering anyone. She tucked her talisman in her jeans pocket—for good luck, she stubbornly thought at the absent Charlie. It had been dim in the store and she hadn't looked at it closely. Making her think the image on the rock had changed was another of those tease-the-newbie games.

Of course there was no theater ghost—just tricks of sound. The opera house had been designed to carry sound of all kinds. With all these rock and concrete tunnels beneath, they amplified and distorted the smallest noise from above even more. And if she wanted to believe that theaters absorbed the energy of performances over the years, the very walls vibrating with old melodies when all was silent, well, that seemed several sane steps above buying that some *entity* haunted the halls, singing of lost love.

Having the monster flashlight helped, too. If nothing else, she could use it as a club.

When she climbed back upstairs at the end of the day, terribly dusty and more tired than she should be, a text message popped up from Roman.

Dinner tomorrow?

"Yay, yay, yay!" Christy did a little dance with her phone. This one would be a no-brainer.

Would love to! she texted back. She hoped that didn't sound too eager. She should probably play hard to get, but that had never been her thing. He'd sent the text a couple of hours before, so that would have to do.

Pick you up at 8? Can't wait, sweet girl. The text came back immediately.

The old pet name gave her a tingle of delight. Maybe she could think up one for him. Something no other girl had called him. She didn't mind that he'd dated around a lot. Of course he had. And it wasn't like they were actually engaged, despite their fathers' bad jokes.

She tucked her phone and other things in her bag, set the BNoD squarely on the middle of her desk, and looked around for her iPad. *Well, shit.* Gathering up her stuff and keeping one hand free for the flashlight, she'd left it sitting on a box by the door. It would probably be okay there overnight, but she really wanted it with her. Quiet evenings in her hotel room were sometimes *too* quiet.

Oh, well—it would only take a few minutes to retrieve it. She'd already checked in with Charlie and he'd headed out, thinking she'd be right behind him. A frisson of uncertainty ran through her and she wondered if she was being the dumb chick in the slasher movies, going back down into the depths of the opera house after everyone had gone.

Yeah, as if the ghost was going to get her.

A quick trip down and back—armed with the monster flashlight. No different from being down there ten minutes before.

Right?

Turning the lights on as she went, she headed back down her favorite spiral staircase. No way would she get in that elevator with no one in the building. On some of the levels, she had to descend into a pool of shadow barely broken by the spear of her flashlight. At least it helped her find the switches. Each series of bulbs buzzed on with sluggish resistance, slowing her progress.

Finally she made it to the lowest level—second lowest, really, but the one below didn't count anymore—and lit her way to her current storeroom. She unlocked the door and there sat her iPad, right where she'd left it.

Only . . . a red rose sat on top of it.

That familiar chill washed over her. *Someone just walked over your grave*, her aunt Isadore's voice said in her mind. Tentative, she reached out to touch the rose. Her hand was shaking. She poked the blossom—it was vividly real, satin and alive. Where did it come from? Her touch had overbalanced it and the rose tumbled off its perch and fell to the floor, dust staining the dewy petals.

She stared at it, like it was a snake coiled to strike her ankle, trying to shake the overwhelming feeling that someone was watching her from the hallway. Thoughts running in frantic circles, she gripped the flashlight, the metal cold and slick in her abruptly sweating palm.

A click. And the hallway light went out.

Shit. Shit. Shit. Shit. Shit.

Had this happened to Tara? Would she be the next to go missing, to have her father demanding that the lower levels be searched yet again for a body that would never be found?

She refused to turn around.

She had to turn around.

Oh God.

She turned.

And screamed.

A shadowy figure stood just past the open door. Tall, broad-shouldered, a dark silhouette against the unlit hallway.

"Don't be afraid, Christine."

That voice. *The* voice. The golden tenor caressed even spoken words, music running through it. Something deep inside her recognized it, resonating with it, with him. The shimmering feeling of *not quite real* made her head swim.

She grasped the heavy flashlight, holding it in both hands, ready to swing.

"I'll scream," she threatened. Most inane threat ever, since she already had. Look at all those people, *not* coming to save her.

"No need." He sounded amused. "I won't hurt you."

"I don't believe you."

"Why would I want to do harm to such a beautiful and vibrant young woman?"

"Oh God—you're going to rape me."

He laughed— a warm breath of sensuality, soothing in a totally irrational way. "I'm not. I never would."

"Then what do you want?"

"To talk with you." He moved, and his silhouette flowed, a long cape around him. "I want to know you, Christine."

"Who are you?" Her voice had strained into a whisper, fear shutting down her throat after her brief enchantment with the sound of his laughter. "Don't come any closer!"

"I won't. I don't want to frighten you."

"Well, you already did."

"I apologize. My . . . social skills are rusty."

She choked out a scornful cough, a ragged sound that surprised her. The flashlight was growing heavy, her arms tiring as she held it up. This was when they grabbed you, though—the moment you let down your guard.

"If you're not here to hurt me, I want you to go away."

"I understand, Christine. This was enough for me, for now."

"I'm not *her*." The words burst out, fueled by fear and a kind of desperation. Who the hell was this guy? Was he really a ghost?

"Who?"

"Christine."

"But that's your name—I heard you tell my stage manager."

"Your stage manager?" Charlie?

"I think of Charlie that way, yes. This is my opera house; therefore you all work for me. You, Christine, are my apprentice. A very special apprentice. It's time for you to relearn what you used to know."

"This is my father's opera house." She tried to sound unwavering, clinging to the part of what he said that made sense, but her voice faltered.

"There are many ways of owning. Not all of them involve names on deeds."

"Who *are* you?"

He shifted ever so slightly closer to the circle of light spilling through the doorway, barely enough to show he wore a half mask, a slash of darker material in the shadow of his face.

"You, my apprentice, shall call me Master."

* * *

She should quit.

That was the clear and obvious solution. Not that she could tell anyone why.

Oh yeah, Daddy—see there's some stalker dude who's probably a ghost living below the opera house and, get this, he thinks he really owns it! And he gave me a rose and said some really weird shit. Say, can you find me another job?

He'd send her right back to the mental ward.

Christy groaned, wanting to bang her head on the bar, and took a deep swallow of her margarita instead. The salt on the rim pricked through the icy, tart concoction, finishing with the dark smoke of Hornitos tequila, seeping into her blood and soothing her as much as the crackling fire and chattering people.

She'd come straight to Del Charro from the opera house. After she'd stood there, clutching that stupid flashlight for forever after the ghost disappeared. Except he'd looked real. What did ghosts look like? And what was up with the you-shall-call-me-Master bit?

She should really just quit.

Maybe she wouldn't have to. Charlie might fire her for leaving all those lights on. Because, when she'd finally screwed up her courage, she'd grabbed the iPad and run all the way up the spiral staircase, certain he might grab her from behind. Or worse, through the gaps between the stairs. No fucking way was she stopping to turn off the lights and climb in the pitch black.

She couldn't face her silent hotel room either, so she'd come to this place, because she'd seen happy people through the tall floor-to-ceiling windows that faced the street, open to the balmy evening. So much better than being alone, cliché as it might be.

"Ready for another one?" The bartender pointed at the empty glass she clutched in both hands.

"Yeah." Christy pushed the glass to her. "Something seems to have happened to this one."

The bartender grinned and set the glass in the sink. "I'll make you a fresh one. Where you from?"

Everyone here asked her that. She wasn't sure if it was because she so obviously wasn't local or because they assumed everyone was a tourist.

"I live here. Well—at the El Rey until I get a place. I'm working at the opera." *Unless I quit.*

"Oh, cool. I've never been—can't afford it—but I hear it's really neat." The bartender shook her unnaturally red ponytail. "One day, when I'm rich and famous. And learn to like opera."

"What do you do—I mean, do you have a job besides bartending?"

The redhead laughed. "You figure I'm not planning to get rich and famous tending bar? No, I'm a starving artist. I paint." She set down a brimming margarita and wiggled her fingers. "Faces, bodies, that kind of thing. This job pays the bills okay."

Christy sipped the margarita—twice as strong this time. She'd have to watch it or she'd be taking a cab home. To the hotel. Whatever. "Do you guys serve food? Dinner food?"

"Sure. Restaurant's attached, or you can eat here at the bar."

"That would be great. To eat here."

The bartender handed her the menu. "Special today is the chicken enchiladas. And we were voted best hamburger in Santa Fe." She wandered off to serve other customers while Christy looked over her choices. Definitely not another burger after the one at lunch. She should have a salad.

"You decided?"

"I'll have the potato chips with the warm blue cheese dressing for now," Christy told her, abandoning any thought of picking something healthy.

"Nothing like comfort food." The bartender tapped in the order.

"No kidding."

"I'm Hally." The redhead held out her hand, shook Christy's.

"Like Halle Berry?"

Hally wrinkled her nose and leaned on the bar. "I wish! No— short for Halcyon. My folks were all into Burning Man and Rainbow Family, that kind of thing. I had a weird childhood. But I can dig a latrine, build a campfire, and cook stew for a hundred people. Plus I'm all kinds of creative."

"Ah." She'd heard of Burning Man, but not the other.

Hally waved a hand at her. "I won't bug you. You waiting for someone?"

"No. I, um, actually don't mind if you want to chat. I didn't want to be alone tonight, pathetic as that sounds."

"Not pathetic at all. I can't imagine moving to a new town by myself." Hally waved back at someone coming in the door and pulled out a couple of longneck Buds. "You must be all kinds of brave."

Remembering the sheer, bowel-draining terror of meeting the theater ghost, how she'd run like a frightened rabbit once he'd left, that black cloak swirling in the dark, Christy shook her head. "Not by half. You wouldn't believe what I saw—" She cut herself off with a shiver.

Hally widened her hazel eyes, dramatically lined with thick eyeliner. "What? Don't stop there."

She had to tell someone and she sure as hell wasn't going to bring up the ghost to Charlie again. She leaned farther over the bar, scooting the margarita ahead of her. "Have you ever heard that the opera house is haunted?"

"No!" Hally glanced at the group down the bar and hushed her voice. "Well, I mean, everything around here is haunted, according to some people. Spirits everywhere. Old city, battles, negative vortexes. Did you see a ghost?"

"I don't know." Christy chewed on her lip. He hadn't seemed like a ghost, but what did ghosts seem like?

"What *did* you see?"

"This will sound crazy."

"I don't care." Hally propped her elbows on the bar and her chin on her hands, cupping her gamine face. "Tell me everything."

"Well, first I heard singing."

"Not unusual for an opera house."

"When no one was there."

"Oh . . . oh! Yes, creepy. Go on."

"And then tonight, he—"

"Dammit! Hold that thought." Hally snagged an order ticket from a waitress and pulled out several bottles of wine. She also slid the potato chips and dip in front of Christy with a cheerful wink. It all seemed so very normal, the jangle of a sports game on the television over the mirror, the rise and fall of conversation. The everydayness of it all grounded her. That man had been no ghost. Nothing creepy or otherworldly there. She'd been rattled. Who knows? Maybe it had been some stage tech, pulling the running gag of scaring the new girl.

"Okay! Sorry about that." Hally cracked a beer for herself, noting it on a tab. "So—'tonight he . . .' "

"You know, I've been thinking, and something tells me I shouldn't talk about it."

Hally nodded, solemn. "You have to honor that. A spirit visits you, that's a special thing."

Christy snorted, then realized Hally was completely serious. "Have you seen a spirit—for real?"

She sipped her beer, her hazel eyes bright as she nodded. "Yes. Of course, I was on a little peyote at the time, but this woman came to me. All pink and purple—that aura is supposed to mean she's a loving spirit—and she told me I should paint naked."

She couldn't help it; Christy giggled. Hally tried to look offended but lost it. "Well, it seemed profound at the time."

"And did you follow that advice?"

Hally waggled her eyebrows. "Never in public."

5

It helped to feel she'd made a friend. Hally promised to meet up with Christy on Sunday—sadly, still four days away—to go shopping and show her all the best places to get clothes at "nontourist prices."

After that, her hotel room didn't feel quite so lonely. Though on Saturday she needed to go look for apartments, so she could unpack some of her stuff. Because she was staying. No way she'd run home with her tail between her legs, crying for Daddy, because the mean guys at the opera played a joke on her.

She went to bed, firmly resolved.

But she didn't sleep well. Maybe it was the margaritas, or the chicken enchiladas Hally had finally talked her into. Christy tossed and turned, wakeful, certain someone was in the room with her. She even clicked on the bedside lamp, not once but twice, to make sure. The second time she took her carved stone with the bear and put it in the bedside table drawer.

When she fell into a deeper sleep, the dreams came.

She was running down the spiral staircase, something chasing her. *Run up!* she begged her dreaming self, but she kept going deeper, her feet skidding off the steps, until she fell. The stairs melted away and she plummeted through the dark, searching for a name to call. If she could only think of who to yell for, she'd be saved.

The ground rushed up and her voice choked in her throat as she braced for impact. . . .

The air thickened, stretching out her fall, cradling her. No, those were arms—strongly muscled, holding her close against a masculine chest. A man, eyes icy blue behind a black half mask, gazed down at her, speaking to her in a liquid language she didn't understand. His cloak swirled around them, and she realized she wore a wedding gown, the bodice tight against her breasts, white lace spilling to the floor.

He laid her on a bed, something out of a medieval castle, and chained her wrists above her head. Her body pulsed with longing. She writhed, drowning in lace, begging without words, while he reached down with black-gloved hands and raised the hem of her skirt.

"Yes, Master!" she shouted.

Christy woke herself with shattering abruptness. She sat straight up in bed, blinking at the dim room, sunshine leaking in around the curtains. Her heart pounded double-time, her skin slick with sweat—and arousal.

She didn't even want to think what that dream meant. Except no more chicken enchiladas, delicious as they'd been.

At least she was up bright and early. She made it up to the opera house before Charlie did. More cars were parked in the backstage lot now, and a crew of people in overalls were carrying stacks of lumber inside. That confirmed it—more techs around, more people thinking it would be funny to give her a bit of a scare. And okay, okay, they got her good. No wonder she'd had nightmares.

Ha-ha. The best revenge would be to act as if nothing had happened.

She settled into her office, taking the time to transfer her data from the previous day's inventory into more permanent files, cross-checking them against entries in the BNoD. Three items didn't seem to be listed anywhere in the notebook. She'd done a good chunk so far—surprisingly so, considering her distraction—but it was a drop in the bucket. It would go faster if she simply entered what she found, marking locations. Then she could compare it to the paper inventory in the evenings.

Except for tonight, when she'd be going out with Roman Sanclaro again.

She might or might not have been doing a happy chair dance when Charlie rapped on the door frame.

"Busy?" He rubbed the corners of his mouth, like he might be trying to wipe away a smile.

"Nope. Just about to head down to the dungeons for more inventory."

"Well, I've got a mission for you."

"Okay." She opened a reminder app on the iPad, ready to take notes. Charlie eyed it dubiously and she gave him her sweetest smile. "Hit me."

"The props manager, Carla—you'll meet her—needs the flute for *The Magic Flute* and insists she needs it yesterday. Something about needing time to refurbish it. Can you prioritize finding it for her so she'll get off my back?"

"I'm on it!" Christy assured him, sounding her perky best. "What exactly does it look like?"

"It's about yea long," Charlie held up his hands a yardstick length apart, "with gold curlicues. Might have silk flowers and ribbons tied on, depending on how it was put away."

"Got it."

"Thanks, kid." He turned to go. "Everything go okay yesterday?"

"Yep—just fine."

"No more . . . incidents?"

She shook her head and shrugged. "Not a thing. Why do you ask?"

"Just checking." He gave her a long look, then left, his jaunty whistle fading down the hall.

Ha. Showed him. If Charlie was in on the joke, he'd tell the others they hadn't rattled her.

Christy paged through the index of the BNoD, looking for flutes, then at broader categories. She found a number of items listed simply as *musical instruments*, which was totally unhelpful. Nowhere did any of the listings say *magic flute*, though there were several plain *flutes*. They were all, naturally, scattered in different storerooms and levels. Resigning herself to searching them all, she made a list and set off on her quest.

She started with the uppermost levels first. Not out of cowardice, but because if she could find the special magic flute with less effort, she'd save herself time and make Carla—and Charlie—happy all that much sooner.

The wig room door stood open when she went past, blazing with mirrors and warm light, row after row of bodiless heads staring into space, each sporting an elaborate confection of gleaming hair. A carpenter passed her in the hall, giving her a jaunty wave while he spoke to someone on his cell about glue. She waved back, feeling full of purpose and enjoying the burst of cheerful activity. It reminded her of an advent calendar that had been all closed up and now was opening, door by door, revealing a whirl of color and promise.

She searched the first storeroom for an hour. Miraculously, she eventually pulled down the box—incorrectly labeled—containing the flutes listed in the inventory. Which turned out to be some lovely champagne flutes.

Not at all what Carla wanted.

By noon she'd searched three more locations to no avail. Stomach growling, she headed back upstairs. Maybe she could run down to the Village Market and get a sandwich to go. Once she got her own place, she could pack her lunch.

"Hey! Hey, you—girlie." A woman's angry voice stopped Christy in her tracks. She turned, reflexively hugging the iPad to her breast.

"Me?"

"Yes, you." A tall blond woman strode up to her, looking her up and down. "You're the new Tara, right?"

"Christy, yes."

"Did you find the flute yet?"

"Not yet." She thumbed on the iPad, turning it to show Carla—for surely this was Carla—her list-and-search method. "See, I've checked—"

Carla waved a dismissive hand at it. "I'm really not interested in your excuses. You may be sucking on Daddy's teat, but the rest of us have jobs to do around here. Jobs that are important to us. I take goddamned pride in my job—do you get me, Chrissy?"

"I'll find it this afternoon, I promise."

Carla held up her hands, making a face of astonishment. "Why the hell aren't you looking right now?"

"I was. I am. It's just, I'm hungry and—"

Making a disgusted noise, Carla rolled her eyes. "And what? Off to have lunch with your little, rich girlfriends?"

"No." Stung, Christy scrambled for a reply to that dramatically unfair assumption.

"But you did go out with Roman Sanclaro, didn't you?" Carla pulled off her glasses, peering at Christy as if trying to see her better. "I can't imagine why—you don't look like much. I heard he took you to Geronimo. Pity date to curry favor for the family's sake?"

"Carla!" Charlie called down the hallway. "You're not badgering Christy about that flute, are you?"

"Well, dammit, Charlie—I told you this morning I need the fucking thing. You might not mind facing opening night with a rusty, decrepit, nasty flute, but I do. And she hasn't even started looking for it yet."

Christy's mouth opened and closed, making her feel like a mindless goldfish gasping for air. Carla glowered at her, daring Christy to say otherwise.

"I'm heading downstairs to search Level 3," Christy raised her voice for Charlie to hear while she returned Carla's glare.

"Good luck with that." Carla shoved her glasses back on and marched down to Charlie's office, thick blond braid bouncing.

What a freaking bitch. She'd show her. Screw lunch. Besides, Roman would likely feed her well tonight, and screw Carla and her opinions. She could date who she liked. Besides, Roman might have offered a pity date for old times' sake, but a second date meant he really liked her. Didn't it? Of course it did. Taking her righteous indignation with her, Christy headed back down the spiral staircase, checking her tablet for the next place to look. Surely she'd strike gold this time.

By six o'clock she was nearly in tears with frustration. She'd found numerous flutes—and a surprising number of various other musical instruments—but none of them were perfect matches. One of the "flutes" had turned out to be a slide whistle.

"Really?" she asked the long-gone anonymous person who'd penciled in that description. "You're truly *that* much of a freaking idiot that you don't know a slide whistle from a flute?"

To make herself feel better, she entered the item into the inventory correctly. At least someone else would be able to find the slide whistle someday; her legacy. The orderly inventory she'd begun had morphed into a patchwork quilt of observations. This sort of thing in one room, that stuff in another. But, by God, she knew where to find champagne flutes and a slide whistle!

A cold draft washed across the back of her neck, the door creaking open behind her. She stilled, frozen, a rabbit in the open. Was it *him*?

"Working hard, I see." Carla's barbed sarcasm came as a relief. An irony the woman would be unlikely to appreciate. "Must be nice to get a job playing computer games."

Christy stood, her knees protesting from being cramped so long while she sorted through the 37th box that day. She knew, because she'd been keeping track. "I've located everything listed as a flute or a musical instrument in the inventory." She nudged the BNoD on the floor with the toe of her now very dusty shoe. "And I haven't found it. I'll have to go through every room systematically."

Carla frowned. Or rather, her usual frown didn't lift. "Did you look under *Mozart*?"

The syrupy tone didn't fool Christy for a moment. "No. I looked under—"

"*The Magic Flute* is a Mozart opera." Carla said this slowly, as if English might be Christy's second language.

"Yes, I know that."

Carla's blond brows flew up. "Don't get snippy with me."

Christy swallowed her pride in the face of Carla's rising irritation. "It's just that it makes no sense to file a prop under—"

Heaving a dramatic sigh, Carla snatched up the BNoD and thumped it onto a carved wooden trunk that looked suspiciously like the Ark of the Covenant, sending a cloud of dust poofing up. She flipped through the pages to the index—though it was hardly deserving of the word—and stabbed her finger at a big, bold **MOZART**. With about five pages of items listed after it. " 'Flute!' " Carla pointed. " 'Antique flute, assorted flutes, flute, flute, flute.' "

Well, shit.

"Okay." Christy withheld her own sigh. "Tomorrow morning I'll—"

"No, now." Carla gave her a stern nod. "Tonight. You can leave it on my desk."

Christy reflexively glanced at her iPad clock. "Um, it's already six twenty and . . ." she trailed off, partially in fascination at the scarlet creep of fury climbing Carla's cheekbones.

"What?" Carla hissed. "Do you have something *better* to do?"

She sure as hell couldn't confess to a date with Roman Sanclaro. Or that she was afraid of a ghost. That bolt of alarm when she'd thought he was behind her proved that she might have convinced her mind he wasn't real, but her emotions were a few steps behind.

Christy gestured weakly at the page Carla still had pinned with one callused finger. "Most of that stuff is on the lowest levels and everyone has pretty much gone."

Carla shook her head, cocked it, and studied her like a mouse that had dared invade her kitchen. "So, explain. You're afraid?"

Yes. "No. I, just, um—"

"Look—I know our petty little problems are likely of no concern to a special snowflake like you," Carla snapped the notebook closed and shoved it at her, "so go do whatever it is that's so important, and I'll explain to Charlie why we don't have a decent magic-looking flute for opening night."

Carla, she didn't give a shit about, but Charlie . . . She couldn't disappoint him. Especially because it would get back to her father. Oh, joy.

She set down the notebook and began stacking her stuff. "No. You're right. This is important. I'll find it tonight and it will be on your desk in the morning."

"Good girl." Carla grinned at her, triumph cracking her dour face. "You see to it."

She stalked off, leaving Christy to lock up the storeroom. And to text Roman her regrets. She hoped he wouldn't be mad.

6

Upstairs, everyone else had gone home, and most of the lights were out. Christy sat at her tiny desk and pulled her cell phone out of the drawer. There was simply no point in taking it below the top level, since she had to turn it off anyway so it wouldn't drain the battery searching for a network connection.

Bad news. Work emergency and have to cancel tonight. ☹

She hesitated over adding the unhappy face, hoping it didn't look too young. But she didn't want Roman thinking she was blowing him off. Hopefully he'd answer soon. Having Carla find her here texting wouldn't go over well.

Maybe she should just call him. That might be weird, though, because they hadn't done phone calls yet. What if he was in a meeting or something? No, she'd wait a few minutes. If he didn't answer, she'd send something else.

While she waited, she opened the BNoD to the stupid Mozart index and recorded the locations of all Mozart-related, flute-type objects. Maybe it wouldn't take long and she'd find it right away. The masked man hadn't bothered her all day. It could be he'd leave her alone now.

Though it hadn't sounded as if he planned to.

The shrill whistle of an arriving text made her jump.

☹

Which made her laugh.

Want to push it back to 9? followed right after.

She wished. *Better not. I don't know how long it will take.* She hesitated, then took the leap. *Maybe tomorrow?*

Can't. Friday?

Friday sounds great!

I'll be thinking of you. Don't work too hard. 'Night, sweet girl.

Reluctantly, she slid her phone back into the drawer. What a great guy. It totally sucked that she had to wait two more days to see him. Grabbing her stack of supplies, including the monster flashlight/club, she headed out the door. Then, feeling a little superstitious—or maybe heeding the voice of caution—she set it all down again and pulled out a notepad. She made a list of the rooms she planned to check and added the time, 6:45. Just in case.

The note looked a little like a bad omen, a stark square of white on her bare desk, and she shivered.

Then she steeled herself and descended to the lower levels.

After a while she stopped jumping at every little noise. The opera house crouched, quiet and still, and Christy decided against playing music. If the ghost—or whoever—decided to visit her, she wanted warning of his arrival. So she could do what, she didn't know.

Starting with the storeroom simply named Mozart, she sorted quickly and efficiently through box after box. Being in the room felt like being in a Monty Python version of *Amadeus*. The wild and wacky props, costumes, and improbable furniture relaxed her more than anything else could have. With a thrill, she located the brightly feathered bird costumes that should go with *The Magic Flute*, but no—it would be too logical to keep the flute itself in the same vicinity.

Nine o'clock. Exhausted, starving, and covered in layers of grit, she finally locked the promising all-Mozart room and headed down the hall to the next location. Reaching the end of the pool of light, she flicked the switch to light the next length of hallway.

And nothing happened.

She snapped the switch down to off, and back on again. The lights flared, briefly, and died again. *Just fantastic.*

It had been enough to see the door to the next storeroom, though, not that far down the hall. Determinedly turning on the flashlight—

she could just see herself telling Carla she had been afraid of the dark—she panned the beam down the hallway to spot her goal and headed for it.

Something black fluttered into the edge of the stream and she snapped the light over . . .

Him.

With a cry, she jumped back, dropping her tablet, markers, pens—but clinging to her only weapon.

"Good evening, Christine." With the flashlight spotlighting him, icy blue eyes glittered behind the black mask. With a rush the dream came back, her blood quickening with the memory, the shimmering sense of unreality and blood loss making her head swim. She hadn't seen his eyes before, had she? He moved, fluid as a cat, the cloak parting to show his lean, masculine body dressed in formal evening clothes. Across his black-gloved hands lay a golden flute with ribbons trailing from it, incongruously fanciful against his grim appearance. "I believe you're looking for this."

"How . . ." She ran out of breath, inhaled, and tried again. "How did you know?"

One side of his mouth quirked up, curving the sensual lips. With nothing else to see of his face, his lips and those crystalline eyes demanded her attention. "I know everything that occurs in my opera house."

"Have you been hiding it from me?" He didn't look like a tech. Or a ghost. All that searching she'd done, and he'd had it all the time. She was pissed off. Which was better than afraid. Or fascinated.

"I'm giving it to you. Isn't that what you want?"

"Beware of strangers bearing gifts."

He laughed, low and sensual. "I believe that's *Greeks* bearing gifts."

"Still applies."

"But we're not strangers, are we, Christine?"

"One very creeptastic and scary meeting doesn't change anything. I amend that. This makes two creeptastic and scary meetings."

"I don't want to frighten you."

"No?" Her pitch rose a little too high. "Then what's with the cloak and mask? Why do you skulk around and torment me?"

"Do I torment you?" He stepped closer. "How so? As you say, we've barely met."

Oh, haunting my thoughts and one extraordinary dream.

"This," she answered instead. "This is tormenting me. Hiding the flute so that I kill myself looking and now taunting me that you have it."

"But I wasn't hiding it. I'm offering it to you." He took another step closer, holding out the flute, like a tribute.

"Don't come any closer." She kept the flashlight beam on him but adjusted her grip, ready to swing it at his face. *Just swing it hard enough to break his nose,* her college "Don't Be a Victim" instructor had said. *You don't have to knock him out—a broken nose hurts like hell and bleeds like more hell. Hit it and run like the wind.* Of course, the instructor had told them to scream, too. Something that would not work for her with everyone gone for the night. Or with ghosts.

"Then you come to me."

"If you really want to give me the flute, set it on the floor."

Those lips curved in amusement and he went down on one knee, laying the flute on the floor with a kind of reverence. Then he looked up at her. "A gift for a beautiful lady."

"Okay." He didn't move. "Um, thanks."

He laughed under his breath, and she had the uncomfortable sensation that he was mocking her. Uncoiling, he stood, and she flinched back another step, afraid for a moment that he might pounce on her, like an enormous black bird of prey.

Instead he swept her a deep and ironic bow. Then faded into the dark, leaving the golden flute behind, shining on the floor, alluring and lovely.

She played the light over the hallway but saw nothing. He'd vanished like the ghost he couldn't possibly be. *Where?* A fine frost of fear brought goose pimples to her arms, even while her blood still surged in response to his sensual presence.

Uncertain what to make of it all, she seized the flute and made her way to leave her hard-won prize on Carla's desk.

7

When she stumbled outside, still in somewhat of a daze, and made her way to her vehicle, a sleek sports car was keeping it company. Head swimming with fatigue and low blood sugar, not to mention the dreamlike hangover of her encounter in the depths of the opera house, she frowned at it. The door swung open and Roman popped out.

"Christy!" He strode up to her and cupped her face. "I was worried sick! I must have sent you a dozen texts and you didn't answer."

"Oh." She shook her head. "Sorry—I was down in the storerooms and left my cell in my office. Didn't even have it turned on."

He smiled at her with affectionate concern. "It's past ten o'-clock. It's not even season yet. You don't have to work this late. I can't imagine what kind of 'emergency' could rate this level of dedication."

"Oh, well, Carla needed—"

Roman held up a hand to stop her, then relieved her of her bag and slid an arm around her back, gently guiding her to his car. "Say no more. Carla is an überbitch. I'll talk to Charlie about it."

"Oh, no! Please don't. It's fine. I found what she needed and—" She stopped in the act of settling into the buttery leather seat. "Wait. I have my car."

"Let me give you a ride home. Have you even eaten? We'll stop and get some takeout. You look like you crawled out of a Dumpster."

She ran her fingers self-consciously through her hair. "I wasn't planning to see anyone," she grumbled when he got into his side of the car. "And how am I supposed to get to work in the morning?"

"I'll give you a ride. I have to head up to Taos early anyway."

He wasn't planning to spend the night with her, was he? It was way too soon for that, even with fabulous Roman Sanclaro.

"Um, what?" She realized Roman had asked her a question.

He slanted her a look. "Head in the clouds? I asked what Carla had you looking for."

"Oh, a flute—why?"

"Just curious." He gave her that charming smile. "Where do you want to stop for food? We'll take it back to the hotel."

"About that—Roman, I'm not ready for—"

He put a warm hand on her thigh, right above the rip she'd somehow gotten in her jeans. No wonder he thought she looked like hell. "I'm not interested in rushing anything with you, sweet girl. I just want to feed you and tuck you into bed, alone. I'll be back in the morning, after you've gotten some sleep and had a chance to clean up."

She amended his plan by asking him simply to drop her off, along with her small pizza from Dion's, saying that she'd left her hotel room a mess. Mainly she didn't want him to see Star, the stuffed kitty she'd been unable to leave behind. It was stupid, but having Star with her reminded her of the times before, when she was happy and the ground had been steady under her feet.

Roman kissed her good night at the door, long and sweet as before, but she felt too jumpy to really enjoy it. She kind of wished she'd just been able to drive herself back, to think about the ghost bringing her that flute—a physical object. What did it mean?

And what did he want from her?

Electing to pull a Scarlett O'Hara and think about it tomorrow after all, she wolfed down her Tuscany pizza, took a long, hot shower—ever more grateful for the pine-scented shower gel to wash away the grime of the day—and fell into bed.

Waking from a deep and blessedly dream-free sleep, Christy didn't even think about what had happened the night before until she had dressed—in a nicer outfit, since Roman was picking her up, even though she'd be back to making her inventory—and was applying her makeup when she paused in the act of putting on lipstick. She stared at her face in the mirror as the memory of the night before came back.

Was she losing her mind?

It all seemed so hazy and dreamlike. A movie she knew she'd seen but couldn't quite recall the details of. As if she'd been under some enchantment, like a Disney Princess.

A sharp rap on her casita door snapped her out of her reverie, and she gathered her things. Roman stood on her doorstep in a gorgeous suit with a bag of pastries and a broad smile. He looked her up and down appreciatively. "Now there's the lovely Christy I know." He cupped the back of her neck and leaned in to give her a kiss. He tasted of coffee and chocolate, sweet and warmly enticing.

"Good morning to you, too," she said, smiling.

He took her laptop bag and handed her the pastries with a wink. "I thought I'd better be more proactive in keeping you fed."

She rolled her eyes and got in the car when he held the door for her. "Yesterday was a fluke."

"I hope so. We can't have you withering away to a shadow of your former self before you even get to see opening night."

"True." She laughed ruefully.

The ride up the hill took practically no time, the sky shining a promising vivid blue against the morning sun.

When they pulled up backstage, however, the glare of multiple police lights greeted them. Flashing red, blue, and white, they were scars against the graceful opera house. Charlie stood by her car, talking with a uniformed officer. A waterfall of relief gushed over his face when he spotted her.

"Christy!" he called. "Jesus Christ, girl, you scared us all half to death."

"Sorry—I, um, got a ride home last night. I never even thought someone would notice I left my car here."

Charlie glanced at Roman, smoothing away a flash of something sour. "Good morning, Mr. Sanclaro. Good of you to take such good care of our Christy."

If Roman caught the barbed tone, he didn't show it, shaking Charlie's hand and smiling with easy charm. "Is that what this is all about?" The sweep of his hand took in the multiple cop cars and tense atmosphere.

"No." Charlie looked grim, shaking his head like a horse shooing flies. "I'm afraid I have bad news. Tara's been found. Or rather, her body has. A tech found her early this morning, on one of the lower levels." His faded blue gaze caught Christy's. "Not far from one of the storerooms you were working in, I think. The detective needs to interview you. You, too, Mr. Sanclaro, I imagine, if you were here."

Her stomach clenched and her thighs turned watery. Roman put a supportive arm around her waist. "Has she—I mean, was she . . . ?"

Charlie worked his lips over his teeth. "The cops aren't saying much, but Danny—the tech—said she looked like she'd been dead a while. And like she'd been tortured."

It was hours before Christy made it to her tiny office. The detectives were kind and didn't really question her story, though the lead detective seemed to suspect she'd left something out. Which she had.

Somehow she thought bringing up the theater ghost might be a bad idea. Given that he didn't exist and that it might make people think she was nuts. Understandably.

At the same time, if he wasn't a ghost, he could be the key to the investigation, into resolving Tara's horrible murder. They were using the word freely now, and Christy's stomach roiled with guilt, confusion, and terror.

Could the ghost have done it?

Was she next?

Just because he'd been gentle so far didn't mean he wouldn't, couldn't turn into a monster. All the serial killers seemed nice to their neighbors. The phantom, with his eccentric clothes—including a cloak and mask—could never be called normal or unassuming.

She needed time to think. If she mentioned the theater ghost without some kind of proof, they'd think she was neurotic. Charlie might even send her home, to protect her.

She opened her desk drawer.

And her heart sank through her stomach, a stone plummeting down an empty well.

A red rose sat inside, as fragrant and flagrantly lovely as the one the ghost had tried to give her two nights before. A note hung from the stem, tied with a bit of ribbon that matched the ones on the magic flute. Three words, in cursive script, graced the thick vellum.

Tell no one.

Ghost Aria

1

Christy didn't tell anyone about the rose.

Or the note. Especially not about the note.

She buried them both in the bottom of her bag and, on her way home from work that night, took a drive down Cerillos and found a Dumpster behind a strip mall and threw the rose in. It laid there, absurdly lush and lovely on a black plastic garbage bag bursting at one long seam with some sort of rotting residue, a gaping wound. Squelching the urge to climb in and take the rose back—what the hell was wrong with her?—she resolutely dropped the lid. The gunshot bang brought her shoulders up around her ears.

Just a little jumpy.

Since the note could be evidence—God, how she hated to contemplate that—she kept it and brought it back to her little hotel room.

Once inside, she gratefully threw the bolt on the door, dropped her bag, and flopped on the bed. Bonelessly, she lay there, her nerves and muscles thrumming with a tension that kept her hyped despite her exhaustion.

It had been possibly the worst day ever, topping even the day in junior high when her mom had taken her out to lunch and broken the news about the divorce. Probably because it hadn't been actual news by that point, just the final confirmation. In some ways—despite the pinched concern on her mother's face and the awful point-by-point breakdown of who would get which houses, cars, and slices of Christy's life—that day had at least provided an end to the unbearable tension of waiting for the inevitable.

Someone finding Tara's body in the bowels of the opera house? That had not been inevitable. Christy hadn't realized how much she'd embraced the fantasy that her predecessor had run off to Acapulco with some cute guy and was romping in the surf instead of dealing with the labyrinthine inventory she'd escaped.

But no. All this time she'd been dead. At least according to the scuttlebutt—mostly gossip from the backstage staff who'd talked to Danny before the police shut him up, though a couple of the other guys said they'd seen the body, too. Everyone watched way too many forensic shows, and some of their discussion of blood pooling and putrefaction had curdled Christy's stomach.

Charlie said that everyone processed trauma in different ways and not to listen to their talk. He offered to let her take off the rest of the day, or even the rest of the week. But she'd told him no, she'd rather work. That it would keep her from dwelling on it all.

That much was true.

She didn't tell him the rest—that she'd lied to the police by omission. She hadn't told them about any of her encounters with the mythical theater ghost. Christy groaned and threw an arm over her eyes.

Despite her fear, she'd felt fascinated, giddy and enthralled just being near him.

And now he might be a psychopathic murderer, lining up Christy as his next victim. Maybe that's why he'd dumped Tara's body—because he'd lured Christy into his net and planned to do her in next.

She needed to tell the police. Only now it would look really bad that she hadn't before this. What did people do? In the TV shows, the witness who later slunk into the police station and confessed to holding back always got in trouble. Or ended up dead.

But just because it made for good television didn't mean it would happen to her. Right?

Feeling a hundred years old, she sat up, every joint protesting, and dug the note out of her cell phone case. Using her nails to pull out the thick vellum by the very edges—because, you know, fingerprints—she set it on the glass-topped hotel dresser.

Tell no one.

When had he left it in her desk drawer? After she'd left the building but before Danny found the body in the early morning hours? The police said Tara's body could have been in that spot for days or longer, but Christy didn't think so. She'd been down that hallway, she was sure. Pretty sure.

Did the phantom put Tara's unlovely corpse there to cement the warning that she tell no one about him? Or was she to tell no one about that?

None of it made any sense, least of all that she'd done exactly as he'd instructed, even before she saw the warning note. She just couldn't bear to see those expressions again, the way people look at you when they think you're crazy. It was irrational and cowardly of her, but there it was. The only thing that made sense for the immediate future was to keep it hidden.

Taking her eyebrow tweezers, she pried out the molded plastic shelf that held her eye shadows inside the pretty case and set the note inside. Face down. She didn't have plastic to wrap it in, so this would have to do. Snapping the shadows back in place, she stowed the whole thing back in the counter drawer and caught her image in the big mirror.

Oh yeah, she looked like hell.

Her formerly saucy pixie cut looked more along the lines of a bad incident with a garbage disposal and the deep circles under her eyes were worthy of one of those meth-addict cautionary billboards. Good thing she wouldn't be seeing Roman tonight; he'd finally left for Taos once the police were done asking him if he'd seen or heard anything, anything at all, while he waited for her in the parking lot.

Speak—or think—of the devil, her phone whistled with a text message from him.

How are you doing, sweet girl? Back safe in your room yet?

The guy worried about her safety more than her dad did. It was a little over-the-top macho, but also caring. The protective, big brother vibe. She'd been glad to have him there that morning, steadying her with a warm hand on the small of her back, giving her reassuring smiles, reminding the detectives that she was a witness, not a suspect, unless he should call in his lawyer for her?

I'm fine! Safe and sound.

She smiled as she sent it, remembering how the police had backpedaled when Roman suggested bringing in his family lawyer. He was kind of her knight in shining armor, rescuing her from prom disasters and police interrogations alike.

I wish I could be there to spoil you. You should have come with me. Beautiful moon tonight.

Here, too, she texted back. At least she figured it was. She pushed back the Indian blanket–patterned curtain and popped open a space between the slats of the blinds. Beautiful streetlights. Her window faced the wrong way to see the moon. Oh, well. *And I needed to work.*

Been thinking, he answered immediately. *I could get you another job. Better pay.*

Whoa. She sat on the end of the bed, taking in that text. Only two nights ago she'd been thinking of that very thing. Would that be the smart thing to do? Charlie wouldn't be surprised. Neither would her father. But then, he'd only arranged the apprenticeship for her because she'd nagged him to death—to prove she wouldn't like it. And because the opening had conveniently popped up at the last minute.

"Why start at the bottom when I can make you my executive assistant?" he'd complained. "There's a reason people do it this way. Do you see Romney's boys working shit jobs? No, you don't."

It had devolved from there, as their arguments always did, ending up with him calling her obstinate and her trying not to cry and failing, as usual. Which always made him feel that he'd won. Or, rather, she'd feel that she'd lost, which amounted to the same thing.

But she'd won this time and gotten this job. She still wanted it. Roman might be happy working with his dad, but she needed to do something on her own. Maybe that made her less mature, but whatever. The phone whistled again.

You there?

Yeah. Gotta go. Phone call from Dad. She winced a little as she texted the lie. *Talk to you later!*

OK. Stay in and stay safe. Good night, sweet girl.

She'd thought she wanted nothing more than to stay in, order food from Dashing Delivery, and soothe herself with comfort food and bad TV. Maybe it was the obstinate side of her, but something about Roman telling her to stay in and stay safe rubbed her the wrong way.

Besides, maybe she wanted to see the damn moon for herself.

Grabbing her jacket and bag, she headed back out, deciding to drive around a little bit. She headed toward the historic plaza and found an open meter. Though the evening had turned chilly, quite a few people wandered around the square, lit with old-fashioned lamps. A couple of blocks away, the glowing tower of the cathedral stood tall against the night sky, the moon serene and nearly full beside the spire.

It did look lovely.

Hands in pockets, she walked along the colonnade, looking in the shop windows now and again, but mostly strolling. Enjoying not having to talk to anyone for a little while.

Beside one of the ancient posts, an older man wrapped in a long leather coat played a violin. The music drew out, echoing against the arcade, sad and sweet. She hummed along, then stopped herself, the notes choking in her throat. It was the phantom's song, the one she heard when the opera house fell silent. Something so familiar yet just out of reach.

She pulled out her wallet and found she had a five. When he finished the song, she dropped it in the man's open violin case. The violinist grinned, a ragged jack-o'-lantern rictus of round cheeks and missing teeth.

"Has young leddy got a request fo' me?"

"Just, um—what song were you just playing?"

"You like? I play again for you."

He launched into the opening chords and she felt bad for stopping him. "No. I mean, I do like. I wanted to know the name of the song."

The man shrugged, no longer pleased. " 'S an old song."

"You don't know the name?"

"I teach meself, yanno? No fancy lessons. Jes' me an' this." He shook the violin at her. "You wanna hear? Then listen."

With something close to a sneer, he played the song again. Feeling trapped, she stayed there. Every once in a while he'd raise his gnarled brows at her, as if a certain note was significant. The melody wound around her, pulling at her, a problem that needed solving. But the answer remained out of reach.

"Thank you," she said when he finished with a flourish.

He cocked his head, shook it with disgust. "Eh. You din't listen. Go 'way."

She resisted the guilty feeling that she should throw more money in his case and walked away from the plaza. Her stomach growled, insistent now, and her feet took her down to Del Charro and some rational company, she hoped.

Hally, the bartender and her new friend, waved as Christy walked in the door and set down a round coaster ostentatiously in front of an empty barstool. Feeling like a local already, Christy hung her jacket on a hook by the door and took *her* seat.

"Was hoping you'd stop by!" Hally did a little dance. "Any sightings?"

"Don't ask." Christy dropped her forehead on her folded arms with a groan. She shouldn't have told Hally about the theater ghost rumors the other night. Never mind that she'd been wondering if she was losing her mind. Heh. Now that it was clear she was, she didn't want to talk about it.

Hally patted her arm sympathetically. "Nothing one of my monster margaritas won't cure!"

"Not tonight. Maybe just a glass of chard or something."

"Coming right up. Menu?"

Christy nodded and took it, tempted to get the chips and blue cheese dip again. She ordered the burger instead—with blue cheese crumbles to satisfy the craving—and a side salad instead of the fries. Half comfort, half healthy.

"Rough day at work?"

"You could say that. Among other things, this one woman, Carla, seems to hate me."

"Ohhh—I know her. She came to a couple of my art classes in high school. She's an expert on calligraphy. And a major bitch. Don't let her get you down."

"Okay. I know it's not that big a deal."

"We still on for Sunday?" Hally set the glass of wine in front of her and leaned her elbows on the bar, a vertical line between her crimson-dyed eyebrows. "Maybe no? You look kind of beat down."

"Gee, thanks."

"I mean that in the nicest possible way."

"Yes, we're on for shopping on Sunday. I could use some fresh air. But I'm apartment hunting Saturday, so it kind of depends on what I find."

"I'm totally flexible. Whatevs."

"I've been looking through the listings—is everything in Santa Fe so expensive?"

"Yes." Hally's red ponytail bobbed with her emphatic nod. "Resign yourself to paying a fortune in rent if you don't want your stuff ripped off every time you leave the place."

"That bad?"

"Eh." She lifted one shoulder. "It's a lifty culture round here. You're not going to get murdered or anything, but don't leave your stuff out. What? What did I say?"

Christy made herself relax her jaw. The police had warned them not to spill details. Just then the Albuquerque news station broke in with a special report—and a shot of the lovely opera house on the hillside, a yellow stripe of caution tape across the image. Christy pointed Hally to the screen. "That."

Hally turned up the volume, and they watched the report, most of the other people at the bar not paying any attention. There wasn't much for the reporters to reveal. No details yet. Police investigating. Hally turned wide hazel eyes on her and twisted up her pink lips. "I take it all back—you look great, considering."

"Sorry. They told us not to talk about it."

"No kidding! But are you okay, honey?"

Hally's sincere concern did more to unhinge the dreadful tension than anything else, even Roman's sympathetic texts. "Yeah. Roman thinks I should work somewhere else."

"Who's Roman—your boss?"

"No. He's an old family friend and I'm kind of seeing him. Roman Sanclaro?"

"*Roman San-fucking-claro*?" Hally jumped back in mock astonishment.

"Yeah?"

"You're dating Roman Sanclaro and Did Not Tell Me." Hally clutched her temples, making crazy eyes. "Who are you? What have you done with my friend?"

Christy laughed, snorting some of the chardonnay down the

wrong pipe. "Hey, I only met you the other night. His family is kind of big around here, so I didn't want to seem like I was dropping names."

"No, honey." Hally wiped the already clean bar. "His family is not big around here. They're *huge*. They're the Rockefellers of New Mexico, only older. They're the Trumps of Santa Fe, without the skyscrapers. Roman Sanclaro is Prince William, if Will were better looking and still unmarried. He's the—"

"Okay, okay. Stop!" Christy held up her hands in surrender. "This is kind of why I didn't mention it."

"Humph. I dunno, Christy. I thought we were close, but it turns out I don't know you at all." Hally pretended to wipe away a tear. "And your families are friends? Is your last name Carnegie?"

Christy sighed. "It might as well be."

"Wow. Then can I ask why you're worried about rent?"

"Because I'm more than my father's daughter, okay?"

Hally gave her a little nod. "Fair enough. But you'll have to make it up to me by telling me abso-fucking-lutely every last detail."

"There's not really that much to tell . . ."

"I don't care. Make it up if you have to."

So Christy ended up eating her comfort burger while telling Hally all about her one actual date (so far) with Roman, plus the prom rescue. Hally declared this tale couldn't be told over salad and ordered the chips and dip for them anyway. All in all, it proved to be a far better way to spend her evening than staying in, staying safe, or even making inroads on organizing the inventory.

And when her cell rang with her father's ringtone, Christy silenced it, deciding to pretend a little while longer that nothing more sinister haunted her world than the possibility of choosing the wrong outfit for the next evening's date.

2

The shrill ring of her room phone woke her from dreams of waltzing.

The phantom, ice-blue eyes intent behind the black mask, held her in his strong arms, spinning her around and around, giddiness spiraling with sensual need. She kept hoping he'd kiss her, bring her in tight against him, but he held her in that rigid balcony of an embrace, never quite close enough to kiss.

Blinking at the dark room, Christy wasn't sure what had yanked her out of the dream until the phone shrieked again.

"Gah—stop!" She fumbled around on the bedside table, the blinking orange light showing her where the phone she'd never once used sat. " 'Lo?"

The receiver was upside down. She reversed it and tried again. "Hello?"

"Christy, dammit!" her father nearly roared. "Where the hell are you?"

She thumbed on her cell phone. 5 a.m. Oops, and still silenced—with a raft of missed calls and voice messages.

"Um—in my hotel room." Obviously, since he'd called her there. "I was asleep. You do know it's two hours earlier here, right?"

"I don't give a shit what time it is there. Why the hell aren't you answering your cell?"

"Sorry—forgot I had it on silent."

He didn't respond right away. A glass clinked and his breath sighed out. Calming himself. Possibly counting to ten.

"We had an agreement." His reasonable tone. Always a red flag that Carlton Davis was incandescently pissed. "I gave you a job I did not agree with—at your insistence—on the grounds that you remained in contact. Your mother is frantic."

As if he cared about her mother's emotional state.

"I apologize." Christy clicked on the bedside lamp, to better focus on what he needed to hear from her. "It was irresponsible of me and it won't happen again."

"Damn straight it won't. You're flying home today. There's a ticket waiting for you at the Santa Fe airport. Leave your car there and I'll arrange to have it transported."

Shit. She needed to play this very carefully. Any glimpse that she was being obstinate or emotional—or unstable—and she'd lose this match.

"Okay, Daddy. What time is my flight?"

He paused. "No arguing?"

"No—I understand that you're worried about me. Is this about the murder at the opera house?"

"Of course it's about the murder, Christy, dammit!"

In high school she used to tell her friends that she grew up thinking her name was Christydammit, like those cartoons with the dog thinking his name was Baddog. By the time she finished college, she'd stopped making the joke. It had stopped being funny.

"I apologize that I didn't call you, but the detectives were most insistent that we not speak to anyone about the investigation."

"Well, it's my damn opera house, isn't it? They damn well spoke to me."

It's my opera house. I know everything that goes on in it. The memory of the phantom's velvet voice seemed so at odds with her father's Type A shouting.

"You're right. I should have thought of that. I still have so much to learn."

"Yes, well . . ." He sounded pleased by that. Point for her. "Your flight is at ten, so you'd better hustle. I'll arrange for a driver to pick you up at JFK."

"Ah. I won't have time to tell the opera-house staff in person then. That's kind of a relief—they'd all been saying I'd bail before the week was out."

"What? What are you saying?"

"Oh, you know." She waved a hand in the air, acting out the role. "The usual remarks about me being a spoiled little rich girl. They had a betting pool going that I wouldn't be able to take real work."

"That's absurd. Who said that?"

Careful—don't get anyone in trouble. "Oh, everyone, really. It's too bad they'll think they were right and I ran at the first sign of trouble. I hope it doesn't reflect badly on you."

"Hmm." The clink again. Not a glass but a china coffee cup. Her father wasn't the type to use a ceramic mug or—God forbid—a paper cup from the coffee shop.

Christy held her breath, making herself stop there. *Don't lay it on too thick.*

"What do the cops say? Are you in danger now? They seemed to think we could go on with the season."

"Oh, yes. With the exception of where they found—" so weird to say it "—the body, we're open. Something about it being a dump site and not the murder scene. They expect to clear it soon." The cops would have told her father that, but it was good to show him she was paying attention.

"A Davis never runs from hard work."

"So you always say, Daddy."

"Don't think I don't know you're playing me on this."

Too thick. Dammit. "I want to make you proud. I want to do a good job and I don't want to screw up my first opportunity and have people in the business saying Christine Davis is a daddy's girl who can't take any knocks."

It was a risk, laying her cards on the table. It might push him over the edge. She waited, winding the phone cord around her finger. At last he chuckled, a bare breath of a laugh, and she relaxed.

"Look who's growing up. Fine. Stay there, if you're determined. But you be careful. Keep that cell phone *on*. And call your mother, would you? I don't need that harpy shrieking in my ear. You explain why I'm letting her precious baby daughter be bait for psychopaths."

"Yes, Daddy."

"Don't you just 'yes, Daddy' me, either."

"Yes, Daddy," she answered around a smile. He harrumphed, but she knew it was to cover a laugh.

Only later did she realize he'd never mentioned the Sanclaros and asking them to look out for her.

She ended up leaving her mom a voice mail, seeing as it was the middle of the night in New Zealand. How her mom had even heard the news while doing her story on the rebuilding of Christchurch, Christy had no idea. Probably her mom hadn't called her dad at all and that had been just another guilt point. Her mom didn't enjoy talking to her ex-husband any more than he wanted to hear from her.

But Christy wasn't going to risk her probation on a technicality. She called as she said she would.

It gave her a little pang to hear her mom's voice, if only on the recorded outgoing message. They'd seen each other at Christy's graduation only a couple of weeks before, but things had been such a whirl, they'd barely spent time together. What would her mom make of all these happenings?

She wouldn't approve of her dating Roman, most likely. Christy snorted to herself, waiting at the light to turn onto St. Francis. She had never liked Domingo Sanclaro and often made pointed remarks about the kind of man who brought his son on all his business trips, but never his wife and daughter. She'd also thought Roman was spoiled and insufferable. Of course, she'd only met him when he was a teenager and not as the man he'd become, so she'd still see him that way.

No, she wouldn't approve at all.

Christy drove up the hill, the city street transforming into a di-vided highway. If she kept going, she'd end up in Taos, where a really great guy had invited her to be. Still, taking the exit at Tesuque and heading up Opera House Drive felt good—it meant she was doing her job.

The new security measures meant she'd be unlikely to encounter the phantom again, regardless. Man or ghost, he couldn't evade the cameras being installed on every level. Until then, Charlie man-dated that no one be alone. Christy had gained an assistant for her inventory.

The hapless soul—a lanky teen from UNM apprenticing for the

summer—lolled against her locked office door. He gave her a one-handed wave, the other buried in the drooping pocket of his baggy jeans.

"Hiya. I'm Matt. Your new slave. What do I do?"

"Aren't you Carla's apprentice?"

He shrugged and grinned, standing out of her way so she could unlock the door. "Was. The Valkyrie Bitch had to give me up so you'd have help—and a constant escort."

"I wouldn't let her hear you call her that." Christy bumped her shoulder on the stubborn door to get it to release, but it resisted.

"Allow me." Matt slammed the heel of his hand on the door above her head. It flung open to show the tiny space. "Not much in here worth locking up."

More like locking out, but never mind explaining that.

"So is Carla mad?"

He snorted. "How can you tell the difference? Near as I can see, she's always on the rampage."

"Still—I bet working with her is a lot more interesting than what you'll be doing with me."

"It's all good." He grinned again, with an easy expression that lit up his somewhat homely face. "I get course credit no matter how I spend my days. Bonus for me if I don't get yelled at."

"Okay, then." She handed him the Big Notebook of Doom. "This is your new best friend. Let's get to work."

The time passed more quickly with company. Matt turned out to be an organized soul, with a keen interest in the contents of every box he pried open. He suggested tagging each database entry with additional keywords, so they could cross-reference by opera and composer as well as item type and location. This was after she told him about her futile search for the magic flute—until Carla mentioned the all-Mozart storerooms.

He snickered at the story, sharing her indignation over such a terrible sorting system, until the thought hit him and he pointed at her in shock.

"Wait—whoa! You were down there that night? Where they found Tara's body?"

"Yeah." She busied herself with typing in a description of a fake sword. "Creepy."

"So . . . did you *see* anything?"

She shook her head, not looking at him. "Nope. Whatever went down, it happened after I found the flute and left."

"Carla was really surprised you found it."

"Really?" She looked up and found him buckling on a scabbard. "How do you know?"

"That morning, right before Danny came running in, all scared and pukey—not that I wouldn't have been scared and pukey, too—I got in before Carla did. So I saw it there on her desk and knew you must have found it. She'd been ranting about how the theater ghost always stole it and seemed to be enjoying that you were on a wild-goose chase. She'd already ordered another one, you know."

"I didn't know."

"Yeah. She's got it in for you. Dunno why."

"So . . . she mentioned the theater ghost?"

"Oh, sure. They all do. Didn't they try to get you with him?" Matt wiggled spooky fingers in the air. "How he haunts the lower levels, searching for his lost love. They say that when the opera house is really quiet, you can hear him singing."

"Have you heard him?"

"Nah." But Matt wasn't grinning now. "You?"

"Maybe." The word was dry in her mouth.

"Spooky."

"It was."

"Some of the guys—they think he's the one who did in poor ol' Tara."

"How could a ghost do that?"

He shrugged and gave his attention to unbuckling the scabbard. "Who else could have done it?"

"Maybe that guy she was seeing—the one everyone thought she ran off with."

"Could be. That was before I started working." He handed her the scabbard and gave her a theatrical salute. "But don't worry, fair Christy, I shall guard you with my life!"

She couldn't help but wish he'd phrased it another way.

3

The day passed without event and Charlie sent everyone home at 3:30, telling them to enjoy the gorgeous May afternoon and relax over the weekend.

Roman wasn't picking her up until seven, so Christy decided to follow Charlie's advice and spend a bit of time looking at the galleries on Canyon Road. She tried texting Hally to see if she wanted to meet up, but she didn't answer. Probably in her studio, getting some work in before her happy hour shift started.

See, Dad? Not everyone picks up their phones immediately every damn time.

Tourists were thick on the sidewalks, spilling over into the narrow streets, clearly arriving for the weekend and the Friday night gallery walk. Christy ended up ducking into a narrow little shop to avoid a group of at least twenty Japanese tourists, blocking the way while they took photos of the historic buildings.

Eyes adjusting to the dim interior, she wandered around the low-ceilinged space, peering at the shadowy paintings on the walls. The authentic adobe held a bit of mountain coolness yet, and a wood-stove crackled with a somber red gleam. Or maybe it wasn't the temperature giving her the chills.

A painting of a bear, one paw cupped, caught her eye. The painter had rendered it realistically, but a shadow of a spiritual skeleton hovered beyond it—reminiscent of the bear etched on the stone still hidden away in her hotel bedside table. That was enough to give her the shivers, but when she moved to the right it became a man, sharp-cheekboned and muscled, with familiar ice-blue eyes. She gasped, and someone behind her wheezed out a laugh.

She whirled, half expecting it to be *him*. No, a bent woman leaning on a wooden staff looked up at her, her neck twisting to fix Christy with her obsidian eyes.

"That one always takes folks by surprise, it does."

"Who is it?"

The shopkeeper cocked her head at it. "Depends, I suppose. He has many names in many cultures. My people call him a name that means Ruler of the People, or Master of the People, more or less. Our legends say he lives under the mountains around here. An artist from my pueblo painted that—she has the sight, as did her granny. Makes for nice pictures." She cackled and shuffled back behind her desk, behind a high counter. "You should buy this. He likes you."

Ah, not so much a spooky encounter as a sales pitch. Christy shook her head. "I can't. I'm just a poor apprentice. Maybe one day."

The woman sat up straighter. "You work up at the opera, then?"

"How did you know?"

"Nobody else calls their workers by such fancy names. I saw what happened to that poor girl up there." The woman sighed mightily and fumbled with a teacup. "Not the first time. Won't be the last," she muttered.

"What do you mean?"

"Eh, don't mind an old woman. Sometimes I mix up my dreams with the real world. And the movies. Oooh—that Bruce Willis. He's still something, isn't he?"

"Yeah, I guess. He's kind of old, but—"

"So am I! Yes, indeed. So am I!" The woman dissolved into a fit of cackling laughter, slapping the desk so her tea spilled. She paid no attention to it.

"What did you mean, 'wasn't the first time'?"

The shopkeeper heaved herself to her feet, leaning heavily on the staff, and fixed that flat black stare on her again. "Tell me, little bird—have you seen him?"

"Who?"

The woman nodded sharply at the painting. "I think you have. I knew he liked you."

"I . . . I don't know."

The woman shrugged. "No. But you will." She snickered, thoroughly enjoying herself. "When he comes for you, remember that it's an honor to be taken by him."

"I don't want to be taken." An odd choice of words. It sounded strangely sexual.

The woman nodded knowingly. "Oh, you will. You will want it. Here. Let me give you something." She hobbled back to her desk. Under her long skirt, decorated lavishly with silver beads, her foot turned out to the side, clubbed and useless. After several minutes of muttering and rummaging, during which Christy seriously considered escaping, she exclaimed happily and held out a chain with something dangling from it. "Come take this—don't make a crippled old woman come to you."

Careful not to touch the woman's fingers—though Christy couldn't have said why she didn't want to—she took the necklace. A pendant hung from the delicate silver chain, a spiral with a turquoise chip set in it. Every other stall in the Indian Market had twenty of the same thing. That'd teach her to fall for the witchy routine and expect some amazing magic token.

"Thank you. How much?" She supposed she owed the woman a sale.

"Not a thing. It's a gift—don't sully it with your money. And don't think I can't read your face like a trashy newspaper. This necklace is special. Wear it all the time."

"Why all the time?"

"Protection, little bird. You'll need it."

After that strange encounter, Christy lost interest in wandering the galleries. The silver pendant felt warm against her skin and her thoughts flitted about like the little bird the shopkeeper had called her.

It's an honor to be taken by him.

What a load of Indian maiden bullcrap. As if she'd be some sort of innocent sacrifice for the bear god under the mountain. She hated to inform everyone, but she hadn't been a virgin for at least five years. Really, who was anymore?

She stopped by Del Charro to see Hally, but the place was mobbed, people spilling out of the doors. The redhead gave her a flustered wave and disappeared around the corner with a loaded tray of margaritas. No barstools open, either.

Instead, she picked up the latest copy of the *New Mexican* and headed back to her hotel to circle rental possibilities. Better to think about getting an apartment than all the strange goings-on. It turned out to be a good thing she had, because Roman sent her a text that they were going somewhere special and to dress up, which meant ironing her silk dress.

When he arrived, exactly at seven, Christy was ready in her amethyst silk sheath, which did dynamite things for her otherwise nondescript blue-gray eyes. He stood on her doorstep, movie-star handsome in his black suit—with a bouquet of red roses. She must have flinched a little, because a look of concern dimmed his wide, white smile.

"Allergic? Afraid of thorns? Hate the cliché?"

She laughed and took the bouquet, letting him in. "No. I was . . . just surprised. They're very beautiful—thank you." In her heels she matched his height, so she leaned in and gave him a kiss.

"Mmm. That's what I've been missing." He snatched the bouquet from between them and tossed it on the bed. "Give me some more of my sweet girl."

His elegant hands roamed her back, warm through the thin silk, and he pressed her close, kissing her lightly and then deepening it. He tasted of whiskey and maybe a hint of Cuban cigar, a surprisingly intoxicating combination. She toyed with the dark hair that brushed the collar of his black shirt, sinking into the kiss.

This felt right and real. He smelled of expensive aftershave, and when he cupped the back of her neck, tilting her head so he could trail hot kisses along her throat, the zing went right through her. Oh, yes.

"You taste delicious," he murmured against her skin. "I could eat you up, sweet girl."

She smiled lazily into his warm brown eyes, feeling languid and more than a little turned on. "We could stay here and order in."

"Tempting. Very, very tempting." He kissed her again, lingering over it. "But I want to do this right. I'm taking you to a special place—I think you'll love it."

He drove them out of town, up through the canyon, refusing to spill the surprise. She'd put her bet on Bishop's Lodge, which everyone said was great, but they went on past it. When he turned in at a road she didn't recognize, she saw the sign for the Rancho Encantado resort. Very nice indeed.

Roman sent the valet off with the car—after letting her out himself—and escorted her into the glass-fronted dining room. The obsequious maître d' led them to a table on the patio, with a perfect view of the amazing horizon and incipient sunset.

"Perfect, yes?" He winked at her, holding her chair, while the maître d' stood back discreetly. "And the moon will be up before long, so we can enjoy both."

"Gorgeous." She rubbed her hands over her bare arms. The bubble coat had stayed in the hotel room yet again, safely out of sight. "I just hope I don't get cold!"

He smiled and flicked a signal at the maître d'. "Now would I let my sweet girl catch a chill? Never. I want tonight to be perfect." The man returned with a box wrapped in gold paper with an elaborate bow, setting it before her and vanishing.

"What's this?"

"Open it." Roman leaned back in his chair, his eyes sparkling in anticipation.

She unwrapped the box while a group of waiters appeared to set up a champagne bucket and pour glasses for them. Inside the delicate tissue paper lay a short white jacket made of butter-soft leather. "Oh, Roman—you didn't need to do this."

"I wanted to." He stood and took it from her, holding it so she could shrug into the satin-lined sleeves. "I saw it in Taos and thought of you."

It fit like a dream and she suddenly felt sophisticated, with the high, straight collar framing her throat. It reminded her of the dress he'd brought her to wear to the prom—grown-up and sexy. Roman lifted his champagne glass. "To the most beautiful girl in the room."

She clinked her glass against his and settled in to enjoy the romantic sunset.

The weekend passed in a whirl. She stayed out late with Roman on Friday, moving to the inside courtyard and the gel fire bed for after-dinner drinks while they talked about old times and caught up on what they'd been doing. For only being in his late twenties, Roman had traveled extensively, and he told her stories about all the places he'd visited. He was plainly shocked that she'd never been overseas, but he didn't know Carlton Davis. The man had no time for vacations. And though Christy's mom had become an international journalist after the divorce, her dad always found a reason why Christy shouldn't go along. Usually to ensure a good future for her.

After drinks they went dancing, and Roman finally dropped her off at her hotel at 2 a.m. She'd invited him in, but he'd settled for a very long kiss at the door, leaving her full of dreamy heat and a promise to call her soon.

Thus she woke up later than she'd planned for her apartment-hunting expedition, barely making it to her first appointment. By the end of the day, she had several choices to run past Hally, who'd promised to give her a final vetting.

They spent Sunday revisiting them and hitting the shops Hally pronounced the very best for deals. Sure enough, Christy returned to her hotel room Sunday evening with several new outfits she thought Roman would like. She also had a signed rental agreement for an apartment she could move into the following weekend, once the landlord cleaned the kiva fireplace and de-moused the place—both on Hally's advice.

She talked to her mom. No surprise there, but she wasn't nearly as concerned about the murder as Christy's dad had implied. Once she'd established her daughter was fine and in no danger—Christy might have stretched that part a bit—Laura Moon let the topic go and instead asked how Christy liked the new job.

"I like it." Christy paced the length of her little hotel room. "This one woman seems to have it in for me."

Her mom laughed, her generous, amused-by-life laugh. "There's always gotta be at least one."

"Really?"

"Really. Fact of life, It's not whether someone will give you shit at a new job—it's which person will it be."

"So what do I do?"

"Heh." Her mom shrugged verbally. "You do the job to the best of your ability. That's what you're there for. Is she someone you answer to?"

"Sometimes."

"Then make her look good. She's only a real problem for you if she gets in the way of you doing a good job. Make sense?"

"Sort of."

"Try it out for a few days and call me. Some people are all about the battle. If you don't fight back, they lose interest."

"Okay. I will." She heard a shout in the background, and her mom yelled something back in another language. "Do you have to go?"

"I have a couple more minutes to dispense motherly advice." Her mom's smile came through the phone clearly. "What else? Men? Clothes? Picking out a couch for the new apartment? Ask me anything."

"Are you—when you go to dangerous places for your stories, are you ever scared?"

"Often," her mom replied promptly. "Sometimes more than others. But fear is a tool. Our early warning system—only a fool doesn't listen to that."

"But you go anyway."

"Not always. Not if the alarm bells are really going off. But yeah—going anyway is part of my job. Getting the story so terrible events will be revealed. That's important to me."

"So how do you know? When it's big alarm bells or just . . . being paranoid."

Her mom sighed. "This is where being a mother is the hardest. I'm guessing you're asking because of the murder, and you want to know how much is being hyped up by all the gossip and what is legitimate concern for your safety."

"Pretty much." *Oh, and a ghost that's taking a strange and possibly obsessive interest in me.* Never mind that part.

"The mother in me wants to tell you to stay home safe, but I lived that life and it nearly killed me." Her mother's voice reflected the exhaustion and depression of her married years. Unlike her ex-husband, she was careful never to criticize Christy's father, except in oblique references. "So my best advice is this: Listen to your instincts. Trust your gut. Trust yourself."

"Okay." She paused, feeling like she should be honest. "I ran into Roman Sanclaro."

Her mother's end of the line went icy.

"We went out to dinner a couple of times."

The connection crackled.

"Mom?"

"I don't like him. You know that."

"I think he might be different now. He's more mature."

Her mother heaved a weary sigh. "I'd tell you to stay away from him, but I know you won't. So just . . . be careful, okay? Don't take everything he tells you at face value."

Christy laughed. "So trust myself but don't trust anyone else?"

"Yes."

And the connection was lost.

4

Monday flew by without a pause.

Over the weekend, the cops had cleared the lower level for staff access again. Rumors ran thick and fast, but nothing else of note had happened. And nobody had any new news—just endless rehashes of the details everyone already knew.

With Matt's efficient help, Christy triumphantly checked off cataloging an entire storeroom. It was a little strange to see the blinking red eyes of the video cameras now installed in every room and at most major hallway intersections. Whether due to those or the partner method, nothing strange happened all day.

Christy felt herself relaxing.

This she could do. Even Carla's "emergency" request for a particular set of curtains seemed to be a challenge instead of a crisis. *Make her look good.* Matt scored the find on those—right before five o'clock, too—and insisted on doing a touchdown dance.

Still laughing at his wild interpretation of an appropriate victory dance, Christy unlocked her office door and dumped the BNoD on her desk. A few more weeks and the thing would be history. She and Matt should make a little bonfire of it.

She pulled open her drawer and jumped back a foot. *Snakebit!* her aunt Isadore would have said.

Another rose. Crimson and in lush, full bloom.

Another note.

Meet Me Tonight.

With no thought of preserving this one, she crumpled it in her fist, a little panicked noise escaping her.

"Pretty flower." Carla leaned in the doorway, her arms folded. "Got yourself a boyfriend, huh?"

"I don't know." Christy waved her hand, trying to look breezy. "Secret admirer, I guess. You know how it is."

"No. I don't, actually. That stuff only happens to the cheerleaders and prom queens."

The sharp edges of the vellum note pricked her palm. "Well, I've never been either."

"The concept still applies." With a close-lipped smile, Carla shrugged up from her leaning position. "Good job finding those curtains—or was that all Matt?"

"Matt definitely gets the prize for that one." *A good manager always gives credit where it's due.* But the praise, faint as it might be, showed that her mom's technique was working.

"And the flute—who helped you with that?" Carla's gaze dropped to the rose and she picked it up, spinning it in her fingers and inhaling the wine-dark scent that already pervaded the little office. Her eyes behind her wire-rimmed glasses were hard as marbles.

"N-no one." Dammit, she never stuttered. Christy shrugged, put her hands in her pockets, and tucked the note deep inside. "Just got lucky in the Mozart room."

Jeez, that sounded bad.

"I'll bet you did. Find anything else interesting?"

Strange question. "Like what?"

"Call it curiosity." Carla shrugged and held out the rose. Christy took it, not really wanting to touch it again, but she couldn't very well tell Carla to toss it on the desk. "Have a wonderful evening."

Christy clenched her fists in her pockets, the note digging into her palm, while she glared at Carla's departing swagger. That woman couldn't possibly know anything. How could she? And how had the phantom gotten into her locked office?

She checked the door to the adjoining room—also locked.

It's my opera house.

Well, she sure as hell wasn't his. No way was she meeting him.

Tossing the rose in the trash and taking her things, she turned off the light and locked the door.

And left without a backward glance.

If she walked at a faster clip than usual, that could be blamed on being excited to be going home for the day. And it wasn't possible to feel eyes following her as she walked down the hallway and out the door. It felt weird having those video cameras everywhere. Who wouldn't get paranoid?

Her rubber soles didn't click on the concrete floors the way her heels had that first day, but each step seemed to blare an alarm. Resisting the urge to run, she rounded the last corner and hit the exit bar on the doors with a bang, emerging into the balmy evening with shredding relief.

The dirt and gravel under her tires spit and hissed on the underside of her car when she backed out with a bit too much spin, and again when she peeled out, passing through the gate.

And nearly ran down Carla.

The tall blonde stood in the middle of the road leading out of the lot, hand up flat like a traffic cop. Of course Christy braked. She barely entertained the notion of running her over. Nice people didn't think that way.

Carla came around to the driver's side, pantomiming for Christy to roll down her window. "Can you come back in for a few minutes? I need some help moving a few things." She leaned down, peering at Christy's things on the passenger seat. "Did you forget your posy?"

It took Christy a few seconds to process that the old-fashioned–sounding word meant the rose. "I wanted to keep it at the office—more cheerful."

"It will die without water."

Christy stared at the woman, her eyes hidden by the glare on her glasses from the lowering sun. "I guess that's a chance I'll have to take."

"Your deal." Carla straightened and knocked a fist on the hood. "Come help me. It'll only take a few minutes, and everyone else is gone."

Christy flexed her hands on the steering wheel, so close to telling Carla to go screw herself. Which wouldn't be following her mother's advice—nor would it mesh with the story she'd given her father about her desire to prove herself to the staff. Above, the soaring roof of the opera house glowed white and gold against the deep blue sky. A shadow fluttered in one corner, and disappeared again. Her heart clutched.

Meet Me Tonight.

But she couldn't tell Carla she was afraid. She parked her car again and turned off the ignition with a deep, sinking sensation. Carla actually smiled at her, and they walked back in together. That was important; they'd be together. And there were the cameras. In another few minutes, she'd be in her car and gone again.

She followed Carla to the prop shop, where two freshly painted totem poles stood waiting next to a handcart. "You can dump your things there." Carla indicated a tall workbench with her chin. "I can move these with the dolly, but I need you to help me maneuver it on there. I'm glad I caught you—two-person job, and the glazers get in two hours before I usually do. They'll have a fit if these aren't in place and ready to go. I really didn't want to get up at four a.m., you know?"

Christy hesitantly smiled back at the unusually relaxed and chatty Carla. Another point for Mom on how to get along at the new job. Together they wrestled the totem pole onto the flat ledge of the handcart, and Christy steadied it while Carla tilted the cart back, letting the statue settle into its cradle.

"Perfect! I'll go drop this and be right back for the other."

"I'll come with you—"

"No need! I can scoot it off easily enough and be back in two minutes." With that, Carla was already in the big freight elevator, the doors grinding closed.

Christy was a heartbeat from running after her, like a timid kindergartner chasing after her big sister. Two minutes. No big deal. The elevator cables clattered, then were silent.

She surveyed the empty prop shop, the off-duty stillness of the opera house settling like a heavy cloak. Shadows deepened in the corners, taking on the darkness of the unlit hallway. A grating sound, like metal against glass, scraped across her nerves. She turned in a slow circle, looking for the source.

Nothing.

She decided to text Roman to pass the time. He had meetings, he'd said, but maybe they could meet for a drink in between or something.

But her bag was gone.

She spun in a slow circle, her heart climbing through her ribcage like a tarantula. The workbench stood empty. Carla hadn't returned. The blank eye of the video camera over the door returned her stare, the red light off.

The sound again. A sparkle of light as a prism fell, spinning in slow motion until it crashed and shattered on the concrete. Her eyes flew up.

Above her, on one of the high shelves, an enormous crystal chandelier teetered, then plummeted.

Her thoughts flashed, a flock of birds changing direction with a thunderbolt clap of wings.

A shadow appeared, seizing her in iron arms, lifting her.

"Christine."

Like a curtain closing across her mind, she lost consciousness.

5

Candlelight, golden and gentle, greeted her when she woke.

She shifted, the glide of warm velvet under her cheek, the brush of a soft fur blanket covering her. So peaceful and cozy. Her lashes looked like black lace against the warm light. Sighing, she snuggled in, drowsy and peaceful.

What the hell?

With a bolt of panic, she sat up, the throw falling away, and tried to absorb her surroundings.

It was something out of a dream.

She sat on an antique chaise, sort of a carved wooden fainting couch, covered in emerald velvet with throw pillows in satin jewel tones. The fur blanket felt real, soft as chinchilla, in a dazzling light pearly gray, nearly a luminescent silver. The rest of the room held similar furniture, an eclectic assortment of Victorian-style lines and fabrics, breathtakingly elegant. Plush Oriental carpets easily worth tens of thousands of dollars covered the floor, one bordering another in a stained-glass pattern of color.

On every surface, white pillar candles glowed, their flames straight and true in the draftless cavern. For a cave it was, rough rock walls a disconcerting backdrop for the lovely pieces. As if she were some sort of exotic animal, displayed in a zoo habitat created by some well-meaning but misguided keeper—who couldn't disguise the impression that the abandoned lion's den of rocks and crags had been hastily converted just for her.

Little doubt who her captor might be. Or that Tara's fate might yet be in store for her.

The stark terror she'd felt in the prop shop had chilled now, coating her insides with a fine frost. Her mind felt crystal clear, sharp and incisive. Some part of her recognized this as an adrenaline high. This was the state that allowed mothers to lift cars off their children or soldiers to continue fighting with fatal injuries.

Fight or flight.

If escape wasn't an option, she would fight. Laura Moon's daughter wouldn't go down without one.

Resolved, she explored the room. Most of the furniture sat at least an arm's length from the cave walls, which allowed her to walk behind the credenzas, desks, and settees, even the tall bookshelves. Though the candles didn't provide much penetrating light, her investigations showed no doors, no tunnels, not even a mouse hole.

She circumnavigated the room twice. Then a third time, just to be sure. The only egress appeared to be the chimney. The fireplace seemed to have been dug out of the wall, large enough to stand in and deeply inset. Behind a gleaming brass screen, logs burned with fierce heat, any smoke whisked up the chimney. No telling how high it might be.

"Christine."

She'd been ready for this, so she didn't startle. Instead, she reached for the fireplace poker and slowly turned to face her captor.

He'd apparently dressed for the occasion, the black cloak swept back to frame his broad shoulders, clothed in a billowing white shirt with poet's sleeves, a waistcoat of swirling gold brocade fitted to his narrow waist. The black half mask obscured his face but not his ice-blue eyes or his sleekly groomed white-blond hair.

In his gloved hands, he carried a tray with a crystal carafe and a plate of some sort of food. His gaze touched on the poker and moved back up to her eyes, his sharp-edged lips curving. "Does the fire need stirring?"

"You think I won't use it, but I will." Her voice sounded even and confident. "You're not raping me without losing some important soft bits, mark my words." She eyed his crotch significantly, which was maybe a mistake because the tight fit of his black trousers left little to the imagination.

"I won't be raping you at all. I told you before, I have no wish to frighten you."

"Breaking news—kidnapping and imprisoning someone is frightening to them."

"I did not kidnap you. You fainted in my arms. I could hardly leave you alone in the hallway."

"Then I can leave whenever I wish?"

"That is always within your power, if you truly want it."

"Like Dorothy, I only have to click my heels and wish to be home?" She snickered. "That's hardly a realistic answer."

He shrugged, the liquid in the carafe sloshing. "What is real?"

She flexed her fingers on the poker. It felt solid. The fire warmed her skin. But her dreams had felt this vivid, too. "I don't think I know anymore," she replied, finally.

His lips curved. "I receive little company, so I would love for you to stay and continue to talk with me for a while."

"Oh, is that what we're doing?"

"Yes. A clever woman like you should recognize a conversation when she's in one." He turned away and set the tray on a low table of glossy wood with frivolous legs that ended in dainty carved hooves.

She lifted the poker. With his back turned, she could strike him over the head. Quick and clean.

"Don't." He said it softly, with stern command, never looking at her. He poured the blood-red liquid from the carafe into a glass and brought it to her. "If you try to attack me, I will tie your hands. I'd prefer you to accept my ropes under other circumstances."

The words sent a pulse of heat between her thighs and her once-clear thoughts whirled. She didn't know what to think or do.

"Come sit," he said, in a much gentler tone, warm and coaxing. "Have some wine. Eat something. We'll talk." He eased the poker out of her hand, set it back in the stand, and wrapped her fingers around the wineglass. Clearly unconcerned that she might disobey, he turned his back and moved to an antique French chair, unfastening his cloak and setting it aside. He settled himself on the chair and stretched out one leg, as if it pained him, his muscular thigh twitching.

Christy clutched the wineglass. Her self-defense instructor had never said what to do in this kind of situation. Or maybe she had. Make him see you as a person. *Trust your instincts.*

"Won't you sit, Christine?" He sounded a little weary.

Forcing herself to move, she took the chair opposite him, at the other end of the long table. In her jeans and Sarah Lawrence sweatshirt, she felt grubby and graceless. She tucked her sneakered feet under the chair, holding her knees pressed tightly together. After an awkward moment, she set the full wineglass on the table and, for lack of something to do with her hands, folded her arms.

"No wine for you?" He always sounded so amused by her.

"I can't help but notice you aren't drinking any. I'm really not interested in being drugged into submission."

He stilled, intensity burning through him. "I'm not interested in using drugs to entice your submission, Christine."

She had to look away. Jesus, why did those things he said eat through her like that? Shifting a little in her chair to ease the ache between her thighs, she caught him watching the movement with avid interest.

With deliberate care, he poured himself a glass of wine and lifted it to her in a graceful toast. "To new beginnings." *To the most beautiful girl in the room.* A shiver ran through her.

He drank from the glass, like a flesh-and-blood man, to all appearances, then cocked his head at her. "You won't seal the toast either?"

"No, thank you."

"I want to earn your trust, Christine."

"Why?"

"So I may pay my court to you."

That stopped her. A frisson of shock, fear—and, curiously, pleasure—ran over her skin. It all felt like stepping into some old story. A fairy tale.

"I don't understand." It came out as a whisper.

He set his wineglass on the table, a bookend to hers, leaned his elbows on his knees, and laced his fingers together. "Surely in even such a modern world, a young woman understands what it means to be courted. I want to woo you, Christine. I want to seduce you, to unfold your petals and open you like the sensuous flower of womanhood you are. I want to peel away every layer of resistance until I hold you trembling and naked in my arms, until I know you more intimately than any other being on this earth."

Her nails were digging into the wooden arms of the chair. Somewhere in that speech she'd unfolded her arms and leaned toward him, helplessly entranced by the images he created in her mind.

It was all so strange, as in the dreams. The urge to go to him overwhelmed her. He held out his gloved hands, opening his arms. "Come to me, Christine. Give me a kiss."

"No." She clutched the chair, as if it would anchor her there. "I won't. I can't."

"But you can. Am I such a monster?"

That cleared some of the spell. "I don't know—if you murdered poor Tara, you are. And perhaps I simply don't want to."

His lips curved, making her wonder how he'd feel and taste. "You want to. You are as drawn to me as I am to you. You're too intelligent to delude yourself on that point. You want to kiss me now, to taste me as I wish to taste you. All you have to do is ask."

Christy shook her head, both in refusal and to dispel the desire his voice created in her. "Gotta point out here that you didn't respond to the part about Tara."

"I didn't kill that girl." Anger rippled through his voice. "It grieves me deeply that you could think it. Have I done the least thing to harm you?"

Christy shrugged elaborately. "No. Not a thing. I suppose the rape, torture, and murder part of our program is still to come."

"Beneath this mask and these clothes, I may be scarred, but I do not possess the twisted soul to do such a thing. I promise you that."

"Okay, then how did her body get there? And so conveniently after you ambushed me in that hallway?"

He adjusted the mask, showing a touch of uncertainty—the first she'd glimpsed in him. "I don't know." He said it softly, a confession.

"How can you not know?" she demanded in a tumult of emotion. "You're the theater ghost! You see all and know all! You come and go like the wind and no doors are locked to you!" Her voice rose perilously high and she strained forward in the chair even as she clung to the arms, as if she might launch herself at him. "Tell me how any of this is possible!"

He regarded her somberly. "I am bound by flesh and blood. I am only a man, Christine."

"I don't believe you," she hissed.

"No?" He stood abruptly and came around the fragile barrier of the coffee table in a single stride. She shrank back in her chair, but he only held out a black-gloved hand. "Touch me and see."

She knotted her hands together. "I don't want to."

"Give me that much." He sounded equally distraught. "Let me at least prove to you that I am not a ghost."

"And then you'll let me go?"

"It is always within your power to come and go, if you want to. Touch me. Trust me."

He stood over her, so tall, his fair hair shining in the candlelight. Hesitant, she laid her hand in his, the leather soft and supple from his body heat. He drew her to her feet with great care, so she stood close enough to smell him. Like cedar chests and pine smoke, warm leather and man.

Taking her hands by the wrist, he laid them flat on his strong chest. Then let go and stood at her mercy. She flexed her fingertips on the brocade waistcoat, feeling the contour of muscle beneath. His breath rose and fell, his strong heart thumping. She trailed her hands down, over his flat abdomen, enticed by his masculine form. But the fabric, stiff and scratchy, got in the way. He wasn't watching her but instead stared steadfastly over her head, concentrating on not moving, perhaps. She unfastened one of the elaborate gold frogs and his breath caught.

Only a man.

That small response, more than anything, emboldened her. One by one, she unhooked the closings, then spread open the waistcoat, freeing the white linen crushed beneath. It was damp from the sweat of his skin, fragrant with his scent. Intoxicated, she ran her hands up his hard belly, ribs, and pecs. All man. When she reached his collar, her fingers found the button there and set about to undo it.

His hands came up, clamping her wrists, holding them there.

"No."

She stared up into his intent, icy eyes. "Why not?"

"I don't want you to see me. Some of it is . . . not pretty."

"Is that why you wear a mask?"

"Yes." He searched her face with a kind of yearning. "Can you look past that?"

"I want to see."

"Not yet."

"Then I want to touch. I'll close my eyes."

He hesitated.

"You asked me to trust you. Trust me." *Trust your gut.*

He breathed a humorless laugh. "Such a simple thing to ask, is it not? And so terribly uncomfortable to give."

For the first time, she felt she might understand him. A ghost pain from her own scars sparked across her belly. "You also asked me to touch you. Let me."

His gloved fingers flexed on her wrists. "I want to blindfold you. Will you let me?"

It seemed the room spun around her in a long, slow whirl, a carousel of exotic beasts whispering to her of dread and exhilaration. The few logical thoughts she could muster all muttered that this was a bad, bad idea.

But something deeper and stronger overrode them. She wanted this.

Trust yourself.

6

She nodded, feeling like the moment when you step off the high dive at the pool. When it's too late to change your mind and all that's left is the fall—and the rush of ecstatic panic that comes with it.

Only that feeling was bright—born of sunshine, squealing children, and cool water on blue tiles. This . . . this came of night-dark pleasure, enthrallment, desire, and a mysterious man holding a black silk scarf.

"Turn around." He didn't smile, and the eyes behind the mask held a challenge. It was part request but mostly command, and she turned, body simmering, heart thumping with the intensity of the moment. Trust indeed. And more.

. . . to entice your submission.

The black silk slithered over her eyes and she pressed her fingertips against it while he tied the scarf behind her head. Gentle but firm. It made no sense, but by giving up her sight, she felt as if she'd turned over something to him. It opened a door inside the depths of her soul, a long, shadowed hallway where she might hand over more and more. A kind of tension drained away, leaving a vibrant hum behind. She was underwater, floating in the dark.

He sighed, brushing the nape of her neck, sending shivers through her. A whisper of sound, and hot fingers caressed her skin. She pressed her lips together against a moan.

"Ah, Christine," he murmured. "You undo me."

His lips replaced his fingers, kissing along her spine, his tongue licking into the hollow at the base of her skull. Her breasts felt full, swollen with the ache to be touched, and moisture bloomed between her thighs. Had he said he wanted to seduce her? Breathlessly, she took in every sensation, listening intently to the rustle of crisp linen, the sound of him unbuttoning the shirt.

"All right." Desire ran hot through his voice. "You may turn."

She pivoted carefully, somewhat unbalanced by her blindness, but encircled by his protective arms. He took her hands and guided her, moving in a step so hot flesh met her questing fingers. She drew in a breath, sharp, astonished, as if being unable to see made the sensation of male skin all the more otherworldly. Moving her palms over his chest, she absorbed the feel of him, and he groaned, a shudder running through him.

"Did you mention torture?" he asked, his voice rough. "Perhaps I am the one to suffer it."

"Do you want me to stop?" But it was a taunt, a flexing of her power over him. She found the change of texture where his nipples were and scratched them lightly with her nails. The skin puckered under her touch and his muscles tensed.

"Not yet." He seemed to be restraining himself, a vicious tension running under his skin, his muscles nearly vibrating under her caress. Even blindfolded, a thrill of possessive triumph filled her, the beast tamed to her touch. She reached higher, thinking to run her hands over those broad shoulders. A ridge of twisted skin met her touch, a cicatrix of pain, and she faltered, her own internal wounds breaking open, oozing old and strange emotions.

With a harsh curse in a language she didn't understand, he stepped away, leaving her swaying without an anchor.

"Wait." She reached out, feeling through the air. "Don't go."

The sharp sounds of him buttoning his shirt and waistcoat answered her.

"What happened?" Her fingers found the knot in the blindfold and she tugged at it. So tight.

"Don't you dare." His growled command froze her and then he seized her, taking her wrists again in his powerful hands, moving them inexorably away from the blindfold and down, behind her back, arching her against him. She struggled a little, but the movement pressed her aching nipples against him, nearly unbearable even through her shirt and bra. She couldn't escape him and the thought excited her beyond reason.

"Please." She turned up her face, whispering the plea.

He adjusted the grip, holding her wrists with one hand, freeing the other to stroke her cheek, feather light. Warm breath flowed over her lips. He must be close enough to kiss, and she strained against the explosive need for more. But he held her tight, so he remained beyond her reach.

"Are you afraid, then?" The question came harsh, full of tearing emotion. "You are revolted by my scars. Admit it."

"I didn't see anything."

"But you felt it. You flinched as if burned yourself."

"I didn't mean to."

"Your honest reaction tells me all I need to know. Remember, Christine, I could see your face."

"Then you saw surprise and nothing more."

"Nothing more than that?" A gloved finger pressed against her lips. "I think you lie."

She wanted to tear off the damn blindfold. It exposed her to him in such a terrible way. He breathed a humorless laugh at her struggles. "Tell me the truth."

She couldn't. She never discussed it with anyone. It made those nightmare days far too real. They were better kept locked away behind the fibrous walls of scar tissue.

Hot lips brushed her cheek. "I can't bear for you to hate me. If I thought you did, I would become a monster in truth and do what monsters do—lock up the fair young maiden and keep her imprisoned to feed their dark, depraved hungers."

"Do you . . ." Her breath faltered. "Do you have depraved hungers?"

"Oh, my sweetly innocent Christine, you have no idea."

"I'm not that innocent."

"No?" The hand on her cheek turned her head and the hot lips moved to her ear, catching her lobe in a sharp bite that made her gasp. The little pain rocked through her, sparking a deep craving. "Does that mean you want what I offer?"

Maybe. "I don't know."

His hand dropped to her collarbone, caressing the skin where her sweatshirt revealed it. Fingertips catching the silver chain, he drew out the pendant, the metal whispering against her neck.

"What's this?"

"An old Indian woman gave it to me."

"Interesting." He caressed it, then let it go, leaving it outside her shirt. "Now, tell me."

"I can't." But the confession beat at the inside of her skull. If all of this was just a dream, perhaps she could open the door here, in this place of shrouding shadows. A protected truth.

"What else did you feel, besides surprise? You looked distressed, pained. If not revulsion, then what? Give me this piece of you."

She hesitated, trying to frame the answer. To explain to him, her dark reflection in the mirror.

"It did pain me. Reminded me of something from long ago. I have . . ." She faltered. Took the simple way out. No explanations, just the plain and final fact of it. "I have scars, too."

He softened, his arms enfolding her in a bearlike embrace, drawing her against his body while his hand cupped her head, like something infinitely precious.

"I know." His voice rumbled under her ear.

"How could you possibly?"

"We know each other, don't we? I see myself in your eyes."

"This is all a dream," she whispered.

The hand cupping her head shifted. "Is it a good dream?"

"I'm waiting to find out."

And his mouth captured hers suddenly, soft on the edges but steel hard in the center. He kissed her as if he were a man in the desert finding water. In answer, the heat simmering low in her belly flared up, lighting her blood, a spark to gasoline. She kissed him back, ferocious, starving in turn for something she couldn't name.

The phantom insisted she keep the blindfold on for the first part of the journey up and out.

"This is my way in and out—not yours," he informed her, with no room for debate. She'd tried anyway.

Somehow he'd gotten her out of the seamless chamber, but he'd led her around it a dizzying number of times so she couldn't know where in the room she'd been. When he stopped to take off her blindfold, he'd turned away quickly, so she couldn't study his expression. Now they moved along yet another dimly lit and narrow hallway; with him leading the way. His light threw crazy flickering shadows against the walls, making him a deeper silhouette. She was more familiar with him now, and she could see the slight hitch in his stride, the catch in his hip as he walked. He continued on, holding her hand in his as he drew her along behind him, his thoughts far away, and she missed the intensity of his regard.

She had, perhaps, already become a little addicted to it.

He stopped so abruptly she nearly crashed into him.

"Listen."

She thought he meant to listen to him, but he said nothing. The shadows stilled and seemed to fold their wings, settling around them with the quiet. Not entirely silent, however; in the singing distance of the acoustics, sounds traveled to her. Not the golden voice, serenading her, but the harsh vocals of police speakers, the whoop of a siren. The tromp of footsteps.

"Oh no."

"Oh yes. The daylight world searches for you."

Shit. She really hoped her father wouldn't find out. All at once she felt thirteen again, getting caught after sneaking back into the house. Her father had accused her of staging the rebellion to make him let her live with her mother and showed her how very badly her plan had gone wrong.

"Have I been gone that long?" It hadn't felt very long. She didn't have her phone, so she couldn't check the time. "Where are my things?"

"Where you left them."

"No—you moved them." She remembered now. The strange sounds, the chandelier falling while she stood petrified below. What had really happened?

"I must go." He still held her hand and now drew her closer. "Give me a kiss."

"Tell me your name."

"Call me Master." He whispered it, like a secret, like a promise, and followed it with a searing kiss that chased the confusion and questions from her reeling mind.

He set her on her feet and she became aware she'd been clinging to him. A gloved thumb rubbed over her lip.

"Close your eyes for a moment."

Rather than risk another discussion about the blindfold, she did. A sound like sandpaper and a whiff of dusty air. Then he pulled her by the hand a few steps and let her look again.

She stood on the very lowest level, outside the sealed door she'd seen on her first day. Feeling an odd sense of déjà vu, she traced the image carved into the door. The collar and whip that had instantly captured her attention.

"I don't understand all of this," she whispered.

Her voice echoed back. She was alone in the empty hallway.

7

The martial thump of boots on metal jerked her from her daze.

She hurried down the murky hall to the central spiral staircase and peered up through the grate. The levels were lit up to three above where she stood. Voices created quite a din, with shouts, doors banging, and dogs barking. They'd brought out search dogs?

Creeping as noiselessly as possible, she skulked up one flight of steps on all fours, keeping her profile low. She made it to the next level up without setting off shouts of alarm and decided not to risk another. Being that far down would help with her story that she hadn't heard anyone.

Unfortunately she needed more of a story than that.

Why would she have come to this level—without her keys, dammit—and stayed down here when Carla needed her help? Could she fake temporary amnesia? The chandelier fell and she hit her head, can't remember what happened but miraculously sustained no injury. And somehow wandered off.

Had the chandelier really fallen? Or had she only imagined it teetering above her, one of its crystal pendants spinning through the air like a snowflake, then soundlessly shattering on the floor?

If it hadn't really fallen, then she'd sound insane.

If none of this had really happened, she had to consider that possibility.

Think. Think. Think.

She slid along the wall, trying doorknobs as she went, underneath the video cameras, out of range of their unblinking black eyes. No little red lights gleamed in the dark, however, so perhaps whatever happened to the one in the prop shop affected these, too. If that had happened.

It all whispered of mental imbalance, a thought that made her nerves cringe, the sensation of fingernails scraping sandpaper. The very worst part of being treated for mental illness was the way you learned not to trust yourself. Every thought could be a fraud, a decoy leading you away from reality and into the ever-shifting realm where everyone looked at you with sideways concern and believed nothing you said.

You were never crazy. Stop that.

Every explanation for her behavior led back to that place, though. Christy didn't think she could bear to go through that again. The careful sympathy and casual dismissal. Worse—she began to wonder if she had dreamed it all up. That colorful carousel of a room and a masked man who intrigued and lured her.

Lights flared from the stairwell and the sounds of stomping boots came clattering down. A dog barked with excitement, his furry shape lunging down the tight spiral. He'd caught her scent and soon would be upon her. The game was up. She stepped out into the middle of the dark corridor and walked back the way she'd come, shading her eyes when the lights flashed on.

The German shepherd came leaping at her, full of doggy joy. She'd once read about how search dogs in major disasters became depressed, finding dead body after dead body. Their handlers would have to hide themselves in the rubble so the dogs could find a living person to restore their hope. She knelt down and scratched under her collar, letting the dog lick her face.

This, at least, was real.

"Christine Davis?" A man in uniform approached. She nodded, and he spoke into a radio. Better reception than her cell, she noted with some irony. Perhaps she should suggest them to Charlie. "Do you need medical attention?"

"No—I'm fine. I, um—" *Moment of truth. What excuse will you use?* "I'm afraid I got lost and, well, I fell asleep. All the noise woke me." *Ah, yes. The too-stupid-to-live defense.* Never underestimate the power of seeming to be an idiot. Far better than crazy.

"Well, let's get you out of here. You worried a lot of people."

"I'm sorry." She tried to sound meek and sorrowful. If her hair were long still, she would have twisted a lock around her finger.

"Never mind that. Though Detective Sanchez will want to talk to you."

Upstairs, the prop shop had been taped off and crime-scene types were closing up their equipment cases. No need to check for evidence now. Detective Sanchez met them outside the door, arms folded, suspicious eyes looking her up and down as she repeated her story. He didn't buy it for a moment, that much was clear.

As she spoke, she desperately wanted to see past him, to crane her neck to peer around the corner, to see the chandelier. Would it be perched high on the shelf, covered in dust? Or would it be a jumble of broken crystal on the floor?

Her heart pounded with the need to know, her neck tense from restraining the urge to push him aside so she could see for herself what was real.

"So, even though Ms. Donovan expressly told you to wait for her return, you decided not to?" At Christy's frown, he clarified, "Carla Donovan, your boss."

As much as she wanted to say that Carla wasn't her boss—and who knew her last name was the same as Charlie's?—she bit her tongue on that and concentrated on being silly. Surely they would have mentioned the chandelier?

"I was worried about her. She was gone a long time, so I went looking for her."

The detective checked his notes. "Ms. Donovan says she returned in five to seven minutes."

"Oh." Christy turned big eyes up at him, pleading. "It seemed longer. And with all the scary stuff going on, I . . ."

"Your story doesn't hold water, frankly." Detective Sanchez kept his hard gaze on her. "If you were frightened, why would you go down to the same level where a murder victim's body was found?"

"I—" It was a good question. "I wasn't thinking."

Sanchez sighed. "Is that the only thing you were afraid of, Christy? Did something else happen?"

Did the chandelier fall or not? She wanted to shriek the question. She clamped down on it, keeping her voice even. "Like what?"

"I understand you're seeing Roman Sanclaro."

It took her a moment to adjust her thoughts. Roman? "Um, yes. He's an old family friend. What does that have to do with anything?"

"He's waiting for you outside. He's been quite concerned about you. Is there anything you need to tell me?"

She no longer had to fake being confused and a little dumb. She had no idea what he meant. Sanchez drew her aside, farther away from the prop shop doorway. "Did Roman Sanclaro hurt or threaten you?"

"What? No." Her thoughts lost some of the fog and she focused on him. "Is he a suspect in the murder?"

His face stayed impassive. "The investigation is ongoing. Do you have information to share with me?"

"Ah . . . no. No! I've known Roman practically my whole life. He would never hurt anyone." Her voice shook, everything catching up with her.

Sanchez's gaze flicked away and, despite his professional poker face, she could practically read his thoughts. They all said that kind of thing, the families—even the wives and girlfriends—of serial killers. She sounded just like those poor people on TV, bewildered, unable to believe the evidence before their eyes.

"I know you have my card already—here's another," Sanchez was saying. "Call me anytime you want to talk."

Christy nodded, folding his card and sliding it into her jeans pocket. His intelligent gaze held both a plea and a warning.

"Even if you feel afraid for no reason, I want to hear about it."

That was a laugh. He had no idea the things that currently frightened her. "Could I ask a favor?"

Sanchez raised an expectant eyebrow.

"I'm really sorry I caused so much trouble, but could you not call the owner of the theater about this?"

"Carlton Davis? Typically I wouldn't, unless there had been an actual crime." Christy breathed a sigh of relief, which the detective didn't miss. "I'm aware he's your father, Ms. Davis, so let me give you a word to the wise. Honesty is always the best policy."

With a little salute, Detective Sanchez pulled down the tape and went into the prop room, asking someone to release Christy's belongings to her.

With trepidation, she followed him. All of her desperation to see had fled, and now she almost couldn't bear to look. Like the girl she'd been, she wanted to cover her eyes and peek through her fingers.

There were her things, sitting on the workbench where she'd left them. Up above, the chandelier rested, regal under its thick coating of dust and cobwebs. Underneath, the concrete floor was bare and clean.

But in the corner, catching her eye, a shard of crystal glittered.

Phantom Serenade

1

Roman met her outside, pushing past the patrol officers who had clearly been keeping him back.

"Christy! I was so afraid that..." He stopped himself and wrapped his arms hard around her, holding her tight and rocking. It felt oddly jarring after the ghost's—the Master's—powerful but gentle embrace. "Where *were* you?"

"Well, see, I—"

"Never mind. All that matters is that you're safe." Roman drew himself up and slung a protective arm around her waist. "Come on, sweet girl. Let me take you home. You can tell me all about it in the car."

"I can drive myself, my car is—"

"I won't hear of it. You're pale and you've clearly had a bad scare. Let me take care of you."

His insistence frightened her a little. The intensity of his eyes and the strength of his grip on her arm. Sanchez's vague warnings echoed in her head, pissing her off. What business did he have, making her doubt her old friend?

"Okay." She smiled at him. "Thank you." And then he considerately turned off his usual blasting techno music and they rode in the car in blissful quiet.

Though it made the uneasiness stir again, she also didn't argue when Roman brought her back to his place instead of her hotel room. Taking care of her seemed to make Roman happy, and it helped to be around him, a real human being she'd known nearly forever. And she did know him, despite Sanchez's oily hints. Besides, she owed Roman for coming to her rescue yet again.

Especially because now, along with everything else, she felt guilty.

She imagined little green wisps of guilt-smoke wafting out of her ears, seeping from her pores as if she'd eaten too much garlic and wasn't fit for romantic company. Roman had accepted her story at face value, sympathetic that she'd felt rattled at being left alone and had gone seeking Carla. If he'd too easily believed that she'd be dumb enough to get lost and then take a nap in the bowels of the opera house, that was her own fault for taking the bimbo defense. *Playing dumb works until you get tired of everyone thinking you're a waste of air*, her father had reminded her the one or two times she'd tried that tactic with him.

One did not want Carlton Davis thinking you were a waste of air.

Roman's place turned out to be a small mansion up Hyde Park Road. He excused it as modest—not like his folks' place—but it clung to the hillside, a jeweled spider, multileveled with balconies and an infinity pool. All the brightly lit windows looked out over Santa Fe valley. The sunset views, no doubt, would be spectacular.

Christy stood in one of those windows, admiring the view, feeling more grounded all the time. The events of the night faded more with every passing moment. She could almost believe her own story—that she'd fallen asleep and dreamed it all.

"Not how I imagined you seeing my house for the first time," Roman called from the open-area kitchen, where he was getting her a glass of wine. She became abruptly conscious of her grubbiness. Somehow she always felt underdressed around him. It wasn't the money—she'd been around enough rich people to know plenty of them bought their clothes at Target.

She smiled over her shoulder. "It's okay. I appreciate you giving me shelter."

"I asked Gloria to start a bath for you in the guest suite." Roman handed her a half glass of white wine. "I'm sure you'll feel better after you've cleaned up."

The wine tasted amazing, a soothing sweep through her bloodstream. It would have been really nice to have more than the child-sized portion he'd given her. She cast a rueful glance at her dusty sweatshirt. "I'd just have to put these back on—not much point."

"I may have bought a few things I thought would look nice on you." He smiled broadly when she protested. "Now, now—no complaints. I love to give you gifts. You might as well get used to it. The guest suite is down that way. Gloria is waiting for you. She has a robe you can put on, too."

"Am I, um, staying the night?"

"I think that's best—what your father would want me to do. You're safe here with me, Christy, I want you to know that. I respect you as a woman. Don't worry that I'll take advantage. I want to do this right. In fact, we're having a family party this weekend. I'd like you to come out to the Compound, see my father again and finally meet my mother and sister. They've been asking to see you. I told them we've been going out as more than friends."

Whoa. Really too much to process all at once. *Guilt, guilt, guilt.* The little guilt fairies pranced around in her head.

"Roman?"

"What is it, sweet girl?"

"Do you consider us to be . . . exclusive?"

He smiled at her over the rim of his much more generous glass of wine. "Don't give a moment's worry to that. I would never cheat on you. It goes against everything I believe in, our families' honor, my church. You can trust in me, Christy. Always."

He was such a great guy.

She didn't know what Sanchez's beef with him was, but she, at least, could show she believed in him. So, while she really would have rather holed up in her hotel room to think about all that had happened, instead she obediently trotted down to the guest wing level, to make Roman happy and to let poor Gloria go to bed.

Roman's housekeeper turned out to be a matronly Hispanic woman who clucked sympathetically over Christy's frightening adventure in the half English/half Spanish patois many New Mexicans seemed to use. Which meant she didn't understand most of what the woman said to her. But that was okay.

Besides, the tub was fabulous.

Big enough for five people, sunken into the floor, and set into a niche of bay windows that hung over the valley, it more than made up for time served with only a small shower stall.

She sank into the steaming water, scented with something reminiscent of orange blossoms. Too sweet, but well intentioned. Gloria bustled off with Christy's clothes, presumably to wash them, leaving her with a fluffy white robe.

"Captive again," she muttered to herself. But then decided she didn't mean it. Roman was only being kind. And the protective thing was because he cared for her. After all, he'd been the one to call the cops when he'd come looking for her and found her car still there, Carla gone, and the place locked up.

Christy swished her shoulders in the water, scooting down to get the heat up around the tight base of her neck. Apparently Carla thought Christy had taken off, and the woman had left without noticing her car was still there.

Gloria came bustling back in to see if she needed anything. When Christy asked for more wine, Gloria nodded with a Buddha smile—and brought her herbal tea and a burrito wrapped in a napkin, so she could hold it.

Suddenly ravenous, having totally forgotten that she'd never eaten dinner, she devoured the burrito, which turned out to be perfectly complemented by the soothing tea. Ferociously sleepy, she forced herself to climb out of the luxurious tub and pulled on the robe. The connecting guest room sported more windows and a California king bed that had been turned down for her.

Her bag sat on the dresser and she checked her phone. Nothing from her father, thankfully. Charlie had left her a voice mail telling her to take a sick day to rest up. He sounded carefully neutral. Hopefully he wasn't angry at her causing so much trouble. She didn't mind the reprieve from getting up early, however.

The phone was down to the last 20 percent of battery, but her charger was back at the hotel. Nothing to be done. Weary, she sat on the edge of the bed. Roman had left a note on her pillow, wishing her good night and sweet dreams. He'd see her in the morning.

Sliding naked between the million thread count sheets, she killed the bedside lamp and gazed at the warm lights of the city in the valley. The moon, the same amber-orange color as the discreet downward-facing lights, lowered herself in serene splendor toward the horizon. Christy toyed with the silver spiral pendant, sliding it back and forth on the chain, remembering the smile in the Master's

voice at seeing it, those chiseled lips curving beneath the inscrutable black mask.

Of course she dreamed of him.

Not of Roman, the handsome, genuinely caring guy who'd been
her prince charming all her life. No—she dreamed of the Master. A
swirl of dreams repeating themselves, a badly streaming movie that
caught itself, restarted, and played again. Over and over, she
waltzed with him, held at arm's length while her nipples stood taut
and her groin throbbed. Then she ran down the stairs, calling,
shouting for someone. And her foot slipped off the metal step. She
fell, dropping through black space, still calling that name.

Then they waltzed again, in dizzying circles. She pleaded with
him, but he stayed remote, holding her only by his gloved hands, his
icy-blue gaze focused on the distance.

She woke, disoriented, in utter darkness. Instead of the rough,
over-bleached hotel sheets, expensive cotton flowed against her
naked skin. Roman's house.

But why was it so dark?

Finding her phone on the bedside, she saw it was past eleven in
the morning. A remote control next to it let her open the blackout
shades that had been lowered for her sometime during the night.
Like blast shields on a spaceship, the blinds all rose simultaneously
in majestic silence along the row of windows, letting in the bright
morning sun.

She found a pink-flowered sundress in the bathroom, along with
a cardigan and ballet-slipper flats. Gloria had washed her undies
and left them on the hamper. No sign of her jeans and sweatshirt,
alas.

Dressing in the clothes, which fit fine but seemed as if they belonged to some other girl, Christy wandered through the sprawling
house, looking for Roman. Or food. Possibly both.

If anything, the place was even more beautiful in the daylight.
Exquisitely decorated in what she'd learned was northern hacienda
style. Not the adobe and Saltillo tile, but patterned brick and wood
floors graced by rugs with colorful designs. The house could have
stepped out of *Sunset* magazine, and very likely had been featured
in it at some point.

It was the antithesis of the phantom's abode, the opposite of the eccentric cave deep beneath the opera house. Roman Sanclaro lived like a king, presiding over a world the Master lurked beneath.

She found Gloria in the kitchen, and the woman awarded her a bright *"Buenos días,"* along with a mug of coffee, then pointed outside.

Roman sat at a table by the pool, shaded under an umbrella, working on a laptop. He waved and smiled at her but was absorbed in a phone call, so she wandered around the pool area.

The day was shaping up to be warm, the tiles of the deck nearly hot under her feet. The infinity pool stretched right up to the edge, water spilling over the far edge to fall into a trough that caught it to recycle back in. Beneath, the high-desert scrub scattered across the sharp incline, a sere contrast to the crystal aquamarine water of the pool.

"How's my girl?" Roman's arms slid around her waist and she leaned back against him. He kissed her cheek and mmm'd appreciatively. "I love your perfume. Sweet, like you."

She laughed. "It's your perfume. Of course you like it."

"I do like what I like. And you—do you like my house? Pretty view?"

"It's breathtaking. The way this pool seems to fall off the cliff is truly spectacular."

"Yes. Though I've thought that when I have children, I'll have to change it—wall it off. Too dangerous, don't you think?"

She shrugged. "I haven't been around little kids much. Surely that's a ways in your future, isn't it?"

He turned her in his arms and she faced him, the sun bright in her eyes so she squinted up at him. The disadvantage of flats.

"I think it's finding the right person," Roman said. "I'll be thirty before much longer. I'll need a son to follow in the family business."

"And what if you have daughters?" she teased, trying to lighten his serious mood.

"Then I'll have to make sure they marry the right boys." He kissed her, chaste and light. "Do you think your father approves of me?"

"I'm not sure he approves of anyone."

"He likes me. I'm sure of it. Come." He grinned with charming confidence and steered her back to the table. "Gloria is bringing out some lunch."

"I should get back to the hotel—my phone is nearly out of juice."

"I'll take care of that." He slid the cell phone out of her hand and disappeared into the house.

Feeling at loose ends, she sat and sipped her coffee. She should be enjoying herself. The digs and the view were certainly far superior to the hotel's—and, alas, better than the apartment she'd rented. But it was weird not to have her stuff. She nearly went to fetch her iPad, just to have something to do, when Roman, followed by a beaming Gloria, reemerged.

She clucked at him until he moved his laptop and files off the table, then proceeded to unload enough food to feed ten people, including a pitcher of sangria. Christy eyed it.

"A bit much for a weekday, isn't it?"

"We're celebrating your being okay." Roman flashed his white teeth and took her hand. "I want you to rest and enjoy yourself today. I have some work to do, but I can do it from here. I thought maybe you could sunbathe by the pool. It's supposed to be sunny and warm all day."

"This dress isn't really right for it."

"I think it looks great on you."

She plucked at the skirt, scattered with blush rosebuds. "I don't wear much pink."

"You should." He poured her a half glass of sangria. "It suits you—very feminine and sweet."

Like you, she finished mentally, then felt bad for being snarky, if only in her head.

"Besides," he continued, "I have some extra bathing suits, for guests."

"All right, then," she capitulated, "vacation day it is." And she added more sangria to her glass, pretending she didn't see his concerned frown.

2

The guest swimsuit was a one-piece, thankfully, if more demurely cut than she'd usually wear. Still, it did the job of covering her stomach, which was the important part.

Roman spent most of his time on the phone or frowning at his laptop, while she lolled—frankly bored—under a blue umbrella, sipping iced tea. Finally she asked Roman for her phone, saying she needed to call her dad and check in, when he looked dubious. Her dad was in meetings, however, which at least meant he hadn't been looking for her.

So she tried Hally. Roman was too far away to hear who she was talking to anyway.

"Hi, girlfriend!" Hally's chipper voice answered. "What are you up to—aren't you supposed to be working?"

"Long story, but I'm taking the day off. Guess where I am?" Christy took in the view, the glassy pool leading to it like a red carpet, only in translucent aquamarine.

"Since you never tell me anything, it must be good. Spill!"

"I am lying by a beautiful pool, taking in the view . . . at Roman Sanclaro's house."

Hally gasped dramatically. "Did you spend the night?"

"Yes, but no hanky-panky. I stayed in the guest suite."

"Well, what's the fun in that?"

"I know." Christy couldn't decide how she felt. "He's all old school and gentlemanly about it. His parents want me to come see them this weekend—and he told them we're dating."

"Shut up! Already?" Hally audibly composed herself. "I mean—how do you feel about that?"

Christy snorted at Hally's halfhearted attempt to be an objective listener. "Well, we are old family friends, and Roman and I are kind of seeing each other. But it still seems really fast."

"Well . . ." Hally mulled it over. Christy could imagine her chewing on the end of her ponytail thoughtfully. "He is close to his family and they are big traditional types. Plus, being family friends, he'd want to keep things on the up-and-up."

"But he's supposed to be this big player and all."

"*Until* he meets the right girl," Hally crowed in triumph. "Congratulations—you have been selected as the Sanclaro Sacrificial Virgin! And you win a billion dollars!"

"Oh stop." But Christy was giggling along with her. From the table at the other end of the pool, Roman gave her a quizzical look, so she waved cheerfully at him. *Just relaxing and having fun. Doctor's orders.*

"So, what happened last night? This must be quite the story. If you're sitting by the pool, you have time to tell it."

The giggles stilled and went quiet in her chest, making the thumping of her heart sound all the louder. This was the part she couldn't talk about. *Tell no one.* She'd been kidding herself, gossiping with Hally about Roman as if that was her entire world. But no. Those two belonged to the sunshine side of her life. To the bars and the pools and the family gatherings.

The ghostly Master belonged to none of that. Through choice or curse, it wasn't at all clear—if he was real at all. And yet she'd touched him and felt drawn to him and his darkness. Was it the self-destructiveness the counselors had tried to make her believe lurked in her soul?

"Christy—are you still there?" Hally sounded concerned. "Was it—" her voice dropped to a deep whisper, though it was hardly necessary on the cell phone "—the *ghost*?"

"I can't talk about it," she whispered back. Aware she was hunching around the phone, she made herself lie back. The blue umbrella stretched over blond wooden slats, radiating out in a spider's web.

"Honey . . ." Hally trailed off. "Should I be worried about you?"

"I don't know. Maybe," she confessed.

"Okay. We need to talk. How long are you staying there?"

"I'm not sure. Roman is being all concerned and wants me to rest. He gave me a ride last night, so I have to get him to take me home—or better, to my car—but he's working, so I hate to interrupt him, and . . ." She trailed off when Hally made a rude noise.

"Will you listen to yourself? You sound the same as my old auntie bitching about getting someone to take her to the grocery store."

"Gee, thanks."

"You're welcome," Hally replied crisply. "Now—you want to blow that joint or what? I'll come get you."

The relief rushing through her told Christy all she needed to know. "Oh yes, please. I owe you big time."

"Yes, you do. And I know how you'll make it up to me, too."

Roman wasn't thrilled at her abrupt departure. When she glided past him, he barely glanced up from his current phone conversation. Talking about that Taos deal again, by the sound of it. If she kind of made it seem as if she was stepping inside to use the restroom, it wasn't exactly untrue. She also changed into the dress and ballet flats again—since her clothes were still nowhere to be seen—and got her things.

When she emerged, fully dressed, Roman raised an eyebrow and signed off. "Too much sun?" He held out an arm, so she went to him for the hug, surprised when he maneuvered her to sit on his lap.

"No—well, yes. I need to get going, run a few errands while I have the time."

"Are you sure you're ready for that? Maybe you should take another day to rest."

"I'm fine." She smiled to smooth out the irritation in her voice.

"Well, okay. But you'll have to wait a couple of hours. I have another call and—"

"Don't give it another thought," she interrupted, not missing the line between his eyebrows when she did. So she leaned in and kissed him. "You've done so much for me. Thank you."

"I understand you're impatient, Christy, but I can't just pick up and drive you around because you've taken it into your head to go."

Sitting on Roman's lap and hearing him sound like her father tipped the scales. She stood up, having to tug away from his hold. "I would not impose further. My friend is coming to pick me up."

"Ah." He sat back and folded his arms. "Thus the phone call. I thought you said you were calling your father."

"I made several calls." *On my own damn phone.* She kept her tone breezy, though this was getting to be a little much. "Do you know where my clothes are? I couldn't find them."

"Gloria has them. Gloria! Bring Christy's clothes," he shouted into the house, and Christy winced at his tone. Was this their first fight?

Gloria came bustling out, wearing her usual radiant smile and carrying a tote bag, not minding a bit. She patted Christy on the cheek and told her to come again soon—or something like that. Roman watched her go with a bemused expression. "She likes you. That's a good sign."

Because Gloria didn't always approve of the girls Roman brought home, Christy supposed. She checked the tote, thinking maybe she'd change really quickly. But she only found her sweatshirt, sneakers, and socks.

"Where are my jeans?"

"Oh," Roman replied, reading something on the laptop screen. "I told Gloria to get rid of them."

"What?"

Roman looked astonished at her sharp question. "They had holes in them."

Christy set her jaw, surprised at the flare of anger. "I wear old jeans to work because I'm going through dusty boxes in old store-rooms. That way I don't mess up my nice clothes."

He shrugged. "I'll buy you a new pair. Heck, I'll buy you as many pairs of jeans as you want. They're just clothes, Christy. It's not a big deal."

"I don't need you to buy me things."

Roman threw up his hands. "Okay, so buy your own jeans. Have it your way. I don't even know what we're fighting about."

She took a deep breath. Blew it out.

"Hey." Roman got up and took her hands, giving her his charming smile. "Don't be mad, sweet girl. I'm sorry." He kissed her cheek. "Okay?" He kissed the other cheek. "Okay?" He kissed her forehead. "Okay? Am I forgiven?"

Feeling like she'd been bitchy, she nodded. Roman rewarded her with a long, sweet kiss on the lips.

"That's my sweet girl," he murmured.

"Hal is here to pick up the missus," Gloria said, popping her head through the sliding glass doors.

Roman gave her a *look*. "Hal?"

"Hally. She's my girlfriend. I mean, she's a girl who's my friend."

Roman's cell went off, playing some techno ringtone.

"I'll let you answer that. Bye!" Christy kissed him fast and took the opportunity to go.

"I'll text you!" Roman called after her.

She tossed a wave over her shoulder and escaped through the glass doors.

Hally lurked on the front patio, leaning a shoulder against one of the hand-carved wooden pillars supporting the portal.

"Hey—you could have come in," Christy greeted her.

Hally gave the front door a brittle look. "I don't think so. I sure wasn't invited in. The housekeeper even suggested I wait for you in the car. Like I'm your driver."

"Baby, you *are* my driver." Christy flounced down the walk, trailing her hand through the air, movie-star–style. "Now, take me somewhere."

"I'll take you somewhere, all right," Hally grumbled. She got in her little VW Bug, plastered with Blessed Be bumper stickers, and reached over to unlock the door for Christy.

"Seriously." Christy tossed the tote in the backseat and ran her fingers through her hair. "I really appreciate you coming to get me."

"That's what friends are for." Hally's customary cheer had returned immediately. "Speaking of which, how much do you love the dress you're wearing?"

"Roman gave it to me. Too granny?"

"*Way* too granny. But with what I have in mind, you won't be wearing it long anyway." Hally bared her teeth in a wicked grin and refused to say more.

She parked in an underground pay lot near the rail yard and they walked a couple of blocks to Hally's apartment, on the second level of an adobe building on a narrow, twisting half-commercial, half-residential street.

"The parking sucks—though they give me a reduced annual rate—but the light is good. Plus I can walk to work." Hally unlocked the door at the top of the rickety pine staircase and pushed it open. "Don't mind the mess. You're not allergic to cats, are you?"

"No, I—" Christy was still petting the brown one that greeted them at the door when two gray kitties came bouncing around the corner, ready to play, followed by an older black cat, meowing for food. "You have four cats?"

"Six." Hally tossed her bag on the counter, took Christy's, and set it there too. "I figure if I add one a year, with natural attrition, by the time I'm 40, I can officially qualify as a crazy cat lady."

"I think you're already there."

"A girl can dream. Want anything?"

"I'm good." Afternoon light shone in the windows on the south side. The apartment seemed to be mainly one large room taking up the southeast corner of the building. Hally rattled around in the kitchenette, tucked in a nook beside the front door. A futon on the floor draped in filmy scarves that hung from the ceiling took up the other windowless corner. Books tumbled from several piles near the bed and an e-reader lay on her pillow, looking small, neat, and precious, like a prayer book. The rest of the space was devoted to painting.

Finished canvases hung on the walls and were stacked against the walls five and seven deep. From all of them, faces looked out at her, gazes veiled or bold, rarely straight on, but sidelong or looking through a cracked-open doorway or dappled by leaf shadow. Some of the paintings showed bodies, clothed, naked, and veiled, but the eyes were always what stood out, dark or bright, all burning with inner fire.

"Welcome to my chamber of horrors." Hally stood next to her, sipping a Coke. "You can tell me you hate them—I won't be hurt."

"They're amazing." Christy searched for more and better words. Then shrugged. "Why aren't you famous yet?"

Hally clapped her hands, squealed in joy—putting a total lie to the won't-be-hurt bit—and kissed her on the cheek. "Goddess bless you! Now take your clothes off. You're my next stepping stone to fame and fortune."

"What?" Christy's stomach clenched and she wrapped her arms protectively around it.

"Don't tell me you're shy." Hally pulled out a partially finished canvas and set it on an easel by the east window. The background had been painted in from the edges, swirling with shadows and suggested shapes. In contrast, a lighter area in the middle waited, vacant and expectant, for a figure to be added. The person—presumably her—would recline on a fainting couch. From what Hally had already roughed in, the chaise looked very similar to the one in the Master's den.

Christy found herself next to Hally, reaching out to touch the painting. "It should be green."

From the corner of her eye, she caught Hally's start and her assessing look. "How did you know I planned that?"

"Why did you pick me to model in this painting?"

"I had a vision." Hally said it as if it was the most natural thing in the world. "I woke up this morning with it in my head and I had to paint it. When you called, I'd been plotting how to get you to pose for it—I figured it was meant."

"You don't have a couch like this."

"I figured you could lie on my futon. Close enough."

"I'm not posing nude."

"But it has to be!" Hally insisted, none of her usual mellow self in evidence. "You're naked, stretched out with your arms over your head, gazing out. Please? I have cookies."

"No. Not nude."

"Chocolate-chip cookies?"

"Not even for chocolate-chip cookies."

"You said you owed me." Hally narrowed her hazel eyes in mock threat. "Don't cross the goddess blessed."

A chill shivered across Christy's skin and she met Hally's gaze. The other girl's face had gone white, with a greenish cast beneath. Christy swallowed the dryness in her throat. "Well, that was dramatic."

"I'm sorry. I don't know what came over me."

"I do." Christy glanced uneasily out of the closed windows. "Still, you shouldn't say such things."

Hally sighed. "I know. Now I'll have to light a bunch of candles and do penance."

"How do you do penance?"

"It's personal—I'll give up something I don't want to. It's between me and the universe." Hally shrugged her acquiescence and started to pack up the paints again. "Probably not being able to finish this painting will be enough pain."

Christy chewed on her lip, tugged between conflicting emotions. The sense of being drawn along by fate both unsettled and excited her. In the painting's background lurked the shadows of furniture that could be the Master's. And one dark form could be his cloaked figure. Would the painting give her some sort of answer?

"I'll pose." She blurted it out before she could change her mind. "But naked from the waist up only. I'll drape scarves over the rest and you can use your artistic license or what have you."

Instead of her earlier excited squeals, Hally studied her with grave concern. "What changed your mind?"

Christy lifted a shoulder and let it drop, tried a smile that came out wobbly. "I want to see how it comes out."

"The painting?"

"All of it." She reached out again, this time toward the shadowy form in the dimness. The suggestion of him faded, became mere brushstrokes. "Remember how I said it was a long story, what happened last night?"

"Yes."

"I was here."

3

Christy undressed in Hally's tiny bathroom. She only had a shower stall, too. Such a long way from Roman's opulent sunken tub. The medicine cabinet mirror didn't reflect below her breasts, so the scars on her belly were thankfully out of sight. She wore Hally's robe back out, and the other girl kept her back turned until Christy had arranged herself, strategically draping the off-limits portions of her body with scarves left handily nearby.

"Okay," she said, once she was reasonably sure none of the scars showed.

Hally scrutinized her, her face absorbed. "Don't hold your breath. Relax."

Easy for her to say—she wasn't undressed in broad daylight for the first time in, oh, eleven years.

Bringing a few more pillows to approximate the angle of the painted chaise, Hally tucked them under Christy's shoulder, coaxing her to lie more on her shoulders, but with her hip turned up so her thigh dropped over in front, hiding the vee at her crotch. When Hally adjusted the scarves, Christy stopped her.

"I'll do that."

Hally knelt on the floor in front of her, her lips pursed. Not meeting her gaze, Christy focused on the scarves. "Surgery scars?"

"Something like that."

"Nothing to be embarrassed about, you know. Our scars reflect that we've struggled—and won."

"How do you know I've won?" The words came out in a strained whisper. Such a small thing, to yank her back to that time.

"You're here, aren't you? That's a win every time. When you're ready, stretch your arms over your head and turn your face toward me."

Christy did, lying her cheek against her arm. Hally frowned at her.

"Something's not quite right. Can you cross your wrists and stretch them up more?"

She followed suit, feeling how the more strained position raised her breasts, her nipples peaking taut even in the warm apartment.

"Now think of him."

Hally didn't have to specify—they both knew who she meant. She let herself think of the Master, imagined lying naked in front of him, her wrists tied over her head. The desire for him, never completely cooled, simmered between her legs.

"Yes," Hally breathed. "Exactly."

Being painted gave her time to think in a way that lying by Roman's pool hadn't. She held still, thinking of the phantom and his mysterious ways, of what he had and had not asked of her. Though she never doubted he could be dangerous, her gut insisted he'd told the truth about Tara. He wanted something else from Christy.

He wanted this.

And, lying there while Hally captured her languid desire for the unknown, Christy wanted him to have it.

She wanted to be his Christine.

The next morning, Carla confronted Christy as soon as she arrived at work, sizing up her too-expensive slacks. With her grubby jeans gone and her only other pair too dirty to wear again before laundry day, Christy had chosen the best of several unhappy options. It would be more than a relief to get her things out of storage and stop living out of a suitcase. Until then, she had only so much to work with.

"Carla, I'm really sorry about the other night. I, um, just—"

Carla held up a talk-to-the-hand palm and looked to the heavens, shaking her head.

"You know, I tried to give you a chance. 'Maybe she's not a spoiled rich girl,' I said to myself. And then I ask you to help me with one little thing. Twenty minutes of your precious time, and what happens? You run off to take a *nap*?"

Christy cringed under the lash of Carla's scorn. Stupidest excuse on the face of the earth.

"I'm sor—"

"I don't want to hear your apologies. I want you to know that I asked Charlie to let you go."

"You—you did?" Misery welled up. All the starry-eyed fantasies about seeing her ghost again shriveled up in the stark light of Carla's anger.

"Of course I did. If it were up to me, you wouldn't have lasted that first week. Hell," Carla laughed bitterly, "you would never have been accepted in the first place. Do you realize you've taken the place of people who've sweated and worked their way for a chance at an apprenticeship here? And you flounce about here, like some fancy accessory we can't afford."

"I want to work hard! I—"

"You don't know how." Carla pronounced her verdict as the worst insult possible. It hung in the air between them, mean and rotten. "You're soft fruit. A hothouse flower that won't thrive in the real world. Go home to Daddy."

Never. That resolve straightened her spine. No matter what happened with this job, she would never live under her father's roof again. He could cut her off, but she was a legal adult in every way. He couldn't force her to do anything.

Not unless they think you're crazy.

But she wasn't a scared adolescent any longer. She had grown up, into a calm, reasonable, and determined adult.

"Am I fired then?" She made her voice as even as possible. She'd find another job. Hally would help her. Other people did it and so could she.

"No," Charlie said, coming down the hall. "Which I told you, Carla."

She stiffened, planting her hands on her hips. "We agreed she'd be on probation."

"Yes, and we also agreed that I'd discuss it with her." Charlie, several inches shorter that Carla, even in his heeled cowboy boots, returned her furious stare with equanimity. "Didn't we?"

Carla threw up her hands in exasperation. "You're a goddamn pushover, Charlie Donovan. Always a sucker for a pretty face."

Charlie grinned at her. "You know it, darling. And good thing for you and your pretty face."

She grimaced at him but, shockingly, giggled when Charlie shooed her along with a pat on the ass. She actually fluttered her lashes at him and then sauntered down the hall, Charlie watching her go with exasperated admiration.

"My wife has quite a temper, but she makes up for that failing in other ways."

"I, um, had no idea."

"Why would you? It shouldn't come up in the work place."

"It must be kind of hard to work together."

"Yes and no. The good outweighs the bad. Now," he fixed his faded denim-blue eyes on her, "you want to tell me what really happened the other night?"

"Detective Sanchez didn't tell you?"

"Oh, he relayed your story, all right. Along with his opinion that there's a lot you're not telling."

Christy shifted her bag, wishing she'd had the chance to at least unlock her office door and set her things down. "I've thought and thought and I don't know what else to say."

He nodded, scratched his bristly chin. "Did you know all the cameras went out?"

Feeling her eyes widen, Christy pressed her lips together and shook her head.

"Sure did. There's you, watching Carla wheel that totem pole out, and pffft," he chopped a hand down, "nothing but static. Every camera in the building became a pricey piece of metal and plastic."

"Wow."

"Yeah. That's what Detective Sanchez said, only in more colorful terms. His people seem to think some kind of massive electrical pulse fried 'em all simultaneously. The Board is going after the company guys who did the install, though they've inspected and they say nothing is wrong." Charlie shrugged and tucked his thumbs in the loops of his jeans. "They'll sort it out. Meanwhile, the cameras still aren't working, so keep that in mind."

"Okay." Christy searched for something else to say—*not* about the chandelier—and dug in her bag for her keys instead.

"Any more encounters with the ghost?"

"What?" The keys dropped from her suddenly nerveless fingers and plummeted into the depths of her bag. *Dammit.* She looked up and Charlie leaned in, bracing an elbow on the doorway and propping his head on his hand. The position created a kind of privacy shield around them. One Christy strongly wanted to step out of.

"I watched one of those Discovery Channel shows and they said ghosts can do that—some kind of electromagnetic pulse that zaps our electronics. Got me to thinking about what you said, and the singing. Our conversation over lunch that day."

"Surely you don't believe that's what's going on here." At last her fingers found her keys again. She had to kind of duck under Charlie's arm to fit them into the lock, but she did it anyway, relieved to escape through the opened door.

"I think there's room in this world for all sorts of explanations. If you encountered the ghost, I hope that you'd tell me about it."

"So you could do what, Charlie?" She dropped her bag on the desk with a thunk of exasperation. "Call in the Ghostbusters?"

"Or a shaman. There are some working ones around here."

"You're serious."

"The spirit world is nothing to toy with. Damn straight I'm serious. Serious as a heart attack." He grinned crookedly.

"Don't say that."

"Bad luck?"

"Yes."

"See—you're as superstitious as any of us. All this," he waved a hand in the air, "started with you. I think you're at the center of it, somehow. Carla thinks so, too, though she wouldn't put it in the same words."

"It didn't start with me." She took a drink from her water bottle to salve her dry mouth. "Tara disappeared before I was even hired."

"Aha!" Charlie held up a finger. "But *after* your dad called about putting you on the roster."

She ran a shaky hand through her hair. Oh. "What are you saying?"

"I think our ghost likes you, *Christine*."

"Well." She neatly stacked her supplies. "Sorry to disappoint you, but I have not met any ghosts." Because the Master was definitely flesh and blood, whatever else he might be. That much she was sure of. Pretty much.

"I wonder."

"What are you saying?" She let her Davis temper flare. *Don't hesitate to let them know when they've pissed you off. Most people back down from confrontation.* "Are you asking me to leave—am I fired after all? Because this back and forth is getting tiresome."

Charlie only smiled, a quiet, closed-lipped grimace. But then, he had to face Carla over the breakfast table. "I'm not in a hurry to anger Carlton Davis, or one of our patron families—or our resident theater ghost either. I was raised to have respect for these things."

Somehow she knew he mainly meant the last one.

"You'd do well to think about that."

4

After Charlie left, Christy sat on the cracked vinyl of her ancient office chair for a moment, toying with the silver spiral pendant and staring at the poster on the opposite wall. Torn, and from a season ten years past, it glowed with sunset colors. The graceful golden lines of the opera-house roof seemed part of the landscape, as if it had grown there.

A good artist could do that—make it seem as if a construct hadn't been built but rather had evolved naturally.

With its own resident spirit, it seemed.

"Ready, boss?" Matt punctuated his cheerful greeting with a knock on the door frame that made her jump, and he grinned, wagging a finger at her. "Daydreaming about Ryan Gosling again? And after a bonus day off, too. That's not the workaholic I've come to know and love."

Christy snorted. "Ryan Gosling is *your* boyfriend."

Matt patted his chest with fluttering fingers. "I wish! Though I'd do Emma Stone, too. Think they'd be up for a three-way?"

"With you? They'd be fools to say no."

"That's what I say. Okay, so here's what I did while you were off gallivanting."

By the end of the day, Christy had made up her mind.

She waved good-bye to Matt and stopped in to see if Carla

needed any help—anything to try to patch things up—but the prop shop was dark, thankfully. The door to Charlie's office stood closed and locked, too, with no light showing beneath. Making a good show of it, she exited with a few of the carpenters from the scene shop and drove off in a mini caravan with several of them.

Then she drove around and parked in the big patron lot, but behind a Dumpster, so it wouldn't be obvious. Through a long succession of texts, she'd convinced Roman that she planned to go down to the mall in Albuquerque, to bypass the Santa Fe boutiques and buy new jeans, among other things. He'd sent her a couple of unhappy faces but perked up when she agreed to dinner the next night and Sunday church and dinner with his family.

If things didn't go well Thursday—or if they went really well with the Master in between—she'd beg off the family deal.

This juggling men thing wasn't easy.

Especially when one of the men was . . . whatever the Master was.

She snuck back in through the backstage apron, letting herself in quietly, then sat in her office pretending to work until the opera house settled into its familiar evening silence.

With a sense of fluttering anticipation, she fixed her lipstick and gathered her things, thumbing off her phone. She'd made a preemptive call to her father earlier, so he shouldn't be looking for her. Mentally, she ticked off all the points to make sure she wouldn't be missed tonight. Sneaking around took great attention to detail.

Turning off the lights behind her and armed with her flashlight, she headed down the spiral staircase.

As she descended, the clinks and whispers of the cooling opera house swirled together in its nighttime song. Weaving up through it, a golden thread reeling her in like a fish hooked on a line, came the phantom's song.

Her body warmed and her blood fluttered in the soft points under her jaw. He seemed to know she was coming to him. Everything in her focused into a sharp point of anticipation. Soon she would see him again.

Anything could happen.

The song intensified as she reached the lowest level, though it still drifted just out of reach of her comprehension. Shining the flashlight on the door, dust motes filtering through the narrow beam that was the only light in the massive building, the emblem carved in it stood out in sharp relief. A whip and a collar.

From the first day, she'd wanted to know what it meant. Now she would.

A whisper of sound.

Then his voice. From nowhere and everywhere.

"Christine."

It shivered over her, her nipples peaking, as if he'd touched her with more than his honeyed voice.

"Kill the light, my love."

Of course. The beam winked out and she set the now useless object on the floor.

"Place your hands on the door, please."

In a daze of rising desire, she did, unsure of why it rocked her so to do such a simple thing. Her palms pressed against the gritty surface, which felt carved from some soft stone. Silk whispered against her face, a blindfold sliding into place, then tied tightly. She whimpered a little, her control slipping away, and gloved fingers brushed her cheek.

"Shh. Trust me. You've come to me for this, yes?"

She nodded. He waited.

"Yes," she finally answered aloud.

"Then come." He took her hand.

The opening door barely made a sound. The sensitive acoustics, though, picked it up and murmured back the echo of stone scraping in protest. He led her back the way they'd come two nights before and, though she tried to memorize the twists and turns, counted the stairs, she soon lost track.

Alice falling down the rabbit hole. But of her own free will.

She knew when they entered his domain, though no sound alerted her to their entry. Once he removed the blindfold, she blinked at the unchanged room, lit by candles, the chaise Hally had somehow known to paint sitting in the center. In front of the fire, a table set for two waited, white tapers in a silver candelabra gracing the center.

"Are you hungry?"

His hand brushed the small of her back and she looked up at him now, the carved lips under the black half mask, blue eyes bright with excitement behind it.

"I don't know if I should."

His eyes dimmed a little, shadowed with disappointment. "Why did you come to me if you don't trust me to care for you?"

"It's not that." *So much.* "It's more that I feel as if I've crossed into another world and that if I eat or drink anything here..." She trailed off, feeling foolish.

"That, like Persephone, you'll be trapped with the lord of the underworld."

She nodded. "Too much theater, I guess."

"Understandable." He gazed around the room. "I am king of all I survey here, yet I am a prisoner of it also. You perceive more than you realize."

"I do?"

"Yes. Here." He laid a gloved hand over her heart, nearly cupping her breast, and her nipples rose inside her bra. But he didn't trespass further. Instead he took her hands in both of his and raised them, kissing each in turn. "I swear to you, Christine, that you may always pass back and forth between the worlds. Though I may be trapped in certain ways, you are not. You enjoy a freedom I do not. I shall always be your willing companion, as long as you'll have me."

"Oh." Warmth bloomed through her at the declaration. It all seemed impossibly romantic, in a way she'd always wanted to believe in. A way the hard lessons of the world wouldn't let her. This, however, was another place.

"Would you care to change for dinner?" He gazed into her face, asking more than that.

"Um, sure. Do you have something for me to change into?"

He gestured to a screen in one corner, one of those old-fashioned kind, with lacy panels tied with pink ribbons to the wooden frame. Stepping behind it, she found a rack of costumes—some from operas she could name, others from a different imagination. Ball gowns, negligees, a slave girl costume, something made of bands of black leather. It was Cinderella mashed-up with *Story of O*.

"What should I put on?" she called through the screen.

He chuckled. "You choose. From that I'll know your mood and we can work from there. Take your time."

Okay. Not the black leather or slave girl outfit then. *Not yet*, a titillated part of her whispered. She sorted through the gowns, something to match the fairy-tale feel, and found one in emerald satin, with a draped neckline, a corset bodice, and a belled skirt. High matching heels sat beneath it.

She shucked out of her pants and sweatshirt, hanging them on a hook, then added her bra, because the off-the-shoulder gown wouldn't allow for it. The bodice wasn't easy to manage, but she laced it up as best she could. The stays clasped her ribs securely, lifting her breasts with demi cups. The tight sleeves went to her shoulders and a sweep of demure satin covered most of her naked breasts. Her cleavage, however, rose higher than she'd ever seen it, the silver spiral pendant nestled just so. In the oak-framed, full-length mirror, she looked lush and womanly.

Stepping into the shoes, she felt aware of her bare legs beneath the hoop of the skirt. The Master turned when she came out, his gaze sweeping her with warm desire.

"A fine choice."

The bodice slipped a little, and she pressed the cloth to her breasts. "I'm not sure I laced it right."

"Allow me."

She gave him her back and he loosened the laces, the gown sagging a bit so she held the fabric clutched to her breasts. Then, working from the bottom, he tightened the corset around her waist, the constriction rising through her chest. By the time he finished, her nipples throbbed from the strangely arousing intimacy of him lacing her into the gown. Laces she surely could not undo herself.

"I can't breathe," she protested.

His hot lips grazed the nape of her neck and his gloved hands drifted over her collarbone, feathering over the upper curves of her breast, displayed more than ever. She knew he must be looking down her cleavage, which made her even more flushed and breathless.

"Yes you can," he murmured, his mouth traveling to her ear. "Don't fight the gown. Give in to it and relax."

While she concentrated on that, he led her to the table and held her chair. She perched on the edge, the skirt billowing around her so she had to tuck it down. Corsets don't allow one to slouch, she discovered, so she sat straight, her breasts outthrust like an offering. From the way her dinner companion watched her, the view wasn't lost on him.

He poured golden wine in their glasses, then held his up in a toast. "To new journeys."

She murmured agreement and clinked glasses with him, aware that he watched her sip from hers, that he relaxed fractionally when she did.

"You are a beautiful woman, Christine. Thank you for coming to me."

The compliment both pleased and unsettled her. No one had ever called her beautiful—except for Roman in his toasts, and that seemed different—and she felt sure it wasn't true. Pretty or attractive, maybe. But never beautiful. Still, the way he said it made her believe that he, at least, meant it in all sincerity.

She toyed with the salad on her plate. "Where does the food come from, if you never leave the opera house?"

"There are more realities than you know. They intersect in many ways."

"Does that even make sense?"

He lifted a shoulder in a half shrug. "It does to me. You will understand in time."

"I don't know about that—I'm still not sure why I'm here."

"Aren't you? Isn't it because I asked it of you?"

"I don't do everything everyone asks of me."

"Not everyone. Me." His ice-blue eyes darkened with intent. "I want you to do what *I* ask of you."

She ate some salad to distract herself from the way her panties dampened at the thought. The corset clamped her tightly and her head swam.

"I don't think I understand."

"I think you do. But tell me your reasons for being here with me, if not because I asked it of you."

"Curiosity. I want to know more about you."

"Give yourself over to me and you will."

"Exactly what does that mean?"

"It's the ultimate expression of trust. When we are together, you do what I ask. Anything I ask."

"What if I don't like it?"

"You will.

"How can you possibly know that?"

"I know you, Christine. I feel your heart and what dark pleasures will thrill you most. Trust me in this."

"I'm trusting you with everything already."

"Yes. I need that from you."

"I don't know if I can." Her salad was gone, so she laid down her fork.

He rose, took her salad plate, and set it on a nearby buffet, then stood behind her.

"Clasp your hands in your lap."

Heart accelerating, she did.

His gloved hands settled on her bare shoulders, easing her back in the chair. With calming caresses he smoothed the skin of her throat. She sighed, closing her eyes. The touches, soothing and arousing, dropped lower. Her breasts, already full and tight, seemed to swell in anticipation. Would he draw the satin down and bare them?

Both afraid and hopeful that he would, she waited. The soft leather covering his hands traced the full curves above her nipples, the fine cloth just hanging off of them. She moaned, dropping her head back against the chair, and felt the cooler air as the fabric fell away.

"So very beautiful," he whispered. "I want you to stay this way while we finish our dinner, so I can gaze on your loveliness and you can find out how it feels to do what I ask of you. Will you do that?"

She opened her eyes to find his, sparking blue above her.

"All right."

"I want you to say, 'Yes, Master.' "

She blinked, uncertain. He caressed her cheek with a smile. "When you are ready, then."

He went to the buffet and arranged food on plates. Feeling odd sitting there with her breasts naked above the green gown that otherwise bound her so tightly, she sipped her wine. Her thoughts and emotions seemed to dance out of reach, beyond analysis. The desire, though, stayed as real and true as the heartbeat pounding in her chest.

"Why can't I call you by your name?"

"That is my name."

"That's a title, not a name."

"What are names but the way we are defined? I am called by what I am."

Setting a plate before her, he took his back to his place and sat.

"Now what?" she asked.

He smiled and might have raised an eyebrow under the mask. "We eat. It's very good."

The chicken smelled heavenly indeed and melted in her mouth when she tried it. The sight of her thrusting, pink nipples distracted her, though. So strange to be having dinner while on sexual display. Thrilling, too.

"I meant, what happens after this?"

"I knew what you meant. And that's one of the rules. I decide what happens. You don't get to know. You only do what I ask."

"So, this is a sex game."

"Oh, no. More than that, Christine." He stilled, drawing intensity to him like a building storm system. "Will you try—just a taste—at least for tonight?"

"Everything you ask?"

"Yes."

"And if I refuse?

"Then it all comes to an end."

"Promise?"

"More than that. I swear it upon my life."

5

"I have a rule, while we're negotiating," she said.

"Is that what this is?" The static charge of his excitement hadn't diminished but continued to build, a thundercloud rumbling down the valley. The thread of amusement in his voice was like the trill of the last bird singing before the storm arrived.

"Everything is a negotiation—most people don't pay enough attention to know it." She didn't much want to think about her father's advice at this erotically charged moment, but his specter haunted her anyway. "I'll only be completely naked in the dark. If it's light, my belly is always covered."

"You don't have to hide your scars from me, Christine."

"I'll show you mine if you show me yours." She flung out the challenge, and it lay on the table between them. A safe bet, there.

He inclined his head gravely, the waves of desire coming off him somewhat diminished. She was sorry for that.

"And we should talk about the detail stuff. I'm on the pill, so I won't get pregnant."

He raised a bland eyebrow at her, and she wondered again what manner of creature he was.

"But what about STDs—do you have condoms?"

"I cannot give you a disease, if that's what you're asking. My . . . afflictions are of another sort entirely."

"Ah." She'd pretty much expected as much, but a girl had to ask.

"Are you ready to begin?"

"We haven't already?"

He smiled, and the tension rocketed up again. "Ah, my Christine, we've only tasted the edges. Say the word and I will show you how we cross the threshold."

Her body throbbed, that smile of his a tangible caress across her skin. Anything was possible. Anything at all.

"I'm ready." And with her words, it seemed the room revolved, then steadied, the colors brighter, deeper, more intense. She'd handed control of herself over to him. It felt like nothing else ever had.

"Come here." He took a box from the sideboard and set it on the table, then turned his chair so she could stand in front of him. Sweat trickled from her armpits and she felt even more that she couldn't catch her breath. *Anything he asks.* On unsteady legs, her thighs damp beneath the belled skirt, she rose and stood before him, breasts bare and swollen so hard they ached.

He opened the box. Inside, resting on royal blue velvet like expensive jewelry, lay a silver collar and four cuffs. She'd seen the collar before, carved into the plaster at the dead end of the hall. Taking up one of the smaller cuffs, he asked her to hold out her wrist. In a trance, she obeyed, letting him lock the smooth metal around her narrow wrist, where it fit as if made for her.

Perhaps it had been.

Once her wrists were both cuffed, he asked her to turn around. Drawing her wrists together at the small of her back, he linked them together. Her breath shuddered in and out, forced shallow by the corset dress so her breasts bounced obscenely. Each moment rattled her more, dissolving her rational thoughts and sending her into a whirl of sensation.

When he had her turn around again, he patted his thigh. "Put your foot here."

He braced her waist, helping her balance when she set her heel on his knee. After locking a cuff around that ankle, his gloved hands smoothed up her calf, and she became aware of how very vulnerable she was under the skirt. His intent ice-blue gaze held her as firmly as his strong hands.

Then he released her and asked for the other foot. This time, once it was locked, his hands rose higher. She held still, a rabbit snared by longing.

"Are you wet, Christine?" he asked softly, one hand holding her calf in an iron grip, the other tracing up her inner thigh.

She nodded, pressing her lips together against a whimper. Why this aroused her so, she didn't know, but her sex felt hot and swollen, open and ready.

"Set your foot down." She did, but his hands remained under her skirt, hidden by the emerald bell of it. "Let's take these off, shall we?"

The leather gloves roamed over her hips, hooking in her panties and pulling them down. Riveted by his gaze, she felt the soaked lace slide down her inner thighs to her knees and calves. At his urging, she stepped out of them and waited for what he'd demand next. Knowing full well what it would likely be.

"Kneel down."

Ah yes.

It wasn't as hard as she'd thought such a thing might be. Daylight Christy might have been horrified, but Christine, in the Master's sensuous nighttime world, could sink to her knees between his spread thighs, her naked breasts displayed for his pleasure. Without waiting for instruction, she lifted her chin and let him lock the collar around her throat.

A shudder of unnamable emotion swept through her. Threshold crossed. Transformation complete.

"While you wear these, you are mine." He intoned the words as if they were a sacred ritual. "Now answer me properly. The way you know I need you to."

"Yes . . . Master."

A breath sighed out of him. Reverence and triumph.

He took something else from the nearby sideboard and held it in front of her. It took a moment for her eyes to make sense of it, for her arousal-soaked brain to understand. The other object from the door—a whip.

She searched his eyes behind the mask, wanting to ask questions, not sure if she was allowed to. He returned her gaze seriously, the unspoken conversation flowing between them.

"Are you frightened?" he asked.

"No," she answered with complete honesty. She should be, but she wasn't. Instead she soared on a hot hurricane wind, moisture surging between her naked thighs. If he asked it, she would give. That's how this world worked.

"Kiss this, then, to show me you accept the pain along with the pleasure."

She bent her head and pressed her lips to the braided leather, transported by how very far past any boundary she'd gone. He set the whip aside and cupped her face with those black-gloved hands, bending down to kiss her, first gently, then more fiercely. She didn't resist, suspended in his grasp, as if she'd given over all her resistance.

She likely had.

Holding her, he stood, drawing her with him so her turgid nipples scratched against the soft linen of his white shirt, his mouth feasting on her upturned lips, steadying her against his powerful chest. She missed being able to touch him, but being helpless added another dimension. All of her focus centered on her mouth, breasts, and sex. A wild urge ran through her, to beg him to take her, to bend her over the dregs of supper and fuck her within an inch of her life.

But she didn't. Because he didn't ask it. There was a purity in that.

Instead he asked her to go over to the chaise and wait for him. Breasts aching as she walked, she went to the fainting couch Hally had painted, noticing for the first time that rings were embedded in it, at the head and foot.

"Hold still." Silk whispered and the blindfold dropped over her eyes. He knotted it tightly, and the world went further into night. A breath of leather, of linen, and then his hands, bare of the gloves, settled onto her skin. She gasped out a breath at the shock that passed between them, skin to skin. He drew her back against him, her bound wrists between them, and filled his hands with her breasts.

She moaned, wild for more. He rolled her nipples between thumb and forefinger, his mouth hot on the sensitive stretch between her neck and shoulder. Then he bit down and she screamed in delight, nearly climaxing from that alone. The arousal seemed to transcend her flesh and she leaned her weight on him, inarticulately pleading for more.

He sat, drawing her with him, to recline on his lap, while his hot mouth feasted on her offered breasts. She writhed in utter abandon as he laved them with his tongue. Drawing her nipples into his mouth, one by one, he sucked them into throbbing points of excruciating sensation. Being bound and blind made it all larger, more extreme, drowning her.

She strained, arching her back, pressing her breasts into his avid mouth, needing more.

His hand spread her thighs then, and she became aware that the hoop had collapsed around her waist, leaving her exposed to his gaze. Relentless, his fingers trailed up her thigh, wet from her abandoned response. His other arm held her under her shoulder blades, raising her up for his hungry mouth on her breasts.

Head dropped back, panting for breath, she waited for the touch that would shatter her.

He toyed with her, though, smoothing the moisture on her thighs, barely brushing the lips of her drenched sex. Sharp teeth scraped her nipple and she groaned, spreading her thighs as wide as she could.

"You are indescribably lovely in this moment. Do you want me to touch you?"

"Yes, Master." The plea flowed out of her, as naturally as the fluids preparing her for sex.

"I'd like for you to let me whip you first. Will you allow it?"

"Yes, Master. Whatever you ask." And she meant it with all her soul.

He helped her rise and bent her over the velvet-covered roll on the high back of the chaise, then told her to spread her legs as wide as she could. With clinking chain, he attached the cuffs at her ankles to the feet of the chair, stretching them widely. She hung over the chaise, the back pressing her hips high in the air, her breasts pendulous and heavy.

He unfastened her wrists and guided her hands over her head, fastening them beneath the seat. Then his hands worked at her waist and the skirt fell free, leaving her bottom and spread sex exposed and vulnerable.

Warm hands moved over the globes of her bottom but still didn't touch her where she most craved it. Her straining thighs trembled with longing.

Another brush of leather. The whip trailing over her skin, an ironic caress. When it left her, she held her breath, knowing the next touch would not be so gentle.

It hissed through the air, then smacked her upturned ass. As if stunned, her nerves didn't relay the pain immediately, delayed by shock. Then rivers of it spread out, hot fire shooting up her spine and down her spread thighs, and burrowed into her starving sex. She clenched her fists and screamed. Was still screaming when the second lash landed, and the third.

She convulsed against the chaise, not knowing anything but the shrieking sensation of pain with such an ecstatic edge. Then his hot mouth was on her open sex, a blizzard of ecstasy that sent her into an immediate and rolling orgasm.

Plunging against his mouth, she rode out the pleasure and pain, gutted by it, ripped open and sent flying.

Surely never to be the same again.

She drifted through a universe of black, with sparking stars and swirls of motion, but little else.

Gradually she became aware that the Master had released her ankles and slipped her feet out of the high heels. He'd unlocked her wrists from the chaise and helped her stand, removing the blindfold, steadying her while she swayed on her feet, then setting her on the couch, the velvet soft against her bare skin, the lash marks on her bottom stinging with new life.

He disappeared from view, then returned with a robe. He'd donned his gloves again, but his eyes were vivid behind the mask, full of blue fire.

"If you like, I'll loosen your corset laces so you can go behind the screen and change."

Blearily, her mind still unanchored, soaring on the pure rush, she took the plush robe from him and waited pliantly as he undid the laces from their tight knots. When the fabric started to slide away, she clutched the robe to her breasts, holding it secure.

He soothed her with a kiss on her bare shoulder, reminding her without words that he hadn't forgotten her rule, even if she had for a moment. Looking up over her shoulder, she caught his gaze and offered up her mouth for a kiss. She tasted herself on him, smoky salt, like a primordial sea. Indulging her, he held her against him, comforting hands on her waist, prolonging the kiss until she pulled away.

"Christine," he murmured, a deep vibrato of emotion thrumming through her name.

"Yes, Master," she answered.

When she emerged from behind the screen, wearing nothing but the silk robe and the collar and cuffs, he had settled into a leather armchair. He pointed to the floor between his knees and she knelt, easily, naturally. In the moment, it all seemed right. She felt trembling and new, still damp from emergence, fragile wings drying.

"Are you all right?" He inquired it of her with gravity, another ritual.

"Yes, Master."

"Excellent. You will return tomorrow night at the same time."

Her mind spun, gaining no traction. What day was tomorrow? It was as if she'd forgotten any other existence but this one.

"Are we done?"

He caressed her cheek. "For tonight, yes."

"But you didn't—" Her face heated. It was foolish to be shy after all they'd done, but it seemed . . . impertinent somehow, to inquire about his sexual release.

"I received so much from you, Christine. More than I'd hoped. It's enough for now. A wise man sips of the nectar, lest he become drunk with it."

She nodded, not really understanding. But that could be because her thoughts were still goo.

"You will return at the same time tomorrow night." He sounded more stern on this repetition, a demand for her willing obedience that made her still sensitive nipples harden against the silk and her throbbing sex to simmer with increased heat. She rubbed her bottom against her heels, savoring the pain. With a rush, she became aware that she still wore the cuffs and collar, which meant she must do whatever he asked.

"Yes, Master," she agreed, reveling in the pliancy of submission. A thought niggled at her, though, something from the daylight world of calendars and appointments. "I'll try," she added, trying to remember what it might be.

He lifted her chin, his eyes serious. "If you fail, you will be punished."

Heart thudding, she swallowed the sudden dryness in her mouth. "Didn't that happen already?"

Under the mask, he smiled, his carved lips curving with a cer-

tain remorselessness. "No. Tonight's whipping was a spice. A first
lesson for you. A test, if you will."

"How did I do?"

"You were spectacular, my love. You respond to the kiss of the
whip as ardently as to the most erotic touch of my mouth."

She shifted, rubbing her wet thighs together. Surely he wasn't really
done with her for the night. She needed more than this.

"Stop that," he chided. "Spread your knees so you don't stimu-
late yourself. You may adjust the robe as necessary."

He didn't release his grip on her chin, so she had to do it by feel,
opening her thighs and making sure the drape of the fabric covered
her belly. Cool air hit her slick and swollen folds, a little moan escaping her.

"We are embarking on a journey together—one that requires intense discipline from both of us. If you fail to do what I ask of you,
punishment is necessary. Do you understand?"

"Yes, Master." With her knees spread at his order and his collar
around her throat, she did understand, to the core of her being. She
trembled with the truth of it.

He smiled, warm now, loving, and brushed a thumb over her
lower lip. "Now go to the mantel and bring me the silver key sitting
there."

She did, aware of his gaze on her, and brought him the key. One
by one, he unlocked her ankles and wrists, not touching her more
than necessary. Kneeling for a third time, she felt the collar slide
away, leaving her curiously bereft.

He set it aside with the cuffs, all in a gleaming pile next to his
glass of wine, and kissed her on the forehead.

"Now do as you will."

It felt odd to put on her pants, sweatshirt, and sneakers again. So
prosaic, the trappings of her daily life, compared to the lush and exotic world the Master claimed as his.

He led her out a different way this time, letting her out a door
she hadn't known existed but that opened near where she'd hidden
her car. It didn't surprise her that he knew where she'd left it—or
that he didn't cross the threshold of the doorway. He vanished, as always, back into the depths, saying nothing more about the next

night. Those demands were for when she belonged to him, and he'd released her to follow her own will again. She understood that much. And discovered her will to be something different than she'd known it to be. Being free to do exactly as she wished gave her power. Flexing with it, she stood alone in the night, under the vast and shatteringly lovely canopy of stars.

She stood there for a while, soaking in the sensation of being dwarfed by the expanse of the sky. Her new self stretched along the interior surface of her skin, coursing along the nerves that sang with stunning sensuality. For the first time in her life, she felt like a woman, not a girl.

For the first time in her life, she understood what that meant.

6

She drove home feeling like her little car had become an airplane. Though the night was cool, she put the top down and let the wind chill her ears and toss her short hair around her eyes with stinging bites. They reminded her of the way the whip had fallen on her vulnerable, upturned bottom, and how she'd been restrained, unable to defend herself. Totally at the Master's mercy and every desire.

The one orgasm hadn't been nearly enough. She wanted more. Much more. In this erotic haze, even the seam of her jeans pressing on her clit could be nearly enough to make her come again. She wriggled, pushing herself closer.

Her cell rang—a jangling new ringtone that nearly sent her swerving off the road.

She grabbed the phone, if only to make it stop, and saw Roman's name on the screen. He must have programmed the ring himself when he had her phone at his house. One of those techno beats that all sounded the same.

She didn't want to answer, but she did.

"Hey there, sweet girl. Are you back yet?"

What had she said she was doing? That was the problem with lies—it took work to remember and consolidate your stories. Oh yes, Albuquerque and new jeans. The glass-and-polished-tile mall with its bright lights and stores full of merchandise seemed so far from where she'd truly been that it made her giggle.

"What's funny?"

"Oh, nothing—the DJ on the radio. And yep, I'm pulling into my hotel now."

"I thought you must be driving back and that's why you didn't answer my texts. Why don't you come over? Model your new jeans for me?"

"Oh, Roman." She faked a yawn. "I'm so tired. I didn't find any jeans I liked, either. I think I'll crash." That was a laugh. She wouldn't sleep for hours, she was so wired.

"I get it." He sounded disappointed. "Tomorrow night, though, I'll have your undivided attention. I thought we'd eat in the bar at Rio Chama—hang out and see who comes by. I'd like you to meet some of my friends, so look your best."

Shit. She sat in the dark car in front of her casita and thumped the heel of her hand against the steering wheel. Time for honesty. Past time. Only immature girls played games.

"Look, Roman, I think we need to talk."

Strained silence.

"I mean, you are such a great guy. Any girl would be lucky to have you interested in her, and we've been friends forever, but I'm just not sure—"

"Say no more, sweet girl. I absolutely understand."

"You do?"

"Of course." His warm voice held a teasing smile. "We've been moving fast and you're nervous about seeing my family as my girl-friend. But you don't have to worry—they won't mind that you're not Hispanic or Catholic. You're like a second daughter to them. Don't give it another thought. We'll talk about it over dinner tomorrow."

"The thing is, I don't think I can make it tomorrow night."

"But you promised."

"I know, but—"

"What—did you get a better offer?"

Yes, actually. Which made her worse than dishonest.

"Are you seeing someone else?" he continued, voice thick with suppressed anger. "Is that what tonight was about? After all I've done for you, you run off to dally with some other guy?"

"No! I mean..." *Yes.* She was a terrible person. She blinked back tears. "I'm handling this badly."

"Yes, you are. I expected better of you, Christy. I expect better of you in the future, too. Now, I think you at least owe me the courtesy of meeting me in person, on the day and time we agreed upon, and we'll discuss our differences."

She rubbed the back of her hand against her eyes. He was right. She owed it to him to break up in person. As for the Master, she'd have to slip him a note. Maybe he would understand and not punish her. Once she had things tied up with Roman, she could go to the Master's realm freely. Turn herself over to his dark dominion.

It was the right and mature thing to do.

She slept poorly, shockingly enough.

All night she twisted, tangling in her sheets, dreams knotting together. In one she screamed and crawled under a lashing whip. But the man holding it was Roman, his face contorted in rage. She begged him to stop, but he wouldn't. Each time it fell on her, it cut away pieces of her flesh. Her breasts shattered like glass balloons, sending blood flying. She flung up her hands to stop him and he cleaved them away, as easily as a knife through warm butter.

The nightmare woke her and she bolted for the bathroom, vomiting into the toilet, the retching convulsive, leaving her weak. Naked, she lay on the cold tile, one arm wrapped over the scarred ridges on her belly, and fell asleep again.

The stairs again. She ran down them, always down into darkness, never up into the light and escape. Her foot slipped and she fell, searching for the name to call, always hovering just beyond her reach.

Cold air whistled past her cheeks, chilling her to the bone. In dread, she tensed for impact. Certain she would die.

Then the Master held her. She clung to him, digging her fingers into the warm fur of his chest. He rumbled comfortingly and she looked up into his bear's face, his icy blue eyes full of love.

Tucking her under the covers, he told her to sleep. She snuggled in, safe and warm, drifting off to the caress of his paw on her cheek.

When she awoke in the morning, she was back in her bed, holding the polished stone bear carving in the palm of her hand.

She arrived at work the next morning feeling as hung over as if she'd partied all night. So not fair to suffer the aftereffects of overindulgence without having actually indulged in much of any-thing. Unless you counted kinky sex.

If she did, she'd have to count it as an indulgence of the wickedest kind.

In the harsh light of her hotel bathroom, she'd peered over her shoulder—looking for evidence of her extraordinary experience—to see nothing. Only the smooth expanse of her skin. Though her whole body ached. It reminded her of the time she'd taken a wild hair to bike with friends out to the seashore. She hadn't been in shape, but the ten miles had felt fine. Glorious, even, with the coastal sunshine and good company.

The next day, though, she'd been depleted. Sore in every muscle and joint, too exhausted to move. And yet she'd wanted to do it all again.

This, too, was like a party hangover. She dragged her feet down the hall to her office, feeling far less than perky, but already her thoughts simmered, imagining what the Master might ask of her next. How exhilarating it would be. She chafed against the daylight, wanting to descend the spiral stairs and find him again. To sub-merge herself in his make-believe realm. But she must wait for the night.

Until after she dealt with Roman.

Sitting at her desk, she found a pad of paper and wrote a note for the Master. But should she write Master? It was odd, looking back at last night, how easily the word had come to her lips. Of course, she'd been half naked, fully aroused, and kneeling at his feet. The rules were different, then.

No, that title belonged to the cuffs and the collar. Right now, her will was her own to exercise as she thought best.

> *M—*
> *Will be delayed tonight. I know this breaks my promise,*
> *but it will ensure I can keep my future promises.*
> *Christine*

She hesitated over saying more, but nothing seemed right. Espe-cially in case someone else found the note. She nearly said she'd ac-cept whatever punishment he decided on but realized with a profound thrill that saying so would be redundant. That was already part of their agreement.

How strange that the idea energized her.

With a thrill of delight, she added "Yours" before her name, meaning it for the first time in her life.

With a light heart and sure-footed in her sneakers, she spiraled her way down the stairs, waving good morning to the various techs who greeted her. The opera house truly bustled with energy now, ramping up with increasing excitement—a project she belonged to. Next week the talent would arrive, taking everything to a whole new level as rehearsals started in earnest.

In the bright lights, she made it to the bottom level in next to no time. Even the twinge from her dreams—that visceral feeling of her foot missing the step and the endless plummet that followed—didn't slow her down.

The lowest level, dim with only filtering light from above, echoed empty and still. At the plastered-over end, she laid her hand over the carved-in symbol, remembering the feel of his collar around her throat and the orgasmic sting of the whip.

She slid the note under the door, finding a whisper-thin crack that allowed most of it under. It was the best she could do. On impulse, she kissed her fingers and pressed them to the image.

A promise.

"Why are you always lurking down here?"

Christy whirled with a squeak, her heartbeat going from zero to sixty in half a second. "Shit, Carla—you scared me!"

Carla swaggered up to her, hands on hips, and peered at the door. Then she slid her glasses down her nose and blinked at Christy with wide, contemptuous eyes.

"What kind of idiot stands in a blind corner?"

Christy pushed past her, hoping Carla would follow and not spot the corner of the note still sticking out from under the door. The props manager, however, stayed put.

"Or do I miss the mark? Maybe you're not the bubbleheaded girlie you want us to see. Could be you're up to something."

Christy threw up her hands in exasperation and spun on her heel. "Oh right! I'm some sort of superspy conducting a deeply laid plan to sabotage you and my father's opera house."

"And Charlie." Carla pointed at her. "He's part of your plan, too."

"For heaven's sake—I was joking. I was being sarcastic."

"Were you?" Carla sidled up to her, meanness creasing her eyes behind the glasses. "Or you were trying to divert me by making my suspicions seem silly?"

"Frankly, Carla, they *are* silly. I'm here to learn and do the best job I can."

Carla made a show of looking all around her. "Oh yeah, I see how you're doing a real good job. Down here where you don't belong. Skulking."

"I was not skulking."

"Then what were you doing?"

Christy opened her mouth. Closed it again.

Carla pounced. Forehead knotted, finger in Christy's face, she shouted, spittle flying, "I will take you down, you little slut! You are done for here. Sashay your cute little ass back to Daddy or I will ruin you. Mark my words, you'll regret crossing me and mine. I want you gone."

The woman was insane.

Christy floundered, uncertain what to say, how to calm the raging monster Carla had become.

The cheerful sounds of work from above filtered into the silence between them. Weaving through it came the song, comfort and longing. The whisper of her name.

Christine.

She belonged here. This was her place.

"I won't leave," she said, bracing herself for more of Carla's wrath.

"Then a disaster beyond your imagination will occur." Carla hissed the over-the-top threat and stalked off, a rigid scarecrow figure climbing the stairs.

Christine.

7

After that, the day couldn't have passed in a more ordinary way.

Christy and Matt worked through the inventory, making satisfying progress. The mindless task gave her time to practice her speech to Roman—far better than indulging prurient fantasies. At one point in the afternoon, Charlie poked his head into the storeroom they were sorting.

"Have you kids seen Carla?"

"Nope!" Matt answered, making a gagging face behind Charlie's back.

"Not since first thing this morning," Christy added. *When she acted like Crazy Bitch from Hell, but never mind that.*

"If you see her, would you point her my way? She missed our afternoon planning meeting."

"Will do!"

Matt waved at the empty doorway, a manic smile plastered to his face. "Sure thing, boss! Right after I rip off my testicles and feed them to your wife on a platter!"

"Oh stop."

"Hey! Maybe she's gone forever. Maybe she met with a Terrible Accident." Matt dropped his voice like a voice-over in a TV movie.

"You shouldn't say such things."

"But I *want* that wish to come true! It doesn't count if I really mean it."

"You're incorrigible."

"I am?" He looked pleased. "If I knew what that meant, I'd probably be all flattered."

Three other people came by looking for Carla over the course of the afternoon. By the time they ascended from the depths up to the main level, organized teams were combing the different rooms, reminding Christy uncomfortably of the search for her. Surely she hadn't been grabbed in a similar way.

Hairs rising on the back of her neck, she thought of the theater ghost singing while Carla verbally attacked her. Had the Master done something to her?

Surely not.

Watching Charlie run a fretful hand through his hair as he talked with a group of techs down the hall, Christy fumbled her keys into the lock of her office door. It gave more grudgingly than usual. She flipped on the light.

A scream of horror ripped from her lungs.

Naked, bruised, and bleeding, Carla's unconscious body draped over Christy's desk. Red lines crisscrossed her flesh, crusted with scabs here, oozing blood there. Black-and-blue marks bloomed like exotic flowers on her Scandinavian skin.

Perched between her breasts lay a redolent red rose.

And a note.

ACT 4

Dark Interlude

1

Sunday could not have been a sunnier, more brilliantly beautiful day.

Everywhere the lilac bushes hung heavy with their panicles of sweet blossoms, lending a drowsy, syrupy feel to the hot June sunshine. Light poured through the stained-glass windows and open doors of the Basilica of St. Francis. Between the soaring music, the bright summer clothes of the people attending Mass, and the venerable beauty of the ancient cathedral, it seemed that nothing unsavory or violent could happen in the world.

But it had.

Christy clung to Roman's hand, and he glanced down at her with a reassuring smile and slid a strong arm around her shoulders. He was happy with her. Pleased that she'd come to her senses and appreciated him and what he so generously offered her. She'd even worn the new dress he'd brought her as an apartment-warming present—without pointing out that a gift like that was supposed to be something for the home, not something to wear.

She copied him on the motions of Mass, murmuring the right sounds under her breath, a sotto voce chorus of general agreement. Overall it wasn't so different from other church services she'd attended, with the possible exception of all the kneeling.

That reminded her, with a deep, painful twist in her groin, of kneeling in front of the Master, and the dark, sexual things they'd done together. She'd felt then that she'd crossed into another world, and now it seemed she stood on the other bank of the river. She had returned to the land of the living, where the sun dispelled the shadows, where nice people went to church on Sunday morning and your boyfriend gave you demure silk dresses to wear to visit the people who'd been friends of your family since you were a child.

Where women weren't kidnapped and tortured nearly to death.

Carla was out of intensive care, at least, and was expected to recover. The doctors had managed to repair the worst damage to her internal organs, and the greatest concern now was the amount of skin disruption and the inevitable infection. Those were the words Charlie used, echoing what the docs had told him. It called images to her mind of the skin suppurating and separating, infection bubbling out, corruption of the flesh.

She hadn't been back to the opera house since they'd found Carla, draped over Christy's desk like an obscene offering.

None of them had. The police had sealed the place and seemed quite certain that what had happened to Carla had occurred on-site. Detective Sanchez had grilled Christy for hours on Friday, asking her over and over what she thought the note meant. As with the others—the ones the police still did not know about—it was direct and simple, cursive script on vellum.

For my love.

Was Christy the object of affection and Carla's bloody, tortured body a tribute to her? Or was Carla the one who was loved? Why was she left on Christy's desk?

She didn't know. It made no sense to her either. The Sanclaro lawyers sat with her through the interrogation, cautioning her on which questions not to answer, insisting she be left alone, since she clearly could not have committed this crime and therefore was not a suspect, frustrating Sanchez to no end.

It had helped, though, to remind her of what truths she danced around.

Including the very real possibility that the Master had hurt Carla. That he'd tortured and murdered Tara, too. Christy rocked from side to side on the hard wooden pew, sure she felt the bruises he'd left on her and she'd enjoyed receiving. Beyond that—she had reveled in it.

She worried, now, that some deep fault in her character had been exposed, that she might be fundamentally wicked at some basic level. Was her ghostly lover truly a cruel and perverted murderer—and had she been so attracted to him for those very reasons? Like goes to like. She'd been running to that and away from Roman, who only wanted to protect her, to hide her from the cruelty of the world.

His arm slid away and he pulled down the kneeler so they could pray yet again.

Not knowing how else to ask for it, she wished to be cleansed of the taint. She eyed the wooden closets along one wall that Roman had said were the confessionals, longing to climb inside one, close the door, and spill out all the secrets she'd been keeping.

It didn't escape her that the only person she hid nothing from was the very being who sat at the center of her web of lies.

Everyone folded up the kneelers, then stood. She followed along, but Roman put a hand on her shoulder. "Just sit and wait," he murmured. "This is communion and you can't take it—you haven't received absolution."

"What?" She said it a little too loudly, and several heads swiveled in her direction with expressions of shock and disapproval.

Roman smoothed a hand down her back. "Just formalities. Don't worry."

She sat and he joined the line of people going up to kneel in front of the priest—God, would she ever rip from her mind the image of her kneeling, bare-breasted and aroused for her masked lover?—and receiving the wafer and a sip from the golden goblet. The altar boy had rung a bell when the priest held them up, declaring them the body and blood of Christ. The miracle of transubstantiation, Roman had murmured, the mundane transformed into the holy in an instant.

For a brief and terrified moment, when Roman said she hadn't received absolution, she thought he knew, that he'd looked into her shadowed heart and seen where she'd been and what she'd done. Silly, because he'd explained it beforehand: Only Catholics in good standing could take communion.

Fortunately, after that the service wound up quickly. The priest stood outside the open doors, resplendent in his robes, as if he'd stepped out of one of the paintings in the basilica. Roman introduced her as his girlfriend and asked if the priest would be coming for dinner later. They beamed at each other, full of holiness and happy grace, anticipating Reina Sanclaro's excellent recipes, and the priest enfolded her hands in his dove-soft ones and blessed her. She felt dirty and wretched and wrong.

This had been a bad idea.

Hally had tried to talk her out of it the day before, in between moving Christy's things from storage into the apartment, which smelled of soot and the astringent flavor of recently disappeared mice.

"You've had a shock, finding a body."

"Not a body, Hally. You only say that when the person is dead."

"Did she sit up and say, 'Oh, hi, Christy'?"

"Don't be ridiculous."

"Just trying to cheer you up. Why are you going to the Sanclaro shindig?"

"They're family friends, and—"

"Read: your father's friends. Does he even care? Besides, you said you were dumping Roman's ass and now you've signed up to be trotted out for Sunday Mass and dinner?" Hally shook her head. "And you haven't even gotten laid yet. This is all wrong, I tell you."

Riding in Roman's sexy car, with his favorite techno tunes blasting, she felt the wrongness.

"Maybe I should skip the family dinner this week," she tendered. "I have so much unpacking to do, and—"

Roman stopped her with a hand on her thigh. "Don't be nervous. And today is a special day, my parents' thirty-fifth anniversary party— I really want you there. They do, too."

"I know, but—"

He squeezed. "I don't want to hear any more about it. You'll have fun when you get there. You'll see. I have a special surprise for you."

They drove on a winding road through a long canyon and turned in to a drive guarded by an ancient stone wall and wrought-iron gates. The Sanclaro emblem, a cross speared by diagonal swords and encompassed by a circle, was split in two by the opening of the gates. They moved smoothly, powered by invisible electronics, a perfect melding of the old and the new.

Huge trees bordered the drive, adding their stately shade to the sense of deep history. They opened up to reveal a massive hacienda, with multiple wings, romantic balconies, and red-tiled roofs.

"It's beautiful," she breathed.

"Yes." Roman beamed with pride, and she took his hand. "The Sanclaros trace their history back to the conquistadors. This land has belonged to us, always."

"After it belonged to whatever tribe they kicked off of it," she joked.

He gave her a sidelong glance. "I wouldn't trot out any of that liberal claptrap around my family. Not unless you want a real history lesson."

She frowned but decided not to argue.

Roman's parents waited on the vast portico of the house, reminding her of the priest standing vigil at the church, side by side, with polite, formal smiles. Domingo Sanclaro was a more silvered, more distinguished version of his son, with a paternal smile and dark eyes. He was also more severe than she remembered.

Reina Sanclaro had the cheerful full-fleshed rosiness of a well-fed matriarch. She took Christy's measure in one sharp glance, a pleasant hostess expression fixed on her face while she brushed imaginary dust from her black skirt.

"Christy!" Domingo held out his arms so she had no choice but to accept the embrace. "I haven't seen you since you were a gawky preteen. You've certainly grown up since then."

"Yes, she has." Roman sounded proud.

"Remember how we used to tease you two about how you should get married so we could join the Sanclaro and Davis dynasties?"

"Of course." She forced a smile. She hadn't been *that* gawky— and the way he was looking her over made her feel itchy. Had he always been this creepy?

"And look at you two now—this is a happy day for us! I'm so proud." He looked between them fondly.

Uncertain how to reply to that, Christy, feeling much like Reina Sanclaro, who stared fixedly into the distance, kept a pleasant expression on her face.

"Will your father be visiting you in Santa Fe?" Domingo asked.

"I don't know, Mr. Sanclaro." *I hope not.* "He hasn't said so."

"He should, shouldn't he, Reina? He's hosted us in New York so many times. He'd be welcome to stay here at the Compound."

The Compound. The capital letter stood out in her head and she wanted to make a joke about multiple wives and where the captive cult children were kept. Roman's hand settled on the small of her back, as if he could sense her irreverent thoughts. She suddenly looked forward to telling Matt about this. He'd appreciate the HBO-miniseries quality of this scenario.

Hally would say *I told you so.*

"What was that all about?" She muttered the question to Roman as he guided her to the ongoing party in the back garden.

He grinned at her, full of some simmering secret. "He's just happy to see you again. To see us together."

Together. The way he emphasized the word niggled at her. It all felt so unreal. How could it be that this sunlit world of happy people seemed like the false one? Her head swam as Roman introduced her to innumerable relatives and family friends, including his very pretty younger sister, named Angelia, after her great-grandmother, Roman said, with an odd note in his voice.

They all looked her over, seeming to know something she didn't, the women giving Roman nods of approval and the men whispering jokes that made him respond with snickers and shoulder punches. Roman gave her a glass of fruit punch to drink, and she wanted to say something about a culture that drinks wine in church but not at the party afterward. She was losing count of the number of things she had restrained herself from saying, but surely those should pile up into some nibble of absolution at some point.

Despite it all—the guilt, the uncertainty, the sinking fear that her grip on her life and sanity seemed to be slipping away—she wanted most of all to go to see the Master. To touch his skin, breathe his scent, drink in his kisses and, like some sort of polygraph, help her separate the truth from the lies. Though he might be the poison spider at the center.

Disaster.

"Here's your plate." Roman jerked her thoughts out of their sickening spiral. "I didn't get you too much because I figure you're like most girls–watching your weight."

She'd never said any such thing, but she supposed most girls were. Roman had his own ways of being considerate. Besides, he was practically doting on her, bringing her food and punch, saying how pretty she looked, and seeming so proud to introduce her to everyone. Normal people acted this way, and something must be profoundly wrong with her—something deeply self-destructive—that she kept thinking she wanted something else.

Roman was tapping his glass with the side of his spoon, like at weddings, when people egged on the bride and groom to kiss. Everyone felt silent, looking toward him expectantly, and he rose, with a smile for her. She shifted, easing her bottom, uncertain what he was up to.

"We all know why we're gathered here today—to celebrate the long and happy marriage of my parents. Let us toast in congratulations and to many, many years more!"

Everyone raised their glasses and voices in jubilant shouts. Christy joined in, relaxing into it and calling out congratulations. Of course, the anniversary.

"And, because today is such a special day, I'd like to commemorate it with my own milestone. Thirty-five years ago my parents married on my great-grandmother Angelia's birthday. As is Sanclaro tradition, my mother has turned over Angelia's ring to me, to give to my bride."

Christy's stomach clenched. Suddenly the sun felt far too hot.

"Christy?" Roman pulled her to her feet.

Oh, no, no, no. This could not be happening.

He opened a ring box, the jewel flashing bright in the sun. "I know this is fast, but my great-grandmother Angelia would want it to be today. In some ways, even when we were kids, I think we always knew. Our fathers certainly did! Will you marry me?"

Everyone erupted into cheers again, applauding and shouting "Christy! Roman!" And other things in Spanish. No one could have heard her answer—nor did anyone seem to expect one of her, least of all Roman. This was like one of those awful flash-mob videos where a guy hires all his friends to do a dance routine in some public place while he proposes, and you can see the girl just staring in that frozen way, knowing she didn't want it that way.

Because how can you say no, in front of all those happy, happy people?

You can't.

He slid the ring on her finger, an antique setting with a glowing opal surrounded by diamonds. He held her ringed hand in his and raised their joined hands high, while everyone cheered, as if they'd won a horse race. Soon someone would run up and hang a wreath of roses around her neck. The absurdity of it would have made her laugh if she hadn't been concentrating so hard on not puking up all that punch.

"See?" Roman said in her ear. "Everyone loves you. I knew they would. We'll get married here, just like my parents did."

Finally everyone wound down and they sat again, though various other relatives—none of whose names she could remember—stood to give toasts to both Roman's parents and to Christy and Roman. She gritted her teeth and waited until she could yank the heavy ring off her finger and give it back to him. She didn't have it in her to humiliate him in front of his family. They would talk later and she would explain.

No one could force her to marry Roman Sanclaro, no matter how fast her life was spiraling out of control.

Her cheeks grew tired from fake smiling, but she soldiered through. Angelia came up to her, all smiles, and asked if she could be Christy's maid of honor.

"Of course you will!" Roman tugged one of his sister's glossy raven curls. "We wouldn't have anyone else."

Christy nearly argued that she wanted Hally for her maid of honor, until she remembered that she had no intention of marrying Roman. They were sucking her into their mass crazy. She didn't want to contemplate the alternative, that all the madness in her world had one common factor.

Her counselor used to tell her that if it seemed as if all her friends were being mean or if all sorts of bad things seemed to be happening, there were two possibilities: either everyone you knew suddenly woke up in a bad mood or you were perceiving it that way. Which was more likely, that the world had turned against you in a mass conspiracy, or that *you* were feeling persecuted?

The answer was meant to be obvious. It was more likely that her head was messed up than that she was fine and everyone else was messed up.

Thus, either everyone else was crazy—or she was.

2

Christy didn't have an opportunity to speak to Roman alone until he took her on a tour of the grounds. Once they were well away from eavesdroppers, she screwed up her courage to tell him the truth. He looked so happy, she hated to do it, but she reminded herself that he'd created this situation. You don't ask important, life-altering questions when the other person can't say no.

"If you like," Roman was saying, "we'll get married in this gazebo. My cousin did and the pictures turned out great."

"Roman, I can't marry you."

She blurted it out loud and fast enough that he actually jerked in shock.

"But you already said yes."

"No, I didn't!" She laughed and threw up her hands, feeling an edge of hysteria. "You didn't give me a chance to answer."

"Because it never occurred to me you'd say no." He looked genuinely confounded. It clearly really hadn't been a possibility in his mind, and Christy felt bad about that. How many girls would be giddy over marrying him?

"I'm sorry," she offered. It sounded weak, even to her.

"But we always *said* we'd get married. I thought that's part of why you moved here!"

She couldn't say he'd seemed beyond her reach; then he'd think she just needed reassuring. "No—I came here because this was where my father could get me in." Or was willing to. Surely he hadn't had this in mind. He might be a controlling tyrant, but he wasn't feudal. Much. "Those jokes about betrothing us were just that—being funny."

"I thought you loved me." His brown eyes held pain, like a dog she'd kicked.

"I don't really know you." That was soft-pedaling, yes, but it was better than saying that she'd liked him more before she got to know him, back when he was more of a fantasy.

"You just need more time, then."

"Well, no. I mean—"

"I know this was fast." He shook his head ruefully and gave her a chagrined smile. Picking up her hand, he examined the gorgeous old ring. "I was so excited about the timing, with the anniversary party, and when the ring fit perfectly, it all seemed so *meant*. Am I a romantic fool?"

Her heart broke a little at his wistful question. Prince Charming, rejected. "No! It's me." *Gah—had she really said that?* "I just have so much going on, with the murder and Carla . . ."

"The thing is—" Roman squeezed her hand, looked away at the house, his face settling into severe lines that made him look more like his father. "The thing is, the lawyers seem to think you could be in a lot of trouble."

"Trouble?" she echoed. The ring felt heavy. She should have wrestled it off while she had the chance. Now, with her hand so firmly gripped in his, she'd have to make it an even bigger deal.

"I didn't want to worry you, but the lawyers say the cops are really looking at you, and they might have a pretty strong case. They spoke with my father and they feel they can't represent you unless your interests are also the family's. Since we're practically already family and I thought you felt the same way about me," he grimaced, as if it all sounded foolish now, "I already told them you're my fiancée. I thought it wasn't even a question—and that you'd be grateful for the protection."

"I . . . see." Wow. None of this had occurred to her. She'd been with Matt all afternoon when Carla was abducted and hurt. And Tara had disappeared before she arrived. "What kind of trouble am I in—what did the lawyers say?"

"I can't really tell you that." He made a regretful face. "They're most insistent that their legal advice is for family only. I don't make the rules."

"Well, I'll just talk to Detective Sanchez, then."

Roman laughed and dropped her hand. "Sure, if you want to get arrested. That will look great for your father. Tell me—does he even know what you're up to?"

She felt the blood drain out of her head. "Up to?"

"Sneaking around. Missing at night. Lying. I don't know, Christy—it looks suspicious."

"If you feel that way, then why this whole engagement farce?" She pulled at the ring, angry that it wouldn't come off fast enough for her to fling it at him. She managed to get it off but scratched her knuckle doing it, and put it to her mouth, sucking away the blood.

He clamped his hands over hers, folding the ring painfully inside. "You're all emotional, sweet girl. Who could blame you with all that's happened? Maybe you should see someone—consider medication."

"I don't need medication." Her voice wasn't strong, though. Roman couldn't possibly know about before. Her father wouldn't have told anyone. None of this made any sense.

"Don't you? I wouldn't want to miss signs of a cry for help."

"I'm fine. It's just been . . . a difficult few days."

"I feel greatly reassured to hear that. But remember, we have doctors we can call in. They're always happy to help a Sanclaro." He unwrapped her fingers from around the ring, extracted it, and put it back on her finger, kissing the bleeding knuckle. "You'll wear this ring and that way I'll know you'll be rational and think about this."

She stared into his handsome face. Was this new sense of threat real—or because she was losing her grip on her emotions? Roman only wanted the best for her, didn't he? It made no sense that he'd be blackmailing her into an engagement. *Did he hurt or threaten you?* Detective Sanchez's words came back to her suddenly. And for the first time, she was afraid of Roman.

"Christy?" He gave her a stern look. Not one that made her giddy with desire, but that made her want to run. Except she was trapped. She needed time to figure a way out of this snare of truth and lies. She looked down at the lush grass that didn't belong in the desert landscape.

"Tell me you'll wear the ring and behave as my fiancée, so I'll know that all will be well."

"I'll wear the ring," she repeated back, feeling like a wind-up doll.

"Good girl." He tucked her hand in the crook of his arm, imprisoning it there. "You've made me a very happy man today."

She went along, waiting for her chance to get away, not sure which of them was insane.

"Do you think I'm crazy?" Christy slid onto the bar stool at Del Charro with a sense of profound relief at her escape, and Hally, taking one look at her, started making one of her famous monster margaritas.

"Not more so than most."

Not the answer she'd expected. "What does that mean?"

"Well, don't you think everyone is kind of crazy, just more or less so?" Hally cocked her head in earnest question.

"I guess I think most people are sane and only a few are crazy."

"See," Hally held up her hands to demonstrate, "it's a kind of spectrum. People on this end," she wiggled the fingers of her right hand, "are all what we think of as sane. They only see the physical world, nothing more." She fluttered her left hand. "On the other extreme are the people who've gone full woo-woo. They're so wrapped up in the spirit world and all the nonphysical aspects of existence that they can't deal with anything concrete. Most of us are somewhere in the middle."

"That makes no sense."

Hally frowned at her, popped a lime on the rim, and slid over the margarita. "It totally makes sense. You have to—Oh. My. God."

"What?" Christy started to swivel on her stool, but Hally seized her left hand and stopped her.

"Tell me that is not an engagement ring. A fucking Sanclaro family-heirloom engagement ring. And an opal! You can't wear this."

"Oh, well . . . it's a long story." One she didn't even understand herself. She packed down the visceral terror she'd felt while looking into Roman's eyes. Of him or her own dark places, she didn't know. "I have to keep it. For now."

Hally blinked slowly, like an owl. "I revise my earlier statement. Yes. You *are* crazy."

Christy sagged. "I knew it."

"Then why did you take the ring?" Hally spaced out the words as if her friend might be a little slow on the uptake.

"Oh, that?" Christy's gaze landed on the ring, held high in Hally's grip. "That's kind of the least of my problems right now."

"Honey, if you really believe that, then we need to talk. Should I be worried?"

Christy tugged her hand away and sipped the margarita, the tang of salt, lime, and Hornitos making her eyes water. At least that's what she told herself it was.

"I think that worrying isn't going to fix my problems."

"You want to talk about it?"

"Maybe. Eventually. Not tonight." She held out her hand. The ring looked pretty, if a little big for her delicate hand. "Everything else aside for the moment, why can't I wear an opal?"

"Bad luck."

"You don't really believe that."

"Okay," Hally amended, "it's more that they hold magic, which can be good or bad, but if you don't know for sure, it's safer to assume it's bad."

"Cynical of you."

"Not really. See—opals are special gemstones. They're more a kind of glass, so they have all sorts of different things in them. That's why you get all the different-colored sparklies."

"Is that what the gemologists say?" Christy asked drily.

"Hush. I'm an artist—you get the paraphrased version. Because of their nature, they absorb personal energy. The personality, emotions, intentions—all the life force of the person who wears it." Hally leaned her folded arms on the bar. "A lot of magic workers use crystals to focus their energy that way. Because opals have that much more stuff in them, they're less predictable. You can pack in a lot more power, but how it comes out again can be all over the place. What matters most is who's worn it before and how they used it."

"Roman's great-grandmother, Angelia Sanclaro."

Hally snorted. "What do you want to bet she was no angel?"

"You can't possibly know that!"

"Exactly!" Hally pounced on her response, pointing a finger up-ward. "You know nothing about her, but you're going to have her distilled essence riding around on your hand?"

"Sounds icky when you put it that way."

"It is. Better not to wear it at all."

If only that were an option.

3

When she got back to her apartment after a reassuringly normal-ish conversation with Hally, who blessedly asked no more about what the hell Christy was thinking getting engaged to Roman, she tried to organize her thoughts.

A message on her cell from Charlie's assistant said the cops had finished and the opera house would be back in business. Monday morning awaited her, with all that would entail.

She couldn't wear the ring to work, regardless. It was too valuable, too likely to elicit unwelcome questions, and too much of a taunt to the Master, who saw everything in his theater. She contemplated his reaction with a strange mixture of fear and remorse, which seemed all wrong when she remembered that he might have been the one to hurt Carla. And Tara, no matter how he'd ducked the question. She couldn't seem to untangle the sticky web of emotions from the growing snarl of events. If only she could get a grip on one thread, maybe she could make a start, but they all kept slipping away, formless, dissolving when she looked too closely.

She unpacked some boxes, hoping the boring task would soothe her jangled thoughts about the two men. Both seemed real, yet also fantastical. The Master felt like flesh and blood, but—by his own admission—he lived in multiple realms. However that was possible. And Roman, for so long her dream man, now a fixture in her life, with a weight of reality as heavy as the ring on her hand. Both charming. Both cruel in their shifting ways.

Which was capable of the horrible attacks?

The ring clunked against something in the box and she pulled out the polished stone with the bear. She'd been as drawn to that as she was to the Master. She fingered the silver spiral pendant hanging around her neck, given to her by the woman who believed in the bear god. Was that who he was—a sort of ancient demigod? She removed the necklace, unthreaded the pendant, and set it next to the stone on a little shelf next to her kiva fireplace. She hesitated to add the third piece, but she needed to see. Wrestling off the ring, she set it next to her other tokens. Then rearranged them, shuffling them in a shell game.

The triangle of her life. Her. The Master. Roman.

It meant something, she felt sure of it. As if they were connected by something deeper than her just happening to take this job. If she were Hally—or one of Hally's spirit teachers, maybe—she would be able to read all these signs and omens. She would know what she should do. But as it was, she couldn't quite grasp what it might be.

It was clear, however, that she couldn't keep ignorantly bumbling about. She needed to do research, and the Internet didn't have the answers she needed. For old stuff, you went to libraries.

She left the three things there for the night, safely in the other room, while she cuddled Star's ragged comfort and pulled the covers over her head.

In the morning, afraid to leave the priceless ring in her apartment and knowing she'd better have it handy if she ran into Roman—she hated the way she mentally cringed at the thought of his displeasure yet couldn't seem to control the reaction—she tucked it into the tight coin pocket of the jeans she'd managed to pick up at the secondhand store near Hally's place. Maybe Angelia's potentially bad juju wouldn't affect her if it didn't touch her skin. She kind of didn't believe that part, but it seemed unwise to pick and choose myths at this point.

Either she believed all of it or none of it.

At the opera house, everyone was upset. The talent—always superstitious anyway—rehearsed unevenly, and shouts of displeasure rang through the building, reproduced by the excellent acoustics, more than a few times. Matt and Christy spent most of their time scouring the storerooms for things the harried, field-promoted assistant props manager couldn't find. Carla had been doing the job for so long that she knew what she needed and didn't keep lists. Undoubtedly a contributing factor to the terrible state of the inventory, a project that had been abandoned in favor of Matt and Christy helping to get five operas up and running in three short weeks.

The atmosphere of dread hung heavy backstage. Pressure and panic combined to make everyone snappish. It didn't help that Charlie hadn't come in—not that anyone blamed him, but the loss of his unflappable presence created a greater sense of chaos.

Matt stuck to her all day like the proverbial glue. He kept reassuring her that he'd protect her, but the way he kept sliding white-eyeballed glances at the door and jumping at the least little thing, she suspected he was more frightened himself than brave.

Often Christy felt the tangible creep of a penetrating gaze on the back of her neck. She refused to look behind her, and stayed with others always. She was the lame gazelle sticking to the center of the herd while the lion paced the edges. She would not be culled from the group, not until she was ready. No matter how much she might long for the ecstasy of the lion's teeth sinking into her throat.

After work—when everyone left en masse by mutual agreement, counting heads once more after the doors were locked—she went to the history museum. At lunch she'd called the library to inquire about local lore. The very helpful reference librarian told her she'd be better off with the New Mexico History Museum for research on the old families of the region. For information on Native American legends, she'd best go to the Indian Pueblo Cultural Center in Albuquerque, a jaunt that would have to wait for the weekend.

It didn't escape her sense of the ironic that she'd lied to Roman about driving to Albuquerque after work the week before. Now it would be the truth and she doubted he would believe her. Especially since she couldn't tell him the reason behind it. The way he'd looked at her when he made her promise to wear the ring gnawed at her. No—he didn't trust her at all.

That was all it was, she told herself. Nothing more sinister than that.

Hally was right that she was crazy to have accepted this engagement. All the reasons—needing the lawyers, keeping her father at bay, not upsetting Roman, needing time to think—none of it made any sense.

The dream images revisited her, and she felt as if she were forever running down those spiral stairs, the monster just behind her. She had no time to stop and think. To make a plan.

Run, her deep thoughts whispered with urgency. *Run!*

She ignored the voices, as she'd learned to. They mostly told lies.

Fortunately, with tourist season in full swing, the museum stayed open until 8 p.m., down at the Palace of the Governors. She had to park in the pay lot on Water Street and walk into the Plaza, the sidewalks thick with people. Passing through the arcade, she spotted the mean violin-playing busker, tourists passing him as if he weren't there. He saw her, however, and his tune changed from a country jig to the song the theater ghost sang. Sweet, full of longing, and beyond naming. Like an aching sense of nostalgia for a happy childhood moment you never really had.

Remembering his scorn from the last time, she swung out into the street, blocked off for the evening's festivities. Music from a mariachi group in the band shell nearly drowned out the plaintive melody.

"Hey, leddy!"

She walked faster.

"Hey, young leddy—you no' deef. Come back here. I gots a message for ya!"

Christy stopped at that. Wasn't she looking for information? For omens and their meanings? Not thrilled, but feeling that she needed to do it, she went back and faced the old man and his gap-toothed, unfriendly grin.

"I wonnert when you'd come back to listen."

"I didn't. I was passing by. What message?"

He played the song slowly, an exquisite tenderness transforming his face into something nearly angelic, as in a renaissance painting. The song, of course, had no words, sung only by the violin. Same as when she'd heard it at the opera house, really, the lyrics unintelligible, just the liquid melody, full of unmet emotion. So much of opera was that way—sung in other languages so you weren't trapped by the words. Words could be used to spin lies, but music—at its heart, music only told the truth.

Even if it was a truth you didn't care to hear.

The song ended, snapping her out of her reflection, and she wiped away a tear that suddenly trickled down her cheek. Like a scab had broken open because she'd moved carelessly, leaking blood.

The old musician pointed his bow at her, his gnarled smile back, the gnome replacing the angel. "Better. You listen."

"But I don't understand the message."

He shrugged. Not his problem. He went back to the sprightly jig he'd been playing before, the crowds flowing around him, a piece of bedrock parting the stream.

Christy walked on to the museum, turning over the song in her mind. Not just the song but the realization that music carried truth that words didn't. Roman's words, the Master's words—they muddied the waters. That meant something.

At the museum she pored through the records on the Sanclaros. The helpful collections assistant pulled several volumes on the conquistadors for her also, flagging the sections about Salvador Sanclaro and his part in the campaigns. She'd vaguely known much of this—mostly from her U.S. history class in high school—how the Spanish and Portuguese had come to Mexico and what would become the American Southwest back when the early colonists were still setting up shop on the East Coast in the late 1500s.

She traced her finger over an illustration of Sanclaro's shield—the same as the emblem on the amazing gates that guarded the estate from the outside world. The notation said the Sanclaros had worn it in the Crusades. The family name likely dated to the same era, probably a borrowed version of St. Clair, a fairly common French surname honoring the patron saint of clarity that bled into the name Sanclaro over time.

The cross honored the Catholic church, of course, the diagonal swords pointing upward to indicate the family's continuing battle against evil. The circle turned out to be a halo, indicating that the family considered themselves to be eternal defenders of the holy church.

The Sanclaro name turned up regularly through the long four

hundred years following the arrival of the conquistadors, the ensuing wars with the Indians and Mexico. A detailed treatise, labeled
as likely an accumulation of several folklore tales, on a particularly
ugly event claimed that Salvador Sanclaro had kidnapped the
daughter of a tribal chief, married her, and declared the tribe's territory to be his. The tribe fought and was destroyed by Sanclaro's
men and allies. Descriptions of the terrible day said the lovely river
valley had been soaked in the blood of the entire tribe, all dead. The
land became the Sanclaro compound and the Indian bride—never
named—died in childbirth, leaving behind twin daughters.

The tribe had been known as the People of the Bear.

Christy almost stopped there, her head reeling, but forced herself to go on.

Several old paintings were reproduced in the documents. One, a
set of portraits that seemed to be made for a cameo necklace,
showed identical young girls with large dark eyes. A flowing ribbon
at the bottom of each named them, Angelia and Seraphina.

Far from suffering for their sins, the Sanclaros prospered. Gold,
ranching, land, politics. Where other families failed, the Sanclaros
flourished. Their fortune grew and their reach widened.

The opal ring was also mentioned in connection with the family.
A letter included in the papers mentioned that Salvador gifted his
twin daughters with identical opal and diamond rings on their eighteenth birthday. Since then, it seemed, the Sanclaro brides always
wore these rings.

An Angelia of the relatively modern era had been born at home
in 1890, twenty-two years before New Mexico became a state. The
photos showed her as a baby, posed with another infant who looked
remarkably the same. In fact, Christy had to read the notation twice
to figure out which was her—and learned the other child was her
twin brother. Angelo, of course.

Another photo showed them, with the same wide, dark eyes and
glossy black hair, pre-adolescent and slender. Then Angelo, serious
in his WWI uniform. Angelia appeared next in her engagement portrait, the luminous opal on her finger, prominently displayed by a
coy hand to her cheek. Her fiancé, interestingly enough, was not
mentioned.

Over the years, she took her place as the matriarch of the

Sanclaro family, ruling all the enterprises with an iron fist, particularly after Angelo died in 1929, under odd circumstances. However, many suicides and accidents had followed the stock market crash that year and, though the family fortunes had taken a relatively minor hit, his death was blamed on it. And on a vein of insanity that seemed to haunt the family.

He left behind a six-year-old daughter, named Angelia, of course—how did they keep them all straight?—who was raised by her aunt, as if the child's mother had never existed. Perhaps she hadn't. One letter hinted darkly that Angelia and Angelo were, in fact, the parents of the girl.

The daughter—a product of incest or not—grew up to be a lovely young woman, glowing in her eighteenth birthday portrait, wearing a mink stole and a saucy hat. Surprisingly, she attended college in New York, a development that sent an uneasy current through Christy. Surely that was a coincidence.

She turned the page to find the chill of the truth. That Angelia had married in college, hastily. The gossip column related the society wedding, which the Sanclaro family had not attended, and managed to make it clear the bride was expecting. The groom's family however, the Davises of New York, footed the bill in elaborate fashion. She recognized some of the names—various elderly aunts and uncles.

Why had she never heard this story?

Perhaps because of the scandal. A divorce came within two years. Angelia Sanclaro—who seemed never to have taken Davis as her married name—returned to New Mexico. There was no mention of the child.

But Christy knew. Knew with crystal clarity what had happened to the child.

It boggled the mind, but the timing was right and it explained so much, including the vague stories about Christy's grandmother dying in childbirth, leaving her grieving widower to raise the child alone. A child he foisted off on his sister. Domingo Sanclaro, only two years younger, would then be her father's half brother. Had her father even known?

Domingo only took over the family business—a sprawling empire of real estate, mining, oil drilling, and similar interests—after his grandmother died in 1996. Christy would have been around four or five then, which would match the time when Domingo began visiting. And when her parents began fighting.

It also explained her father's deeply loyal interest in the Santa Fe Opera House—and how the Davises had managed to obtain an island of property in the vast Sanclaro holdings—which he refused to sell, even during the various economic downturns and despite the fact that all his other businesses were on the East Coast. It had to be a bequest from his mother. A woman who'd left him without a backward glance and later died in a car wreck on the road to Las Vegas, according to a yellowed newspaper article.

All those jokes about betrothing them—and Roman was her cousin, albeit via half brothers. It made her stomach turn.

"Catching up on your research?"

She jumped, as if she'd been caught doing something wrong, slamming the volume closed in pure reflex. Detective Sanchez stood on the other side of the table, smiling in a way he probably thought was friendly but conveyed his suspicion. He surveyed the stacks of books and files.

"Doing a little background check on the new fiancé's family, huh? Aren't you supposed to do that *before* you accept the ring?"

"Wow—news travels fast."

"When the Sanclaro lawyers call our offices to instruct us to leave you be as you're now family, yes. Yes, it does."

Always had been family. She couldn't quite assimilate it.

"Then why aren't you leaving me be?"

"Free country, right? Museum is open to the public. Mind if I sit?"

Before she could answer, he'd pulled out the wooden chair and made himself comfortable. He spun around a reproduction of an etching thought to be of Salvador Sanclaro, surrounded with Christlike rays of light, noble in his Spanish armor. Sanchez made a rude noise at the image.

"Don't care for the Sanclaros?"

Sanchez screwed up his face and considered. "Hmm. Rapists, pillagers, robber barons. Not a lot to admire."

"Is that why you're harassing me?" *Always accuse first*, her father counseled.

"Just saying hi to a friend." Sanchez produced the friendly smile again, folded his hands over his ample belly, and tilted back in his chair. "So, tell me—how does a nice *gringa* like you manage to get engaged to the heir to one of the most powerful families in New Mexico within weeks of arriving in Santa Fe? That's quite a feat, even for an old friend."

"Just lucky, I guess."

"You are lucky, Ms. Davis. What happened to Carla Donovan— that could have been you when you disappeared. Why her and not you? I wonder."

"Because she was abducted. I wasn't abducted. I got—"

"Got lost and fell asleep, right, I know the story. We also both know it's a lie."

"Why would I lie about that?"

"*That*, Ms. Davis, is exactly the part that bothers me."

"Has Carla woken up yet?"

"Why—what do you think she'll tell us?"

"I want to know as much as you do."

"I'm betting that much is true. But you want to know for different reasons."

"We're all concerned about her."

"Why didn't you want your father contacted? Surely he'd be concerned."

Her stomach clenched and she resisted the urge to reach under her shirt, to touch the scars there. "Because he'll be worried about me and make me come home. I don't want to go home." Was this what her father had been afraid she'd find out? Then why get her the job here at all?

"Yeah." Sanchez dropped his chair back onto all four feet with a clatter that made her start. "See, Christy, a good liar knows to lie about everything. Mix it up, you know? But you're not a good liar—and I know that because when you tell the truth, which is most of the time, it's very clear that you're being honest. That was the truth right there. Tell me, does your father know about this 'engagement'?"

He actually made air quotes around the word. If she didn't have the same surreal attitude about it, it would have made her angry. Still, her tone came out irritated.

"No—it's supposed to be a secret from him for now."

"Not much of a secret."

"Don't you have to keep it confidential? Like a lawyer or a . . ." She floundered, looking for the right terms.

"Like a priest and the sanctity of the confessional? No, I'm a cop. I'm the one who decides which information to release and which to keep close to my vest. Why do you ask, Christy—do you have something to confess?"

The image of those shadowed, private confessionals in the cathedral flashed through her mind. *You haven't received absolution.*

"If you do, I swear to protect you," he pressed. "Help us out here. Carla can't tell us what happened to her. Tara will never be able to tell us. You're the only one who can."

"I can't tell you something I don't know." Her lips felt numb, and she tried to show the shining truth of that—she really didn't know what had happened to them—but she felt the cloud of the lie, of what she did know and felt a gut-deep loyalty not to reveal.

"Have Roman Sanclaro or his father threatened you?" Sanchez asked in a low voice that wouldn't carry. "Blackmail, maybe?"

His perception startled her and she felt sure it showed. Not trusting her voice, she shook her head, pressing her lips tightly together.

Sanchez looked disappointed, scrubbed his scalp with it. "Has it occurred to you that an alliance with your father would be greatly valued by the Sanclaros?"

Ha! If he only knew.

"I'm not an idiot, Detective. People have been using me to get to my father all my life." It came out more bitter than she expected, and she rubbed her arms, chilled in the museum's careful climate control.

"No. You're not an idiot." Sanchez eyed her, as if trying to peer inside her skull. "I suspect you're even smarter than you seem. Maybe you're one of those pretty girls who learned early on not to threaten the men around them. Growing up under the thumb of a guy like Carlton Davis would do that."

"Wow—that was such a mix of insult and compliment that I'm not sure what to say. Do I say thank you or fuck you?"

Sanchez laughed, leaned on the table. "Ah. There's the real you. And I have a hundred bucks that says you never talk to Roman Sanclaro that way."

"Keep your bet because it's none of your business."

"*You* are my business. You're neck deep in my case. And there's something you're not telling me. I can smell it."

"I really don't see how you could think I'm guilty of—"

"Not guilty," he cut in. "No, I don't think that. Of course, I can't completely rule anyone out. But my gut says you're an innocent. Which is why I can't leave you to the wolves."

"I'm not a babe in the woods." Why did everyone keep implying that she was some virginal ingénue?

"No. You're no helpless infant. You're the princess in the tower."

"What? Is that some kind of police code?"

Sanchez laughed, stood, and tipped his cowboy hat to her. "I was reaching for the story metaphor. You've got princes and dragons fighting over you, don't you? I do believe that makes you the trophy."

4

The words stuck with her, as Sanchez likely meant them to. They wound together with Roman's vague threats about her needing the lawyers, and how the Master spoke of needing *her*. In her apartment she pulled out the opal ring from where it had ground uncomfortably against her pelvic bone all day. The polished stone with the bear image had ridden in her back pocket, so she got that out, took off the silver spiral pendant, and set the three together again on the shelf beside the kiva fireplace.

She stared at them, trying to perceive the wordless message there, as in the melody of the song. Though the engagement ring was a lie, it carried a certain truth about the Sanclaros. The Master hid himself behind masks and mystery but swore to be true.

And she? Well, her whole life was pretty much a lie.

She mulled her options all morning. Now that she was over the shock, she thought about what else she'd learned from the files at the museum. The Sanclaros, even after all this time, were the invaders. The Master—half man/half bear?—was tied into the tribe that was destroyed, perhaps. The gods of the land before the conquistadors brought Catholicism with them. Princes and dragons.

It all seemed absurd. A fairy story of battles and murders. And yet the pieces fit.

Except for why he seemed trapped under the opera house. Why there?

Christy took her sack lunch out on the back deck, where the opera house looked to the west over the valley. She sat on the edge, dangling her feet over the drop, eating her peanut butter and jelly sandwich.

Was Roman the prince and the Master the dragon? Or vice versa?

Roman had lied to her. About the lawyers protecting her, for sure. Maybe more, if he knew about their shared blood.

She stared out over the breathtaking landscape, remembering when she'd arrived, full of hope, determination, and, okay, quite a bit of naïveté, it turned out. The ingénue enters, stage left.

Well, this was her story. She hadn't wanted to be locked up in her father's castle and she wouldn't be anyone's trophy.

She dusted the bread crumbs off her hands. No more waiting around—for rescue or abduction.

Time to take matters into her own hands.

She performed her trick of pretending to leave but circling back to park behind the Dumpster. This time, fear rode high on the edge of her excitement. *Trust your gut.* Repeating her mother's mantra helped, but she still felt that tension her mother must feel, stepping into a war zone. Something no damsel in distress ever did.

Amazing how much courage it gave you—the determination not to be a pawn.

With her keys, she let herself in, descending the spiral stairs, the heavy flashlight Charlie had given her in hand, down to the lowest level and the door to his world.

He came without song, without warning. Just a presence in the shadows. Saying nothing.

Silence throbbed between them and, despite her new determination, Christy found she had no idea what she wanted to say. Instead she only wanted to fling herself against him, to feel him wrap his strong arms around her, to hold her tight and close. Why was it that standing here with him in the near total darkness, him a man in a mask and cloak, forever hidden from the light, felt more solid and

more real than the last few days had? That she felt no fear of the
monster, while terror had filled her at the look in Roman's eyes?

"Christine."

The whisper of his voice, full of longing, regret, joy, and grief
echoed off the walls, eagerly repeated in a susurrus of sound, like a
religious chant. It wrapped around her, melodious, hypnotic, a song
without words.

"I'm sorry I didn't come back."

"I knew why you didn't come."

"Did you do it?"

"You wouldn't be here now if you thought I had. You know the
truth in your heart."

"Do I?"

"It's in you to know it, Christine. You have to listen."

"Who are you?"

"I've been trying to show you. But I need your trust for that, and
I've lost it."

"Who hurt Carla? Who killed Tara? You see everything in this
opera house, you say—who dumped Carla's body on my desk with
a rose and a note in your handwriting?"

He stilled, the sudden coiling of a predator hearing the heedless
footstep of his prey.

"What note?"

"Like the others you left me. 'For my love' this time."

"I've never left you notes."

"Yes—and two others."

"No. I can't write, Christine. Not in your language, anyway. I
never learned."

The fine hairs on her arms stood up, her skin goose pimpling.
"Then who did?"

He laughed, dry and unamused. "Someone who escapes my
sight."

"But you said nothing here escaped your notice."

"Clearly I was mistaken." He paused and she waited, feeling him
consider what to say. "I am not what I once was. I am . . . crippled."

"I know," she whispered.

"Beyond the scars. I have been weakened and it has taken me so
long, perhaps forever, to find my way again. When you arrived, I
thought, I hoped that—"

"That what? Why me? I'm an ordinary girl."

"No." He laughed, then rolled into another, deeper laugh. "You are an extraordinary woman, on the cusp of becoming who you will be. You are my muse, my priestess and avatar."

"This is a very strange conversation."

"I cannot help that. You are a child of the modern world. These things aren't part of what you understand."

"No. They're definitely not."

"I need to touch you."

She took a half step back, the open hallway behind her. "I don't think that's a good idea."

"I've missed you, Christine. I thought you might never come to me again." His voice came out hollow, devoid of its usual richness. "My life can be a lonely one. I was only half alive before you arrived. Now I feel every moment we're apart like the keen edge of a knife in my heart. I crave the sight of you, the scent and taste of your skin."

The earnest passion reached inside her and found its mirror, touching her in a way that none of Roman's avowals ever had. She responded to him from the core of her being, the desire for him spreading through and suffusing her. Her sex pulsed in answer when he spoke of tasting her.

And yet . . .

Wasn't that only physical? The cravings of the carnal flesh the priest on Sunday had spoken of with such derision. Not to be trusted. To be rejected as the work of the devil.

She felt so alone. Like him. Crippled. As if a piece that should make her whole had been stripped away early in life.

"Would you . . . hold me?" she tendered. "Only that?"

"Yes." Like a vow of love, the affirmation breathed out of him. In the shadows, he opened his arms.

She slipped inside his embrace, relaxing as his arms folded around her, holding her close, like something to be cherished. As if she was as precious to him as he claimed. She wanted to stay right there forever. She wanted him to sweep her up and carry her off, to take her away from the jangling world and all the petty annoyances and looming horrors.

But that would be fleeing to the tower. Just another one, where she'd be kept safe. A pretty trophy for the mantel.

So she pulled away from his reassuring heat, the solid comfort of his body. She missed him immediately, as if she'd left a layer of skin behind, leaving her exposed to the cold world.

He seemed to feel it, too, his arms still outstretched, embracing the space she'd left behind. "Christine . . ." he said on a long, musical breath. "I love you."

The confession emptied him, and his arms dropped. The deep, primal part of her wanted to fling herself at him again. To make him wild promises. She held herself back with the bare fingernails of reason.

"Why me?"

"It's always been you. Only you can make me whole again."

His words uncannily echoed her thoughts.

"I don't understand." Her frustration welled up. "Why are you trapped in the opera house? What can I possibly do to help you?"

"It's not something I can explain in words. You must experience it to understand."

"What kind of experience?" She had to ask the question, but she knew. Her sex flared to life, responding instantly to the thought of being with him again.

"Like we did before, yes."

"I can't trust you that way again." Besides, she wanted it too much. It couldn't be right, wanting that, his dark world and cruel-edged sexuality. Was it the Sanclaro blood that made her want this? Her fingers drifted to the opal ring in her coin pocket.

"What do you have in your pocket?"

She started, guiltily. "Are you a cat, to see in the dark?"

"The night is my domain. I may be weakened in many ways, but the dark serves me. I can see you clearly, yes, and the conflict on your face when you touch what's in your pocket. What is it?"

"A ring."

"Show me."

Honesty wasn't the easiest path to take, but she'd resolved to it. She dragged out the ring, the prongs holding the circle of diamonds catching on the seam. Laying it in the center of her palm, she held it out for him to see.

His breath hissed out, followed by a grunt of pain, as if she'd plunged a sword into his heart.

"Angelia's ring."

"You know it?"

"Why do you carry it if you don't know?"

"It . . . was a gift."

"Ah. I should have known. You will learn the ways of your blood and you will serve those who keep me trapped for their gain."

"I won't do that. I don't even know what you mean."

"Christine." He sounded weary now, the vitality bleeding away, all music gone from the dry husk of his voice. "You cannot halfway vow. It makes no difference that you carry the ring in your pocket instead of on your hand—you are fooling only yourself. You cannot serve two masters. It will tear you apart."

"I don't serve any master," she shot back, stung.

"We all serve someone or something. The trick is in knowing who or what it is. Some spend their whole lives discovering that."

"What do you serve?"

"When you learn my true nature, you will know the answer."

"But I can't be with you that way."

"Not while you're engaged to another man, no. I may not have much, but I have my integrity." A whisper of a footstep as he turned away.

"That's it? This is good-bye? I'm doing the best I can here."

"No, your best lies in *your* true nature and you don't know it yet. Until you do, you're as crippled as I am."

"How am I supposed to find that out, though—it's not like I can Google it." The joke, a desperate attempt to alleviate the tension, fell flat.

"Go in peace, Christine. Know that I love you and I wait for you, should you be free to love me in return."

"Wait!" She could no longer see or hear him. "Don't leave me. Please."

Only silence answered her plea.

5

The week dragged on, each day feeling like a river of mud to slog through. Carla came out of the coma but remembered nothing of what had occurred, or so said the scuttlebutt around the theater. Rehearsals continued and Charlie came back to work for short periods. He didn't speak to Christy. She tried not to mind.

She'd been relocated to Tara's office, since hers was now sealed and the police finally agreed that nothing more could be gleaned about the former intern. Though it was a bigger, more pleasant space, she felt eerily as if she'd shuffled into Tara's shoes in a final way. As if she'd come some sort of circle and the story was beginning again.

A foolish idea, but her head was in a strange place.

She still hadn't talked to her father, deliberately ducking his calls and leaving return messages that went directly to his voice mail. She couldn't bear to hear what he might have to say.

She went out to dinner with Roman in the evenings, wearing the ring and the clothes he bought her, pretending to be the cheerful companion he liked best, while she felt around the edges of what he knew. She wanted to know what his stake was in marrying her, why Sanchez suspected him so. It felt like more theater. *Wear the costume, be the character. Don't make him angry. Don't tip your hand.* All the while she heard the Master's mocking voice, so accurately noting that she didn't know who she was.

She was a hypocrite—which should be her father's role. Not hers.

When he took her home after their dates, Roman kissed her at the door and she faked enjoying it, sliding away as fast as she could without insulting him. He despised her apartment—calling it dingy and beneath her—and refused to step inside. She knew he said it mainly to convince her to move to the Sanclaro compound. But she liked her cozy place, so she was just as happy not to have him calling attention to its faults. It also meant she didn't have to hide Star, and it steadied her to come home and see the bedraggled stuffed cat waiting on her pillow.

Most importantly, since she managed to find excuses not to go to his house, it kept things from progressing between them sexually. She'd looked it up, and first cousins could marry in New Mexico— and in a surprising number of other states—and she and Roman were only half cousins, or however that worked. Still, she couldn't bear for him to touch her. Her skin crawled and her thoughts went to the Master and how he'd turned away, certain of her eventual betrayal.

By Friday night she knew nothing more. Roman dodged all her probing conversational sallies with a smoothness that made her question everything. Maybe he truly did care for her and want to marry her. He acted like he did. And, all week long, there had been no sign of the cold-eyed and demanding monster she believed could have killed Tara.

Surely if Sanchez suspected Roman, he'd have been questioned. But nothing had happened. She felt as if she'd been holding her breath all week and was finally running out of oxygen.

Maybe she had imagined all of it.

So, unable to think of a reason not to, she let Roman take her back to his house—just for a nightcap, he said.

She stood in the bay window again, overlooking the jeweled valley, while Roman poured drinks for them. They'd met with some of his friends—all handsome and full of business talk—along with their girlfriends, lovely and polished. The girls didn't talk about their professions and nobody asked what she did. Instead they kept to social topics and local politics. They were friendly and articulate, but not particularly interesting. Christy wondered what they might have to say, away from the guys.

But Roman was pleased with her for fitting in, for the way the guys had complimented him on his "catch." She liked it when he was happy with her—something that bothered her on a deep, unspoken level. It sometimes reminded her of her growing-up dance, of keeping Carlton Davis in a place where he approved of her. Still, it made her feel a little more sane, more like the person she'd always been.

She tried to ignore the taunting idea that she was somehow only as half alive as the Master, waiting to be redeemed. She missed him profoundly. Thought about him constantly, with a physical ache.

Roman handed her a glass of champagne, his brown eyes warm and admiring, and she drank that in, letting it block the disappointed echoes of the Master's golden voice in her head. "To my beautiful fiancée," he said, clinking his glass against hers, and she started a little, having forgotten who she was with. Roman kissed her, and she tried to like it as she once had . . . but ended up turning her face away. A cold anger stilled his face. Just as it had the previous Sunday. "Sometimes I feel as if I don't know who you are anymore, Christy."

Part of her froze. A rabbit facing down the wolf. She didn't want to meet Tara's fate. *Keep it light and get out*, she told herself.

Run, whispered her internal voice.

She stepped away. "How could you? We've only known each other for a few weeks."

He shook his head, a dog shedding water. "That shouldn't matter. My parents barely knew each other. You and I have belonged together since we were children."

"Why do you think that?" She warned herself to tread lightly, but this could be her chance. "Nobody has arranged marriages anymore. Those were just jokes. No one expected us to end up together for real."

"My father did." Roman's reply came with a dark anger and he tossed back his wine. Went to pour more.

"We don't have to do what our fathers want."

"Easy for you to say. I live in my father's pocket."

"Then don't! We're adults. Free to choose."

"I choose you," he insisted.

"Why? It makes no sense."

"Are you saying you've changed your mind?" He shifted into the dangerous self again, brown eyes congealing to an alien darkness. Drawing closer, he backed her against the white leather couch while her heart hammered. He wrapped a lean hand around her throat. "You know I can't allow that."

"I—" she stammered, out of breath. "No. Please don't hurt me."

"Why should I hurt you? As long as you behave, we'll be fine. Have you forgotten already?"

"No. I mean, I'm wearing the ring."

"But what is in your heart, Christy?" He leaned closer, flexing his hand. "God sees what's in your heart. Maybe you need to talk to the priest."

"I'm not Catholic."

"You'll need to be, before the wedding. That would be a good show of what's truly in your heart, my sweet girl. Start your catechism classes so you can convert and have your confirmation. That will help you find your true self and put these doubts to rest."

"You think I need to find out who I am?" The words cut through the haze in her mind, the fog of self-pity and sorrow that had clouded her thoughts since the Master had walked away. Another message.

You won't listen.

"If you're going to be my wife, you need to cleave unto me. Do you understand?"

"You're right, Roman." She employed the humble tone she used with her father, and Roman straightened, releasing her throat and patting her cheek. Relieved at her escape, she scrambled for the right thing to say, to appease the beast who prowled in his cold gaze. "I'll take the weekend to meditate and purify my thoughts."

"I'm so proud of you." He kissed her on the cheek. "I think it's the right thing to do. I'll have Gloria prepare the guest room."

"I think I should go home. I don't feel right staying here. How would it look?"

He didn't like that. "You stayed here before. It would be fine."

"But that was before we were engaged—and before we agreed to purify ourselves for the wedding. Shouldn't we be beyond reproach, especially in the eyes of God?"

He softened at that and smiled, the sweet Roman again. "So serious about everything. We'll do this your way—though, if you moved into the Compound, this wouldn't be an issue. My parents would approve, too."

She managed to smile back, exhilarated that he seemed to be letting her go. "I know. I'll think about it."

Roman drove her home and kissed her at the threshold. As soon as she shut the door, she wrenched the ring off her finger and called Hally.

6

"But *why* Bandelier?" Christy complained. "Everyone at the opera said it would be crawling with tourists on a Saturday. How can I possibly find myself with ten thousand brats crawling up my ass, screaming that they want candy?"

Hally threw her an amused look, then turned her attention back to the highway. "This is how the future Sanclaro matriarch talks?"

"Ha ha. I never said I was going to actually marry him."

"What exactly *are* you doing?"

"Today? Finding myself, as weird as that sounds."

"That's not what I meant."

"I know." She hadn't told Hally about how much Roman frightened her. Or about the strange mystery of their families, which sounded crazy, even to herself. "It's hard to explain."

"That much is clear." Hally glanced at her again. "I mean, I'm no great fan of Roman Sanclaro, but I don't really get what game you're playing here. Is it just about the lawyers?"

Christy shifted uncomfortably in her seat, easing the seat belt away from its tight grip across her shoulder, and looked out the car window.

"Hokay . . ." Hally blew out a breath. "Let's try this. Why *are* the cops so interested in you? They can't possibly think you're a suspect."

"Because I lied to them."

"You did?" Hally honked the horn. "My good girlfriend lied to the pigs? Color me shocked and delighted."

"You make no sense. One minute you're scolding me for my fake engagement and the next you're happy I lied—*outright lied*—to the police."

"Yeah, well. They're different things. Different kinds of truths."

"Truth is truth—how can there be a difference?"

"Here." Hally tapped her breastbone. "In your heart. If I know you, you had an excellent reason for lying to the *poh*-leece."

"And you don't think I have a good reason for what I'm doing with Roman."

"I dunno. Do you?"

Christy plucked at her seat belt again, wishing it had one of those lock mechanisms that kept it from strangling you. "I need to tell you a secret."

"Yay—finally!" Hally did a little seated dance behind the steering wheel. "It's been killing me not to ask."

"You can't tell anyone."

"Yeah, yeah—Cone of Silence. I get it."

"I mean it."

"Right. Spill."

"Not anyone. Not even . . . your cats." Christy seized on that, unable to think of who else Hally might be tempted to tell.

Her friend looked somber and shook her head. "That might be a deal breaker. I tell my cats everything."

Christy punched her on the biceps. "Be serious. You can't speak the words out loud, ever."

"Jeez, okay." Hally rubbed her arm, pouting, even though Christy had barely tapped her. "Don't be psycho girl about it."

"That's just it." Christy ran her hands through her spiky hair. Since she wasn't seeing Roman that day, she'd added extra gel to make it stand up. If she was going through some ceremony in the sacred something to discover her true self, she needed every boost of spunkiness she could get. "I might *be* psycho girl."

"I doubt that."

"Remember that thing you told me the other night—about how people who get all involved in the unseen get nutty because they lose their grip on reality?"

"Sure."

"And remember how I asked you a long time ago if you'd heard stories about the opera house being haunted?"

"I knew it!" Hally thumped the steering wheel but didn't set off the horn this time.

"You did?"

"Well, yeah. I'm not an idiot. Tell me what happened."

So she did. It felt strange, under the blazingly sunny sky, amid the red cliffs and deep evergreen valleys, to talk about the phantom's shadowy world. Hally listened without her usual commentary—which said something, right there—and her silence created a kind of vacuum that drew more of the story out of Christy than she'd planned to tell. She left out the more erotic details but told her pretty much everything else.

By the time she'd finished, Hally had parked her VW Bug in the lot at Bandelier National Park—after interrupting only once, to make Christy pay the entry fee at the gate. The redhead, her hair down for her day off, sat with her eyes closed for a few minutes.

"Wow," she finally said.

"That's all you have to say?" Christy popped the buckle on the annoying seat belt.

Hally cracked one eye at her. "It's a lot to assimilate."

"You're telling me."

"No wonder you want to look inside your heart. I think I brought all the right stuff."

"So—you believe me?"

"You believe you, right? That's all that matters."

"I don't know that I do."

"That's why you're here, then."

"You never did tell me why *here*." Though the lot was full, it didn't seem to be the three-ring circus most national parks usually were. Of course, that was mostly back east.

"You'll see. I was more right than I knew." Hally got out and began cheerfully rummaging through the bags piled in the backseat. "That's a good sign."

"I don't have any Native American blood—I won't have a connection to this place, even if it *is* all sacred and spiritual." Even as she said it, she realized it wasn't true. If what she suspected was true, she could be descended from that long-ago kidnapped Indian girl. She hadn't told Hally that part, however.

Hally shouldered a bright patchwork bag and flipped her hair out of her face with a huff. "Are you a human being?"

"Maybe not. My dad sure isn't."

"Ha ha. My point is that human is human. It's not necessary for you to match up recent ancestry to harmonize with something. Besides, we don't have the time to head off to find whatever stone circle your ancestors used to commune with the spirit world. We'll stand on someone else's ladder. They won't mind."

"How do you know?" Skipping a little to keep up with Hally's long stride up the path, Christy took in the imposing cliffs, shifting tones of red, yellow, and orange sending striations of rock to challenge the deep blue sky. The sheltered valley felt quite warm already and she was glad she'd worn shorts. Even though some families were running around, a kind of cushioned silence fell over the area. A special feel.

"I know because I'll make sure of it." Hally tucked a blowing strand of hair behind her ear. "This is why you need me. I'll provide the protection and make sure we show the proper respect. The rest is up to you."

"I still have no idea what I'm doing," Christy muttered.

"Yes you do. Trust yourself."

"Easy for you to say—you didn't get yourself accidentally engaged to a guy you don't even like all that much. Or indulge in a secret affair with another guy who may or may not be some kind of ghost. Either of whom might be a serial killer."

Hally slanted her a foxy grin. "There is that."

"See?"

"Sorry. No out for you. You still have to do this yourself."

By this time they'd made it up to the cliffs, bypassing all the excavated ruins and informational signs. Sometime she'd come back and read them all. The cliff itself was pockmarked with cave holes, some with ladders leading to them. Hally surveyed several, then picked one and dropped the soft bag on the gritty soil. She pulled out a rope and a laminated sign.

CLOSED FOR RENOVATION

She slung the rope around the ladder and hung the sign at eye level.

"Clever," Christy commented.

"Not my first time to the circus. Climb up. Mind your head, the ceilings are low."

Intrigued, Christy ascended the ladder into the ancient cliff dwelling. She'd never actually been inside one and it felt . . . different. As if she'd crawled inside someone else's skin. Inside the domed room, a glimpse of blue came through the perfectly centered smoke hole, and she knew with visceral truth what it had been like to live here. The children running outside belonged to the tribe. This room sheltered them during the colder winters and from the summer monsoon rains. It was as if the walls themselves had absorbed the energy of all those lives lived here.

Hally crawled through the low doorway, the natural hush of the place absorbing the sound of her movement. She pointed to the floor directly under the smoke hole and Christy sat, the smooth stone surprisingly warm and comfortable beneath her.

"Give me the opal ring." Hally held out her hand.

"You can't lose it."

"I'm not going to lose it, but you can't have it inside the circle with you."

"What circle?"

"The one I'm about to draw to protect you. Now hand it over."

Christy dug it out of her pocket and placed the glimmering ring in Hally's hand. It looked odd in this simple place. Gaudy and wrong. "What about my necklace, or this stone?"

"Do you associate those things with *him*?" There was no mistaking which *him* she meant.

"Yes."

"Then keep them—they'll help. He's tied to this place, and they're related to it, too."

"How do you know he's tied here?"

Hally rolled her eyes. "He told you, remember?"

I am king of all I survey here, yet I am a prisoner of it also. She didn't remember telling Hally that part, but she must have.

"I think he meant the opera house."

"Geologically speaking, we're not that far from there."

"Says the nonscientist."

"Yes, I know. Now let me concentrate."

Starting on Christy's left, Hally began drawing a circle around her, scratching a line in the stone, muttering under her breath. When she connected the circle, nothing changed. Christy hadn't known what to expect, but not nothing. Then Hally set four stones around her, one of them directly in front of her, between her and the mouth of the cave.

Hally took the bag and backed out, her feet on the ladder. "Now, keep your back straight—imagine your tailbone growing roots into the rock beneath you. Energy runs through you, through your skull, out the smoke hole, and into the sky."

"Then what?"

The redhead smiled, but with a certain intensity. "Ask your question and wait for what comes to you. Be respectful and grateful. I'll be out here, doing my part. Call me when you're done."

"Wait—how do I know what question to ask?"

Hally didn't laugh at her. "Be honest with yourself. Ask what you really want to know. This isn't a test. You're not here to impress anyone. Ask what's in your heart."

At one time Christy might have felt silly, but that same feel about the place settled like a mantle over her shoulders, warm and full of an ancient serenity.

She sat with hands on knees, gazing out of the dwelling opening. Looking straight out across the valley, only trees, basking in the sunshine, met her eye. If nothing else, it was peaceful. Not unlike the peace the cathedral had offered, but of a different flavor. In this place, absolution felt possible.

Relaxing into it, she let the world fall away. It reminded her of how she felt when she was with the Master—transported to another place, suspended in time. The familiar warmth flooded her, sexual and spiritual. Alert while asleep.

In her mind, she asked the question: *Why me?*

She'd been afraid it would sound whiny, too "poor me." But, in the silence of her skull, the sincerity came through. How had she become the pivot of so much?

In the valley below, ancient people worked the fields, their brown skin baking under the sun, singing a song she'd heard before. Dogs ran past, a group of kids shouting gleefully after them. Then the sun went behind a cloud and a shadow fell over the people. Men in armor spilled into the valley, silver swords cutting through wooden spears, splintering them.

The people fell to the earth, like so much harvested wheat.

She walked through the aftermath, her bare feet sinking into the blood-soaked soil, bits of crushed plants spattered on her calves. Not far away, a creature bellowed in pain. She found the bear, shining white and pinned to the ground. An enormous silver cross pierced him through the stomach, as if he was no more than a hapless butterfly, stuck to a collector's board.

The bear's icy blue eyes were glazed with pain as it writhed, unable to free itself from the silver spike. The cross at the top, encircled with a golden halo, shone in the sun like a beacon.

Sorrow welled through her—for the crippled bear, the murdered people, the ravaged crop. All that life, senselessly destroyed, all for wealth. The rage rose in her heart, anger against her father, always so determined to have his way, no matter what it cost. An image came to her of her thirteen-year-old self, pinned under her father's weight and determination, while he pulled up her shirt to reveal the slices across her tender belly.

"Cutting is a sign of mental weakness and emotional pain." He spoke in even tones, not caring if she heard him over her tears and cries. "You shouldn't have done this to yourself. I had no idea the divorce had affected you so deeply. But we'll get you the help you need. If you can't be happy living a normal life here with me, then we'll find you a nice group home, where they can help you recover your sanity."

That had been the real her. She'd never been insane. Just injured.

Like a wounded creature, she'd tucked away her pain and never told anyone what she'd done. But the truth shone through, didn't it?

She wrapped her hands around the silver spine of the cross and it shifted under her grip, writhing like a serpent. Drawing on her deep stubbornness, her own determination, inherited from him but inverted, used for life, not power, she pulled. It tried to squirm away, but she held on, using all her sorrow and fury to pull it to her.

It came free with a scream. From her, from the bear, from the earth itself.

She fell, plummeting through darkness, trying to remember the name to call. Glittering discs of gold and silver fell around her, nicking her skin, drawing blood. She fell into the arms of the bear and he sank his claws into her. Crying out in ecstasy, she threw back her head, giving him her throat.

He took it and her blood flowed free, sinking into the earth, pulling the maimed bodies with it, drawing them under. In their place an unnaturally lush green lawn grew. Among the endless sameness of grass, stalks of another plant grew here and there. She lay in the bear's embrace while the crops grew up around them, luxurious, reaching for the sun. The stalks grew tall, their leaves spread and waxed, offering their shade. Through the patchwork green, buds burst into full sunflower bloom, turning their faces to their namesake shining above.

In the blessed depths of the shadows, she smiled.

7

Hally didn't ask what she'd seen. Which was good, because Christy didn't think she could put it into words. The redhead picked up her stones and scuffed away the circle, moving in the reverse of what she'd done before. They walked back down the path in silence, Christy turning over what she'd seen and felt, still under the spell of it all.

She knew without doubt that somehow, somewhere, she hadn't dreamed that. It had been real. No innocent maiden, her ancestress, some ancient echo of herself, had given herself to save the Master from ultimate destruction. Whether the tribe's god or totem spirit, he'd survived, but weak and crippled. Scarred.

And somehow, whatever she'd done, the magic of blood and love had fixed a piece of him forever in this realm.

A young boy—yelling at the top of his lungs, face covered in melted ice cream—barreled up the path and between them, forcing them apart. Hally watched him go, her eyebrows raised. "Guess you were right."

"Eh." Christy shrugged. "It's good for there to be life here."

"Look who's less grumpy now."

"What does it mean, when an animal is white?"

"In most mythologies, it means that it's a spirit form."

"Like the white stag in the Arthurian tales."

"Exactly."

They got back to Hally's car, the sun sinking low, and she pulled back out to the highway. "Where to?" Hally asked in a chipper tone.

"Would you drop me off at the opera house?"

"Thought so."

Though it was late on a Saturday, people were there working—mainly the props and scenery crews—putting in extra hours. With dress rehearsals kicking into gear in the next week, it suddenly seemed as if a mountain of work loomed. Nobody was surprised to see Christy and, likewise, nobody paid much attention when she tossed off a wave and headed down the spiral staircase.

"Just popping in for a minute!" she called out to one of the props guys, just in case. That way they wouldn't look for her if she went "missing," especially without her car in the lot.

She simmered with anticipation—and a kind of joy, she realized. The same surge of deep vitality she'd felt lying in the bear's embrace in the shade of the sunflowers. This, then, was what trusting your gut truly meant. Even what Roman believed in when he said people "just knew." It went beyond thought, she understood now. Beyond words.

She knew.

And trusted.

She hadn't even brought the flashlight because she didn't need it—for light or for self-defense. The shadows grew deeper. Round and round she rattled down the spiral stairs, the lower-level air chilly on her bare arms and legs, the rubber soles of her sneakers squeaking on the metal steps.

In her haste her foot slipped, skidded, and flew off the edge. Her stomach plummeted, the gasping terror of the fall flooding her.

The hard jerk of her shoulder flashed sharp pain as her grip on the rail yanked her back, her butt slamming against the steps, knocking the breath from her lungs.

"Shit," she gasped. Not so invincible, after all. "Pay better attention, Christy, would you?"

"Yes." The golden voice rolled up from below. "Have a care. You're counted as precious by others."

She peered down through the stairwell grate but couldn't make him out. "Master?"

"Who else?"

"Sometimes I'm not sure if all the voices I hear are yours."

"Understandable."

"Is it?" She pulled herself up, strained shoulder protesting, and descended the last few spirals. "Do you hear them, too?"

"Of course."

"Who are they?"

"Come with me and see. They wait to meet you." A shadow separated itself from the darkness. He removed his hat with a sweep, to bow to her. In the bare light filtering from above, his half mask concealed his face and his white-blond hair gleamed.

A small silence fell between them.

"Have you come to me?"

It felt like the moment the proposal should have been. The question asked as a formality because both hearts already knew the answer.

"Yes."

"Then come."

He opened his arms and she hurtled herself into his embrace. She pressed herself to him, drinking in his scent, man and more. The vibrant energy that infused him streamed through her and she wanted him, so deeply she thought she would weep from need. She raised her face to his and his mouth descended on her, feeding on her lips in turn, like a starving creature.

He murmured, deep in his throat, a sound of wordless longing. One strong arm held her tightly against him while a gloved hand splayed over her jaw and cheekbone, as if testing the reality of her presence.

"I want to be with you," she told him between kisses, "in every way imaginable."

"You know how it must be. There are rules."

"Yes." She remembered offering her throat to the bear—the fierce and extraordinary surrender and ecstasy of the moment. "I'm yours."

In truth, she always had been. She saw that now.

He drew a length of silk from his pocket, presented it over his upturned palms. "Do you surrender yourself to me?"

Offering herself in sacrifice to the bear. Blood without death. Ecstasy and pain. Her blood surged with her pounding heart, nerves burning bright and arousal flooding her senses.

"Yes."

"Yes, what?"

A wave rolled through her. She turned up her face, offering her throat to the beast.

"Yes, Master."

He bound her wrists together and she watched from a curious remove, already feeling that meditative sense of giving herself over to the forces of the world. Of all the worlds, whatever and wherever they might be. The place she truly existed. Her breath rose and fell with aroused intensity, the full sides of her breasts swelling against her inner arms.

When he blindfolded her, it became another level of yielding.

He led her along by her tied wrists, never faltering, her unfailing guide. Trusting him was no longer a conscious exercise. He would make sure of her footing and her way. She smelled water, and the always cool air of the lower levels grew damp on her cheeks, with a more penetrating chill. She shivered and he paused, then wrapped his cloak around her, cozily warm from his body heat, his musky scent filling her nose.

"Step into the boat." It was the first time he'd spoken since she'd called him Master.

Boat?

But she followed his lead still, finding her footing in the small boat that rocked on water so still it made no sound. He helped her to sit and she folded her bound hands in her lap, while he tucked the cloak around her. They moved, gliding, and the sound of oars dipping in and out of the water added to the surreal feeling.

"How is there a lake here?"

In answer, he sang a song she'd never heard, of deep waters that ran under the mountains of time. She floated, on the water, on the music, on the surging desire that made her thoughts melt away.

All she really wanted was for him to touch her again.

But she had cast herself into his power as surely as she'd stepped into this boat that carried her across an unknown underground lake. If she struggled against it now, she'd surely drown. No, the key was to ride along, not to fight it.

She felt strangely serene, giving up the need to fight everything.

Calm and free.

The hypnotic dipping of the oars ceased and the boat ground

lightly against a dock. The air seemed warmer here, nearly balmy, as if they'd crossed into another world.

Then the Master was beside her, slipping strong arms under her knees and lifting her against his muscular chest. He stepped up onto the dock, his boots thunking on the wood, then set her on her feet.

"Warm enough now?" His breath feathered across her cheek. She nodded, and he pulled the now stultifying cloak from her. Then he removed the blindfold. "Look."

She gasped at the beauty of it. The dock fed onto a boardwalk and all along it white pillar candles lit the way. They glimmered off the black mirrored lake water and ascended in tiers up stairs and winding walkways that ran through archways of black-leaved trees. The candlelit paths traced a route up a hillside to a series of towering stones set in a circle. Torches ringed them. The place glimmered with magic and clarity.

"Fairyland," she said on a breath, then felt silly.

The Master wrapped his arms around her and laid a cheek against hers.

"Welcome home."

ACT 5

A Haunting Duet

1

Christy didn't question it.

When the Master said "welcome home," she felt the truth of it. However impossible the reality might be. She belonged here, to him. That was all that mattered anymore.

It helped that she'd moved beyond thought into pure sensation. Now that she'd given herself over to him, she felt consumed by the need to be taken. With her hands bound, she couldn't seize him and urge him into her aching core.

But she would have.

He untied her hands, as if answering the thought, but held her wrists in a tight grip, ice-blue eyes sparkling in the candlelight.

"I would have stripped you naked at this moment, except for my promise to you. But the rules remain the same—you must submit to me, understand?"

She nodded mutely. She did understand, in a way she hadn't before. To free the bear was to make him the master. He inclined his head toward one of the dock pilings. They weren't wood but seemingly carved from polished rock. Obsidian, perhaps. Draped over one was a sheer white gown.

"I shall turn my back while you undress and put that on. It will cover your scars, but little else."

"Thank you, Master."

"As you respect my scars, so I respect yours." His lips feathered a kiss over her forehead, a kind of benediction. Of absolution.

True to his word, he turned his back, staring off over the mirrored black lake. She toed off her sneakers and wriggled out of her clothes. The ridged scars across her abdomen caught the light, silver lines that, strangely, were not that ugly. In a way, they were her own battle scars.

She pulled the gown over her head, the sheer silk falling over her in a cloud. A wide belt of gold fabric gathered it at her waist, holding tight against her midsection. Above it, the bodice parted, falling open in loose sweeps that ran over her shoulders but left her breasts bare. The skirt was really two slim triangles of cloth, gliding along the outsides of her thighs, completely revealing her front and back.

A concession only to her scars. Otherwise, she might as well have been naked. Nervous, she stared at the black-cloaked figure waiting for her to finish. It would have been easier, she realized with dawning perception, if he'd stripped her with her hands bound. She could have relinquished this uncertainty. It seemed unthinkable to tell him to turn, to see her. On impulse she knelt on the glassy black surface and waited, hands clasped in her lap.

His gloved hand drifted over her hair, smoothing it with tenderness. "I feel that I've waited forever for this," he mused in a soft voice.

She looked up at his forbidding figure. "Have you?"

"Pain, I think, has no time. Its impact is infinite, but we also have no memory for it. Once it ceases, we forget the intensity. Over time, we lose it entirely."

"That's physical pain—not emotional."

"True. Grief lessens, but never disappears entirely. Are you ready?"

"Yes."

He offered his hand and she rose to her feet. The ice-blue eyes glimmered in the light of the thousands of candles as they traveled over her, his gaze palpable as a touch. Her nipples peaked and her sex dampened. His lips curved in a smile.

Telling her to turn, he once again bound her wrists behind her back and then roped her ankles tightly together. As if the binding of the ropes on her body somehow set her inner self free, her mind drifted once more into that dream state. The world where no thoughts mattered, only feeling.

He swept her up, one arm under her shoulders and the other under her knees, carrying her like a bouquet of roses up the walkway. She let her head fall back, pliant and relaxed, her breasts upthrust, the transparent silk scarves trailing around them. The candlelight felt warm on her eyelids, the air cool on her naked skin. Supported only by the Master's strong grip, she floated through the air to her fate, yielding to it—and to him—without reservation.

She opened her eyes when he laid her on a polished slab, warm, as if heated from within. They were inside the stone circle she'd seen from below. Around her, obelisks carved of the same rock towered. The Master untied her hands, then bound them again above her head. He also anchored her roped feet to the bottom of the slab, so she was stretched between the two poles, like a sacrifice.

And yet she felt no fear. She felt more centered in herself, more truly certain than perhaps ever before in her life.

The Master ran his gloved hand up her thighs, letting the translucent fabric frame her body. Cupping her breasts, he kissed her taut nipples until she moaned, scissoring her thighs, needing so much more.

Shadows appeared behind him and surprise rippled through her. "Who—?"

"They are the voices. Those who cannot be silenced. Like me, they live on, half in one world and half in another. You know them also. They are here to witness and to celebrate. Yes?"

She nodded, her heart swelling, unnamable emotion dampening her eyes. He drew back and people surrounded her. Her people. She couldn't see them well, despite the blazing candles all around. They were silhouettes, glimpses of flowing dark hair and soft black eyes. Hands traveled over her skin, touching and caressing with reverence. They fondled her breasts and dipped between her slick thighs, increasing her pleasure. Lips kissed her and tongues lapped, stimulating and teasing her so she squirmed against the ropes that bound her so tightly, that made of her an offering to them.

Unable to resist, she forfeited trying to. She gave herself over to it. It was like being worshipped—overwhelming, humbling, and relentlessly exciting.

With stone blades and loving caresses, the shadowy figures cut away the draping scarves of silk, leaving only the belt of tight cloth at her midriff. The many hands then rubbed oil into her, coating her skin so it gleamed golden. They turned her over, spinning her inside the bonds, and oiled her back, delving even into the cleft of her bottom. She writhed on the glassy surface, wishing the Master would return soon. The thought dissolved in the endlessness of the moment, and it seemed she would be this always, forever anointed and aroused.

She became aware of a drumbeat in the background, a low thrumming that echoed the pulse in her groin, the pounding of her heart in the cage of her ribs.

At last, the hands shifted, freeing her of the slab and carrying her to a pair of standing stones on a raised area capped by a horizontal piece. Lifting her, they hung her by her bound hands to a hook in the top, so she dangled like a decoration beneath.

Or like a priestess presiding over a ritual.

From her vantage, it became clear that many more eyes watched. The hillside thronged thick with dark-haired people, holding candles and observing with hushed reverence. The thick scent of flowers twined with that of hot wax, and more shadowy people brought red roses, in full bloom, piling them at her feet and around the slab before her.

The Master emerged from the crowd below, making his way up the slope, his pained limp showing as they parted for him. Unlike them, he was fully fleshed, crisply real. In his black formal wear, cloak, and mask, hair and shirt like slashes of white burning through the surreal gloom, he seemed ever more some creature out of place and time. She imagined the icy glitter of his eyes showed even from that distance, always locked upon her nearly naked form. Her blood churned in her ears and she swung on her hook with an involuntary convulsion of longing for him.

He seemed more pained than usual, moving more slowly. When he came close enough, she saw why: a silver knife protruded from his midsection, blood seeping out to soak his white shirt with the dark, rusty red of an old injury.

With difficulty, he climbed onto the slab and stretched himself out where she had been. The shadow people swarmed around him, binding him spread-eagled to it. With the stone blades cupped in their hands, they cut away his clothing. He rolled his head to the side, watching her, waiting for her reaction, she knew.

It had been this way for her, before, back when she carelessly let someone see her scars. The instinctive revulsion on their faces, the horrified curiosity and the sympathy that nearly broke you. Sympathy worked like an acid, corroding the locks you kept over the festering, secret wounds.

So she didn't wince when they cut away the gloves and the ruin of his hands became apparent. The one leg, muscular to the knee, then withered, as if it had been gnawed to the bone by wild dogs. They stripped him naked and vulnerable, carefully cutting around the blade buried in his lean abdomen, revealing the shining white hair and quiescent cock at his groin. They took everything from him. All except for the knife and the mask, leaving that as a stark black reminder, his blue eyes shards of glacier, burning through the holes.

A shadowy figure approached her, covered more in hair than skin. Armbands, thigh bands, and a chest plate of worked gold shone brightly, the glow obscuring its features. It stood before her and held up a length of leather, just under her chin. She frowned, uncertain, and the creature lashed her on the thigh with it, a sting that turned her suspended body in a slight circle. It held up the strap again. The Master watched, his body tense with the strain of his position.

A question then.

Eyes on his, she bent her head and kissed the strap. Agreeing to what he asked of her. The creature smiled, a glitter of fang in the hairy countenance, unfolding the leather strap to a long length. With a whistle through the air, it landed again on her thigh. The drumbeats quickened at her cry of pain, and an echo of it ran through the assembly. She found the Master's burning gaze, full of love and desire.

The lash fell again on her tender skin, sending her spinning. Again and again, the leather found her sensitive flesh, landing now on her bottom, there on her calf, then across her breasts. The last made her scream and fight the bonds, the crowd yelling with her—in encouragement or anger, she couldn't tell. But it became a symphony, a concert of agony. The whoosh and slap of the whipping, her cries and the reverberations of her pain from those watching.

Sweat ran down her body and melded with the tears pouring from her eyes.

Whenever she could, she locked her gaze with the Master's, like a ballerina finding her steady point as she pirouettes. Gradually, it seemed his body transformed. Sometimes she saw the great white bear, pinned to the altar of the black slab. Other times he seemed radiantly masculine, his limbs perfect and untwisted. His cock grew, unfurling with lust until it thrust high and hard against his belly.

Transported by the pain and egged on by the crowd, her own desire exploded, each sting of the lash a spur to drive her up higher and harder. The strap of leather crashed against the closed triangle of her mound and she nearly came from it, panting and pleading with inarticulate noises.

The Master, too, longed for her with his body, straining against the ropes. He pumped his hips with the throbbing of the drums, going faster and faster now, along with the speed of the lash and the ululating wail of her cries for relief.

With a final, sonic boom of a beat, the drums and the crowd and the lash all ceased.

Only her panting sobs broke the silence. Her tenders rushed forward, supporting her and cutting the ropes on her ankles and wrists. They carried her to the slab and set her on it, so she knelt between the Master's spread legs. His scrotum hung heavy and she, at last free to touch him, cupped it, rolling his heavy balls in her hand. He groaned, almost more of an ursine growl, his glittering gaze fixed on her.

Tears drying on her face, her flesh alive and singing with the extreme stimulation, she leaned over and licked the length of his cock, careful not to bump the knife still piercing his abdomen. The blood welling from the wound ran bright red now, fresh and full of vitality. She took him into her mouth, sucking the broad head, the long length too much for her to take fully. Her vulva cramped with the thought of being stretched by it and she could wait no longer.

Powerful, confident in her sensual hunger, she straddled him, holding his cock and guiding it into her. His gaze remained fixed on hers, filled with a fierce need that took her breath away. She sank down on his shaft, letting it stretch her, enjoying the sensation of opening wide while he filled her. The wild, feral pleasure of their sweat-slicked skin meeting nearly sent her over the edge. She held on, though, knowing there was more.

With him inside her, it seemed they merged. Skin to skin, the physical blended with the metaphysical. The sense of the bear's fur on her naked breasts as his jaws sank into her throat became the fine white hairs tickling her pussy when his cock thrust into her with a bolt of pleasure so keen she shuddered with it, crying out as she had under the lash.

The tension between them built, each stoking the other higher. His muscular thighs bunched under her raw bottom, spearing his cock into her deepest core.

She rode him, her nails digging into his taut abdomen on either side of the offending blade, blood slicked, sweat wet. Their gazes meshed, held.

On the precipice, they poised together.

And she grasped the knife in her bloodied hands.

With a roar, he flexed his powerful hips and thighs, lifting her into the air. As she had in the vision, she pulled on her own deep wells of courage and pulled the blade from his flesh, thrusting it point first to the infinite black sky and screamed, wild and free, while she climaxed, riding his bucking body, a feral steed carrying her to another world.

2

Mind reeling, wrenched nearly out of her body by the shattering orgasm that had rocked her on every level, she clenched the knife over her head, the drying blood welding her fingers to the hilt.

Her thighs protested the strain of straddling the Master's muscular hips. He lay beneath her, peaceful, a beatific smile on his lips beneath the black mask that remained the only thing he wore. The terrible wound in his midsection no longer bled. The flesh was torn, blackened near the center, where it had touched the silver blade, but spreading out it showed the healthy pink of healing tissue.

Her own cuts—so much more shallow, not nearly so crippling, at least not physically—had been that way. They'd knitted themselves together of their own accord. Over time, angry red turned to healing pink to the crystal white of the scars that never fully disappeared.

Peeling one hand off the sticky hilt, she braced herself and lifted off him. She missed the sense of him inside her immediately, and his seed followed, sliding down her inner thighs.

She'd never had condomless sex before. A funny thought, given all that had occurred. Abruptly she became aware that they were alone again. No drums, no hairy creature with a leather lash, no shadowy figures. The prosaic concerns of disease and unplanned pregnancy hadn't mattered in that realm.

Moving around the immense slab, she used the broad-bladed

knife to sever the ropes binding him to the altar. Which of them had been the sacrifice?

Or had they sacrificed themselves to each other, somehow?

He lay still, though his chest rose and fell with his breathing. Once she'd freed him, she climbed over him again, knife still in one hand, and straddled that massive chest. The even thump of his heart resounded against the sensitive, open tissues of her spread sex. He seemed larger now than he had back in that strange carousel living room of his. An anteroom to this world. His skin glowed alabaster against the obsidian slab, his white-blond hair piled beneath his head. Leaning over him, she kissed him, soft and sweet.

Wake, my prince.

The icy-blue eyes opened, warming at the sight of her, and his big hands slid up her back, one cupping the nape of her neck, urging her down to kiss him again. They savored one another for a while, mouths interweaving like melody and harmony, desire rising again between them, growing out of every spot their skin touched, candlelight dancing over them in a warm blessing.

She sat up. Gathered herself. It was time to show all of herself to him.

Working the knife blade under the fabric wrapping her waist, she sliced it away. The Master watched, his hands on her thighs. She shrugged the gold belt away, along with the shard of silk that had been trapped beneath it. Without judgment he took in the chain of scars across her belly, where she'd carved out her pain.

The Master's hands slid up her thighs and feathered over her belly, caressing her, touching the soft skin between the evil lines. Accepting them as both part of her and unimportant. Holding her like this, his large hands nearly spanned her waist, holding her safe and loved.

Gravely, the Master wrapped his hand around hers, holding the blade through her agency. He brought it up to the side of his head, turning his face away and sliding the point under the ribbon that bound the mask to his face.

Steadying the massive knife with her other hand, because she trembled with the surging emotions tossing her on their waves, she cut the ribbon.

The mask fell away.

He rolled his head back to face her fully, the crystalline blue of his eyes deepening with the same tide of feeling, his heart thumping against the wet core of her womanhood.

Whatever had happened to his face had been different from the knife wound. His cheek and temple on the left side looked partially melted away, like chocolate left in the sun. Finally unwrapping her hand from the knife they no longer needed, she tossed it aside and cupped his face in her palms, fingers caressing the scars and the whole skin alike, and kissed him.

Straightening her legs, she stretched herself out over him, their mouths joined, each holding the other's scars. She felt like a tea cozy, a bit of lace draped over the top of his powerful body.

Her sex throbbed for more of him and his cock rose hot and hard against her belly. Their kisses grew deeper, more demanding, more desperate.

He rolled her over onto her back and she barely registered the sting of abraded flesh and bruised muscle. He took her wrists in his hands and stretched her arms above her head. She spread her legs and took him between them, raising her hips in welcome.

He plunged into her slick and willing flesh, swallowing her cry of intense pleasure with his mouth. Setting the rhythm to a strong and steady percussion, like the beat of his heart, he worked his cock in and out. Her legs wrapped around his waist, held fast by his hands and mouth, she opened to him, yielding with each thrust, opening for him like the roses piled around them.

She must have fallen asleep, because she woke, still on the polished black altar, cuddled into the curl of his body, her sore bottom pressed against his muscular thighs.

His hand smoothed her hair back from her cheek and he pressed a kiss to the top of her head. Then he sat up and stepped down from the slab, gathering his clothes. She sat, her knees curled to the side, watching his powerful muscles gather and bunch as he dressed. He moved better, now, more smoothly, though the wound in his gut looked much the same.

He replaced the mask, tying the ends of the sliced ribbon together, his icy-blue gaze growing inscrutable behind it. The gloves, though, he left off, and his hands traveled over her nakedness as if savoring every touch, as he gathered her once again in his arms, carrying her like a bride over the threshold.

She wrapped her arms around his neck and burrowed into him, placing little kisses along his temple, cheek, and throat. He carried her down the hill, along the switchback path that led to the glassy lake. Over his shoulder, she could see the candles wink out behind them as they passed. It saddened her, as if something precious were being swallowed up again.

At the dock, he set her down, wrapped his arms around her, and kissed her, white hair and black cloak falling around them.

"My priestess, you've served me well. Allow me to serve you."

He knelt, dropping kisses along her throat and collarbone, then gathered her breasts in his hands and rained licks and kisses on them. Under his ministrations, their ache lessened. His hands ran over her back as he kissed her belly, never once hesitating over the horrible scars. Cupping her bottom, he eased the sting there, too, and his tongue between her thighs sent wings of rolling pleasure through her limbs.

She buried her fingers in his silky hair, her thighs flexing as the sweet, slow orgasm suffused her limbs. His mouth drank from her, strong arms holding her steady as she sighed and moaned.

With grave gallantry, he swung off his cloak and draped it over her nakedness. Stepping into the boat, he held out a hand to help her in.

He rowed her back across the lake, darkness deepening as the last of the candles winked out behind them.

Time to return to the other world.

"Does it have to end?" She stopped him, after he removed her blindfold but before he could dissolve or slip away or however he disappeared. She wound her fingers into his still loose hair, white in the shadows. "Come with me. Or let me stay."

He wrapped his hand around hers, those lips she knew so well curving while he cupped her cheek. "I cannot. And you cannot. Our worlds are divided. I cannot live in yours and you cannot live in mine. Though your sacrifice, the pain and pleasure we shared, has changed much, it hasn't altered the chains that bind me."

"What will?"

His thumb passed over her lower lip and he followed it with his mouth, tender and sweet. "To ask the question is to answer it."

"I don't understand what that means."

"You are both the lock and the key."

"Are you saying that I'm keeping you trapped?"

"In a way." His lips found the urgent pulse beat in her throat and she lifted her chin, offering herself again and again. "I smell it in your blood—both my captor and my savior."

"I don't understand enough."

"You will. You have brought me gifts beyond price, my priestess. My Christine."

"I love you." She said it in a rush, wishing she had better words than the bare phrase that had to represent the depth of emotion rushing through her like a river.

"You are forever my love. Nothing will ever change that. Though I'm trapped below, I am with you in thought and feeling at every moment. Remember that." And then he gave her one last kiss and slid from under her hand, a drift of white sand sliding from the shore and out to sea.

Her prince, trapped in the tower.

But not forever. Because she had the power to save him.

3

She stepped out of the opera house into the cool June night, locking the doors behind her. Overhead, the Milky Way stretched in a brilliant glitter. Stars flickering with prismatic color seemed to wheel in spirals like the swirling galaxies depicted at the planetarium.

Her body ached in every way imaginable and inside she felt as sparklingly alive as the night sky. The two seemed to be reflections of each other. What had Roman's priest called it? *Mortification of the flesh.* Somehow Christine knew he hadn't been thinking of the kind of carnal ceremony she'd just gone through. Ursa Major, the great bear, strode through the glittering stream of stars and she smiled to think of him. They would find a way. She knew it.

Love conquered all, didn't it?

It couldn't be just a cliché.

Shivering, she pulled out her phone to call a cab company. Then she spotted Hally's little VW Bug, not far away under one of the muted, downward-facing parking lights. Inside, Hally slept in the driver's seat, tilted back nearly horizontal, her unnaturally red hair catching glints of light and slanting shadows giving her face a witchy cast.

Reluctant to startle her, Christine knocked on the window with a light tapping. Hally's eyes opened, not seeing her at first, then sharpened, and she plucked the seat lever, springing herself upright. She rolled down the window.

"Get in," she hissed, though no one could possibly hear them. "We've got problems."

It felt odd to talk to someone from the regular world again. To be wearing her shirt and shorts and to sit in a car while Hally drove it down the road. Her body still pulsed from that last orgasm, her mind spinning from all she'd witnessed and learned, her heart brimming over with sticky-sweet emotion. She hummed a tune, the ancient melody part of it all.

"What song is that?" Hally cocked her head like a bird, listening. "It seems so familiar."

"A really old one. But I don't know the name. Names don't matter anyway."

Hally slid her gaze over, the whites of her eyes catching the streetlights, then back to the road. "Hoookaaaayyy."

"What?"

"You haven't been smoking the peyote or anything, have you?— 'cuz you're acting pretty whacked."

Christine giggled, the giddiness spilling over, sparkling stars spilling through the darkness. "No. I don't think any drug could induce what happened to me tonight."

"Jeez." Hally shook her head. "I'll have what she's having."

"I wish you could." Christine turned in her seat. "It was the most incredible experience, but I don't think I could put it into words."

"Well, we don't have time for it now, anyway. Time for you to sober up and deal with the non-numinous. Gritty reality awaits, *chica*."

"Where are we going?" Christine blinked as they passed Tomasita's, now closed for the night.

"My place." Hally sounded grim. "Hopefully they won't look for you there again tonight."

"Who?"

"Christy! Focus, would you?"

"Christine."

"Huh?"

"Call me Christine, okay?"

The whites of Hally's eyes gleamed again, this time as she rolled them. "Okay, fine, whatever, Miss I'm a Whole New Person."

"I feel like I am! I'll call you Halcyon, if you want me to."

"Dear gods, please no."

"Why not? It means peace and tranquility, especially around the winter solstice. I looked it up."

"I'm perfectly aware of what it means."

"You're that for me, an oasis of calm."

Hally pulled into a parking spot surprisingly close to her apartment, then dropped her forehead to the steering wheel. "We need to bring you down. I wonder if yogurt would work? I might have some acidophilus in the fridge."

Christine wrinkled her nose and got out of the car. "I don't like yogurt."

"Well, it's not as if you took mushrooms, anyway. Did you?"

"Nope. I haven't had anything." She grinned. "Except the most phenomenal sex of my life."

"That explains a great deal."

Hally unlocked her apartment door, peering around the edge before she let Christine in. "A hot shower should ground you. Sorry I can't offer you a glam sunken tub like Roman's got. Make sure you get the mud out from under your nails, okay? The cops might wonder about that."

She looked at her hands. Lake mud was caked in nearly black crescent wedges under her fingernails. Hally was in the kitchenette, cooing a singsong to her kitties, giving them some extra supper.

"The cops are looking for me?"

Hally turned, propping a fist on her hip and leaning against the counter. "Aha! There's a working brain in there, after all."

"Why are they looking for me?"

The redhead suddenly looked exhausted. And worried. Not a good sign. "Go shower. Pull yourself together and we'll talk. They've already questioned me once, so it's entirely possible they'll come looking for you here again. I would really rather you didn't look like you've been crawling around in the bowels of the opera house when they find you."

"Oh." Christine obediently headed for Hally's closet of a bathroom.

"There are clean towels on the shelf. Get started with soap. I'll bring in some clothes for you to borrow."

She did feel as if she was coming down from a high. The squalid bathroom, with its stained linoleum, helped. The plastic floor of the shower—one of those cubby kind cheap landlords bought in one piece to create a full bathroom out of a toilet stall—bubbled under her feet. Making the water as hot as she could stand it, she shampooed repeatedly, scratching at her scalp to loosen the dirt under her nails. She couldn't think how it had gotten there. Maybe from the boat?

"I'm coming in!" Hally called through the door. "Turn your back or whatever, but I won't look."

Funny. She'd forgotten about hiding the scars. As if, now that the Master had borne witness to them, they no longer mattered. Maybe they didn't.

Hally, face averted, set some folded sweats on the toilet seat, then handed her something over her shoulder. "Here's an orange stick."

"A what?"

"You know—to clean under your nails."

"I get that. I just never heard that name before."

"My grandmother called it that. I have no idea why. What does it have to do with oranges?"

"I never knew my grandmothers—either one of them." A sense of loss she hadn't realized she carried swept over her. Loss composed of lies, as much as anything.

"Really—both? Did they both die when you were young, or what?" Hally took down her ponytail, brushing out her hair.

"Well, my mom was an orphan. She never knew who her parents were. She was adopted by this foundation that picks out bright kids and sends them to boarding schools."

"Sounds lonely."

"She said it was better than the foster families she lived with. And then she met my dad when she was young and there were a lot of Davises, so she said they were more than enough family."

"But no Grandma Davis?"

"Died in childbirth," she repeated the old story, not ready to venture into the very strange but entirely possible alternative "There aren't even any photos of her. My Aunt Isadore raised my dad."

"Wow."

"Yeah." Christine turned off the water. "Okay. I'm ready to dry off." Hally kept her gaze on her image in the mirror. "Go ahead."

"Hally—you can look."

"Are you sure?"

"Yeah, I want you to see it. What I was hiding."

Hally turned, her eyes screwed shut, then slowly opened one, her gaze fixed on her friend's belly.

She bent over and studied the scars. "You're a cutter?"

"No." Christine blew out a long breath and made herself look. "Or maybe yes. I guess it's like being an alcoholic—there's always the danger of relapsing. But I haven't done it for a long time. My dad found out, and I was in this rehab place for a while. I hated him for that."

"Oh honey—did your mom know?" Hally handed her a towel.

"She knew I'd hurt myself, but not how. I didn't want her to know. I was so embarrassed. I felt like a failure."

"It's not a failure. Everybody has different ways of dealing with pain. You should be proud for overcoming it."

"I wasn't crazy. And I'm not crazy now. I've learned that much."

"Okay." Hally's bland look reminded her of her promise never to judge. Christine sighed.

"It helps that you know. And . . . and I wanted you to understand at least this part of things. Why I didn't want my father here. Helping me."

Hally regarded her quietly. "I get that. But he did the right thing, didn't he? Even though you were angry then."

"Maybe. I'm going to need his help, though."

"Everyone needs help now and again."

"Well . . ." She sighed and toweled her hair. "I can't count on the Sanclaro lawyers, and if the cops are talking to my friends, then I need help. What did they seem like they were after?"

"The cops are hinting around that they think you could be part of it."

A chill from more than the cool tiles sank into her heart. She pulled on Hally's sweats. "What? Why?"

Hally sat on the toilet and bit her lip. "It's bad. Carla apparently remembered what happened. And now the cops are talking as if she said you did it."

"I didn't."

"Well, it hardly matters, does it?" Hally snapped and tightened her ponytail. "They might have enough to arrest you now. That Detective Sanchez wanted to know where you were. And Sanclaro wants to know where you are. Let me tell you—you're a popular girl tonight. Come morning, you won't be able to duck them."

Christine stood frozen, unable to gather her thoughts.

"What did Carla say I did?"

"Well, we don't know, do we? Here, comb your hair."

She did, hissing at the snarls she hadn't known were there.

"See—they won't tell us exactly what Carla said because they're trying to draw you out. That Sanchez kept saying 'don't you want me to help your friend?' and 'the truth will exonerate her, but it looks bad without it,' and so on."

"Shit."

"In a word, yes. You'd better start thinking up your story."

"My story is that I was with him."

"Can you prove that?" Hally kept her face and voice studiously neutral.

"How?"

"Exactly. Only you have ever seen him. Unless he's planning to testify on your behalf, you have a problem."

"You don't believe me?"

"It's not me you need to convince. I'm not interested in judging you."

"Hally, can I ask you something?"

"I already told you—no judgment."

"Not that. If someone wanted to bind a spirit to a place, how is that done?"

Hally gave her a considering look. "You're not the kind of person to want to commit a heinous act like that, so I'm guessing you want to know who trapped your guy and how to undo it."

Christine nodded. Then shivered.

"Let's pour some wine. Then we'll talk."

4

The few hours of sleep Christine and Hally managed—sharing her narrow futon with one another and the six cats—were nowhere near enough. Hally had wanted to talk alibis, but Christine wouldn't. She did get the opal ring back from Hally, who grudgingly dug it out of the drawer in which she'd hidden it.

"You need to get out of that farce of an engagement," Hally grumbled the complaint as she slapped the ring into Christine's palm.

"Not yet." She slid it onto her finger, remembering how it felt to be the tribal priestess, her feet sinking into the mud of the bloody fields, the ghost tribe gathering around her in that dreamworld below the opera house—and the twin daughters who carried her blood and wore rings like this one. The lock and the key. It started and ended with the Sanclaros. "I need Roman."

Hally was busy scraping her hair into her usual ponytail but fixed her friend with a gimlet stare. "I hope you know what you're doing. That Roman—there's something off about him. When he came by last night . . ." She snapped a barrette in place and shook her head.

"Does he strike you as capable of murder?"

Hally glared. "I cannot believe you can just stand there and ask a question like that about a man you're seeing."

A knock banged on the door, carrying unmistakable police authority.

It wasn't Sanchez, though, just a couple of street cops whose eyes lit up at the sight of her. "Miss Davis, we need you to come down to the station with us."

"Okay." She smiled at their consternation. "You guys want a cup of coffee first?"

They tried to look stern and made noises about this not being a social occasion, but she only shrugged and grabbed her bag. Hally hugged her, hard.

"You want me to come with you?"

"That's not permissible, Miss Roberts." One of the cops frowned at her. "And what happened to you contacting us as soon as you heard from your friend?"

Hally twirled her ponytail around one finger and widened her eyes. "It was three in the morning, I didn't want to wake you guys. I know you need your beauty sleep."

Christine laughed at her, earning an innocent, beaming smile in return.

"You two think this is a laughing matter, but it's not." One cop bunched up his shoulders. "A woman is dead and another is gravely injured. You are both persons of interest, so I'd watch my manners if I were you."

Feet pounded up the wooden stairs and Roman stood in the open doorway. "What is the meaning of this?" He looked handsome as always, perfectly groomed.

"Mr. Sanclaro," said the cop who hadn't been getting all riled up, "we're escorting Ms. Davis here to the station to answer some questions."

"Is my fiancée under arrest?" Roman's gaze traveled over her borrowed gypsy dress before meeting her eyes. Under the studied bland expression on his face, a chilly anger brewed.

"Not at this time."

"Then she doesn't talk to you. Come on, Christy—I'm taking you home so you can get cleaned up for Mass." He held out a preemptory hand.

"Ms. Davis," the nice cop faced her directly, "I'm asking you to come with us now. Call your lawyer, if you need to, but don't force us to arrest you just to have a conversation."

"I already said I'd go and I'm going. I want to talk to Detective Sanchez."

"I'm calling our lawyers, Christy. Don't say anything until they get there." Roman's charged presence had tilted the population of Hally's smallish space from tight to seriously overcrowded.

In front of her intimate, avidly interested audience, Christine did her best to play her part right, the ingénue appealing to her hero. She widened her eyes and moved close to Roman, stroking the sharp lapel of his suit jacket.

"Don't be angry with me, Roman. This is so difficult. I just want to get it all over with."

He softened, as she'd hoped. He loved to play her rescuer.

"I was worried when I couldn't find you last night," he murmured, taking her hand and passing his thumb over the ring.

"I was praying." She spoke the lie without a trace of guilt. "I'm so sorry to miss church, but let's go see your parents tonight. Send the lawyers and I'll answer questions."

"Are you sure?"

"Yes—you go on to church and I'll call you when I'm done. They won't let you sit in, anyway. I'm innocent of any wrongdoing. And your lawyers are the best, right?" She beamed a trusting smile at him and he fell for it, slipping a protective arm around her shoulders.

"You are under the wing of Sanclaro." Though he ostensibly was speaking to her, he stared down the cops as he said it. They looked unimpressed.

"Ms. Davis—if you're finished?"

"Yes. Let's go."

She didn't wait for the lawyers but agreed to talk to Sanchez immediately.

"You need a sweater?" Sanchez asked her, tossing a file on the interview table. "The AC is pretty strong today."

"I'm okay for now," she answered.

"So, where were you last night?"

"With my lover."

Sanchez sat back slightly. She'd surprised him out of his fatherly mien. "I take it you don't mean your fiancé, Roman Sanclaro."

"No. I'm cheating on Roman. Are you going to tell on me?"

"How about you give me the name of this guy?"

"I don't care to tell you that, Detective."

"You don't, huh? What about when you need an alibi for where you were last night—will this prince of a guy quit hiding then?"

"Do I need an alibi for last night?"

"I don't know. Do you?"

Christine sighed, the lack of sleep settling on her shoulders like heavy snowflakes. Long enough and they'd bury her under their weight. "Look, Detective Sanchez, I know you're trying to do the right thing. I want that, too. I'm here voluntarily, aren't I?"

"You're here because my officers picked you up and we damn well both know it."

"But I haven't lawyered up, have I? They'll be here soon, though—so we should probably discuss what you really want to know."

He fell silent, waiting for her to say something. She knew this from theater. The long silence that prompts the guilty party to confess because she can't stand the shouting of her inner voices. Or the imagined *thump thump, thump thump* of the undying heartbeat of her victim under the floorboards. Except the police station was floored with tile. She smiled, amused at her train of thought.

"Something funny?" Sanchez looked irritated.

Score one for Christine—he'd broken the silence first.

"Just waiting for you to ask me questions."

"I already did—who were you with last night?"

"My lover, and then my friend, Hally Roberts."

"You'll say her name but not his."

"That's right. But you already know her name."

"We'll find out his, too."

"I doubt it."

"Why's that?"

"You wouldn't believe me if I told you."

"Try me."

"Okay, he's a semicorporeal being who lives under the opera house. Last night he took me to another realm, where we performed ritual sex magic to help restore his strength as a demigod." She reviewed it in her mind. "At least, I'm pretty sure that was the purpose of what we were doing. We didn't really discuss it in detail."

Sanchez made a note in the file, not looking at her. "Are you waiting for me to tell you how crazy that story is?"

"Yes, actually. I know how it sounds."

"And you've been down this road before, haven't you, Christy?"

"Christine."

"Excuse me?"

"I prefer Christine now. Or Ms. Davis would be fine."

"I have your records, Ms. Davis." He closed the file and tapped it with a blunt finger. "This wouldn't be the first time you've experienced mental and emotional difficulties."

The AC was cold, drilling into her stomach. She stared at the file, willing the dread away. The sight of those old papers, what they likely said about her, robbed her of her courage.

"You're a cutter. I understand that doesn't go away." Sanchez was trying to sound kind. Back to the fatherly approach. "Maybe the stress is making you cut again. Or you're purposely seeking out dangerous situations."

All the protesting she'd done in the past—no one had ever listened. That was the thing about people starting to think you were crazy. Everything you said sounded bad. Some of the old panic began to eat away at the edges of her newfound confidence. Christy the cutter was her crippled self. Christine didn't want to be her anymore.

"I'm not." But her voice wavered, ever so slightly, and Sanchez heard it.

"Maybe I should take you into protective custody, have you evaluated—for your own safety."

Asking for a sweater now would be a sign of weakness. *I'm not a cutter. I never was a cutter. A few little cuts and that was how my father punished me.* The tears pricked at her eyes and she fought them back.

Sanchez's face wore the fog of sympathy, but the truth of his canny maneuvering shone through. Sanchez thought this was the way to get to her. By making her feel crazy. Just as her dad had.

Words lie. But her gut knew the truth.

"Thanks, but I'm fine."

"If I think you're a danger to yourself or others, I can have you involuntarily committed."

She laughed, and it warmed her considerably. Now she rubbed her arms briskly. "If you read my file, you know I've been down that road before, Detective. Believe me, I know the rules. I'm also no longer a frightened and confused thirteen-year-old girl. You'd need a hell of a lot more than what you've got to do that."

"I can do a lot."

"Yes. But not that. You can arrest me, but you can't make me insane."

He leaned in, but she thought she saw a gleam of respect in his eyes. "Even if I don't arrest you, you'll be placed on administrative leave at the opera. The board feels there's enough suspicion to keep you away."

Her spirits sank. They thought she was a danger? "Why?" The question sounded plaintive.

"It's not unusual—and totally up to a private business to make that choice, regardless of the nature of the criminal investigation. You'll still be paid."

As if that was all that mattered. Still, she would find other ways to see the Master, other ways to support herself. It would be better, anyway, not to have any connection to her father. She could see that now. It was time to be truly free of him. No more half steps. The idea, though, pained her deeply. "Seems to me that if you were going to arrest me, you would have done it by now. Why bother with the psych stuff if you could just lock me up?"

Sanchez sighed heavily. "A woman's life is in danger. Do you understand that? Can't you find it in your heart to care about her— no matter how badly she treated you?"

"I thought Carla was doing better."

"Someone tried to kill her last night. Again."

Christine blinked. "At the hospital?"

"No, she was released yesterday and was at home."

"Wow. What happened? Is Charlie okay?"

"I can't tell you anything other than Mr. Donovan is fine. Now you tell me—where were you last night? And think very, very carefully about your answer."

5

Sanchez didn't arrest her. They went round and round for hours—without and then with the lawyers—getting nowhere. After a while, it became clear to Christine that Sanchez, while certain she knew something about what was going on, couldn't pin much on her. He didn't believe she'd been with another man the night before, but he did ask several times where she thought Roman had been. She honestly didn't know. She nearly asked why Sanchez wasn't interrogating *him*, but she suspected she knew the answer to that.

Especially after Sanchez cautioned her three times to be careful.

He thought she'd been with Roman—and that she'd helped him attack Carla. Twice. She saw the conviction in his eyes.

The same officers gave her a ride home in the afternoon. She left a voice mail for Roman, grateful that he hadn't answered his phone. She needed time to compose herself to face him and his father tonight. To build up her courage to do what she needed to do.

After she showered—she might forever associate the scent of Hally's sandalwood lotion with the sinking fear of being recommitted—and changed clothes, they were still sitting in their car out front. Oh well, let them follow her. She waved cheerfully, then slid into her car, bouncing on the hot seat. Putting the top down helped air it out from being closed up but felt kind of frivolous.

She drove to Trader Joe's. Sunday afternoon was *not* the time to shop, but she needed groceries. Plus it amused her that the cops had to deal with the chaos of the parking lot to keep an eye on her. It felt safe and normal to be amid the press of people, even the impatient ones, and the harried others with whiny children. This was how it ought to be for people. Living their lives, feeding their families.

Not relegated to being extinct shadow people, sacrificed for someone else's greed.

She'd been ignoring her phone, except to text Hally that all was fine.

Her father had called a number of times. No surprise there. She deleted the voice mails without listening. No doubt her father knew she'd been put on administrative leave. But there was no way in hell she was going home. And she still wasn't ready to tell him what she'd found out. So there was nothing to discuss.

When she returned to her apartment, Roman was waiting on her doorstep. The tension immediately crawled up her neck. He'd changed out of his church clothes and wore faded jeans and an open shirt. No doubt he'd bought the jeans that way, but he still looked younger, more like a guy her age. Except for his flat eyes, beady and without remorse, like a spider's. His dangerous mien.

He straightened up when she came up the stairs and gave her a rueful smile that did nothing to warm his eyes. "I missed you, so I came early."

"That's sweet of you." She pecked him on the cheek to avoid more of a kiss.

He took a couple of the grocery bags from her, giving an irritated look at the cheerful Reusable Bag! cartoons on them. "Let me help you," he said, and they both pretended this wasn't the first time he'd ever entered her apartment.

"Want a beer?" Christine held up the six-pack she'd bought. She tried not to fret about him coming into her apartment. Why the sudden change of heart? Did he suspect she was lying to him? "They're not cold, but they're air-conditioned-store cool."

"Yeah. Okay, thanks."

He sat in one of her faux Southwestern-antique bar stools, painted a garish orange she planned to change one of these weekends, and watched her put the groceries away, his eyes speculative. When she finished, she popped a beer for herself, leaned her elbows on the counter, and raised her eyebrows in silent question.

"I see the cops are sitting outside."

"Yeah. I guess I'm of sufficient interest that they want to see what I buy at Trader Joe's."

He snorted, then searched her face. She kept hers smooth, no cracks for him to crawl into. "They treat you okay? I hated to think of you being down there all alone."

"I'm fine. It wasn't too bad. I don't know anything, so that helps."

"You know something." When she straightened, he tilted his head, giving her that charming grin. "The lawyers said they asked about me. And that you talked to the cops before they got there. What did you tell them?"

The fine hairs prickled on her arms, but she played it cool. And stupid. "What would I say? You don't know anything. You're only involved in all of this because of dumb ol' me."

"Yeah." He shrugged, drinking his beer, his eyes on her. "Where did you go to pray last night?"

She started to say "huh?" but stopped at the flat look in his eyes. Hard-edged, full of venom.

"You didn't have your car, so where did you go? Are you seeing someone else?"

"No!" But she heard the lie in her own voice.

"Because I'll kill him, if you are. And then I'll make you sorry. Do you understand?"

"I'm not seeing anyone else."

He laughed, a hollow sound. "You sound oh so guilty. Tell me the truth. Confession is good for the soul."

Her sunny kitchen dimmed and exhaustion crept in, a headache throbbing in her temples. She rubbed one, aware of Roman's cruel smile. He rose and patted her on the ass on the way to the refrigerator. "Want another one, sweet girl?"

"I think you should go. I need to rest before dinner tonight."

"But we haven't finished talking. You're a terrible liar, you know. Makes me wonder whose blood you carry after all."

That remark chilled her further.

"What do you mean by that?"

"I think you know." He raised an eyebrow and leaned against the counter; elegant, confident. "You've been doing your research, haven't you? The merger of our two families will be quite profitable for us all. It's fated."

"I don't believe in fate." But her mouth was dry around the words, full of sticky cobwebs.

Roman popped the top on the beer and carelessly dropped the cap on the floor. "You don't have to believe anything. You just have to be a good girl and do what you're told. Are you being a good girl, Christy?" He helped himself to the bag of chips she'd planned to pack in her lunches. "I know what my fiancée told me—pillow talk, you know. You felt so guilty, confessing to me about your secret lover. Maybe he's the one who hurt the lovely Carla, whose only crime was to piss you off."

She stared at him aghast. He tossed the bag aside and, in a lightning-fast move, grabbed her by her wrists, wrestling them behind her and crushing her against the counter. He tried to kiss her, but she turned her face away, struggling to get loose, so he sank his teeth into the cord of muscle beneath her ear, grinding his erect cock against her tender mound.

Christine inhaled to scream and he spoke through his teeth. "Go ahead. Scream. The cops can't touch me and I can always punish you later. Believe me—I know how to do it in ways that won't show. You have belonged to the Sanclaros since you were born. Since before that—no matter what your stubborn father says. No one else will have you. I'll kill you first."

She stilled and he chuckled, licking where he'd bit her. "Just a little love bite, huh, sweet girl? Now tell me the truth."

"There's no one else." She tried to make it sound true.

He smiled and let her go. For a moment she thought she'd convinced him.

Then he slapped her, hard.

She clapped her hand to her cheek, helplessness and rage rising up, choking her. Roman studied her, filing away her reactions. "Have you read *Story of O*? A dirty slut like you would have, I'd think. In there they say you should never spank a girl a little bit, because she grows to enjoy it. No, beatings should be reserved to break her spirit. Otherwise you risk not having perfect obedience. That is what I require of you, Christine. If there *was* anyone else, you will never contact him again. You understand the consequences if you do?"

She nodded, still holding her flaming cheek, feeling shattered by it all. Maybe she wasn't strong enough to see this through.

"Good." He smiled and kissed her on the nose. "Now, go put on a pretty dress, a decent one that I bought you, and do something with your hair. You're coming with me now. Pack an overnight bag. It might be a late evening."

Stunned, she went to get dressed, grateful for a last reprieve of privacy. At least she'd managed to convince him. She was going to the Sanclaro compound.

"Oh, Christy?" Roman called from the other room. "Call your father and tell him about the engagement. He'll know what to do next."

6

They drove out to the Sanclaro compound without speaking. Of course, with Roman's techno music blaring at top volume, conversation wouldn't have been possible. He seemed in fine good spirits now. Now that he figured he'd won.

He'd made her change three times, clearly enjoying putting her through her paces, like he was training a dog—*sit, stay, roll over, beg*—until he was satisfied with the dress she chose. Long-sleeved, with matching ruffles at the wrists and high collar. With the black stockings he'd insisted on, he'd managed to make her look like a maiden aunt.

The cops followed behind, and Christine wondered what they made of her and all this.

Inside, she trembled.

So much for her warrior-priestess self. One slap and she crumpled in fear. She hated herself for it. She could no more stand up to Roman than she could to her father. Just the tone of voice Roman had used had turned her into a crumbly thirteen-year-old again. Nothing had really changed.

She tried to firm her resolve with the image of the Master—not his bear self, but the man she'd made love with—speared through with the Sanclaro silver cross . . . even though it filled her with a paralyzing dread.

A tear escaped and ran down her cheek. Roman saw it and

turned off the stereo. Her ears rang in the abrupt silence. He sighed and reached over to take her hand, lacing his fingers with hers.

"Don't cry, sweet girl. You'll see that this is all for your own good. This will be the salvation of your immortal soul."

"My soul?" she echoed blankly. The scrolled, wrought-iron bars of the Sanclaro gates caught the sunset light, the silver crucifix gleaming with red highlights, as if painted with blood.

"Resist the devil and he will flee from you," Roman intoned. "You have been wandering in the wilderness, without guidance, without your real family. Right now you feel confused, but soon you'll see that all we've done, all we're doing, is because we love you."

Her father had said that—that he wanted her in his sole custody because it would be best for her. Her mother's itinerant lifestyle and liberal/media-elite ideas would only corrupt Christy's thinking. With a pang, she missed her mother, needed to talk to her. Her mother would know what to do. Had her mother known about the Sanclaros and whatever agreement they had with her father? It would explain so many things.

"You don't really believe in demons, do you?" she tendered.

Roman cast her a sideways look. The grand house loomed ahead, ablaze with light, music wafting on the evening breeze.

He squeezed her hand and let go, patting it. "The Sanclaro family is old and has many secrets. We don't discuss this in public, but we have things to teach you. It's time for you to reach your destiny—under my loving and protective guidance."

He parked the car in front of the wide, curving staircase that led up to the hacienda doors, the police unit crunching on the gravel as it pulled up behind them. "Wait here—I'm going to talk to the cops about you, see if we can stand for your good behavior. Then I'll escort you inside."

She waited, tense, her thoughts working furiously. Above, the hills rolled up to the pinking sky, a flare of copper catching the light. Peering at it, she felt as if she knew that shape and color. It reminded her of the opera house. But could that be? She'd still never driven herself here, so she wasn't totally clear exactly where the Sanclaro estate sat in relation to the city. It was a long, looping drive, around hills and through a canyon, and—yes, they absolutely could be in the valley below the opera house, on the sunset side.

And the music she'd thought came from the hacienda instead floated down from above. Someone rehearsing a duet—the light and dark voices winding together, now clear, now torn apart by an errant breeze.

Geologically speaking, we're not that far from there.

The roads tended to follow the valleys, making big loops around the high ridges. That was the opera house, from the other side.

The car door popped open, startling her. "Come on," Roman grunted, taking her arm and nearly pulling her out of the car. The police officers waited nearby, deliberately relaxed smiles on their faces.

"Do you need assistance, Ms. Davis?" one inquired, with a significant glance at Roman's grip on her arm.

"She's fine," Roman snapped. "As you've already been told."

"We'd prefer to hear it from Ms. Davis, if you don't mind," the other officer told him, steel behind the smile.

She could ask for their help, Christine realized. Roman would be angry, but the cops would protect her. Protective custody, Sanchez had suggested. Now she wondered if he'd suspected this. She could escape this way—run from the Sanclaros *and* her father. Which would mean abandoning the trapped spirit under the opera house, too.

"Perhaps we should speak with Ms. Davis alone," the first cop suggested. "Over here, Ms. Davis?"

Reluctantly, but with a fierce warning glare, Roman released her arm, and Christine went with the cops, walking a short distance with them, as if out for a summer stroll.

"Are you being coerced or abused, Ms. Davis?" The one who'd asked if she required assistance cut to the chase.

If she said yes now, they'd take her back to her apartment—and she might never discover what the Sanclaros knew about the Master. It would be the coward's way out.

"No, I'm fine." They looked at her dubiously, and she knew she sounded like the girl who gave in to her father, who wore Roman's cursed ring. *Stop being weak*, she ordered herself. *Overcome it.* "I appreciate your looking out for me, but I'm in no danger." She really hoped that was true.

The first one handed her his card. "You have your cell phone?

Good. We'll be right out here in front. If you're the least bit worried or afraid, call or text my cell. Text 911 to me and we'll come right in."

"Trust your instincts," the second cop urged her. "There's no shame in asking for help."

"Thank you." The emotions of the past few days threatened to swamp her with these two officers so earnestly concerned for her safety. They watched as she programmed the number into her phone. "I'll call if I need you."

"Can I be of assistance, Officers?" Domingo Sanclaro jogged down the hacienda steps, looking like Ricardo Montalbán in his white suit.

"Mr. Sanclaro." The first officer tipped his cap. "We're here to see to Ms. Davis's continued well-being."

He sized them up, dark eyes glittering with ill-concealed malevolence. "Do you impugn the reputation of my family?"

"No, sir. Just following orders, sir. We were instructed not to let Ms. Davis here out of our sight, but your son informs us that we're not welcome inside the house."

"My son is correct. Unless you have a search warrant, you must leave the grounds immediately."

"Is that what you want, Ms. Davis? It's not too late to come with us." The cop ignored the rage suffusing the elder Sanclaro's face.

"Thank you, yes. I'll be in touch." She tucked her phone into her pocket, glad the granny dress at least offered that.

The police officers turned back down the drive while the three of them watched, Christine flanked by the Sanclaro men. In the low heels Roman had chosen for her, she felt short and vulnerable. Part of her wanted to run shrieking after the cops to save her. The other part—a confident part that had survived after all—made her stay.

"Well, Christy." Domingo Sanclaro looked her up and down. "It's always a pleasure to have you here. Welcome to your new home. It's good that you understand."

Roman took her hand and tucked it possessively in the crook of his arm, then slipped her phone out of her pocket and put it in his own. "She does. As you predicted, your arguments were most persuasive—she's ready to take her place in our family."

Domingo smiled, his glittering teeth white. He leaned in and kissed her on the cheek, right on the bruise his son had put there.

"Of course they were. My future daughter-in-law is no fool. Now come along; dinner is ready and Reina will be displeased if we continue to linger."

They all sat around an enormous wooden table that seemed straight out of the Spanish Inquisition. The dining room, lined with oil portraits of the illustrious Sanclaro ancestors, was full of shadows. A stern-faced woman stared down at Christine from one, the opal ring prominently displayed in the center of the painting. The reproduction of the twins in the museum had looked richer; in real life the old oils had cracked in the desert heat. It probably should have been properly archived. They seemed to stare back at her as she ate, Angelia and Seraphina, with their father's Castilian nose and the broad, flat cheekbones of their mother.

They had grown up without her temporizing influence, connected to their crippled god as their priestess mother had been put under the cruel and ruthless hand of their conquistador father. Perhaps he had loved his daughters, the extension of his empire. But the cold expressions on their faces belied that hope. They sat, side by side on an austere pew, in black dresses like nuns, their hands overlapping to show the twin opal rings. Looking at them, Christine couldn't remember which was which.

Domingo sat at the head of the table, of course, with Roman at his right and his wife at his left. Christine sat next to Roman with Angelia across from her, wearing a demure white cotton dress. With her long, soft black hair held back by a pearl headband, she seemed to be an angel indeed. The rest of the long table stretched down at least twenty more place settings.

Just an intimate family dinner at the Sanclaros.

They ate chicken mole and fresh guacamole, the other two women chattering happily about the upcoming wedding and other family. They seemed determined to set Christine at ease, complimenting her hair and her dress, and telling charming stories about Reina's nieces and nephews.

Christine nodded and smiled, acting the role Roman and his father had assigned her, while she turned over the family history in her mind. Some detail of the wedding ceremony niggled at her, combined with what Hally had explained about circles and bindings. Then she knew the right question to ask.

"How can the wedding be here?" she asked. Reina closed her mouth primly, and Christine realized she'd interrupted a story about the most precious niece's First Communion in the gazebo, where Roman and Christine would be married. "Shouldn't we be married in a church, under the eyes of God—on consecrated soil?"

Domingo gave her a long look. "Our land is already consecrated. All of Sanclaro property has been blessed and dedicated to the One True God."

"Oh." And wasn't that something. "How did that happen?"

Roman frowned at her, shaking his head slightly, and she shrank back, not having to fake a ripple of fear.

"The Sanclaros owe their fortune and prosperity to God," Angelia recited, sounding far younger than seventeen. The puppyish way she peered hopefully at Domingo for approval gave Christine a tremor of revulsion. Too familiar. "Right, Daddy?"

He didn't answer his daughter and she sat back in her chair, wilting like a flower without water. Instead he addressed Christine. "Never doubt that God stands behind the Sanclaros. We will do whatever it takes to maintain the purity of the family. Now, let us retire to the chapel for prayer."

The prayers were interminable. They all knelt on hard stone that came from a dismantled monastery, she was informed. That should have been interesting. If the Sanclaro ancestors had been part of trapping the Master, then any kind of religious artifact could do it. Hally had said to look for circles or stars. Or stones set at four points of a circle, like she'd drawn to protect Christine in the cave.

But these stones were only gray and hard, the little chapel a windowless room, barren of anything but a plain wooden cross, the height of a man, hanging on the blank wall.

Domingo led them in reciting the same few phrases over and over, until the Our Fathers and Hail Marys ground into her brain, numbing her into a trance. Twice she fell asleep, and Reina viciously pinched her arm to wake her. Roman glared at her in warning from the men's side of the small chapel.

Finally, Angelia was tasked to show Christine to her room. It was a pretty room, with glass-paned doors that opened onto a balcony overlooking the front drive. Those doors, however, were closed and bolted. So much for fresh air.

"Am I a prisoner?" Christine asked, driven by exhaustion into speaking the thought aloud.

Angelia closed the bedroom door and leaned against it, pulling off her pearl headband and shaking out the soft sweep of black hair. "Pretty much. It really depends—how stupid are you?"

7

"Excuse me?" Christine gaped at the sharp-eyed girl, who no longer looked docile at all.

Angelia sighed. "Maybe you *are* that stupid. Never mind."

Christine held up a hand, realizing as she did so that it was Hally's gesture. "Give me a minute to catch up." Was this some new gambit of Roman's? Get his sister to work on her next? "Why don't you tell me what you're talking about, Angelia?"

"Call me Angie. Just not in front of the family. I'll help you if you'll help me. But we have to pinky swear or something. I'm trusting you, here."

"Okay, what shall we swear on?"

"Tell me a secret. That way we'll be even."

Trust your gut. "I'm only pretending to be engaged to Roman. I won't marry him, even if I have to kill myself to prevent it."

Angie grinned and sat on the white coverlet of the massive four-poster bed, bouncing happily. "I knew you couldn't be that stupid. Careful what you promise, though. It could come to that."

Her scalp prickled. "How? It's the twenty-first century. They can't force me to say vows or sign contracts."

The other girl sobered, a haunted look dimming her vivacious eyes. "You have no idea. The Sanclaros always get their way. Or they'll make you wish you hadn't crossed them."

Christine sat next to her. "Are you okay?"

"Hells to the no. But that's where you come in. They need one of us. I thought maybe when they finally got you here, they'd let me have my own life, but they need a backup. I was willing to let you take the fall for my freedom—sorry about that, survival of the fittest and all—but now we might as well help each other."

"I think you need to back up and explain. I have no idea what you're talking about."

"Don't you know *anything*?"

"Let's pretend I don't."

Angie flopped back onto the bed with an exasperated sigh and stared at the canopy. "Okay, you know we're cousins, right?"

"I suspected." More than suspected, but hearing it from this snarky teen rocked through her, pricking open the anger she carried. *Damn her father.*

"So, according to family tradition, there's always supposed to be a direct descendant of the first Angelia in charge of the family fortunes. Right now that means you or me, baby. I'm too young still and they don't dare give you the reins until Roman has you on a short leash." Angie snickered at her choice of words.

"But there's not a woman in charge now."

"Exactly!" Angie popped up and pointed at Christine. "My icon of a father scoffed at superstition and put himself in charge when Great-Grandmother died. I was just a baby, but I've read the books. Guess what's happened to the vaunted Sanclaro fortune since then?" She turned a thumb down and made a long, whistling noise that ended with a loud and unpleasant raspberry.

"I had no idea."

Angie shrugged. "I'm sure a smart financial person could dig it out if you need proof. It's not common knowledge, as you can imagine."

"How do you know about it?"

"I live here, don't I? They think I don't listen, but I do. It's always been the plan for you to marry Roman—in case you didn't know—but something's gotten in the way. They did something huge to get you here now. Dad is getting desperate. I haven't been able to ferret out why, but he's convinced that getting you on board will stop whatever shit is about to hit the fan."

"Why not put you on the paperwork under his guardianship?"

" 'Cuz then I'd have to marry my brother—as my father's manly pride demands—and even the Sanclaros can't pull off that shit in this day and age."

"So this is all about family superstition?"

Angie paced over to the window, stared out at the rising moon, then turned around, her fingers knotted together. "Way weirder than that."

The angel hairs lifted on the back of Christine's neck. This was it. What she'd hoped to find. "Tell me."

Angie shook her head slowly from side to side. "It's one of those you-gotta-see-it-to-believe-it things."

"Okay, then show me."

"Doing this is very risky for me. You're not supposed to know any of this until after the wedding. First you have to promise to help me escape."

"But you're a minor."

"Tell me about it." Angie held out a hand, looking into her memory and ticking points off on her fingers. "I need you to get me a cell phone and guarantee it for me. I have money I'll give you—don't worry. What I don't have is a credit card. If you'll co-sign one and let me use your address, as soon as I have the cred, I'll transfer it to me. Meanwhile, I'll give you cash for that, too. I have a fake ID worked out—as an adult, thank you very much—but I need a ride to pick it up from the guy, since I don't have a driver's license, much less access to a vehicle. I'll worry about shoring up the rest of my papers later, after—"

"Whoa, wait, wait, wait." Christine held up her hands to stop the torrent of instructions. "You're faking your identity?"

"You *have* met my family, right?" Angie raised her eyebrows and spoke slowly, as if Christine might not properly understand English. "They don't let people go. If I'm going to escape, I have to disappear completely and forever."

"And you've already figured out all the logistics?"

"Thank the Holy Mother for the Internet, huh? I might be home-schooled, but the state still requires a certain level of socialization. My mother has no idea how easy it is to circumvent parental controls."

"I'm impressed."

Angie waved a hand at her. "No, if you'd grown up with a tyrant of a father, you'd have figured this out, too. We do what we have to do, right?"

Right. "Okay. You have a deal. I'll help you." She stuck out her hand and Angie, with an impatient shake of her head, folded her fingers over and gave her a fist bump.

"Girl power!" Angie grinned, then produced Christine's phone. "Voilà."

"How did you get that?"

"I've been taking my brother's stuff for years. He's oblivious. But he'll probably come looking for it in my room, so be ready to call whoever to come get you if we get caught."

"What about you?"

"I'd appreciate it if you'd figure out a way to rescue me as soon as possible." She flashed Christine a gamine grin, but the face behind it was haunted with dark foreboding.

The big house loomed quiet, with sconces along the floor showing their way. Angie led them down the grand stairwell to the entryway, then farther, the way they'd gone to the family chapel.

The chapel sat at the end of a corridor, the waxed Saltillo tile reflecting the foot-level lights. A sculpture stood outside the closed doors, a female avenging angel with a stern face, naked breasts, and carrying a sword. When Christine had seen it earlier, it seemed to be an odd icon for an ostensibly Christian place of worship—almost pagan. The twisted iron handles were looped with a length of chain and a padlock. But why, with nothing of value inside?

With an impish smile, Angie produced a ring of keys, trying several before the lock gave. She held a finger over her lips, commanding silence until they were inside, with the doors closed.

"How—?"

"I've been collecting extra keys for years. My mother keeps nine copies of every damn thing. I figured I'd never know when one would come in handy. And see?"

"Okay, what next?"

"Secret passageway!"

"Really?" Christine surveyed the barren room. "Where?"

Angie deflated slightly. "Well, I'm not exactly sure how to find it. I've been blindfolded every time. I tried to spy on my father and Roman once, when I was eight. Boy, did I get a beating for that."

"A beating? You mean a spanking?"

Angie gathered her hair into a tail and tied it into a knot at the nape of her neck. "I mean a beating so bad I couldn't get out of bed for a week."

"Jesus."

"Jesus had nothing to do with it. Whatever god it is my father prays to in here, he has no love in his heart." Angie's voice cracked, bitterly sharp as broken glass. "That's the day I decided to leave. Ten years ago. Freedom will be sweet. Now help me look."

She was wrong, Christine thought. He wasn't an unloving god. Just an unwilling one.

Angie knew the general location and thought the trigger must be on the men's side. Remembering how sternly they'd all told her never to stray from the women's side, Christine was inclined to agree. They searched the floor, running their fingers along the cracks, then the stone risers that led up to the wall holding the wooden cross.

In her pocket, Christine's phone vibrated with a text message.

Where are you?

"Shit!" Christine cursed softly. "Roman knows I have my phone."

"No, he just knows he doesn't have it," Angie pointed out with calm reason. "Your room is locked, as if you're inside, but he'll be looking for me. I have to lock you in here, and I'll pretend to be praying outside. I'll come back later, once it's safe, okay?"

"What if I get in—what do I look for?"

Angie laughed without mirth. "You'll know it when you see it. Then if you get me my secret cell phone, we can discuss as much as you like!"

"Thank you, Angie."

"No—thank *you*. Believe me, I know helping me won't be easy. I'm glad to pay it forward a little."

The chain rattled in the iron bars of the doors, sealing her in. Without Angie's spunky presence the narrow chapel seemed to press in on her. With only the floor sconces and a recessed ceiling light shining on the cross, the stark room felt dim and forbidding. At least this cross wasn't the sharp, silver spear of her vision—or the one on the gates. Odd, actually, that it wasn't, since the Sanclaros seemed to cling so fiercely to that symbol. Several replicas of it graced the house above.

So, why this simple monk's cross here?

Stepping carefully, because it felt like a bit of sacrilege, she climbed the prayer steps and touched the rough, red-black wood. A thrill of revulsion went through her as she imagined for a moment that it had been stained with blood. She nearly yanked her hands back but controlled her fear. When she pushed, nothing happened. So she pulled.

And with a low, grating sound—much like the entryways to the Master's domain—the entire wall moved, pivoting and opening to a short hallway, and a brilliantly lit alcove beyond.

She stepped over the threshold and found a handle to pull the door closed behind her, just in case Roman checked the chapel, despite the chained doors and Angie's likely interference.

The passageway was narrow enough that she trailed both hands along the walls as she walked toward the light. Halfway down, her fingers met empty air on both sides. Additional hallways led off in other directions—all pitch black. She continued toward the lighted room. Stopping at the doorway, she surveyed the circular alcove. A spotlight, recessed into the high ceiling, illuminated the room. In the center, a pedestal was affixed with a silver dagger, like the old sword in the stone. Three silver crucifixes—the Sanclaro cross— hung on the walls, to the sides and directly opposite the door, each with a different stone inset where the arms intersected.

The floor, inlaid with an intricate mosaic, echoed the pattern. A solid border outlined the circle, with silver crosses below the ones on the walls, reflections in a lake of tiles. One stretched out from the doorway, too, presumably echoing the one over the door. The long legs of the crosses stretched to the central pedestal, as if pinning it in place.

In between the mosaic crosses were animals—a bear, like the one on her stone, along with several others. Instead of their usual depictions, in movement, these lay quiet and still. Everything in the room pointed toward the pedestal. That was the center of it all, and she had to see what was there.

Wary but seeing no way around it, she stepped inside the circle.

If she had expected the room to shake or arrows to fly out of the walls or lightning to strike, the result was disappointing. Like walking on any other floor, into any other room. Except for the dread that ran down her spine and the persistent smell of blood—a dusty, metallic trickle.

She crept up to the pedestal, steeling herself against what she might see. The pedestal seemed to be a pillar of red sandstone, the silver dagger buried nearly to the hilt. In between the two lay a withered paw. Bits of white and golden fur had fallen away, barely clinging to threads of ancient sinew here and there, but the other parts were clean. Claws. Shards of bone.

Revulsion crawled through her. She knew who had done this. She had been there, in a way.

The ancient priestess, desperate to save some ghost of her people, had created this altar, anchoring her god and the restless spirits of the slaughtered tribe here. She could taste the memory in her vision. The fields full of blood, the bear spirit breaking with the loss of the people who'd called him Master.

Preserving what she could, perhaps to restore them someday.

But the priestess had died in childbirth, hadn't she? Unable to teach her daughters what they needed to know. Inadvertently giving them the power over a harnessed god that kept the grass unnaturally green and the family fortunes rich.

As long as one of her daughters held the bear's leash.

Well, if her hand could hold him there, then she should be able to break the circle.

The other option—suicide—would also work, but that would require Angie's death, too. At this point, Christine felt comfortable shedding her mortal body, if it meant she could be with the Master forever, but Angie was young. And sane, still.

She grasped the knife, ready to pull it free. She pulled, yanking with all her strength. But unlike the vision or the ritual, here she seemed to lack the power.

Disrupt the circle, Hally had said. *See if you can find some sort of encircling marks and break the borders. Remove the guardian stones. Anything like that.*

Ruefully, Christine examined the room. She'd found the damn circle, all right—circles within circles—but they could hardly be broken. She fingered one of the silver crosses on the wall. It seemed to be embedded there, deeply sunk into the stone of the walls. The chamber might as well be made of poured cement.

Likewise the mosaic floor. She knelt, digging her fingernails between the tiles, the opal flashing with obscene splendor on her hand. Her nails splintered and her fingertips snagged on the sharp edges, blood smearing on the glassy colors. Aware that she was breathing frantically now, she scrabbled around, a desperate crab searching for some way to disrupt this circle of metal, stone, and glass.

She stilled, listening. Was that the sound of voices, shouting in the distance? Working faster, she searched around the bottom of the crystal dome, feeling for a seam. A brass ring—or solid gold— seemed to hold the entire assembly in place.

It wasn't made to be breached. It was made to last forever, to bind and contain a god and the combined power of his people.

Then her fingers slipped into a groove, her left hand finding a place that seemed made for it, fingertips and palm fitting into the side of the carved pillar. She peered at it, temporarily perplexed by the round divot in the center. With a burst of realization, she rotated the ring so the egg-shaped opal faced in—like a key in a lock.

Sure enough, a similar handprint showed on the other side. Also for a left hand, with a place for a matching ring. Made for twins.

But where was the other ring?

Voices cut into her reflection, sending her pulse racing. Roman and his father, arguing bitterly from the other side of the chapel wall down the hall. Stone grated, and she knew she was out of time.

So close. So very close to fail so utterly.

But she couldn't let them find her here.

She ran back down the hall, every instinct shrieking against going toward them, which she ruthlessly overruled. So she turned on instinct down one dark alley. With her shoes in one hand, she ran silently, listening to their voices escalate as the door allowed them in.

Then she stopped, pressing herself flat against the stone wall, grateful for the utter darkness.

First Domingo, then Roman strode past the opening. Straight into the alcove.

"See?" Roman sounded relieved. "No one has been in here. She probably walked out and is back in town by now. She can't affect anything with only the one ring anyway."

"You had better hope she doesn't find the Angel's Hand," Domingo Sanclaro snarled, all urbane gentleman gone from his voice.

"You're the one who let that fucking Carla steal and hide it."

"She's not exactly in a position to give it to anyone, is she?" Domingo's voice oozed sarcasm.

"That's not my fault." Roman sounded petulant, repressed anger coming out on a whine.

"You need to learn damage control—starting with your fiancée. A man who can't control his woman is no man at all. I'll handle Carla. Go talk to the cops—tell them you two had a fight and she might be hysterical. Hint that she's unstable and you're worried about her. She could be anywhere, and who knows what wild tales she's spreading."

Christine didn't dare linger a moment longer. Creeping on all fours along the floor, in case of a sudden drop, she felt her way, being as quiet and speedy as possible. Her skin crawled with the anticipation that the lights would flick on, exposing her in all her subterfuge.

She forced herself to keep going, praying that she wouldn't end up trapped or, worse, fall into some dank hole and slowly die with broken bones. She had to see this through, to rescue Angie and to make right what had gone so wrong. To somehow turn the horrible events of the past into something good. She wasn't crazy. All of this was.

She needed to survive this, too.

A warm breath seemed to flow over her, a wordless song soothing and guiding her. The scent of blood faded. The dread dropped from her shoulders, replaced with the sweet promise of love and home.

It reminded her of a friend she'd had, back in early high school. They'd walked to her friend's house when school had closed early for the day due to a sudden, intense snowstorm. Her driver hadn't been able to get through the traffic and her feet had been cold and wet, so she'd gone to her friend's place to warm up and wait for the car.

The brownstone hadn't been much—narrow, and the furnishings weren't great—but her friend's dad had met them at the door, setting their wet things out to dry. He'd offered them hot tea and he'd made cookies by slicing some premade dough from the freezer and sticking it on a pan. She and her friend had sat at the breakfast counter while her friend's dad asked about their day and they griped together about the city's inferior plowing plan.

Then her friend's mom made it home and she kissed her husband, teasing him about the freezer cookies, rolling her eyes behind his back. But she ate one anyway, then snuck another. They invited Christine to stay for dinner, but by that time her driver had made it through the slowly clearing roads and she had to leave.

She never forgot the smell of those cookies, though. And she always thought that maybe that was what love smelled like.

For an eternity she crawled along, until the floor grew damp under her hands, then soggy, then downright wet. She splashed through the water, finally standing when it grew too deep to crawl. Slogging through the water, she made out a candle glow ahead, at first so faint she thought her light-starved eyes imagined it. But no, the whispered song grew also, weaving around her, welcoming her.

Then shadows moved and hands touched her skin, drawing her along, steadying her. Reassured, she let them lead her until she saw her way clear. They left her, whispering back into the shadows they were born of. And she stepped out of the water onto the shore of the creek that emerged from Sanclaro land.

She was free.

She stood there, wet and muddy, shivering with reaction. At least now she knew what she needed to do. Find the Angel's Hand and finally restore the Master to his rightful place, and let the ghosts of her ancestors move on. How she would do any of this, she didn't know.

She just knew she had to.

Pulling out her cell phone, she pressed the number for the cops waiting for her, her guardian angels.

And, while she waited for them to pick her up, she finally called her father.

Crescendo

1

The sound of banging on her front door woke Christine from a dead sleep.

Clad in her purple unicorn pajamas, she checked the time: 7 a.m., so she'd been asleep for four hours. She shoved Star's raggedy self out of sight under the covers and blearily made her way to the door.

That demanding knock undoubtedly belonged to her father. When she'd awakened him with her phone call, he'd answered with an immediate "What's wrong?" She rarely caught him off guard, so his uncalculated concern had been exactly the right way for him to respond.

So much so that she'd burst into tears, releasing all the pent-up fear and strain, to her utter shame and embarrassment. Never much for displays of emotion in general, much less on the phone, her father had simply told her to cry herself out and that he was getting on a plane, no matter what she wanted.

She hadn't even argued.

"No more running," she muttered to herself, pasting a bright smile on her face and yanking open the door. "Good morning, gentlemen!"

Carlton Davis stood at the top of the narrow stairs, flanked by the two officers who'd been kind enough to pick her up out on the road the previous night and bring her home. They hadn't asked questions or commented on her tears—except to ask if she needed to go to the hospital, which she'd refused—for which she'd been grateful.

They did tell her what time Detective Sanchez expected to meet with her. Fair enough.

All three men looked irritated, with her father taking first prize. "Christy, dammit—"

"Ms. Davis," one of the officers cut in, "this man says he's your father and wants admittance to your apartment. Do you wish to let him in?"

A blood rage suffused her father's face. It might have made her a small person, but she enjoyed the moment. *The Santa Fe cops don't care who you are, Daddy.* She decided to play the protective-custody thing for all it was worth. If she was going to confront her father, she wanted him off balance and both of them on neutral ground. Just because he'd been nice when she'd called the previous night didn't erase all past history.

"Actually, I would be more comfortable meeting in public. How about the Starbucks on the Plaza in fifteen minutes? I imagine you guys wouldn't mind getting out of the patrol car and having some caffeine, either."

"Not acceptable!" Her father tried to push in the door and was astonished when the officers stopped him. "You dare—!" he sputtered.

"We're doing our best to protect your daughter, sir, and to oversee her status. The department considers her a flight risk. We'd prefer to keep a public eye on her also." The young Hispanic officer gave her a wink on the side away from her father. "It's your choice whether to meet with her, but that sounds like your best avenue."

He didn't like it but finally agreed. To be sure, Christine bolted her door while she quickly dressed. Her father wasn't outside, but her ever-present guardians were, standing outside the patrol car, enjoying the warm morning sunshine.

"Thanks guys," she called out. "Don't you ever go off shift? You've been up all night."

"We'll switch off once we escort you to see Sanchez at eleven. Until then, we're to stick with you."

She lingered a moment, fiddling with her car keys. They weren't exactly her friends, but they weren't the enemy, either. "I don't suppose you've seen any sign of the Sanclaros?"

They exchanged looks. "We couldn't speak to that, but certain suspicious vehicles did visit this area. They continued on after noting the presence of the patrol unit." The report sounded formal, coming from the genial cop who'd winked at her—the general facts anyone might read in the public record.

"Thanks," she repeated. "Coffee's on me."

"Make it less than five dollars' worth and you're on."

Her father waited at a table, a coffee and oatmeal in front of him, cellophane packets of fruit and nuts unopened. He glowered when she waved, then drummed his fingers impatiently when she took cups out to the cops.

"Okay, missy." He folded his hands on the table when she sat. "You've played your games long enough. Why did you force me to come here?"

"Here meaning Starbucks, right? Because I didn't force you to come to Santa Fe—you offered."

"You know exactly what I mean—treating me like a stranger who can't be allowed in your home."

She shrugged and took a bite out of the pink Cake Pop she'd bought herself for breakfast, savoring the sweetness. "I didn't feel like being yelled at this morning, and even you won't make too much of a scene in public."

He sat back, his jaw clenched, then took a deep drink of his coffee and used the cup to gesture at her. "What the hell are you eating? That's hardly a healthy breakfast."

"It's nummy." She grinned at him, hoping her teeth were covered in bright pink sprinkles. "How come we never had cookies?"

"Oh, I see." Her father nodded knowingly, and then spoiled it by frowning at the ragged guy shuffling past selling sage bundles. "You're playing the poor little rich girl now. You had everything anyone could desire, but Daddy didn't love you. I call bullshit."

"Do you?"

"What—love you? Of course I love you. You're my daughter, my only child, my heir. Why else would I have gone to such lengths to make sure you stayed by my side?"

She cocked her head, sucking off the last of the frosting from the stick. "I think there are lots of reasons to want to control people, and not many of them have anything to do with love."

He shook his head, an old dog shooing away flies. "I don't have time for your shit, Christy."

"Then make time." She said it crisply, as he would have—and took satisfaction when he acknowledged the point.

"Well, look who's grown up." He spoke without irony. With grudging respect, even. It was enough to make her realize she wasn't ready to hear what he knew about the Sanclaro connection. They had other business to get out of the way first.

"I hated you for a long time, for what you did to me."

"Perfectly reasonable attitude." He thumbed open the oatmeal, tried it, and made a face. "I'm supposed to be eating this for my heart. I tried to tell the doc I don't have one."

She folded her arms and glared at him.

"What do you want here—an apology?" He stabbed the spoon at the table, breaking it. "I apologize! Does that change anything? It doesn't bring your mother back. It doesn't make me a better father or even a decent man. It doesn't change a damn thing."

"It changes something for me."

"Does it? Then have my apology—I don't expect your forgiveness. I did the rehab, the counseling. Everything I could do. I tried to make it up to you, but I did a shit job of that, too."

"This is a good start."

"Is it? Good. What's next on the agenda?" Back to business immediately. She felt a surge of affection for him, with all his flaws and difficult ways.

"Let's talk about the Sanclaros."

He eyed her and sat back, wiping his mouth with the flimsy paper napkin. "Is this about your supposed engagement to Roman Sanclaro?"

She should have known he'd find out without her telling him. She held up her left hand, where the opal glittered. "This is the engagement ring. Anything to say about it?"

Davis shrugged, nonchalant, but she knew him better than that. Tension rode his shoulders. "Doesn't surprise me that he tried. Sanclaros always were snakes in their dealings. What does surprise me is that you agreed to marry the boy in the first place. Doesn't sound like you. Your mother, at least, taught you to be smarter than that."

"I thought you counted Domingo as a friend."

He made a rude noise. "Of course not."

"They visited all the time."

"Keep your friends close and your enemies closer." He sipped his coffee. "That, however, does not mean marry the bastards."

"Are the Sanclaros your enemies?" She pressed the issue, needing to know where he stood in all of it.

He narrowed his eyes. "What did they tell you?"

"It's what I found out on my own. Was Angelia Sanclaro your mother—my grandmother?"

Her father blew out a long breath and scrubbed his hands through his thinning hair. "Your mother didn't want you to know."

"She knows, then."

He nodded, popped the top off his coffee, and added another sugar packet. "I'd say she'd hate me for telling you this, but she already does. You want the full truth?"

Part of her wanted to stand up and walk out. Her new self, Christine, wouldn't let her. Not trusting her voice, she nodded.

"You got it right—though how you found out, I don't know. I didn't know about it until after you were born. You know how the family always acted like my mother's name couldn't be spoken? My father was never right. Heartbreak, they all said. Growing up, I learned not to ask."

She hadn't expected to feel sympathy for him, her blustery father. But she'd never thought about the little boy he'd been. How cold his childhood must have been.

"Only after you were born and Sanclaro showed up with the documents did we both find out the truth about our pasts."

"Both?" she echoed.

"You know that foundation that raised your mother? Sanclaro funded it. They gathered up all the Sanclaro by-blows and kept track of them. They practically threw us together. Your mother called it cross-breeding when she found out." He grimaced, shaking his head. "She was mighty pissed."

"Wow. I can just imagine." The memories of their angry shouting matches reverberated in her memory.

"She made me promise not to tell you." Carlton Davis held her gaze. "I wanted to, but she hated the Sanclaros. She felt you were better off not knowing. Especially when Domingo first proposed the engagement. I'm breaking that promise now."

She nodded, a knot in her throat. "But we're not . . . engaged by the families, are we?"

"Don't be an idiot!" Her father reined himself in, wiping the words from the air. "This isn't a feudal society. You're not chattel, are you?"

She smiled weakly. "You always joked about it . . ."

He barked out a laugh. "That Sanclaro is a tenacious bastard. I wasn't above stringing him along. I figured if we teased you enough, you'd be contrary and go the other direction."

"So you never wanted me to marry Roman?"

"You think I want to hand away legal rights to what I've built?"

Ah yes. Always back to the money.

Then he did surprise her. "Besides, he's not good enough for you."

"How do you know?"

"How do I know?" He laughed and pointed at her. "Because I know you. And you want more out of life than marriage to some punk-ass junior exec who'll expect you to stay in the kitchen and pop out babies. I might not have given you cookies, but I did raise you better than that."

He had, she realized. Despite everything, he had at least given her that.

"You're right. I never wanted to marry him."

"But you're wearing that ring around. I'm guessing it's not to impress your girlfriends."

"Safest place to keep it. Didn't want to start an incident over a family heirloom."

"Heh." Her father wiped his mouth with the paper napkin. "You're playing him. He has something you want. Not stuff, because you never did care much about that. Information. Something to do with these attacks you're hip deep in."

She gazed at him, scrambling to assemble her thoughts. How had she forgotten how quickly he, the master wheeler-dealer, saw through the ins and outs of a situation? But he couldn't have guessed it all. The truth was too strange.

He laughed. "Don't act so astonished. Your old man's no fool."

"Why do you think the Sanclaros want me to marry Roman so badly?"

"Three things." He held up beefy fingers and ticked them off. "The opera house and land is part of a trust. I checked into it after Domingo first darkened my doorstep. Maybe it was guilt or whatever, but my mother gave it to me via the trust, and it goes to my direct descendants and so on.

"Second, Domingo is superstitious as all hell. There's apparently some family tradition about having a woman of so much blood at the helm of the business or it's bad luck, business won't be good and so forth."

"But does that make any sense?" She asked it carefully. Her father was a practical man. Would he believe . . . ?

"Hell no. It makes no sense at all! That's point number three: the Sanclaros are crazier than coots. All that inbreeding. Insanity runs thick in that family." He didn't meet her gaze. "That's why I . . . might have overreacted some, when you had your *troubles*. I was afraid you'd inherited that crazy gene. It's a great relief to me that you've fully recovered."

His hand covered hers in a rare gesture of affection and it was her turn to look away. Like Persephone, she felt like she had descended to the underworld, where she'd eaten magical food, drunk of the wine, and fornicated with a god. Her parents, no matter their grief, could never fully extract her now.

"So," she fumbled for the right question, "why the long wait? Why did Roman leave me alone for so long, if they were dead set on this marriage?"

"Now that's an odd thing. When he turned up to take you to your prom—which was a surprise I wasn't happy about—I thought for sure he'd be courting you nonstop. But he dropped out of sight. Domingo quit coming around, too. I frankly thought they'd moved on. Then that apprentice got herself killed, Donovan was desperate for a replacement, and you wanted a job so badly, I thought, why not?"

"Charlie called you?"

"No—the other one."

"Carla?"

"Yes. Unusual, but she said Charlie was tied up with the investigation."

A curl of deep regret settled in her gut at the thought that Tara might have died just to create a job opening. "But why now, all of a sudden?"

She realized she'd wondered out loud when her father answered. "I did some sniffing around when I heard your supposedly happy news—not from you, I might add, since you never answer your damn phone anymore."

He waited and she gave in. "What did you find out?"

"Heh." He looked pleased with himself. "Sanclaro's got himself on the edge of bankruptcy. Bad home loans. Apparently rooked a hell of a lot of people and now the Feds are sniffing around, looking for evidence of fraud. The Indian bureau, too, and several tribal councils, including Navajo Nation, which is not without some clout these days."

"Sounds as if the Sanclaros have upheld the family tradition of screwing the Native Americans."

"And the natives are restless!" Her dad pointed a finger at the sky, a wicked grin on his face as he shouted the old cliché, startling several tourists buying New Mexico mugs.

There was nothing he loved better than taking down a business rival. She had to laugh.

He handed her a twenty. "Now go buy us some more of those pink Popsicle things and let's plan our strategy."

Fortunately, her father had been more interested in managing the Sanclaros than grilling her about her other issues. They'd established an odd truce over the Cake Pops, letting the sleeping dogs of her growing-up lie under the table.

For now, it was enough. He didn't need to know about her other life, other worlds. They would deal with that later.

If there was a later.

She walked into the police station and the on-duty desk cop nodded, waving them back to Sanchez's office. Once her escort saw her safely there, they headed off, clearly relieved to be off duty.

To her surprise, Sanchez stood when he spotted her, putting on his cowboy hat. "You're right on time. Come on, let's go."

Bemused, Christine turned and followed the detective out to his car. "No Interview Room A for me today?"

"How's Roman Sanclaro? Nice bruise you got on your cheek there—I've seen his work before."

Self-consciously, she fingered the tender spot. She'd layered on a load of foundation—enough that her father hadn't seen it. "What if I told you I wanted to press assault charges?"

Sanchez tipped his hat with one finger. "I wouldn't be surprised. He seems to think you're unstable and might do that very thing."

Nice.

"Get in the car. And put on your seat belt—I shouldn't have to tell you."

"Yes, Mom." She smiled to herself at his sour look. "Where are we going?"

"Carla Donovan wants to talk to you. I want to be there to hear what she has to say."

2

Charlie and Carla lived outside of town in the unincorporated community of Eldorado. Houses dotted the landscape, turning up in various hollows and on hilltops, amid a winding maze of dirt roads.

The Donovan house was big by East Coast standards but nothing like Roman's place. A pretty, adobe-style place, it enjoyed sweeping views of the mountains and an eclectic interior. Opera posters and other memorabilia decorated the walls. Santa Fe's version of suburbia, she supposed—with the exception of the uniformed cops standing guard.

"I'm surprised you're letting her stay at home," she remarked to Sanchez. "Wouldn't somewhere else be safer?"

"Refuses to budge, and Donovan backs her all the way. I don't like it, but nobody's doing me any favors these days, are they?" He slanted her an accusing look and she smiled sweetly.

Carla sat propped up in bed, looking out into a patio garden. She still looked like hell—a mass of healing cuts over purple and yellow bruises worthy of a harlequin's motley. Turning her head when Sanchez called out a hello, she looked Christine up and down, unfriendly as ever. She burned with curiosity over why Carla wanted to see her—especially since Carla might know where the other ring was. Charlie was nowhere in sight.

"I'm really sorry for what happened to you," Christine said in a rush. The lawyers would never have let her say anything along those lines. It implied guilt, they said.

Carla nodded slowly, acknowledging. "Have things gone to hell without me? Please say yes."

"Pretty much, yes. But the opening night's a few days away. I imagine they'll pull it out."

"They?" Her face sharpened. "You're not helping? You bailed after all."

"I did not bail!" Christine's irritation with the woman rose, superseding any sympathy. "I'm banned."

"Not anymore," Charlie said from the doorway. He looked considerably older. It didn't help that he wore gray sweats that sagged like limp rags on his skinny frame. "I just got off the phone with Carlton Davis, who insisted I either present convincing evidence that Christy is a danger or let her back in."

Carla looked at Sanchez, who stuck his hands in his front jeans pockets and shrugged. "If the boss says let her in, I have no dog in that fight."

"And that sure ain't me," Charlie grumbled. "I better get dressed and get up there. We'll be expecting you shortly, Christy."

She watched him go, sorry he seemed to think so little of her. It looked bad that Daddy had pulled strings. And yet, just this once, she was glad for her father's interference. The knot of worry over how she'd get back to the Master had dissolved a little.

"I need to speak to Christy alone," Carla announced.

"Now, Ms. Donovan—it would really help the case if you'd share your information with me also and—"

"This is still my private residence, right? I want to talk to her alone."

With a heavy sigh, Sanchez shook his head and walked to the door. "I'll be right outside. Just shout if you need me."

"Which one of us are you worried about?" Carla shot back.

He shut the door. Carla turned her somewhat feverish gaze on Christine. Carla's cheekbones were still swollen enough that her eyes watered behind the puffiness. Her own minor bruise throbbed in sympathy, and Christine wondered if the same fist had caused both.

"Have you found the Angel's Hand yet?"

The bluntness of the question took Christine aback. "I'm not even sure what it is."

"Shit." Carla shook her head and then appeared to regret the sudden movement, pressing her fingers to her temple. "I figured Sanclaro would have had you in there looking for it as soon as I was incapacitated. Then they came after me again, so I knew they must be looking still."

"Roman did this to you?" She imagined them, Roman and Domingo, beating Carla in their snarling anger. Christine felt the need to sit, lowering herself onto a buckskin director's chair.

"I don't know." Carla sank into herself, her fire gone as she remembered. "They wore masks and apparently gave me some kind of Ketamine derivative. It keeps you paralyzed, but you're awake and . . ." A tear ran down her uneven cheek. "They kept threatening to rape me if I didn't tell them where the hand is, but they kept pummeling. You have no idea."

"I do, a little." Christine wanted to take the older woman's hand but knew Carla wouldn't like it. "Did you tell the cops about it?"

"No, I didn't tell the stupid police!" Carla snapped. Clearly the pain meds hadn't sweetened her personality. "I know who has the power around here even if you don't."

"Then why did you say I did it?"

"You're wearing the ring, aren't you? I wanted to make it hard for you to have the other one, too. They should have been mine—and now I'm trapped here." She plucked at the blankets, drug-hazed eyes bright with fever.

She was like a rabid animal—wounded and out of her mind.

"Why do you want the rings?" Christine asked in a soothing tone.

"I've worked at the opera house since I was a little girl. You've heard him. Those songs that wrap around your heart and squeeze. Sometimes, late at night, you hear it. *Christine*. He wants the rings. I could have been her. That would be real power. But he wouldn't give me the flute. They saved their roses for you. It's not fair."

"What do the rings do?"

Carla rolled her head on the pillow, her face creased in despair. "Now they'll never be mine." Her lips curled back in a vicious sneer. "But you won't have it either. I'll never tell where it is. You tell them that. Tell them to leave me alone. I'll die before I tell."

"Carla—I don't want the Sanclaros to have it either. Tell me where it is and I'll bring it to you. What does it look like?"

"Just give Sanclaro the message. Is it time for my Oxycontin yet? Nurse!"

Sanchez popped the door open, followed by a hefty home health care nurse carrying a paper cup, who shooed them out with much fussing and clucking.

Sanchez drove Christine back into town. His cowboy hat sat on the seat between them. "You going to give me anything here?"

"She seems pretty whacked out. I'm not sure exactly why she wanted to talk to me."

"Pain meds will do that." But he tapped the steering wheel thoughtfully.

"She thinks the Sanclaros did it to her."

He nodded. Said nothing.

"Aha. And so do you."

"No comment, ma'am," Sanchez said in an exaggerated western drawl and grinned at her. "What do you think?"

"Was Tara raped?"

Sanchez got very serious very fast. "Now why would you ask me that?"

"I just want to know. I thought since I told you something, you'd tell me something."

"Doesn't work that way."

"I think she was killed for some other reason. Not part of a rape and all."

"No comment."

"That means yes."

"That means no comment."

Sanchez dropped her off at her apartment, where she collected her things and her uniformed escort. She put the top down on her convertible to let out the hot air, though the midday sun shone down with fierce intensity on her head.

The sight of the copper peaks of the opera house rising on the hillside filled her with a happy sense of homecoming. When he saw her, Matt literally jumped up and down.

"She's back! She's back!" Then he clutched his hands to his chest. "You're not going to kill me, are you?"

"Oh stop."

"Seriously," he dropped his voice to a stage whisper, which still projected nicely, "things have gotten creepy around here."

"Like what?" She waved to her companion cops, pulled Matt into her office—Tara's old office, bleh—and shut the door. A lush red rose on the desk gave her pause, but she pretended it was no big deal. "Spill."

"Do we have to talk in here? It kind of has a weird vibe." Matt fiddled with some of the figurines on Tara's bookshelf. "Kind of morbid that she's dead and her stuff is still here."

"That's not her stuff—it was probably here before she was. I'm sure her parents took all her belongings."

Matt was shaking his head, his lips pressed together and his eyes huge. "That's not what I heard. Steve told me that Charlie locked up her office before anyone even knew Tara was gone. In fact—that's how most of them found out, 'cuz her office was suddenly closed up. And then, after the, you know, body, the cops sealed it. Steve was going to come in, get her things to send to her folks, but Charlie said it would just upset them."

"Weird."

"See?"

Christine studied the room. "So I wonder which things were hers and what was here."

Matt curled his lip. "I don't want to know. The whole thing is too creepy. Like the roses."

"Roses?"

He pointed at the one on her desk. "What I was telling you. Turning up in odd places. The talent are getting all superstitious about it. And stuff is moved. Props we had ready for the rehearsal are missing or exchanged for the wrong versions. Can you believe that stupid magic flute has gone missing again? It's a good thing Carla the Valkyrie isn't here, because she'd be having a total shit-fit about it."

"Or is that a handy coincidence that she's not here?"

"What do you mean?" Matt looked both horrified and reluctantly intrigued.

"I need your help. There's something I need to find."

"In the old inventory?" He made dubious noise but grabbed the enormous notebook on the shelf. "You know as well as I do that the

BNoD is practically worthless. I take it you already checked the searchable portion?"

"Yes."

"What is it?"

"An Angel's Hand."

"What the fuck is an Angel's Hand?"

"No idea—that's part of the problem."

"I can see how it would be. Okay—which opera is it related to?"

"I don't know."

"Fabulous. How are we supposed to find this thing when you don't know what it is, it's not in the searchable inventory, and we don't know what it would be with?"

Christine gave him a sweet smile and pointed at the notebook in his hands.

"No. No and no. I am not reading this . . . *tome* looking for one phrase."

"It's important, Matt. Or you can go through the storerooms looking for it and I'll read the BNoD, but I might recognize it when I see it."

"How, when you don't know what it is?"

Self-consciously, she fingered the lump of opal ring in her coin pocket. Probably mentioning an antique jeweled ring might be involved would be a bad idea. She sighed. "Hard to explain."

"Yeah." Matt drew out the word. "This might be too much crazy for me. And I have twenty million other things to do."

"I think this thing has to do with Tara's death."

Matt dropped the notebook on her desk as if it had bitten him. "Absolutely not, then!"

"Please. I can't do this alone."

"I don't want to die!"

"I'll make sure you get a year-round position here."

"You can do that?"

"Yes." Yes, she could. She'd make sure of it. Her dad owed her at least one more favor.

"Deal."

3

Matt went off to read in a "less freaky location." Before she did anything else, Christine examined everything in the office. She even asked Steve to come in and point out which things had been Tara's, but he refused, saying he wasn't going to cross Charlie.

So she did it herself. The usual opera posters hung on the walls, along with black-and-white shots of famous patrons and opera divas, signed with black Sharpie marker to people who weren't Tara. The desk held an assortment of pens, some sticky notes with phone numbers and obscure reminders that must have meant something to her. The cops would have taken anything that seemed to be a clue, she supposed, so these must be detritus. Though the drawer held empty file folders, there were no actual papers, so the police must have taken some stuff.

Tara had likely had a laptop, too. Christine's fingers itched to get into that.

Sanchez would tell her to go to hell.

No, anything useful in the desk the cops would already have. Methodically, she went through the bookcase, checking the texts on musical theater, the history of costume design, Georgia O'Keeffe's biography, landscapes of New Mexico.

Maybe Tara had just been in the wrong place at the wrong time, worth killing just to bring Christine to the opera house. But the fact that Tara, too, had been working on the inventory just seemed too coincidental. Especially if Carla had really hidden the Angel's Hand.

Tara had known something. "Come on, Tara," she muttered under her breath, "If death is just a doorway into another world, would you peek back in here and give me a stinking clue?"

"Who are you talking to?"

She shrieked and jumped a foot, her heart slamming into her throat. Charlie stood in the doorway, a strange look on his weathered face. She gazed pointedly at the keys in his hand. He tucked them in his pocket.

"Sorry—didn't know anyone was in here," he said, not sounding sorry at all.

So he opens the door as quietly as he can?

"Did you need something, Charlie?"

"Yeah, the inventory."

"Matt has it. I'm not sure where he got to, though."

Charlie gave a half nod, his bushy brows lowering. "What about you—looking for a book?"

She shrugged. "Doing a little research."

"Well, the props guys could sure use some help if you're done collecting pay for doing nothing."

There was a time that dig would have stung. Now it just made her mad. Charlie knew full well that being kept away from her job wasn't her idea. So she made herself smile, mentally giving him the finger. "Sure enough! I'll be out there in a few."

"Sooner rather than later would be nice."

"Uh-huh. You might look for Matt and the notebook out on the loading dock."

He hovered in the doorway, clearly not wanting to leave her in there. She stood in front of the bookcase, unwilling to back down.

"Fine," he finally muttered.

"Close the door, would you?" She flinched when he slammed it. A loose heating vent screen over the door rattled, a screw falling to the floor and rolling across to her feet. In the ensuing silence, she heard her own accelerating breathing. And music, echoing through the opera house. Human voices merging with that unearthly golden melody and the scent of roses.

She pulled over her rolling chair and climbed up. Not able to see in, she felt around the dusty space, trying not to picture spiders. Her fingertips brushed something. Paper? Stretching up, she got a grip on it and slid it out. A little spiral notebook, with a neatly printed TARA SMITH on the cover.

"Thank you, Tara," she breathed.

Just then the door swooped open, hitting the chair, which spun away on its oiled wheels. The notebook flew out of her hands and she grabbed at the vent and the top of the door, her stomach dropping as her feet went with the chair and she fell, the stabbing terror of her dreams catching up with her.

Strong hands grabbed her—but they were the wrong ones.

"What the hell are you doing, Christy?" Roman's angry face filled her vision and she wrenched herself away from him.

"Me? What the hell are *you* doing here?"

Roman grinned viciously, and a chill of terror shot down her spine. "Looking for you. I hear your father's in town. I hope you can explain why you so rudely *vanished* from the Compound last night. We were frantic about you. Not very considerate of you at all."

"Yes, well—my father called and said he was on his way. I didn't want to wake anyone, so I left as quietly as I could and called a, um, cab."

"And here I thought I had your phone in my pocket. I forgot to give it back to you." His eyes had gone that flat black. *The Sanclaros are insane.*

"It was in my room." She shrugged in nonchalance. "I figured you left it there for me."

She would not give up Angie. Hopefully she'd escaped the punishment she'd feared.

"What *were* you doing up on that chair, sweet girl?" Roman switched subjects rapidly, as if hoping to catch her off guard, his gaze swinging up to the open vent and speculatively back to her.

Where had Tara's notepad landed?

"The vent cover was loose."

The red cover of the notepad peeked out from under her desk. She swooped down and snagged it.

"What do you have there?" Roman looked predatory, and she shoved it in her back jeans pocket.

"Notes. I need to get to work here." She ducked past him into the hallway.

"I'd be interested to see your notes—get to know my fiancée better. Maybe I'll discover why she leaves my home in the middle of the night and then avoids my calls and texts."

She wanted to fling the awful ring at him and shout that she wasn't, would never be his fiancée, much less his wife. Damn that she needed the ring still. So she did her best to smile, if only for the benefit of her uniformed escort, watching their exchange with great interest.

"I already told you why."

"I think you're lying."

"You're free to think anything you want to. My father is in town and wanted to discuss my engagement." She couldn't help throwing that out there. A little dare.

Roman's gaze turned speculative. "So that's what he's up to."

Go, Dad! Sounded as if her father hadn't wasted any time smoking out the Sanclaros.

"Up to?" She raised her eyebrows and tried to look innocently casual even as Tara's little red notebook burned a hole in her pocket.

"This cocktail party on the dock tonight is for all the talent and opera staff, but we're all invited."

"Sounds pretty straightforward to me."

"You listen to me, sweet girl." He hissed the endearment and flexed his fingers, glancing at the cops and away. "All of this is bigger than you are. You're only a tool. And, if you're lucky, you'll enjoy it. But I can make sure you don't, too."

It took all her resolve, but she cast her eyes down, trying to appear meek. Funny that she didn't feel afraid now. Annoying, too, because showing a little fear would be useful.

"Yes, Roman."

He picked up her left hand and kissed the ring. "That's my good girl. See how easy it is for you, if you think only about pleasing me?" He squeezed her hand, hard enough that she gasped. Arrogant ass, to threaten and intimidate her while the cops watched. "This is a new beginning for the Sanclaros. You and I will lead the family into a bright new future, sweet girl. Just as Angelia and Seraphina did."

Holding her hand in the same tight grip, he cupped the back of her neck, his fingers vising the tendons there so she couldn't turn her head. He kissed her, hard, possessively and without the least amount of affection. He might as well have struck her across the face again.

"Until tonight." He smiled. "I'll send a dress over for you to wear. There will be photographers."

4

As soon as Roman exited, discreetly followed by the uniforms, Christine dashed down to the lower storerooms, the keys on her belt loop jingling as she ran down the spiral steps. It wasn't easy to find privacy. Every tech seemed to be going crazy, in and out of all the rooms in the last-minute frenzy of opening week.

Several people called to her, asking for help with their jobs. She was sorry to lie, to shout back that she was on an important errand. Worse, she had effectively removed Matt from the pool, too.

Well, a good manager learns to set priorities, right? Never mind that hers had little to do with opening night.

She escaped into an empty storeroom—empty of people, that is, but crammed full of stuff—shut the door, and slid to the floor, leaning against it to prevent any more surprises. Pulling out Tara's little notepad, she held it in her hands, feeling a sense of reverence and a little grief for this woman she'd never known. Christine had never been all that big on praying—and after the prayer marathon with the Sanclaros, she felt even less inclined toward it—but she offered up a heartfelt wish that Tara's spirit would find its place. In whatever world.

Then, with another urgent wish that this would be it, she flipped open the notepad.

Tara's now familiar lists filled the first few pages, her familiar boxes drawn to the left of each item, most with big checkmarks in them.

It didn't really differ from the lists and notes Charlie had given her that first day—the stuff already passed over by the police and, now she felt sure, Charlie himself. Mostly it was her daily tasks, notes about what needed doing next.

Then she hit it.

☐ *Find magic flute*

A chill of certainty ran over her scalp. The flute—and Matt said it had gone missing yet again—that Carla had been so determined to find. Her heart thumping, she flipped over the next sheet. These were hurried notes, not at all orderly.

> *Found flute—<u>not</u> in Mozart room. Bad news: I think I've found human remains. A mummified hand with an opal ring. Glass-topped box. I have a bad, bad feeling about this. Just by looking at it, I know it's not a prop or an artifact. Will discuss with Carla. Keeping this record as CYA.*

Eureka.

"Only it didn't save your ass, did it, Tara?" Christine murmured. She turned to the next page, but it stared back at her, resolutely blank. *Where* did she find it? The note was dated the day before she disappeared. However Carla had reacted, it had been enough to scare Tara into hiding the notepad.

A loud knock right behind her head made her jump, and the doorknob rattled. She held her breath, hoping the person would go away.

"Christy?" Matt yelled through the door. "Are you in there?"

With a sigh, she carefully closed the precious notepad and pushed it deep into her back pocket, then opened the door. Matt, a brilliant grin transforming his somewhat homely face, held the notebook, one arm wedging the pages open.

"How much do you love me?" he demanded.

"Get in here!" She hurried him in, checked up and down the hall, and locked the door again.

"I meant love in a metaphorical sense." Matt's gaze followed her nervously. "You know I don't bat for your team, right?"

"Hush. Show me."

He laid the notebook on a gilt credenza and pointed ostentatiously to the line. It was inked in between two other lines, nearly illegible. *Angel's Hand: Egyptian artifact, possibly for* Aida. *CJD L6-Verdi.*

"So are we going to look for it?"

"No!" Christy slammed the notebook shut, as if prying eyes might see too much. "I mean, we still don't know what it really is or what it looks like—and the Verdi room is worse than the Mozart room." It was amazing how much easier lying became, the more you did it. It also felt, however, like removing yet another brick in the divider between reality and fantasy. How would she remember which version was true?

"Mostly because someone stuck all that stuff from the Cavalli operas in there."

"No kidding! No—you go help Steve and the other guys. I'll look for the hand after I find that flute. Who keeps moving it?"

Matt did his spooky finger wiggle. "The theater ghost! Where will you look?"

"I'll start with where I found it last time."

"Where was that, anyway?"

"Oh," she waved a vague hand at the floor, "in that one storeroom downstairs, at the far end."

After he left, she waited a while; wanting to be sure he wouldn't double back. Or head to the Verdi room himself. While she waited, she made herself a fake list, so if anyone stopped her, she could look busy. Though she wanted to check the hallway, she forced herself to play the role of busy props assistant instead.

She dodged various groups, taking her preferred route down the spiral staircase, rubber soles squeaking against the metal grate. The big freight elevator was in constant use, clanking and grinding with protests, so she ran into a few other people on the tight curves—one of them teetering on the narrow inside edge, while the one on the outside turned sideways and pressed against the handrail to slide by.

The negotiating happened mainly via smiles and quick hand signals, as the cacophony of last-minute rehearsals, buzz saws, and other electronic tools screaming away made conversation next to impossible.

Inside the relative quiet of the storeroom, Christine locked the door and pulled out her iPad. She'd done the Verdi room early on, one of those first quiet, creepy days. She was sure of it. Scanning her database, she found the listings. Nothing about the Angel's Hand. It had been written in after she'd been through there.

By someone who had access to the Big Notebook of Doom. And who knew she'd been adding to the database as she went and so wouldn't look at it again.

She wouldn't waste another minute looking for the red herring there. No, it would be here, in the Mozart room. In the cabinet where the magic flute was supposed to be and never was. Carla's game of chess.

To be safe, she spent a few minutes pushing a leather-bound sea-man's chest against the door. Then she went to the back of the room, to the antique armoire with roses carved in the doors, the stained wood dark with age, the red of the petals the rusty black of old blood. She'd looked in this cabinet before, on the first hunt for the flute, and remembered the glass-topped box. But she'd been fo-cused—hell, she'd been frantic—on finding the flute, so she'd pushed it aside, one of the many things she'd touched and never added to her lists.

There it was. Hidden in plain sight.

Covered in old leather, the box smelled like something dead but felt like something alive with magic. The glass of the top, though dusty, showed the contents clearly.

A human hand.

But there was no ring. Then she glimpsed the white gold band that matched hers and knew the opal and diamond ring had been turned in, toward the palm.

No wonder Tara had known immediately how wrong it was. Though Victorian in design, the hand was no English family's mummified relic. Its nails were long and carefully oval, the shape of the hand a lady's, preserved in all its refined delicacy. The ring a relic of recent centuries. The twin of her own.

With a deep sense of certainty, she knew these fingers, immor-talized in the box and hidden in the opera props, would fit the other handprint on the pillar and break the binding that held the Master and the shadow people captive.

Taking a table runner from a box—and squelching the urge to note in the database that she'd done so—Christine wrapped up the box and stuck it deep in her big shoulder bag. It seemed insane to carry it around but worse to leave it here.

If the Master wouldn't let her use it, she'd at least keep anyone else from finding and using it. She would hide the horrible artifact away where it could never be found.

It was nerve-wracking, spending the afternoon running errands all over the opera house, the various rehearsed solos, duets, and choruses jangling together in her head. The excitement and stress over the imminent opening night seemed vapid compared to the crazy drama her life had become. When she had a few moments, she added her own notes to Tara's and hid the notepad in the vent again—with a coded reference to the object's new hiding place. Then she sat at her desk with the door invitingly open, ostensibly working on the iPad inventory—but writing down everything that had happened. It felt like the right thing to do. She hoped that following in Tara's footsteps this way wouldn't lead her down the same doomed path.

But her fate would never be the same as Tara's, because she had the Master.

Tara hadn't really had anyone.

This was the worst part—how badly she wanted to go find the Master. To tell him what she'd found out. To be with him. But this would be it: her final performance as Roman's fiancée. Tonight she would lay the trap for the Sanclaros. She'd draw them out with the promise of the Angel's Hand, then either expose them as murderers or blackmail them into silence.

Then she could leave the sunlit world, with all of its thorns and sharp edges, forever.

Her father was taking care of the financial end. Detective Sanchez would take care of the law.

"Wardrobe delivery service!" Hally chirped from the doorway. She'd curled her hair for the party so the unnaturally bright red spiraled wildly. Her dress, in glaring daffodil yellow, clung to her slim figure.

"Wow!" Christine commented. "You look hot. And bright."

"Yellow is the color of regret." Hally smiled thinly. "It seemed appropriate. For you I brought black."

"Thank you! I so didn't want to wear what Roman thought up for me."

Hally wrinkled her nose. "Dove gray. Full length. I saw it in the messenger bag outside your apartment door. I left it there."

"Good. Get the door, would you? I'll change." Christine took the garment bag from her friend and raised her eyebrows at the chichi store name embossed on it. "Can I afford this?"

"Oh, didn't I mention? I met your dad. He showed up at the bar at lunch hour. Handed me a credit card and told me to buy whatever. He also said I'd been a good friend to you and wanted to see my paintings—gave me the number of *his* art buyer."

Christine clutched the dress to her. "Oh my God, you didn't show him *that* painting, did you?"

Hally clucked her tongue. "No, silly. Besides, it's not done."

"Okay." She breathed out her relief. "I'm glad he was nice to you."

"Isn't he always?"

"Absolutely not."

"Yeah. Well, it's nice when people turn out to be better than you thought."

"I didn't think things worked that way." Christine pulled the dress over her head and turned for Hally to zip it up.

"Wouldn't it be a great world if people became better all the time? It should work that way. That fits perfectly. I impress myself."

"It's short!"

"So what? You have fabulous legs." Hally dangled a pair of silver strappy stilettos from her fingers. "And these shoes will top it off."

"Ooh!" Christine seized them. "You really bought Jimmy Choos? My dad will have a fit."

"Hey—don't hand me your credit card and tell me to have at it if you're on a budget."

"So noted."

Hally fished out Christine's makeup and jewelry from the bag and set them on the desk. "I didn't know which jewelry you'd want, so I brought anything silver. That way you can keep your protective sacred spiral pendant on. And all the makeup—shit!"

One of the eye shadows tumbled off the desk and shattered on the concrete floor. She crouched to gather up the pieces.

"What's this?"

Hally was holding a piece of heavy paper. The first note from the rose, which Christine had hidden away under the eye-shadow tray, just in case.

"Give me that."

Slowly, she looked up from it, assessing Christine. "This was one of the notes you got?"

"Yes. But it doesn't matter now, because I know who's been doing all these things."

"Oh, yes. It matters very much."

The little office fell so silent; the soprano aria wafting from the main stage seemed to be in the room with them.

"I know this handwriting."

5

The party was all it should be.

Carlton Davis, master manipulator, had managed to dovetail the "special celebration" with a planned cocktail reception for patrons while the public opening-night tailgating festivities ramped up in the parking lot. Tourists and locals alike set up folding tables by their cars, broke out the fine linens, silver, and crystal and ate and drank, enjoying one of the best sunset views Santa Fe had to offer.

It was surpassed only by the opera house loading dock, with its sheer edge dropping over the valley. Christine's father had supplemented the catering with excellent champagne and a string quartet, bribed down from Taos. Quite the expense to assemble all the players in one spot, but he seemed to be enjoying himself.

Christine's father handed her a flute of champagne. "Ah, and the Sanclaro clan arrives. All of them except the wife, who declined, complaining of a migraine. This is going to be fun."

She glanced over her shoulder to see Domingo Sanclaro, flanked by Roman, Angie trailing meekly behind, clapping shoulders and working the crowd.

"I'm surprised you call it 'fun.' I can't wait for it all to be over."

Her father chuckled. "You have to understand, when you've been in big business for a long time, it's like a duel. You find better and better swordsmen—and women—" He interrupted himself to toast her. "—to pit yourself against. To test yourself. What has Sanclaro Corp. done? It's the financial equivalent of going to the schoolyard and hacking up little kids with a machete."

"Nice image, Dad." Christine grimaced and he grinned, happy to have gotten her goat.

"Apt one, too. I despise fraud. Especially the kind that takes advantage of people who already have next to nothing. Taking Sanclaro apart before his peers will be sweet indeed."

"It doesn't bother you that they're family?"

His face turned hard. "They are not my family, or yours. We share a genetic connection, nothing more profound than that. I was spawned by a coldhearted bitch who spread her legs, popped me out, and dumped me like an unwanted puppy at the pound. That's not family. Never forget it."

He didn't have what she had, however—that racial memory connection to the tribal priestess who'd started it all. Christine wished she could share that with him; tell him that there was something meaningful and valuable in it all. But she kept the secret close.

Davis went on, not noticing her quietness. "If that Detective Sanchez can also nail him and his vile son for murder that will be a bonus. But it's the financial ruin that will hurt him where he lives."

"About the murder, I don't think—"

"Carlton!" Domingo Sanclaro stepped up next to her, shaking her father's hand and ignoring her completely, little tool that she was. "I haven't seen you in ages. I thought we'd never get you out to our part of the world."

Sanclaro wore a perfectly tailored tuxedo and scanned her father's not-Armani suit with a barely veiled sneer, completely falling for his gambit. *Never underestimate the power of seeming to be an idiot.* "You remember Roman. Once he and Christy marry, I'm making him VP."

"He's young for it." Carlton frowned at Roman, giving him the same dismissive glance Domingo had given Christine. She wanted to kiss her father.

"He's a bright and capable young man. He'll make a fine husband for your daughter," Domingo replied smoothly. "I assume sweet little Christy here is still your only heir?"

Her father frowned at her, as if just noticing her presence. "Yes, well, though she's only interested in *some* aspects of the business," he managed to make her sound flighty, "you know how girls are. They try on new occupations like dresses, isn't that right, dear?"

"Oh, Daddy," she took her cue, "that's just mean. I prefer to say I'm eclectic in my pursuits."

He ruffled her hair affectionately, something he used to do a long, long time ago. Before they started fighting all the time. "That's my girl."

"A girl needs a strong guiding hand," Domingo inserted, glancing at Roman. "I'm as delighted as you are that these two kids have finally seen the light. Given Christy's affection for the opera house, I imagine you'll want to deed that to her—perhaps as an engagement gift."

She could see her father's point. Sanclaro wasn't even working for this one. Carlton Davis tossed back the rest of his champagne, knitting his brows, looking a bit befuddled. "That reminds me. I have an announcement to make."

Domingo and Roman exchanged satisfied glances, while her father made his way to the string quartet, tapping on his empty flute with the wire rims of his glasses. Roman moved to slide an arm around her waist.

"What happened to the dress I sent for you?" he murmured in her ear.

"Daddy bought me this one," she answered, keeping an eye on her father. Not far away, Hally and Angie were deep in conversation. Good. Hally would handle the realities of that situation.

Inside the opera house, the shadows grew deeper as the sun dropped, its rays stretching long and red, splashing the copper surfaces with crimson light. A flutter of movement caught her eye, the sweep of a cape, dark on black. Warmth stirred deep inside her.

Soon this would be over and she and the Master would be together.

"Don't get used to it," Roman was saying. "I won't have my wife dressing like a slut."

The music stopped and Carlton Davis cleared his throat loudly into the mike, making everyone cringe and look his way. He grinned, loving every moment.

"Good evening, ladies and gentlemen! Let's all make a toast, please." Waiters passed through, pouring the excellent champagne liberally, and Roman smiled down at her, nearly giddy with his triumph. Carlton Davis held up his now-full flute. "To another fabulous Santa Fe sunset!"

The crowd laughed, then everyone turned to toast the sky. Roman's arm tightened on her waist and Domingo refused the toast. Bad luck, that.

"Now that we've acknowledged nature's contribution to this exciting evening," Davis continued, "I also want to thank the many, many people who made this opera season happen. From the board," he held up his glass to the cluster of elegantly dressed board members, who nodded solemnly, "to the talent," the soprano, already in costume, fluttered her fan, "to the lowest apprentice." With that last, he tipped his glass toward Christine with a long wink.

"She happens to be my daughter," he pretended to confess, gaining another laugh. "Today is a very special day for her—seeing the fruits of her labors in her very first job. I wish I could go back and enjoy that again. I'm proud of you, Christine."

People clapped politely, and she found herself unexpectedly weepy at the words.

"He's taking forever," Roman complained.

"Hush," she replied without thinking, and his displeasure manifested in a sharp pinch at her waist. Learned that one from his mother.

"I think we should all have a moment of silence, too, for the tragic events of this season. For the loss of a young woman on the verge of a new life, a new career, senselessly cut short. And for Carla Donovan, longtime loyal employee of this opera, who couldn't be here tonight due to her injuries." Charlie, in an older-style tuxedo that he probably pulled out every year, acknowledged the words, a deep frown knitting his brows.

"I've come to a decision. Not because of the unfortunate mishaps of this season, but because the world turns and times change. I want you all to hear it first here."

Domingo Sanclaro rocked from heel to toe, beside himself with excited energy.

"As many of you may or may not know, I came to own this opera house via a trust from my mother, Angelia Sanclaro."

Gasps of surprise ran through the crowd. Domingo frowned and Roman slid an uneasy glance at her. She tried to look confused.

"Yes—though it's never been common knowledge," Davis said, acknowledging the shocked response of the gathering. "In fact, it's been something of a deep, dark family secret. But it's time for us to come out of the closet. Christine, honey, you need to know that Roman is your first cousin. While strictly legal in this state, I find such a marriage distasteful and cannot condone it."

People in the crowd glanced in her direction and away, shaking their heads. She bit her lip for them to see her public consternation.

"As penance for keeping this secret, I have investigated the trust and discovered a way to break the terms. As of today, I've sold the opera house."

"What is he talking about?" Roman demanded in her ear.

She put a hand to her temple, acting out traumatized grief and shock.

"I can give you all the details later, but as of," he glanced at his watch, "three-thirty this afternoon, Davis Corporation no longer owns the Santa Fe Opera. An exciting, new company, Star Entertainment Enterprises, will be taking over. I think you'll be in very good hands."

Roman swore, letting her go hard enough that she stumbled.

"What's the meaning of this, Davis?" Domingo Sanclaro shouted far too loudly. The whites of his eyes seemed to bulge with unbalanced rage. "That trust is ironclad. The land belongs to the Sanclaros. Always has and always will. Besides, you can't make this kind of move without the board and the shareholders."

Carlton Davis put on his glasses. "Are you referring to your shares, Sanclaro? The ones I bought out from under you?"

Like a lash, Domingo's gaze cut to his son, who shrank back, shaking his head in denial.

"You haven't been watching your financial house, my old friend. And the board convened an emergency meeting today. Upon seeing evidence of the federal investigations underway into Sanclaro Corp., the good people unanimously decided to divorce themselves from your influence."

Several of the board members nodded in agreement, sending black looks in Sanclaro's direction.

"In fact," her father looked pleased with himself, "I believe there are some folks from the FBI and the Bureau of Indian Affairs here right now, eager to discuss some of the information I sent their way."

Domingo looked as if he wanted to run, torn between keeping his public face and escaping the agents moving in his direction.

A bell chimed and Davis nodded. "And now it's time for the real show to begin—everyone to their seats!"

He held out a hand toward Christine and she went to him, leaving Roman and Domingo conferring furiously in whispers. "That was brilliant," she told her father, who folded her hand over his arm, patting it. "Though I'm sorry to see the opera house pass to someone else."

"You love it, don't you?" Her father gave her a keen look. "I could hear it in your voice from the day you arrived."

She looked up at the soaring roofline, still shining with glints of light against the deepening sky. Like the visible temple on the hill, gateway to the Underworld. "I do, yes."

"Good. Don't tell anyone yet, but Star Enterprises is yours. I set it up for you. The trust really is ironclad. I just transferred it to you early."

She gaped at him, at a total loss for words.

"Maybe now that you don't live with your allergic old man, you can get a real cat and throw away that scrappy piece of fur you've dragged around since you were four. Don't think I don't know you brought it here with you."

"I'm never getting rid of Star. You gave her to me."

"Only because your mother insisted. She always knew better than I did how to make you happy."

Christine leaned over and kissed his cheek. "You've done a damn fine job of it today."

"Well," he cleared his throat with a loud cough, "let's go watch this show then."

6

"Christy!"

She turned as Matt came running up to her. "Christy, the fucking magic flute is missing *again*! Hi, Mr. Davis, nice to meet you, sorry for cursing, but we need to find it *right now*. Curtain goes up in fifteen."

"I thought we had it on the set."

Matt set his jaw and bugged out his eyes at her. "We *did*. And now it's *not*."

"Shit!" Christine ran a hand through her hair, only to snag on the spikes Hally had gelled into it, insisting they made her look "extra-specially hot."

"You go ahead and take care of it," her dad said. "I'll be fine. Don't mind this old man."

She rolled her eyes at him and took off after Matt, struggling to keep up on the high heels. Following him down the concrete side stairs, she dashed onto the set that would soon rise one story to the theater level. Everything was set and in its place—including the flute.

"Matt! What the—"

A hand clapped over her mouth and a muscled arm clamped over her chest, painfully crushing her breasts and lifting her off the floor. She struggled, flailing behind her with her fists, and her captor swung her around to show her Hally, gagged and round-eyed at the knife pressed against her throat. Matt, his hand wrapped in Hally's hair, pulled her head back and pushed the blade against her fair skin with a hand that visibly shook. "Shut up, Christy, okay?"

She stopped fighting. "Good girl," Carla crooned in her ear. "Now you're going to give me the Angel's Hand or your friend here will be the phantom's next victim. Understand?"

Unable to do anything else, she nodded. She'd always known Carla was a big woman, but her strength was astonishing. She wasn't supposed to be here or Christine would have made sure to tell someone about the notes. Matt glanced away when she looked accusingly at him. He must have called Carla and told her about the Hand. He'd been her spy all along.

"Mattie, bring the little witch—after all, we can't interfere with the opening, right? Charlie, let the stagehands in as soon as we're gone."

Charlie, his frown deeper than ever, moved into view.

"Just be—"

"Shut up, Charlie." Carla's voice sounded weary. "I've done the brunt of sacrificing for this. You can at least get out of my way. March, Christy."

Setting her down, Carla pressed a knife against the small of Christine's back. "Take me to it. If you fuck around, you lose a kidney."

They went out and down, Christine and Hally walking ahead of Carla and Matt. Was the Master watching? Surely he'd help her.

"You can't possibly think this will work," Christine said. "It's a full house out there. People inside and out. You'll be caught. It's all over."

"It's not over." Carla cuffed the back of her head and she staggered. "You brought us to this, you stupid cunt. Where are we going?"

"To where I hid the Hand."

"You'd better be telling the truth or I'll show you where Tara died—and demonstrate the technique on you."

The truth sighed through her, the puzzle piece fitting. Carla, not the Sanclaros, had killed Tara.

"I am." Christine unlocked the door to the ballet studio, now quiet with all the dancers off because tonight's opera had no dancing. The roomful of mirrors reflected the four of them over and over, with the bruised Carla looking like the crazed monster in a funhouse. Christine unlocked the door to her old office—the first little closet Charlie had stuck her in.

"I thought the police sealed this room." Matt sounded confused. A little scared, too. This kind of thing couldn't possibly have been his idea.

"They did, but only from the hallway. Now let Hally go."

"No way," Carla sneered, blocking the doorway. "Not until I have the Angel's Hand."

"How do I know you won't hurt us?"

"We will." Carla nodded at Matt.

He looked a little green.

"Do it, you little shit, or you'll pay," Carla growled.

He took a deep breath and stabbed the knife into Hally's arm. A shallow, glancing slice, but she shrieked and clobbered him. He dropped the knife and they fought over it, Hally scratching and pummeling him furiously. Finally he solved his problem by sitting on her and holding the knife point down between her breasts.

"This was a brand-new dress," Hally hissed at him. "The nicest one I've ever owned and you got blood all over it. Karma will get you for this."

"Enough already!" Carla snapped, pointing her own knife at Christine. "Where's the Angel's Hand?"

Christine.

Matt looked worried. "Did you hear something?"

"The show has started," Christine told him. Then she opened the closet, reached under a pile of old posters, and brought out the box.

Carla took it from her and examined it. Then looked up at the security camera near the ceiling and nodded.

Shit. A few minutes later, Roman appeared in the doorway to the ballet studio, followed by his father. Domingo strolled up to Carla, took the box from her, and handed it to Roman. Then he smiled, cupped the back of her neck, and kissed her, a savage, sexual kiss. She submitted to it, though it was clear the pressure pained her battered face.

Christine and Hally exchanged revolted looks.

"Well done," Domingo told Carla. "Though you should never have stolen it from me."

"I just wanted to be with you." Carla wrapped her hands in his lapels, crushing the expensive cut. To Christine's shock, the tall blonde wept. "I carry the blood, too. I can be the Sanclaro hand. Please, Dom! Haven't I shown my loyalty?"

Domingo eyed Christine, then backhanded Carla with enough force that she flew off him, despite her apparent death grip. "Yes. I will be forever grateful that you eliminated that foolish girl and brought the prize I'd only dreamed of within my reach. However, because of you and your games, the fucking Feds are breathing down my neck. We need to act fast. They may dare to arrest me if we don't take steps. Roman, bring her. Meet me in the sacred chapel. I'll prepare the wedding ceremony."

"You can't force me to marry him!" Christine shouted the words, feeling the wild sense of things spinning out of her control.

Domingo smiled at her condescendingly. "With the Angel's Hand restored to me and yours at my disposal—dead or alive, I might add," he waggled the mummified hand at her mockingly, "I am priest and king. I *will* marry you to my son, under the eyes of the only god that truly matters, and we will both watch you consummate that marriage."

Roman leered at her, and she imagined herself beneath him as he raped her on the chapel floor, his father watching. "It won't be legal," she protested.

"Once we have control of our pet god again," Domingo intoned, his face suffused with an insane light, "I will be above the law. You have no idea the *miracles* I can work. If you obey and are pleasing, we might let you live. At least until you bear a daughter or two."

He snapped his fingers at Roman, who reached out to grab her arm. She punched him in the nose and he tried to backhand her, but she ducked.

Just then Matt gave out a strangled wail and fell over, clutching his balls. Hally scrambled up, pushing him over, and sat on him, raspberry nails pointed at his eyes. "I'll do it. Don't push me, karma boy!"

Domingo snarled, pushing the box to Roman. "I'll take care of them. Get going."

Seeing her chance and following Hally's lead, Christine drove the sharp point of her Jimmy Choo heel into Roman's shin, grabbed the Angel's Hand, and ran. On sheer instinct, she ran toward the one person she trusted to save her.

The Master.

Christine.

If running on the polished concrete floor of the long, curving hallway wasn't easy in the high heels, plunging down the spiraling metal stairs was infinitely worse. One of the soaring arias followed her, the song pitching higher and higher as she descended. She held onto the rail with one hand, going as fast as she dared, holding onto the box with the other.

Heavy feet hit the grid of stairs over her head: Roman coming after her.

Impossible, but she went faster. Her body knew the rhythm of these steps, she'd been up and down them so many times. Round and round she rattled down, going deeper into the darker, unlit levels, careful not to let the spikes of her heels fall through the openings in the grate. Roman had slowed, not as confident as she, but still gained on her. Wishing she'd had time to take off the damn shoes, she imagined she felt his harsh breath and the brush of his fingers, grasping for her hair.

She went faster. Stilettos clanging against metal.

And then it happened.

Like the dream. Her heel caught on the edge of the step.

For an endless moment, she hung there, overbalanced.

And fell.

Plummeting over the edge and down. Roman yelled out in fear and panic. Surely not for her.

Time slowed. Her lungs clenched in the vacuum of panic. She fell endlessly, down and down, through the infinite shadows, reaching for a name.

"Master!" she cried.

Strong arms caught her.

"Right here."

She buried herself into his muscular chest, sobs wrenching out of her. He held her close, murmuring comfort in her ear while his warm lips brushed her cheek.

"Watch out!" she warned him, recalling the urgency. "He's chasing me!"

He turned so she could see. Light filtered through the grated steps in lines and squares. No one pounded after her. Only the galloping chorus of the end of Act I followed her, faint strains of the world above that could no longer reach her.

"It's only you and I, my love."

"As it should be."

"As was always meant."

"I want to free you. Free the shadow people so you can't ever be used again. I want to make it right again."

The breath sighed out of him, holding centuries of waiting. "Yes." He strode down the hallway, carrying her along, and the solid door dissolved into smoke before them. So that was how he did it.

"Isn't it real?" she wondered.

"What is real in one world is intangible in another," he replied. "When we pass through the doorway, remember your feeling of submitting to me. Give over. Don't fight it."

Despite the adrenaline pumping through her, it felt easy to relax against him and go into the state of yielding.

"Good," he murmured. And they passed through. "Remember— whatever happens—you cannot change the fact that the river flows, but you can change its direction."

"What do you mean?"

"The things you and I have done—it's like a river of life. You strengthened me and our people."

"But will it be enough for you to go back to being what you were?"

His face stilled into quiet lines behind the mask, his muscled arms carrying her without effort. "The past is gone. We have only the future."

She thought about that as he carried her through the maze of tunnels and passages, now on dry land, now wading through hip-deep water. Looking over his shoulder, Christine saw the shadows gather and trail after them, the dark eyes and flowing hair of the people moving in and out of substance as they, too, seemed compelled to follow.

Gradually she recognized the hallways, the ones under the Sanclaro compound that led to the secret room.

"They lost control of some spaces of land," the Master murmured. "It let me escape some of my prison, to roam my opera house."

"Angelia," Christine realized. "When she bequeathed it to my father."

He nodded. "Her gift to me. Like you, she wanted to do more. But they stopped her."

With a sick sense of sorrow for the grandmother she'd never known, Christine remembered the article about the car wreck. How she'd died in a freak single-car rollover, leaving behind a son who'd thought she hadn't cared.

They all crowded into the tiny alcove, spilling back into the branching halls, the hosts of the people who'd lived and died on the land long ago. The Master's head nearly brushed the ceiling of the chamber, with awe and a tinge of gratifying fear.

The Master set her on her feet, then framed her face with his gloved hands and kissed her, long and deep. Her body throbbed for him and she regretted that they'd had so little time together.

"Thank you, Christine." He brushed his thumbs over her cheekbones.

"I haven't done anything yet."

"For wanting to."

"What do I do?" She surveyed the pillar nervously. She needed Hally.

"Trust yourself. It's in you. In your true heart."

Reverently, she opened the box. The scent of dying roses filled the room, full of decay and old bitterness. She hesitated to touch the mummified hand, but the shadow people shuffled, brushing her with whispers of encouragement. It felt like old leather, delicate and dry.

It wasn't easy, but she held long-dead Seraphina's hand against the pedestal, then pressed her turned-in ring into the depression on her side.

"Nothing is happening." Disappointment, metallic and bitter, flooded her.

"Wait. The magic is already in motion. Like a waterfall down the mountain. Remember: you cannot change the fact that the river flows."

But you can change its direction.

A whisper of melody and the scent of roses and sunshine. The glass dome over the artifacts misted away, the sense of great power humming into the room, like lightning about to strike. It filled her with a viscerally sexual hunger. Over the pedestal, she gazed at the Master. Longing thrummed between them, but he seemed transfixed, unable to move. His black hat, his mask, his cloak, his suit, shifted and became smoke. He stood, powerfully naked and iridescently white, a shining star in the small chamber. His face, still half melted, became a blank canvas for the numinous blue of his eyes.

Golden music filled the room, winding through the stones and artifacts. That so-familiar song. The shadow people were singing. They moved around her, now visible, now blending through the edges of the circle. As they crowded closer, she became aware that they held roses. Lush and full of unearthly beauty, their petals like living flesh, brushing the skin of her exposed arms and legs. The thorns, sharp as blades, caught and dug in, cutting her with small slices.

The pain sharpened her awareness and fed the hunger. Blood—Sanclaro blood, tribal blood—red and hot as the roses flowed down her skin. She nearly pulled away, afraid, but kept her gaze locked on the Master. Obedient to what he'd asked of her, without ever asking it.

She felt the opening of the binding, like letting go of anger, releasing grief. With a collective sigh the people breathed out their relief and, swirling around her in a tornado wind, became a torrent of hair, feathers, and shadows. They swirled out and disappeared into the wider universe.

The Master shimmered, breaking into innumerable shimmering specks, like a pixelated image losing resolution.

"Wait," she cried out. The magic poured out, rushing away. "I want you to be what you were."

"That time is gone." His words wrapped around her like that long-forgotten melody. "Be strong enough to let me go."

"I can't." She was sobbing. Tears filling her vision, flowing away also, like the magic, like her blood.

"Christine." He sang her name, reaching his powerful arms to the sky far above, his muscled chest cording, his cock standing proud. He radiated joyful sexuality, exultant. Free.

His face shifted and coalesced, into the shining perfection of an old god.

"Free me, Christine." He smiled, asking her in the same tone of voice that he'd asked her to abandon herself to him.

With a last wrenching sob, she gasped out her agreement.

"Yes, Master."

7

Everyone treated her carefully after that.

No one quite understood how she'd survived the fall that killed Roman. They'd found them when Domingo sent up the alarm and she woke up in Christus St. Vincent much later, with a concussion and multiple lacerations. The nurses said she looked like she'd gone through a plate-glass window. Shards of crystal lay around them, but no matter how many delicate questions everyone asked, Christine didn't remember what had happened.

Well, she did remember.

Just differently.

Sanchez didn't much seem to care and mostly questioned her about what had happened before her fall. He seemed totally unsurprised at Carla's involvement. Turned out he'd suspected her for quite some time. They'd matched her well-known calligraphy to the notes—both the ones Christine finally turned over to the cops and the one found on her body.

Sanchez couldn't say much until the DA finished compiling evidence, but he'd let drop that Carla had been obsessed with making Christy leave. The final note, it seemed, had been part of a gift intended for Domingo Sanclaro, who returned the favor with the massive beating.

Charlie, apparently, was a remorseful mess, having been both suspicious of his wife's affair with Domingo and desperate to keep her. Being sorry wasn't enough for Sanchez, though, and he'd arrested Charlie as an accessory. It looked like his fate would depend on how much he'd really known—and if he would bear witness against his wife.

The actual charges against Matt were relatively minor—especially since Hally said karma would be plenty and she didn't want to press assault charges. Once the police cut him loose, he took off for some theater group in California. As for Domingo, he appeared to be catatonic with shock and grief over Roman's death when Sanchez took him into custody. Angie was happy to provide adequate evidence for the state and Feds to take him down for a long time, if he recovered.

It might be small and mean of her, but Christine liked the idea of him tucked away in a mental institution. A bit of Hally's karmic justice.

Time passed, and Christine healed enough to leave the hospital and resume a normal life.

Even though this had been a hospital for physical healing—not like the other place—she had felt much the same there as she had then. Like her skin was too permeable for the world.

Hally had talked her into a celebratory lunch, and they were sitting on the porch at El Farol, eating tapas and watching the Saturday tourists flow in and out of the art galleries. A guitarist played acoustic flamenco, bright notes that fit the hot afternoon. Christine hadn't seen the fiddler again. Nor had she heard that song, anywhere but in her heart.

Absentmindedly, Christine rubbed her ring finger, which was healing well but still ached. They'd had to cut the ring off her hand because it had somehow cut into her skin, creating massive swelling. At one point they had worried that her hand would have to be amputated at the wrist, to stave off the blood poisoning from the infection, which gave her the shivers as she imagined it immortalized with Seraphina's. Though several people had pointed out that she could have the stones reset because the ring, as a gift, legally belonged to her, Christine gave it to Angie.

It was nothing more than a set of rocks now.

"It's good to see you out and about again." Hally made cooing noises over the freshly arrived deep-fried avocado. "You look good."

"Do I?"

Her voice sounded young and kind of piteous, the question squeezing around the lump in her throat. Hally squeezed her hand and poured more sangria from the pitcher. "Yes. You're doing great. You know it."

Christine wasn't sure about that. The last week—busy as it had been, dealing with the season ramping up, despite serious holes in their staff roster and freaked-out talent, working with her father to uncover the various shortcuts in accounting that had accumulated over many years, and giving testimony to Sanchez and the Feds, all while she was still recovering—had been eerily quiet. The only music came from human throats. No roses appeared in unlikely spots. Things stayed put.

So many life forces that had infused the opera house had vanished, leaving it emptier.

The Master, too, was gone.

She'd looked for him, tried to find his passageways and various places, but they had vanished as if they never were. As if all of them had been part of his dream and, without him, had all wafted away like so much smoke and shadow. She almost thought none of it had been real.

Except that her broken heart stood evidence that it had been.

"Remember how you said that everybody lives on a spectrum of crazy—that some are more than others?"

Hally nodded in reply, her hazel eyes full of sympathy.

"I think I found my spot on the crazy scale. But now it's too late."

"I know you're still grieving," Hally said, choosing her words carefully. "But you did the right thing, letting him go. Spirits like him aren't meant to be trapped. He's gone to a better place. He's gone to where he should be and you're still here, where you should be.".

"I don't want to be."

"You don't mean that."

"I thought you said he's in a better place," Christine accused, though she knew it wasn't fair.

"Better for him." Hally said it slowly, with great patience. "You belong here."

"I know." She took a deep breath. "I know, but it hurts."

"Have more sangria."

Christine laughed through her tears. "I think people would frown on you suggesting I use alcohol to salve my emotional wounds."

"Hey—I'm a bartender and you're finally off the pain meds. Comes with the territory. And I'm suggesting it more for the tattoo. Belly work can be ouchie."

"Is that a technical term?"

"Actually, yes. Cheers."

Hally stayed with her all afternoon while the tattoo artist did his work. Sometimes holding her hand, sometimes snarking at her when she whined. The artist had suggested she do it in stages, but she wanted it all done at once.

Working with silvery grays and deep blacks, he spun the myriad scars across her abdomen into a spiral. Through the lines, a bear strode, one paw lifted, a skeleton of white rising from his body.

Though her father had offered to pay for it, she used the money she'd earned working at the opera. It seemed fitting.

Besides, it hadn't been her father's fault. She needed to accept responsibility for who she'd been then, as well as who she was now—and who she'd become.

Alone.

She hadn't wanted to say it to Hally, because her friend would be hurt by it. But she felt unutterably lonely, as if a piece of herself had been cleaved away. Worse, it had been a part she'd never known was there before. And now it was gone.

Without the shadows, the sunshine felt glaring and empty.

"I have a present for you." Hally broke into her thoughts. She was driving Christine home after the tattoo was done, as if she were still a patient emerging from surgery who couldn't take care of herself.

"Why do I get a present?"

Hally wiggled her shoulders, parking in front of Christine's apartment building. "New tattoo present? A you-didn't-die-or-get-locked-away-for-a-murder-you-didn't-commit present?"

"Not your standard gift-giving occasions."

"That's what makes this one all the more significant."

She used her key to open Christine's door, making her keep her eyes closed. Then a purring ball of fur was deposited in her arms.

Christine opened her eyes to find huge yellow ones, bright as a harvest moon, staring back at her from a black-and-white face. "A cat?" she squeaked.

"Your dad brought him over while you were getting the tattoo. He said you'd be pleased. And you know me—I'm all about world domination for kittehs everywhere."

"I am. I am pleased." The purring hummed through her, filling a little bit of the ache inside. "Thank you, Hally. For everything, really."

The kitten slept beside her, a warm comfort in the night. And she dreamed. Sweet, peaceful dreams. Waltzing with the Master while rose petals rained around them. In her dreams he wasn't dead. They danced and he held her.

She awoke to warm light on her face, the cathedral bells tolling for Mass. She wondered if Angie would go, as sole representative of what remained of the core Sanclaro family. Her mother's "migraine" had taken on permanent status. Nobody seemed to know how much Reina Sanclaro had or had not known, but the woman had been hospitalized and remained unresponsive.

Angie herself was doing surprisingly well, applying herself with grim determination to the Sanclaro books. She had appealed to Christine's father for advice, and the two made an unlikely but somehow apt pair, discussing disposition of stocks and how to keep the Feds from taking damn near everything.

It made her smile to think of them, and Christine rolled over, her new tattoo stinging as she moved, reaching for the kitten.

Her hand met warm flesh instead.

Her eyes flew open, her heart thudding in recognition.

The Master.

Blindingly real, he lay sleeping next to her. At her touch, he blinked his eyes open, a familiar ice blue. And he smiled at her. He was whole and beautiful. Where once his leg had been wilted, it was now a fully formed pillar of muscle. Behind him, the kitten sat on the bedside table, observing with bright eyes.

She had no breath to speak. He raised a hand and caressed her cheek.

"Christine."

A laugh escaped her. A bubble of sheer joy suffusing her entire being. "How? How are you here?"

"I promised I would always be with you."

"I know, but . . . but you were gone."

He shook his head and leaned up on one elbow, the muscles of his arms and chest flexing. Blond hair spilled over his shoulder, still white but no longer ethereally so. He drew down the sheet and stroked his hand over the bandages.

"Blood and symbols—you invoked me. I'm in your blood. Where once I was anchored to rock, now I'm bound to my totem in your flesh. To you."

"Oh." She chewed her lip, thinking over the ramifications. "That could suck if we ever broke up."

He laughed, then sobered. "On the other hand, should you ever wish to be rid of me, it would be easy enough to do."

"I don't. I will never want that."

"You don't have to promise me that—for now it's enough. To touch your skin, to feel the sun."

He cupped her breast and lowered his head to kiss her nipple. Good thing she'd gone to bed naked. Much more romantic than the purple unicorn pjs.

She ran her fingers through his hair, letting her body warm to his touch. His hair, his skin, even his scent, all seemed slightly different. The same in essence, new in manifestation. Hally would probably understand it all.

"If you're anchored to me, what happens when I die?"

The Master lifted his head. "Is there time for me to make love to you first?"

She thumped his strong shoulder. "You know what I mean. Someday."

"Then I will die with you."

"But I thought gods are immortal."

He rolled onto his back, bringing her with him. "Right now I'm mortal, as you are. Once we shed this flesh, we'll move on to being other things again."

"We? I'll go with you?"

He lifted her and let her sink onto his rigid cock. She groaned, her morning-wet tissues stretching to accommodate him.

"All humans have divinity in them, and you more than most now. We'll walk the earth together for a while, and after that, other worlds. My home is always your home."

Her heart melted like a baking freezer cookie. "We'll have to come up with papers for you. You'll need a birth certificate and—" She broke off on a gasp as he thrust up inside her, shattering her thoughts.

"Later," he demanded. "Or I'll tie you up and make you pay attention."

"Oh." She bent over and kissed him, long and deep. "Yes, Master."